EDEN

Candice Fox is the middle child of a large, eccentric family from Sydney's western suburbs. The daughter of a parole officer and an enthusiastic foster-carer, Candice spent her childhood listening around corners to tales of violence, madness and evil as her father relayed his work stories to her mother and older brothers. Candice won back-to-back Ned Kelly awards for her first two novels *Hades* and *Eden*, and her third novel, *Fall* was shortlisted for the Ned Kelly and Davitt awards. She is also the author of the critically acclaimed *Crimson Lake* and co-writer with James Patterson of the *Sunday Times* No.1 bestseller *Never Never* set in the Australian outback.

Praise for Candice Fox

'A bright new star of crime fiction.' James Patterson

'Definitely a writer to watch.' Harlan Coben

'A fast-paced, expertly crafted read with a cast of colourful characters.' *Guardian*

'Gritty and compulsive.' Jane Harper

Candice
FOX
EDEN

arrow books

1 3 5 7 9 10 8 6 4 2

Arrow Books
20 Vauxhall Bridge Road
London SW1V 2SA

Arrow is part of the Penguin Random House group of companies
whose addresses can be found at global.penguinrandomhouse.com.

Copyright © Candice Fox 2014

First published in Great Britain by Arrow Books in 2018
(First published in Australia by Bantam in 2014)

www.penguin.co.uk

A CIP catalogue record for this book is available from the British Library.

ISBN 9781784758356

Printed and bound in Great Britain by Clays Ltd, Elcograf S.p.A.

Penguin Random House is committed to a
sustainable future for our business, our readers
and our planet. This book is made from Forest
Stewardship Council® certified paper.

For Tim.

The night of the boy's murder he was working, wandering along Darlinghurst Road in the crowds of workers, picking pockets, begging, doing tricks for coins. Later the boy would think of his life in the city streets as the Winter Days, because even in the summer they seemed cold and damp, the daylight short. The skin of his feet was hard and black, but the midnight hours penetrated this husky exterior, brought a chill through the asphalt into his skinny legs. The mornings rang with wet silence and the afternoons were heavy with foreboding, the promise of darkness bringing with it yelling, laughter, running footsteps, sirens.

It took years for the boy to forget how to remember, when one day ate into the next and nothing broke the monotony except the stabbing death of a whore or the chance find of a coin on the concrete. The sun shuttered above the buildings, on and off, counting the days. The boy wandered, head down, practised at sniffing bins outside restaurants to identify treasures hidden within, at slipping through the Minerva Theatre and the Metro Cinema fire exits to fossick for popcorn and sweets, at scaling tall buildings to raid clotheslines strung across cramped balconies.

Sometimes the boy felt he could have been ancient because all that came before the Night of Fire and Screaming was darkness, and it had been months since he had known what day it was. Now and then when he slept he returned to the fires, saw the faces of the woman and the man he supposed must have been his parents against the windows, heard their pounding on the glass behind the bars. Whenever he tried to remember how long ago the fires happened, who those people were and why they had died, how he had survived and how he had got to the city, he was confronted by blackness and silence – a door closed, locked, impassable. He didn't know how old he was or the name those screaming people called him. When the police and the St Canice nuns who had spotted him came to take him, they said he looked eight and that he was mute and malnourished, whatever that meant. He'd fled the van they put him in and kept his eye out from then on. He didn't like the police. He didn't know why.

The boy was lost to himself. He wandered and tried to forget.

On the night he met the French Man, the boy was sitting on a set of steps down from Les Girls, which was alive with laughing and shoving, the toppling of glasses, the slapping of beer caps onto the pavement. The stage ladies with their exotic snakes were yet to perform down at Pink Pussy Cat's, so men lingered in the street, easy targets. It was the boy's favourite spot. To his left he could look down the curve of Darlinghurst Road towards the police station, watching for brawls and arrests when coins could be spilled or wallets lifted, and to his right he could trace the progress of long-legged sailors from Woolloomooloo, jostling and sniggering and trying to grope passing girls, a fine source of small change for a boy with a sweet face who could sing and dance and tell dirty jokes. Most of the jokes he'd read in the underground magazines he found in the streets, The Whisper, mostly. So he guessed he'd been to school once – he didn't remember being taught to read but he could do it. He looked at the dirty pictures and the photographs from the war, all cut up and pasted and drawn over with lines. The men and women in the magazines wore their hair long and dirty, and so did he. The boy thought maybe one day he'd find himself.

2

He rested his heels and counted the trams passing on the line, cluttered with men and women on their way to Potts Point and the dockland suburbs, with their oiled hair, painted lips and leather bags full of papers. It was early enough for the whores who leaned on walls, filing their nails and hooting to each other across the street, late enough for the bums to have staggered in from the parks to curl up for the night on dirty street corners and shopfronts. All the dancers were inside under the bright lights of the upper floors, flashing bare chests and feathers in the windows, curling their hair and perfuming the breeze.

The French Man came walking up the hill under the Moreton Bay fig trees, the smoke from his cigarette winding around a row of sailors advancing behind him. The boy hardly noticed him. He moved off the steps and headed down to meet the sailors, stretching his dirty face into his brightest smile. The French Man caught him by the elbow and spun him in a half circle. The sailors parted to let him through.

'What's the hurry, petit monsieur?'

The boy wasn't fussy who his marks were. The French Man didn't look like a cop so he would make an easy meal. His accent was slurred and heavy. Perhaps he'd been drinking down at the waterfront. His clothes looked slept in. He smelled of cigarettes and wine, but his hair was neatly combed so that the ridges stood out across his curved scalp.

'Hello, sir! Got a coin?' the boy asked. 'I can dance, I can sing, I can tell jokes. I can balance a penny on my nose.'

The boy did a handstand and walked in a circle on his palms on the dirty pavement. His black-soled feet waggled in the air. The French Man folded his arms and laughed, and a couple walking their dog stopped to watch.

'That's very good, monsieur.' The French Man smiled. 'What else can you do?'

'I can make a coin disappear,' the boy grinned.

The couple laughed. Two other men stopped to watch. The French Man fished a penny from his pocket and handed it to the boy.

'Abracadabra, hocus-pocus!' The boy swirled his arms in the air. Everyone smiled. He slipped the copper into his sleeve and dropped to one knee.

'Ta daa!'

'Magnifique!' The French Man clapped his long thin hands. 'Now give it back.'

'I can't.' The boy grinned. 'It's disappeared.'

More laughter. The boy did another handstand as the crowd clapped and then dispersed. The French Man remained, watching, his thin upper lip curled slightly at the corner.

'Another coin for the show?' the boy asked.

'I'm afraid I'm fresh out. Plucked me dry. Are you hungry, boy?'

'Starving.'

'Come on, then. This way. I've got a fresh batch of sausages waiting for me at home. Two streets back.' The French Man flicked his head towards the crest of the hill. 'You're welcome to a bite, little friend. Most welcome.'

The French Man kept walking as though he didn't mind leaving the boy in the windswept street. The boy looked down the hill and saw no more sailors coming. As it swung back and forth, the French Man's wrist glittered with a silver wristwatch. The boy licked his lips, brushed aside his fear and followed.

The boy huddled close to the French Man as the wind rippled through the huge figs on Ithaca Road. He tried to get a feel for a wallet or a coin purse as he brushed and bumped against the man's side. There was none. The watch fastening was a double-fold clip, built for surviving the slip. The boy circled the man, sometimes ahead, sometimes behind, breaking twigs into pieces and strumming them against painted iron rails. The French Man laughed and ruffled his hair.

'You're a small boy. Got to bend to get a hold of you. Quick as a ferret.'

'How many sausages will there be?'

'Enough for a belly as small as yours. You've got an accent to you. Sauerkraut, is it?'

The boy shrugged. He knew he spoke funny but he didn't know why.

Rain was dripping in silver streams from the corrugated iron roof of the terrace house. They stepped up onto the porch. The French Man jangled his keys. Inside, the house smelled damp, as though something in the walls was rotting and about to drip out of the wallpaper. The boy skittered down the hall to a table under a grimy kitchen window. There was equipment here – machine parts and bottles of oil, lenses and cloths. The table was covered with shining, glimmering things. The boy looked over the mess in awe and tried to pick something to lift before the man caught up. He pocketed a shiny lens. There was a paper bag stuffed with small square photographs. The boy glimpsed bare limbs, naked chests. When he put his hand on the bag the French Man brushed it away.

'What is all this stuff?'

'This, my small friend, is the Polaroid 110B, the Pathfinder. Newest thing on the market. It develops pictures instantly. Poof! Right in your hand. Like magic,' the French Man said, and winked. He picked the camera out of the clutter and held it in the light. 'You don't have to go to a store. You can develop your own pictures, right here, at home.'

'Are you a photographer?'

'Sometimes, yes.'

The boy let his eyes wander to the French Man's face. There were scars on his cheeks from burns or acne, marbling the surface of his high cheekbones. The boy thought of the moon. How long had it been since he'd looked up at the moon? 'Here. You take a picture of me and I'll take one of you.'

The boy giggled and took the heavy camera in his small hands, turned it, looked through the viewfinder. The French Man struck a pose. The device hummed and zinged in the boy's hands, seemed to zap like an alien thing. Light exploded off the walls. The camera spewed out a blank picture, which gradually rippled with light. The boy watched it develop with barely contained rapture. Magic. In the picture, the French Man's eyes were black. The boy let the camera go with reluctance.

'Your turn.'

He smiled and struck a pose. The flash burned against the backs of his eyelids. He wondered if he'd ever had his picture taken in the days before the Night of Fire and Screaming, if there were pictures of him somewhere still, smiling and playing. The thought made the boy a little sad. The French Man snapped another picture of him standing and staring at the floor.

'You ever seen Sugar Ray? The boxer?'

'Course I have!'

The boy clenched his fists and hung them above his head, his puny biceps flexed as small lumps on his stringy arms. The French Man laughed and snapped a shot. The boy growled and brought his fists together at his belly. Another zap, hum, a spewed picture. The French Man flipped the photos onto the table without looking at them. The boy laughed nervously, shifting from foot to foot. The room seemed a little small, suddenly. The French Man snapped another picture, and the boy forgot to pose. He was simply standing there. Being him.

'Take your shirt off.'

The boy frowned a little. He slipped the shirt over his head, smelling it as the cloth passed his nose, untold days of sweat and scum and rain. The boy cupped his hands and did a pose of his side as he had seen the boxers do. The French Man snapped him.

'I'm hungry.'

'Just a few more.'

The boy sighed. More pictures. The air in the room was heavy, hard to breathe. His cheeks felt hot. He didn't know why.

'It's no fun anymore. Let's eat.'

The French Man snapped him again, crouching by the table, eye-level with the boy. The light made the boy's eyes water. He reached out and pulled the camera down. The man lifted it again.

'A few more.'

'No.'

'You want to eat, you do as I say,' the French Man grunted, showing teeth. The two front ones were grey as steel. The boy looked down the hall at the front door, so far away the darkness swallowed it, giving only a slice of silver at the bottom where the moonlit street blazed. 'We're friends, aren't we, boy? Good friends. Friends don't argue with each other.'

The camera flashed again. Now the pictures were falling on the floor. The boy picked his shirt up. His fingers were numb, aching, blood was raging in his ears. Embarrassed, somehow. The French Man's hand flashed out, ripped the cloth from his fingers and flung the shirt by the pile of pictures. The boy's face stared up from the photos. Afraid. In the street a siren wailed like a child. The boy in the cramped kitchen drew a breath, fighting a pressure on his lungs.

'I've got to go.'

'You're not going anywhere.'

'I said, I want to go!'

The slap came like a burst of heat, soundless, over before the boy knew what had happened. His ear pulsed, hammering against his head. The French Man shook his head slowly, sadly, then reached up and took the boy's face in his cold hand. For a moment the room shimmered in the boy's eyes. He had been drunk once before, on dregs from bottles he found behind The Goldfish Bowl. He felt drunk now. The French Man held him upright.

'Don't disappoint me, pretty one.'

The boy turned, twisted, tried to scramble away. The French Man's arms were around him. They collapsed to the floor, the man a dead weight. The air was squeezed out of him. His stomach churned, clenched, he tried to suck oxygen into his lungs. His mouth was on the floor, lips collecting dust.

'You do what I say, when I say.'

The French Man pinned the boy's neck against the boards, righted the camera in his other hand. The camera flash caught remnants of polish on the floor, making them glimmer like pools of water on desert sand. The boy kicked out, struck the table leg, pain flooding through his bones. The man snapped another shot, then placed the camera beside the boy's face.

The boy reached out, sweeping it into his arm. In the same movement he rolled beneath the weight of the man and used the momentum to swing the camera up and over, into the side of the man's head.

Then the Silence came.

He had felt the Silence only once before – on the Night of Fire and Screaming, when he had stood in the street motionless and watched the people burning. It felt something like being under water, sounds pinging softly, all else an endless nothingness, slowed by numbness, decaying moments, the dripping of time.

The boy was on top of the French Man, the camera in his hands, beating it down on the man's face over and over without sound, without sensation. The face was breaking, losing shape, becoming wet. The earth was turning beneath the boy's knees, swaying like the deck of a ship. The man's hands were fumbling at his face and neck, scratching, wringing, twisting, punching. Time passed. The camera fell away. The boy used his fists.

When the door of the terrace opened the boy was standing by the table, looking down at a picture of himself standing by the table, looking down. When the men's voices finally broke the Silence the boy lifted his head.

'Jean? Jean? You fucking frog prick. I know you're here. Time's up. I want my money, you hear me, cocksucker?'

There were shadows in the hall, one larger than the other, a great hulk of a man whose shoulders scraped the narrow walls and head ducked beneath the ornate frame of the kitchen door naturally, as though he'd been there before. A smaller man walked in front, cast completely in shadow by the beast. The boy wiped at a tickle on his upper lip. He looked at his hands. The blood was smeared to his elbows.

The first man was wearing a suit the colour of grey ocean, a collar stiff and peaked under his thick square jaw and white as a flash of lightning. Beneath the suit, old muscle languished to fat, making him look like an elderly retired war captain, his once-powerful frame ruined by peacetime. His hair was grey and a deep groove was cut into his chin from a clean knife wound that had split his bottom lip in two. The giant was not as well dressed but gave the same impression of darkened skies and old wars, a bearded bear with a nose that dominated his face, broken and twisted, a fighter's nose.

The boy and the two men looked at each other for a long moment, before all eyes fell away. The men took in the smashed and broken thing that had been Jean the French Man, lying twisted at the boy's feet. There was a gun in the old captain's hand, hanging by his side, forgotten. No one spoke. The boy lifted his palms and examined the blood on them, the mangled knuckles already swollen twice their size, the wet and watery almost-orange blood sliding down his wrists. His stomach was pumping in and out, sucking air, the naked ribs protruding, sinking, protruding for the men to see. He searched for his shirt. It had disappeared.

'Well, would you look at this, Bear,' the Captain said.

The Bear said nothing as the Captain wandered forward and crouched beside the boy. He lifted a photo from the floor and flicked the blood from it. The boy standing. The boy with his biceps bared. He looked at them all carefully, considered each in turn, laid them in a neat pile. Jean wasn't breathing. The Captain stood and looked down at the boy.

Slowly, a smile crept across the Captain's face. Then he began to laugh. The Bear wasn't laughing. He wasn't even smiling. The boy wiped his nose again. There was more blood, running off his chin in inky streams.

The Captain laughed and laughed, and then cocked the hammer on the pistol and put two bullets into the French Man's face. Jean's body bucked twice as though electrified. The boy thought of the burning bodies on the Night of Fire and Screaming, the way they spasmed and shook. The Captain laughed again, a gentle snort, shook his head and walked into the short hall that led to the other rooms.

'We'll deal with him in a minute,' he said to the Bear. 'Put him in the car.'

Hades woke thinking he'd been shot. The great weight that seemed to fall and then wrap around his chest, the noise, the pain. He'd taken a bullet before and this was how it felt. But the thump on his chest was only the cat. The pain was his old man's bones snapping into action, the noise his perimeter alarm sounding, an old fire alarm screwed to the wall above the door. Someone had entered his property. Hades groaned and rolled onto his side, flopping out of the bed like a swollen fish. The cat weaved around his stubby ankles, suddenly full of affection after the terror of the alarm. It was usually a bitch of a thing. Hades kicked it away and slipped his thongs on.

It had been months since he had been visited this late. He'd put the word out that he had officially retired, that all the problems he had once been happy to fix were to be taken elsewhere. He wanted to spend his declining years free of harassment by cops, forensics specialists, journalists and true crime writers. During the day, the workers at his tip kept these scavengers away – Hades' dark past was common knowledge among them and was at the heart of a brotherhood of loyalty and silence. At night he was vulnerable. Before, the first sign of company would be the howling of the tip's wild dogs but he'd begun to sleep through this morbid night music. His daughter,

Eden, had insisted on installing the alarm when she had managed to walk all the way up the dark drive, into the house and right to his bedside without waking him. Eden, always the predator, had made the alarm loud enough to induce a heart attack.

Headlights swept the kitchen. One of the few clocks in his extensive collection that actually kept time chimed an hour past midnight as he reached the screen door. He picked up a Ruger Super Redhawk that was sticking out of a flowerpot and tucked it into the back of his boxer shorts. The double-action magnum tugged at the waistband, felt cold against his arse crack. Hades was not a tall man. He walked with a wooden cane. The gun was far too big to be practical, but if he was going to go out one night in a revenge attack, a shootout with the police or a dance with burglars, all of which were equally likely, he was going to do it with a gun proportionate to his reputation.

The cat followed him out and bolted into the blackness. He hoped it wouldn't be back, but knew it would. A red Barina with plastic eyelashes hanging over its headlights gripped its way uncertainly over the last rise before his shack and stopped with a jolt in the dust. Hades scratched his stubble and waited for the driver to emerge. If this was some kind of attack he was pleased by how undignified the approach had been. It didn't speak of organisation. When the driver slid out of the seat and came into the murky lights, he let his head hang back and looked at the stars.

'Oh god. Not you.'

'Hades!'

She fell on him, rock-hard breasts against his chest, nails in his hair, an assault of smooth limbs and wet kisses, cigarette smoke, perfume. Hades pushed her off. He resisted the urge to smile. It would only encourage her.

'Get off me, Kat.'

'I've missed you. God, I've missed you. It's been too long. It's been ages.'

'What are you doing here, for chrissake? I don't have time for you. I'm retired. It's the middle of the night.'

'I love you, Hades.'

'Go away.'

'No, Hades, I love you. I need you.'

'Oh, don't tell me.'

'Please, Hades.' She stood back and clasped her hands like a child. 'Please help me.'

He looked at her, let the silence hang the way he used to with Eden when she was a teenager, disappointment so deeply felt it could not be squeezed out into words. Just like with Eden. Standing there, Hades was struck with the sense that he was in the presence of a creature in disguise, a spider pretending to be a leaf, a snake coiled in the shape of a rock. Kat had come in her usual get-up – the six-inch heels and cheap nylon mini-dress, the half-dyed black hair falling out at the sides in wispy singed spikes. It was more than that though. The track marks on her ankles weren't from smack, as she'd have you believe. Hades had seen these marks faked plenty of times by undercover cops – a little cayenne pepper and ink under the first layer of skin and irritated welts pop up like the angry sores of the addicted. Kat's 'grown-out' hair extensions were clipped in for the night, a part of her run-down camouflage. The mascara was intentionally clumpy. The multiple piercings in her ears were magnets. Underneath the manufactured cheapness was a very beautiful woman, a clever woman. A seasoned killer.

Hades had caught Kat out once. She was sitting in a cafe in Glebe with a girlfriend, fresh-faced and vibrant, the make-up gone, her hair short and neatly bobbed, a gold watch she'd probably stolen hanging a little too loosely on her wrist. She hadn't seen Hades watching from the traffic lights. There was a newspaper under her perfectly manicured nails and a briefcase by her side. The helpless Bambi act was a put-on too. Hades had heard somewhere that she was a financial advisor or something. He wasn't sure. He didn't care.

Whenever she turned up, he played along with her little game because Kat was just one of many actors, hustlers, con artists and tricksters who came to him in the night with bones to bury. Over the years Hades had been awakened by numb-headed drug mules who'd waited for their moment to cut down their bosses, lady-killers in expensive linen suits, hit men with cold eyes and false charm. Wasn't he one of them too? Hades had spent decades carefully crafting his tired old man image. Sure, he was getting on. He ate too much and fell asleep in front of the TV more than he actually watched it. But Hades was deadly. So was Kat. Under the stars that night they played out the roles of a worn-out ex-warlord and a skinny prostitute. It was too early in the morning for the old man to think about it any more deeply than that.

'What have you done now?' he asked.

'It was an accident.'

'It's always an accident with you.'

'Oh, Hades!'

'Come on.' He waved at her impatiently. 'Get on with it.'

She clopped back to the car, all guilty eyes and pouty lips. Hades watched her struggle with the boot. Nickel bracelets jingled on her wrists. She thrust the boot open and the overhead light flickered. Hades looked in and let a sigh ripple out of him.

'How many times I got to tell you, Kat? How many times?'

'What?'

'You're not wrapping them right. I've told you this.'

'Hay-dees!'

'Look.' Hades leaned over and lifted one end of the tarp that contained the body. 'You leave the ends open like this and you get DNA in your car. Hair. Eyelashes. Blood. Piss. Dirt and plant fibres from the tread in his shoes that will put him in your street, in your driveway. They can take a single hair, do a mitochondrial degradation test and tell you whether or not the guy was dead when the hair fell off him. They can put a body in your boot from a single flake of fucking dandruff, Kat. You know this.'

'So what am I supposed to do about it?'

'You tuck the ends in before you roll.' Hades illustrated with his hands. 'Lie the body out flat, arms down. Like a burrito. Tuck, tuck, roll. Tape. Tape, Kat, not fucking Occy straps. You shouldn't be using tarp, either. You should be using plastic drop sheets. I can give you some. Tarps have a weave in them. They're not airtight.'

'Hades, I'm not as clever as you, okay?' she whined.

'You never rolled a fucking burrito?'

'I don't even know what a burrito is. What do I look like?'

Hades shook his head, felt exhausted.

'The whole car will have to go. They'll have your DNA in the front and his in the back. You need to start thinking about these things, Kat. Listening when I talk to you.'

'You talk too much, Hades,' Kat said, patting the side of his head, letting her fingers follow the rim of his ear to the nape of his thick neck. 'You're always talking. You're always mean to me.'

Her breath felt warm on his face. Hades cleared his throat.

'I do it because you're going to get yourself caught one of these days. And I don't want to be the one who has to come after you before you testify.'

'Would you hurt me, Hades?'

'Probably not.'

'Sometimes I like being hurt.'

She was against him, kissing him, before he knew it. She'd got into his arms the way a fox will slip through a gap in a fence without slowing momentum, gliding, bones following a natural path one after the other until she was all around him, everything he saw and felt. Feral. Dangerous. He sighed again and surrendered. She always did this. He always fell for it. But in a way he kind of liked falling for it, knowing it was coming, wondering how she would make it seem spontaneous and wild and completely out of his hands each and every time. The concubine. Hades imagined that this was what it was like with the men she robbed and killed, leaving work and smoking on the corner, being approached by a cute, vulnerable, irresistible little whore in a painted-on dress. Cold, tired, gullible. Give me your jacket. Take me home. Play with me. She was like a child in his hands now, insistent and needy, surprised by her own passion. Hades withdrew from her and rolled his eyes. Such a snake.

'Get in there.' He cocked his head towards the house. 'Make me a goddamn coffee while you're at it.'

'Don't be long,' she grinned, victorious. Hades grumbled and shut the boot. His hard-on was almost painful but he never put play before work, even when the play was just a ruse to get out of his body disposal fee. A twenty thousand dollar fuck. He would need a couple of coffees. It was cheap and nasty but he didn't mind. It had been years since a woman had genuinely wanted to jump Hades' bones. He wasn't fussed. Women made things difficult, and the last thing he needed was more difficulty in his life.

First things first. He would drive the car back to the new fill grounds where the complex layers of rubber, vinyl, industrial biochemicals and trash were not yet finished. He'd slip Kat's nameless victim in there, where the compressed layers, encouraging the development of leachate acid as a natural biodegrader of human waste, would eventually completely dissolve all trace of him as it had with hundreds of others over the years. He would grind the car's identification off, leave the vehicle to be crushed into a cube and finished off in an industrial incinerator in the morning. Then he'd go to bed with Kat. Hades wondered gloomily if the reward would be worth the effort as he wrestled the keys from the lock. She'd take everything she wanted out of him in a matter of minutes and leave while he was asleep. He was making a mental note to put his wallet and keys away somewhere safe when he noticed the dark shape at the bottom of the hill.

At first he wondered if one of the workers had broken down, left the car and taken a ride with a mate, but it would have been more logical for them to park in the sheds where the car would be protected overnight. Hades took a short wander to the crest of the hill. Stood. Listened. The car was idling, its headlights off. He felt a twinge in his chest, a leftover spasm from the fear that the alarm had generated twisting in his heart. Hades began to walk again, a little faster this time. The car's windows were down, blackness in the cabin, impenetrable. He got no further than ten metres before the car began to move, passed the gates in a blur of dark grey, or blue, or silver, he couldn't tell, before disappearing between the trees.

Hades stopped, suddenly out of breath.

The television was on, but somehow the knocking broke through the chatter of morning programs, the laughter and music and cooking tutorials, to snap me awake. The first sensation was the wetness under my face. Cold drool. Camel mouth. The place smelled damp and reeked of kitty litter. But still bearable. I could leave it a couple more days. I sat up and felt a nudge in the small of my back. I fished around and retrieved an empty Jameson bottle. The pain – dull, heavy, everywhere.

The knocking came again. It was her. She came every day. I hung my head in my hands and groaned, long and loud, so she could hear me. She knocked again. The day before I hadn't let her in, and she was waiting for me hours later when I went to get a pizza for lunch. Immaculate, in grey jeans and a knitted top that hugged the top of her perfect arse and fell to the backs of her cold pale killer's hands. Sitting on a bench in the foyer, reading a magazine. Waiting. Watching.

Eden knocked again.

'Go away!'

She knocked. I crossed the tiny apartment in two steps, kicked newspapers out of the way and flung open the door. Her hand was raised for more knocking. She took me in with those expressionless crow eyes, head to toe, let her hand fall and waited for me to go on my usual tirade. I did. She listened to my swearing quietly, thinking. I don't know what I looked like but I know what I smelled like. I'd expected the performance to get rid of her. When I tried to slam the door, her boot was in it.

'We've got an appointment.'

'I'm not going. Are you listening? Are you fucking stupid? I wasn't going yesterday. I'm not going today. Eden, I need you to leave me alone.' I walked away from the door. She closed it behind her, wrinkled her nose just slightly at the smell.

'Have a shower,' she said. 'We leave in twenty.'

I went into the kitchen and popped myself some Panadol, chewed them, angry. Her eyes wandered over the dirty plates balancing on the back of the couch, the dusty curtains blocking the mid-morning light, the grey cat pawing at the balcony door. Martina's cat. Yes. Alright. I'd let things slip since Martina died. Since I'd been shot and Eden had saved my life. It had locked me to her, silencing me forever on the true nature of her being, the nights she spent stalking Sydney's killers and rapists and molesters. Her playthings, the only way she could vent the uncontrollable and unstoppable evil that was as much a part of her biochemistry as the blood that circled her veins. I'd shot and killed a serial killer, deliberately, and Eden had stood with me through the investigation that followed with her untouchable self-assurance. We were bound, Eden and I, and I hated her for it.

She came into the kitchen and watched me swallow two more Panadol and an Endone. I liked the Endone, had got onto it after the bullet. My shoulder was mostly healed now, but I kept up the act to get the drug. I was supposed to go to physiotherapy to get rid of a twitch that sometimes developed in the last three fingers of my right hand, the only real leftover from the wound, but I wouldn't go. Anything to get the Endone. Lovely, sleepy Endone. There were three sheets left in the packet. I pocketed them.

'What are you staring at?'

'A problem.'

'Am I a problem for you, Eden?' I raised my eyebrows, shook the twitching from my fingers. 'You going to do with me what you do with all your other problems?'

She licked her teeth, looked almost bored. Not answering actually struck a chord with me. Deep down inside I knew she could do it, I suppose that was why. One of these nights I could wake up and find her standing over me. I liked to fool myself sometimes that Eden had a heart, that I'd wrung a laugh or two out of her over our months together, that she would at least have trouble killing me. Most of the time I wasn't so sure.

'You need to have a shower and come to this shrink's appointment with me,' she said quietly. 'You need to do this two more times so you can get signed back on duty. You need to go back to work and get over this thing with Martina. Until you do all these things you're a problem for me, Frank.'

'Don't talk about fucking Martina.'

'Martina is dead. She's dead, Frank.'

I shook my head at the floor.

'I don't like your unpredictability right now. I want you to get off the drugs and stop drinking.'

'Honey, my mother died years ago and she was the last woman who got to tell me what to do.'

'Have a shower.'

'No.'

'Have a shower.'

'No.'

She stood waiting. I considered my options. The first was picking Eden right up off the floor and carrying her out of my apartment. In my mind that was fairly easy – even with all the weight I'd dropped after the shooting I still had a good thirty kilos on her. But she was slippery, I'd seen her put down men twice my size with minimal effort. I didn't know if she had trained in any martial arts but I wouldn't be surprised. She'd also been known to pull knives and guns from secret places on her body, which was always a shock because she dressed like she knew she had a kickarse body – athletic and spritely with curves only where they were absolutely necessary, and where they were, well, just divine. I scratched my neck and looked at her, summoning all my Jedi power, and willed her silently to budge. She didn't. I also knew she could hold a Mexican stand-off for days. She had no emotions. No needs. I shook my head, spewed some more venom under my breath and left her.

I took half an hour in the bathroom just to piss her off, to get something back. I finished up and actually stood there in front of the mirror, counting off the minutes on my watch. Then I went out into the living room and grabbed a shirt from the back of the couch.

'Not that one,' Eden said, handing me a clean shirt she'd plucked from my wardrobe. 'You didn't shave. You need to shave.'

'You need to stop beginning sentences with *you need*.'

'You will shave.'

'Leave me alone, Eden.'

She relented a little and held open the apartment door for me. In the car she flipped the radio on and turned up the air conditioning. I rolled down my window, let the warm autumn air come rolling in. There were people jogging in the park across the road from my apartment block. A couple in matching red-and-black lycra, the woman struggling, her boyfriend egging her on. Some people look like jerks, even from a passing car, even from a hundred metres away.

We turned onto Anzac Parade and headed into the city. At the lights outside UNSW we stopped and students flooded the asphalt in front of the car, some of them carrying iPads and nothing else, slouchily dressed, pierced. An old man with thick-rimmed glasses and a plaid shirt buttoned to his throat wheeled a suitcase across the road towards the gates. Mature-age student.

'Look at this dork,' I laughed. Eden ignored me. She was listening to the radio. Had that intensity about her – a cat about to strike, unnatural stillness, eyes fixed.

'We're going to get put on this, you and I,' she said.

'On what?'

She turned up the radio.

'. . . *the third woman to go missing from the area in as many months. Police won't say at this stage whether the cases are related but are asking the public for any information about . . .*'

I reached over and flipped the radio to a station blaring celebrity news.

'I'm not on duty.'

'You're going to be put on duty if they link this missing prostitute to the others. We're the serial killer team now, Frank.

That's us. Jason Beck gave us that title. They're going to sign you on and put us on that case, whether you like it or not.'

'Does that mean I don't have to go to the shrink?'

'No.'

'I'll refuse the case. My shoulder's no good.'

'What is your plan exactly?' A little frazzle seemed to edge into Eden's voice for the first time that day. I felt slightly uplifted. 'You're just going to languish away in that hellhole of an apartment eating shit and listening to Chris Isaak until you depress yourself to death?'

'Sounds good to me. If no one bothers me for long enough the cat will probably dispose of my corpse. Ah, the circle of life.'

'You're not funny.'

'Depressing myself to death would be very artistic of me. I always wanted to be artistic.'

'Just stop.'

'You stop.'

'I asked Hades if he would give you some work,' she said. She was driving one-handed, hanging her French-manicured nails over the edge of the centre console. Now and then she rubbed them together, the only outward sign of her irritation. 'He said he had plenty you could do.'

'Why do you call him Hades? He's your dad. You should call him "Dad". It's very weird to do otherwise. You don't want people to think you're weird, Eden. They might catch on to you. To your little game. Is that why you ended up a serial killer, Eden? Was Hades a weird father? Did he train you in the dark arts?'

'You better watch your tongue, boy-o.'

We looked at each other. My jaw felt locked.

'You're completely without friends or hobbies right now,' she said after a time. 'Binge drinking is making you totally ineffectual.'

'Oh dear. I wouldn't want to end up ineffectual. That would be ghastly.'

'Hades needs help. He's old. You need something to keep you busy.'

'I'm not working for Hades, honey. That's my final word on that.'

Eden swung the car out of the traffic. The car behind us honked. She pulled up behind a taxi and I jolted in my seat as she yanked the handbrake.

'Listen, Frank, here's how it is,' she said, clasping her hands. 'I'm going to keep coming to your apartment until you do as I say. I'm going to keep calling you on the phone. I'm going to follow you down to that disgusting pub where you spend your nights and I'm going to get in the way of those sluts you take home with you. If all that doesn't work, I'm going to start hanging around *inside* your apartment, and you won't be able to get me out. I've had a key for weeks. I'm not going away, so you make the decision now to get up and get moving or the consequences are going to get more and more inconvenient for you.'

A little colour, a light pink, had come into her cheeks while she was speaking and then it dissipated as quickly as it had come. That was the only indication that she meant what she was saying. I had to give her a little smile. For all the terror and heartache and frustration she brought to my life, for all her intrusions, her insults, her propensity for the word 'dead', I couldn't deny that Eden cared about me. If she was forced to kill me, she was going to make it her last option. I felt a little loved by Eden at that moment. Maybe love was going too far. She wasn't indifferent to me. That was nice.

'You've got a key to my place?'

She sighed.

'Seriously, how'd you get a key to my place?'

Eden pulled the car back into the traffic.

I'd made it clear early on that I wouldn't be having private sessions with the shrink. Eden and I were required to have ten tandem sessions before we could be signed back on to work. The private ones were optional. The shrink had encouraged me to sit alone with her so she could address issues with me that she thought were 'too private' to discuss in front of Eden. I told her plainly that she had my permission to discuss anything she liked in front of Eden and that she'd have to shoot a tranquilliser dart into my arse and hogtie me to get me to do any more than was required. I'm a man of my word, so when I said I'd only do the minimum, that's what I did. The paperwork Captain James handed to us stipulated that we needed to *attend* ten sessions. It said nothing about participation. For the first session I'd simply sat in the chair and hung my head back over the headrest, examining the water stains on the ceiling. Since then I'd been stonewalling Dr Stone, using all my years of training as a detective to keep a conversation going while revealing absolutely nothing about anything. It was kind of fun. I'm not sure Stone agreed.

Surprisingly, Eden was with me on this one. The last thing Eden wanted was anyone examining her past, or even her present, lest they should start scratching their heads about her, as I had begun to do when we met. Eden had a strange vibe that I'm sure she worked hard to keep under control. She was either very attractive to people or oddly repelling, like a pretty but deadly insect. I didn't know much about Eden's childhood, but her father, Heinrich 'Hades' Archer, had been one of Sydney's most powerful criminal overlords back in the late sixties and early seventies. Eden and her brother, Eric, both joined the boys in blue for some reason, even though the two of them had made records in academia while completing their undergraduate degrees and been offered countless scholarships and fellowships to further their studies in science and forensics. Eden's partner, Doyle, had taken a bullet in the face from an unknown drug dealer and she'd barely blinked an eye at his loss or made any effort to catch the guy who did it. To my knowledge she'd never entertained a boyfriend, though wherever we went men walked into lampposts at the sight of her. Her colleagues at the station were deeply afraid of her, and no one would say exactly why. No, any digging by our shrink into Eden's character wouldn't have been pleasant for the moonlighting serial killer. While I was usually fairly brazen about my refusal to participate in our psychologist's appointments, Eden gave up just as little, albeit more politely.

Dr Imogen Stone's offices were on Kent Street on the third floor of an old narrow office building squeezed between a monster architectural design firm and the glass-fronted palace of a mega import company. The stairs were steep and the carpet smelled as if it had been really wet once. She didn't have a receptionist.

27

Eden and I sat in the waiting room. She pretended to read a magazine, flipping through the pictures, those predator eyes fixed and unseeing and her clockwork mind quickly ticking away. I watched her, bored. She really had quite a pointy look to her when I examined her carefully. She appeared in no way friendly, possessed none of the roundness and softness you would associate with approachability. Streamlined and fluid, like a shark.

When Dr Stone walked out she made me think of a big-eyed kitten. She was blonde and golden-skinned with a sprinkling of freckles on her small nose. Short and pretty, the girl next door. 'Stone' hardly fitted her as a name. She suited something soft and pretty like Lily or Pippi.

I shook my head when I realised she was speaking to me. Eden caught me checking out Dr Stone and looked embarrassed. It was the Endone slowing me down.

'Frank?'

'Yeah, yeah, I'm coming.'

'Coffee, either of you? Tea?'

'Frank will have a coffee,' Eden said. Dr Stone made the coffee in a little kitchenette behind her desk by the huge windows. I could see a slice of the harbour between the buildings across the street. The place was bright. When she handed me the cup I got a whiff of some delicate perfume. I wondered if she could smell me. There was still scotch in my veins.

'You've lost weight again, Frank,' she said as she took her seat. There were folders in her lap beneath her usual notebook. I felt dread.

'Keep your eyes off my body, Stone. I'm not a piece of meat.'

'Are you experiencing a loss of appetite?'

I sipped the coffee. Dr Stone waited, her legs crossed and hands on her notebook. She really had coordinated her shoes well with her outfit. She was all cream today. Went well with her skin. The cashmere on her shoes was touchable, like the shimmery stockings.

'You're going to stare at my shoes all session again, are you?'

'You really do have good taste in shoes.'

'Thanks,' she said. Stone was easier to frazzle than Eden. She shuffled the folders and the notebook. 'I've just got the report back from the inquest into the shootings at the Avoca Street church. Looks like your colleagues are prepared to accept your account, that Eden's brother, Eric, accidentally discharged his weapon at you, Frank, and that Eden, you mistook Eric for the killer and shot him dead. They're still puzzled as to how six bullets from Frank's weapon ended up in Mr Beck's head at a trajectory that would suggest he was lying on the floor and you were standing over him. Is this something you think we can talk about today? Either of you? Eden?'

I looked at Eden. She was sitting perfectly upright in her chair, which I assumed must have been difficult, because they were excessively squishy, the kind of chairs that swallow coins, chips, sets of keys, remotes, dining-room sets.

'I'm afraid I don't recall anything further about the moments before the shooting that I haven't already put in writing to the inquiry board,' she said.

'Listen to you,' I looked at Eden. 'You could read the news.'

'Let's get away from actions,' Dr Stone said. 'Let's talk about feelings. How do you feel when you remember that time in the church? Can you remember entering the building?'

Eden said nothing.

'Frank, what about you?'

'I'm sorry, Doctor. You lost me at "Let's talk about feelings".'

Dr Stone licked her bottom lip. I sat sniggering at my own joke for a minute or so. I nudged Eden to see if she'd heard it. She was rigid as pine.

'Tell me how you feel. Seriously. It will have no bearing on your masculinity, Frank, I promise you.'

'You women and your lies,' I sighed.

'I want to know if either of you are returning to that day in your minds, either voluntarily or involuntarily, because I think it's important that we put a name to how the event made you feel so that we can deal with it properly. Eden, you need to deal with your brother's loss and any blame you might have assigned yourself for accidentally killing him. Frank, you need to deal with having been injured so traumatically and with whatever caused you to shoot Mr Beck. Until we deal with these emotions neither of you are going to be fit to move on with your lives.'

Eden pulled a thread out of her jeans and curled it around her finger. She rolled it into a ball and placed it on the arm of the chair. I watched carefully.

'Frank, you're obviously not coping with what's happened,' Dr Stone said.

'What are you picking on me for? Pick on Eden. She loves it.'

'I'm picking on you because whether Eden has dealt with the trauma of this event or not she is clearly still functioning. You're not functioning, Frank.'

'I'm deeply offended by that. I'm here. I'm not even that late.'

'You *reek* of alcohol,' Dr Stone said. She rolled her eyes up in her head on the word 'reek' to illustrate her point. 'And I heard pill packets crumple in your back pocket when you sat down. You're doing the stand-up comedian act to deflect attention. I think you're on the edge of something big here. A big ditch, to put it plainly. We've played this game seven times now. I'm over it. I've got two more sessions with you guys after this one, and I really would like to stop beating around the bush if we can, please, just for the fun of it.'

'Jesus. You're pretty ballsy for a shrink,' I laughed. Eden gave me a warning look.

'I'm a cop shrink, Frank. I'm used to being fucked around. It gets boring.'

I laughed more. I'd never heard her get this fiery. It didn't suit her. She looked very gentle. She formed the words with perfect coral-pink lips and they zinged in the air like electricity. It was hilarious.

'Let's talk,' she said.

'Alright. I'm talking. I'm doing it. What do you want to talk about?'

'Tell me about Beck's last victim, Martina Ducote. I understand you and her were close, Frank.'

I stopped smiling. Eden watched me put the coffee on the small table between us and hang my head back over the edge of my seat again. For the rest of the session, I was silent.

The boy wasn't sure how he got to the car, how long he had been sitting there in the front seat beside the Bear, if the Bear Man had spoken to him or what he had said. He stared at his palms for a long time, at the blood. Eventually he came to himself.

The Bear was watching the boy with interest, a cigarette wedged between his fingers and his huge elbow resting on the sill of the open window.

'What's your name?' the big man asked. The boy's jaw ached, seemed impossible to move. He ran his fingers through his hair and tried to control the shaking in his bones.

'I don't know.'

'You don't know?'

'I don't remember.'

The man drew on his cigarette, blew smoke out the window thoughtfully. Ahead, the orange light of street lamps danced in the rain. The man and the boy turned as they heard the front door of the terrace house slam. The Captain was a dark shape in the night, adjusting the cuffs of his shirt.

'What's he going to do with me?'

'I honestly don't know,' the Bear said.

'Is he going to take me to the police?'

'No,' the Bear laughed. The boy watched as the Captain closed and locked the front gate behind him. He carried what looked like a linen bag over his shoulder.

'Did I kill that man in there?' the boy asked.

'If you didn't, Caesar did.'

'I didn't mean to kill him.' The boy's teeth were chattering.

'I wouldn't worry about it,' Bear said. 'No one's going to cry over him.'

Caesar thrust open the back door of the car and hurled the linen bag onto the seat before sliding in. Instantly it was hotter in the car. The boy sunk deep into his seat. Neither the Bear Man nor Caesar spoke as the car glided into the night. The men smelled foreign to him, of smoke and salt and blood. It was an almost chemical smell, metallic, reminding him of abandoned factories full of rust. The boy felt afraid. There seemed to be no possibility of escape, but he was assured by the Bear Man's calm driving, the cigarette slowly leading to another, the sigh he gave now and then as they pulled up to empty traffic lights burning red.

The boy only realised he was falling asleep when the car came to a stop. The man named Caesar got out and stood smoking by the car with the huge hairy Bear.

'You won't do it even if I ask you to, will you?'

'I don't do children.'

'Then we have an interesting little problem here, don't we, Bear? Because I don't dirty my hands like that either, and I don't want you driving him somewhere and leaving him. If he doesn't remember me, he'll remember you.'

'This doesn't need to be a problem,' the Bear said. 'He's a good kid. He's obviously got spunk. Let him hang around a bit and see if we can use him for something. Doesn't look like he's got an owner.'

'You can't watch him all day long.'

'Yes I can.'

Caesar stubbed his cigarette out on the ground. The boy squinted into the night, could see a building behind the two men all lit up with red and gold lights. People were going in and out of the front door or standing laughing and watching the rain. He could smell dope burning somewhere, clouding into the car through the driver's open window. The boy rubbed his eyes.

The door beside him opened and the Bear Man encircled his arm with his huge hand. He stumbled and grabbed the man's trousers. Caesar was gone. He was being led towards the house. Light, noise. A turntable just inside the door was playing 'Georgia on My Mind'. He brushed against a woman's bare leg. She looked down as she went past him, her painted lips falling open and eyes frowning.

Bear's hand loosened, slid to the boy's wrist, held his hand. There were people everywhere, most of the men clothed and the women not. The boy looked into a dark room and saw bodies moving and smoke curling. Somewhere he could hear a game of pool, the crack and tumble of balls. He was at the back door of the house when he saw the girl standing in the kitchen holding a glass of water and staring at him.

The boy only saw her briefly but the first thing he thought was that she was painted gold, that someone had sprayed her the way he had seen cars being sprayed in the city – with a perfect sheen on her cheeks and the tops of her arms, the soft curves in her throat where the skin dipped over bones and ridges. That was the second thing, the shape of her, like a fleshy bug, with bones speaking their poetry from beneath the gold in the armholes of her loose singlet and in her knees, her bare feet straining as she turned and started to move. Her wide nose and huge black eyes told the boy that she was at least partly Aborigine. He looked back at her as the Bear took him down some stairs into a lush wet garden. There was a greenhouse here with a tiny work shed attached. The Bear stopped and reached up and there was light. The boy was lifted onto a bench covered in tiny pots, seedlings, jars and bottles of every conceivable size and shape, tools rusting and half-polished, strips of fabric and tubes of ointment.

The girl bumped into the Bear's leg and he yelled out suddenly.

'Jesus, Mary and Joseph. Sunday, you scared the shit out of me.'

'Bear, who's that?'

'Never mind who he is. Were you born in a tent?'

The girl named Sunday shut the door of the little shed. The boy watched her curiously, tried to guess how old she was. She mustn't have been much older than him, he guessed, but he couldn't be sure. Bear heaved a heavy sigh and soaked the boy's face in the smell of ash. The big man switched on another overhanging lamp and wet a cloth in a sink by the door.

'Follow me around like a fucking puppy, you do. Always underfoot.'

'What's your name?' Sunday asked.

The boy tried to control his shaking. Bear wiped the blood from his cheeks and neck roughly with the cloth.

'Oi! I'm talking to you!'

'I don't know,' the boy said.

'Whattaya mean, you don't know?'

'He doesn't have one,' Bear said, irritation in his voice. 'Sometimes people just don't have names, okay? His mama got too busy to give him one, just like I'm too busy right now to listen to all your jabbering. You want his name? You sit quietly over there and think of a good one to give him.'

Sunday perched on the edge of the sink and looked at the boy with her head cocked slightly, trying to fit the perfect name to him. Bear took the boy's nose carefully in his huge fingers and felt where one half of the bone had slid up and over the other.

'This is going to hurt,' he said, before sliding the bones back into place with an audible crunch. The boy wailed.

'Francis,' Sunday blurted. 'We can call him Francis.'

'We ain't calling him Francis. He ain't no nancy.'

'Thomas.'

'I got too many Thomases in my life already.'

'What about Henry?'

'He's German. He needs a German name.'

'What's German for Henry?'

'Heinrich.'

'Good,' Sunday said. 'Heinrich is an ugly name. An ugly name for an ugly, smelly boy.'

'This ugly, smelly boy is going in your bed tonight,' Bear said. 'There ain't no other place for him.'

The girl gasped. 'No, he's not.'

'He sure is.'

'He's not, Bear. He's not.' Sunday slid down from the edge of the sink and slupped the big man hard on the shoulder. He didn't seem to notice. He was examining the boy's right hand in the light of the overhead lamp. The tiny bones behind his knuckles had been crushed, and two fingers bent at strange angles, deeper towards the palm than they should have been.

'You really made a mess of this,' Bear said. 'Somebody better teach you how to punch, boy.'

'Bear, he's not really sleeping with me,' Sunday continued. She turned to the boy. 'You're not sleeping with me.'

'Sunday, you shut your trap or you go straight back where I found you,' Bear said. His voice was soft, but the certainty in his words left no room for negotiation. The girl waited for more, a concession of some sort, and when none came she stormed out of the shed, slamming the door behind her. Bear snorted with laughter as he gently massaged the bones in the boy's hand back into place.

'Women, uh?' he said. 'Painful.'

I told Eden I'd think about doing some work for Hades. It was about all that would make her let me out of the car, stop her driving me around and lecturing me on my drinking, on what I could catch from the pub skanks, on what Martina would have wanted me to be doing.

I started to ask her how she felt about Eric's death and that shut her up real fast. I felt bad. I got the impression not that she missed Eric or that she loved him but that somehow her lack of emotion, her natural inability to feel anything for her brother or for any other human being, made her afraid. I sat quietly and tried to imagine what it might be like to be unable to love. I had no doubt that I'd loved Martina. I'd only known her a few days but I'd loved her. No matter how much of a tough guy I spend most of my time being, some part of me still believes in things like that.

When I swung open the apartment door I was shocked by a wall of perfume. I walked in and heard myself grunt in disbelief. Someone had cleaned the entire place – scrubbed it, washed it, bleached it, organised it beyond recognition. There were books in a bookshelf by the bedroom door that I'd forgotten I had, a vase of my mother's that had been wrapped in paper for years was on the polished glass tabletop exploding with flowers. *Actual* flowers. The kitchen was gleaming and empty of all things – the filthy sandwich-maker was gone, the dishwasher empty and airing, the window open. I went into the bedroom and sat at the foot of the bed by the cat, which was curled like a circular cushion. All my clothes had been washed and ironed and hung in the cupboard. The sheets were new. This must have taken a team of people. I called Eden.

'I'm driving.'

'I want my keys back,' I said.

'No,' she answered.

'I'll change the locks.'

'That would be a waste of time.'

'You want to mother someone, Eden, you should go and have a baby.'

'Stop acting like a baby and I'll stop mothering you.'

She hung up. I threw the phone on the bed and went to order dinner.

Driving into the Utulla tip made me nervous. It had made me nervous before I knew that Hades Archer, the Lord of the Underworld, was Eden's father and that everything the police suspected of him over the decades was undeniably true. Utulla tip had been referred to by police as 'Utulla Cemetery' since Hades acquired it back in the eighties, but dozens of searches had failed to confirm suspicions that Hades buried people there for a fee as a retirement hobby. Knowing Eden's secret, knowing how she spent her nights and what she and Eric had done in the past, confirmed for me that Hades had been the one to show the two fledgling killers the ropes. I'd never found a body to fit Eden's killings, although Eric's attempt to kill me was confession enough. Hades and his children were a superior breed of urban predator. However afraid of Eden I was sometimes when she gave me a crooked look or when I heard noises in my apartment in the night or when I walked home from the pub and felt eyes on me from the dark, Hades made me more afraid. He had been doing it longer. But it wasn't that. Hades didn't exhibit the same cold, emotionless, obviously detached murderous persona that Eden did. I'd met him once and he'd been charming. He had a number of friends in the police force, acquired simply through his friendly, giving, likeable character. He was funny, I'd heard. Really funny. I felt somehow that at least with Eden, I'd feel something before she did away with me. That rush of coldness surfers feel when a shadow passes beneath them. With Hades, I wouldn't feel anything. He was that good.

The huge gates, constructed as a complex filigree of twisted metal, chains, bottles, car parts, tyres and strips of melted plastic, were open. On the first turn towards the hill I passed a group of kangaroos made from mismatched mosaic tiles. They looked so real in their shape and posture I actually slowed down, instinctively expecting one to panic and leap in front of the vehicle. On the next bend, two stainless steel and coloured glass komodo dragons guarded a lump of sandstone as big as my car, one basking, one clawing at the air as I passed. A massive mango tree hung with dozens of glass and tin and copper mobiles filled the car with tinkling music.

As I drove up the hill I got a sinking feeling that I was wandering into a trap, that I was edging closer and closer to the point of no return, that I was changing things about my life. People would hear that I was working for Hades if I did it long enough. I was in no doubt about that. It would circulate in whispers around the office, slide under doors like smoke, glimmer in eyes as I walked through the offices. A connection made. Linked in. Hooked up. Frank Bennett and Hades Archer – known criminal association. But I shrugged the feeling off. I was being reckless. It was something I'd become comfortable with.

I told no one I was coming in an attempt to make an inconvenience of myself, but there was a man who appeared to be waiting for me as I pulled up under a 'No Parking' sign made from bottle caps nailed to a wooden board. He was carrying a mug of coffee and wearing a battered cap. Two small piggy eyes were wedged between the cap and his dark beard. He looked at his watch as I approached.

'Morning, Frank,' he said.

'Uh, morning . . .?'

'Steve. Hades told me to wait here for you. Show you what you're doing.'

'I didn't tell Hades I was coming.'

Steve shrugged. He had that 'Let's get on with it' look that a lot of labourers get in the morning. I reached into the back of my car and took out a water bottle. The heat was already oppressive, made heavier by the previous day's rain. I felt the hangover stir in my stomach as I leaned over. I popped two Panadol and shut the car.

'You had breakfast?'

'Not really a breakfast person,' I said.

'You need breakfast. We've got a barbie on.'

You need.

'Yeah, maybe later,' I said. Steve shrugged again and led me down a dirt path. We crested the hill in front of Hades' shack and I could smell bacon cutting uneasily through the tip stink. There was no sign of the old man. He had a strange garden going on around the house, disorganised, like he'd just been throwing random seeds on the ground and letting them survive or die as they wished. A huge pumpkin vine was woven around white roses towering over what looked like chives. A rabbit as big as a golf buggy had been constructed out of a wrought-iron frame and furred with knitting needles – there must have been thousands of knitting needles on the thing. It reared on its hind legs, its huge head turned back towards the gates.

'Look at that thing,' I said as we passed.

'Yeah,' Steve said.

He led me over another hill and through streets carved between piles of trash as high as two-storey houses. Car bodies, bookcases, ladders, toolboxes, washing machines, television sets, compressors, gas bottles, toys. Council street signs, rusting and bent where cars had run into them, had been resurrected and placed at the intersections of bare earth pathways. We emerged into a clearing at the bottom of the hill and were confronted by a huge pile of metal, three metres higher than me and at least twice as long.

'Hades wants you to sort this.' Steve nodded towards the pile. 'It's mostly donation material. He wants three separate piles – copper, aluminium and steel or iron.' He slapped a pair of gardening gloves against my chest. I took them and put them on.

'You got a hat?' he asked.

'No.'

'Not real prepared, are you?'

'Preparation is for boy scouts.'

Steve sniggered. 'I'll get you one. If you change your mind about breakfast, the work shed is on Marine Parade. Really recommend it.'

'I'll be right,' I said.

I started at the bottom of the pile. Copper pipes, lead pipes, a car axle. A shopping trolley, an engine block, various gears and cogs. Rusty saw blades, washing machine barrels. Steve came back with a hat and I quickly soaked it with sweat. The sun was beating down, almost ringing in the silence with its intensity. My hangover stayed away for the first hour and only my joints and the muscles in my back gave me trouble. I stopped and drank half the water, which was warm as a cup of tea. There was no shade. Sweat itched in the hair on my calves and tickled as it slid down my ribs.

My thoughts wandered. First there was the curiosity brought on by what I was doing – what sort of machine this battery might have come from, how old that set of sink taps was, why someone might have thrown out this perfectly good set of bolt cutters. As the work became monotonous I found myself thinking about Martina, about the first night we spent together, the way she held my eyes as I moved inside her. I shook these thoughts away for a while and thought about other girls. She returned to me, this time in the box they'd put her in, the half dozen or so people who had attended her funeral. I wondered how someone so beautiful could have been so alone in life.

When I couldn't get away from Martina in my mind I went to a tiny slice of shade that had developed by a stack of cars nearby and popped two Endone. I wondered if it had been a mistake to get away from my apartment, my television, the booze. I wondered if Hades would tell Eden if I simply left after a couple of hours. If he would even know. I stood in the shade and felt sickness swell in my stomach. The hangover. I told myself that working harder would get rid of it. Get rid of Martina. I drank the rest of the water and went back to the pile, stripping off my wet shirt.

Hours passed. I tried to control my thoughts. Surely the shrink had given me some strategies for that. Alright. My earliest memory. My dad. My dad taking me fishing, sitting under a bridge at Illawarra, yelling as loud as I could when the train went overhead and not being able to hear my voice. Catching toadfish and kicking them back into the water. What did I remember about Mum? Animals. She always had animals around. Baby bats plucked from the fried bodies of their mothers hanging on powerlines – stinking squeaking things, furry, leathery balls of bones. Bones. Martina's bones. Martina's bones in the ground. I'd left her. I'd left her. I'd fucking left her.

I went back to the shade and stood there for a full minute, breathing in, breathing out, sweat dripping off the tips of my fingers. It didn't stop the vomit. There was nothing in me but booze. I stood there gripping the bumper of a half-smashed Corolla and spitting.

Hades' laughter reached me through my throbbing ears.

'You didn't eat anything,' he said. He was leaning on a cane at the entrance to Tropicana Avenue, a few metres away from me, his eyes dazzling in the shadow of his heavy brow. I spat, couldn't catch my breath. He laughed again.

'Come on,' he said, and cocked his head.

'I'm fine. I'm right. It's just a hangover.'

The old man continued walking. I followed reluctantly. He led me back through the piles of trash towards his shack.

The sickness rose again. I didn't want to go in there. I didn't want to be alone with him. It wasn't fear, but a deep trepidation at what he might tell me, what he might want me to know, that heavy mutual understanding that I knew and didn't like what he was, what he had been all his life, what he had raised Eden to be. I'd been built for catching killers. We were supposed to be natural enemies.

He held open the door and I entered. I hoped he couldn't see that all my muscles were twitching, not just the fingers, the way they danced against my thigh. Sun spots clouded my vision, emerald green and swirling. It was cool and dark there. I wondered where my shirt was.

'Sit there,' he said and pointed to a chair at a small table by the wall. He took a water bottle from the fridge and set it in front of me. I drank greedily, looking at the things hanging from the ceiling – ornate glass Christmas baubles and hand-painted teacups, a lizard skeleton still fully assembled by cartilage, spray-painted gold. A huge glass pipe filled with a thousand coloured marbles was wedged between the floor and ceiling by the door to a tiny living room stuffed just as tightly with paperback books. I wanted to go over and look at the marbles. By my shoulder, hundreds of coins had been nailed to the wall, slightly overlapping like fish scales – American quarters and English shillings and Malaysian ringgits.

Hades put a roast beef sandwich together on a plate. I took it, thanked him and shoved it in my head.

'Bet you feel like an idiot.'

'It's nothing new.'

I finished the sandwich and worked on the water. It was painfully cold in my throat. Good. So good. Magic water straight from the hand of the devil.

'Lost weight since I saw you last,' he said. 'Lots of weight. You must have really liked that girl.'

'I did,' I said.

I was struck by how similar talking to Hades was to talking to my father. There was a battle raging inside me – a desire to hear what he thought I should do to fix all the problems in my life tangled up with an old hostility, a need to make sure he didn't find out anything about me he could use. Pride and anger and guilt at nothing. He turned the handle of a mug on the table towards him and resumed a coffee my presence must have interrupted.

'Funny what hard work will bring out in you,' he said.

'I needed it.'

'You want some more?'

'I think Eden will nag me to death if I don't come at least a couple more times, and that's not how I plan to die.'

'Not that kind of work,' Hades said. 'Something more in tune with your official employment.'

I frowned.

He smiled.

The old man folded the newspaper on the table between us with one hand and set it aside. It was a stalling gesture. A bit of silence, in case I hadn't caught on yet, to help me realise that offering me trash-sorting work had been a ruse all along. That was how Hades did things, after all. Set up games and created shadows. Observed, listened, tested you. Broke you down until you were vomiting from the heat stroke you'd brought on yourself. Embarrassed you in front of others, offered you a redemption ticket with something more dignified. That was how Hades operated. Ten steps ahead of everyone else, moving pieces around a game board you hadn't even realised was under your feet. Setting aside the newspaper was a metaphorical setting aside of everything we both knew and need not say in polite conversation.

You're on the edge, Frank, and you're making Eden and me nervous. We own you. I need you to do something for me, and you're going to do it whether you like it or not.

'I've got a problem,' Hades began. 'It's something I'd usually deal with myself, but seeing you're more skilled at this sort of thing I thought I might entrust it to you. I've been thinking of you almost as part of the family for some time, you know. You're my daughter's partner. It comes easily to me.'

Part of the family. Sharing in the secrets. Obligated. Till death do us part.

'What's the problem?'

'I'm being watched. I don't like it.'

'Who's watching you?'

'I don't know,' he sighed. 'Someone slippery. I've laid a couple of traps and come up empty. Seen the fucker only once with my own eyes. I know he's around though. I can smell him.'

I sat back in my chair and thought for a minute. Hades watched me carefully.

'Just watching? Nothing else?'

'Nothing yet.'

'Why would someone want to watch you?'

Hades gave a small laugh in answer.

I felt stupid. 'Okay. What have you seen?'

'A car, a couple of weeks ago. A Commodore, grey maybe. Nothing so brazen since but I feel it going on – and I know about these things.'

'He a cop?'

'I've been assured he's not.'

'Are you assuming he's male?'

'Yes. All I've seen is the car.'

'You got cameras out there on the road?'

'I do now. Haven't caught anything.'

I thought for a while more. The food had really cleared my head. I was almost excited. It had been a long time since I'd been on a case. I was hungry for it.

I reminded myself where I was, who I was talking to.

Hades watched me thinking, sipped his coffee, set it down and looked at it.

'Journalist?'

'They're not usually this persistent.'

'Is it a threatening kind of watching or a curious kind of watching?'

'How am I supposed to know a thing like that?'

'It's an instinct, I guess.' I shrugged.

Hades was silent for a moment.

'I'd say threatening. But maybe I'm just a cynical old man. I feel like letting me see the car was a kind of hello. Now there's uncertainty. Worry. It's not a very nice thing to do, even by my standards.'

I nodded. Made like I was considering. Weighing my options. Mentally sifting through the pros and cons. We both knew I had very little choice but the nodding seemed necessary.

'How much?' I asked.

'Ten grand to start you off, ten grand again when you catch him. Plus expenses.'

'I won't be catching anyone for you, Heinrich,' I said. 'And I'll need to think about this a little. But if I do agree to it I'll tell you who he is and why he's watching you. That's it. You want to hire me as a private investigator, I'll privately investigate. You want an accomplice in whatever you plan to do to him, you can go elsewhere.'

'Good enough,' the old man smiled. 'And please, call me Hades. Everyone else does.'

I went silent again. A deep discomfort had begun to grow in the top of my stomach, under my ribs, hard like a stone. I knew instinctively that nothing short of finding Hades' watcher would shift this discomfort, this ball of anxiety. I was in this now. The mere fact Hades had told me he was being threatened meant I was on the case. A man like Hades didn't air his dirty laundry for just anyone, and he certainly didn't make propositions when he even half thought the answer might be no. I'd been signed up the moment Hades thought of me.

I wondered if Eden knew. If she had planned this all along. I must have sighed, because Hades laughed as he got out of his chair. He sounded like a man who liked trapping things, watching them bash around the cage.

'Coffee?' he asked.

That evening I was feeling pretty good. A combination of sun exposure, a couple of long ice-cold beers and a new project to work on had me pretty upbeat. I sat at the bar in my local with a coaster and pen and began planning how I would tackle Hades' problem – what I would need, what it would cost. I made a couple of calls, just to be certain that there wasn't a pending investigation, state or federal, that might mean that someone was surveilling Hades. My list of things to do was pretty extensive when someone brushed against my shoulder. I looked up into Eden's eyes as she sat down beside me.

'Jesus, Eden, you're like a bloody stalker.'

'Lovely to see you too.'

'What have I done now? I've been an absolute angel today. I didn't trash my place. I went and spoke to Hades. I surrendered to his blackmail with a handshake and a polite smile. I've had two beers. Two.' I held up two fingers.

'If I had a doggy biscuit I'd give it to you,' she said. 'I'm here to brief you on the missing girls case. We've been signed up, as predicted by yours truly.'

'I've got two sessions with the shrink left yet.'

'And you're doing them, back to back, tomorrow morning.'

'Oh fuck off.'

She nodded to the bartender. 'Merlot.'

'What do you mean I'm doing them tomorrow morning? You're coming with me, aren't you?'

'I did mine this afternoon after Captain James signed me on.'

I exhaled with disappointment. The tiniest smile crept to the corner of her mouth as she took the wine from the bartender and sipped it.

'I can't believe you'd leave me alone with that woman when you've seen how she bullies me,' I said. 'You obviously have no regard for my spiritual well-being.'

'You're right. I don't.'

She took a slim shoulder bag from beside her and brought it to her lap, slapped a manila folder on the furry bar runner in front of us.

'Happy birthday to you.'

'Urgh. I'm not doing this on an empty stomach. Can I get you dinner?'

'As long as you don't go telling anyone.'

'Oh. Should I take it off Facebook then?'

She smiled wider.

'Relationship status: It's complicated.'

She laughed. It was a deep and soft musical laugh, some-thing I'd heard only once or twice since I'd known her. Two or three beats and it was gone. It was thrilling, getting Eden to laugh. Something I imagined circus trainers feel when they get a tiger to stand on its hind legs for the first time.

We moved to a booth and ordered steaks. I accompanied mine with a scotch. I was surprised when Eden slid onto the leather seat beside me. She smelled good. I'd been attracted to

Eden when I first met her – she was beautiful and dark like an enchanting witch from a fairy tale, and as with all practised evil beings she could look like a child in the light of one room, a queen in the next, a she-wolf in the dark. But over our time together the attraction had changed. My fear of Eden, of what she had done and what she was capable of, bound me to her like a magnet. I felt a natural curiosity around her. In some ways I wanted to know everything she had done but was afraid of letting her get her claws deeper into me. She was irresistible, like the carnage of a road accident. Something inside me wanted to see the blood, hear the screaming. I wanted to know exactly how bad she was.

'These are our missing girls,' Eden said, opening the folder and laying out three photographs.

I looked at the girls carefully. They could have been sisters but for the tiniest of details – one's nose was a little upturned, one had curly hair, one smiled with big square white teeth while the others brooded. They were all in their late teens or early twenties. One was posing with another girl at what looked like a nightclub, one was sitting on a milk crate smoking a cigarette, one was taking a melodramatic half-profile self-portrait. They were all blonde.

I didn't feel anything, not then. I didn't know these girls, and nothing so far told me that they were dead. I sipped my scotch and tried to memorise the faces.

'This is Ashley Benfield. This is Keely Manning. This is Erin Kidd.' Eden pointed to the photographs in turn.

'Uh huh.'

'Missing sixty-four days, missing thirty days, missing four days.'

'Any movement on the bank accounts, online accounts or phones?'

'No.'

'Check the bedroom cupboards of all their boyfriends?'

'They were all single at the time of going missing.' Eden shifted Keely's photograph up above the others. 'Last seen leaving her mother's house in Narellan to meet a friend in the city. That was the story, anyway. We've confirmed that she was actually going to Bankstown to get drugs and go on a three-day sex binge. She wasn't a fulltime prostitute – she'd get her pimp there to rent her a motel room and she'd take as many customers as she could over the three days. Live off the money for a couple of months.'

Keely was the curly-haired one, smoking a cigarette on a milk crate, skinny bare arms curved forward against the cold in a stripy grey-and-orange hoody. She was a pretty girl under all the make-up. Eden set her photograph aside and put up the photo of the profile shot.

'Ashley was a fulltime prostitute,' Eden said. 'She was couch-surfing between girlfriends' apartments when she slipped through the cracks. No one reported her missing for five days because everyone thought she was somewhere else. Last seen leaving Penrith Panthers alone at midnight after playing the pokies there for four or five hours. A crew of locals was with her and offered her a ride but she said she wanted to walk.'

'Silly girl,' I said. I looked at her photograph.

'Now this one,' Eden said, moving to the last photograph, 'gave us our most promising lead. Erin was a recreational pros-titute. She's been in and out of a few different jobs over the years but she was sleeping with a couple of guys in Camden for rent just before she went missing. She was supposed to have been seen hitchhiking on the Pacific Highway out of Camden four days ago, but we can't confirm that.'

Erin was in a nightclub in the photograph, smooshing her face against another girl's for the picture. Her eyes were bright and wild, the pupils huge.

'What's the lead?'

'One of the guys she was sleeping with is Jackie Rye,' Eden said, flipping through the folder and extracting another photograph. 'Jackie's got a permanent girlfriend, another young girl, but they're on and off again all the time and it looks like Erin might have slipped in there to knock boots with Jackie in the off period. She was only at his farm a short time. Over the past year Keely and Ashley have lived there too – for a couple of months each. It's the one thing all three girls have in common.'

I looked at the photograph of Jackie Rye. It was a mugshot, so the pale, washed-out look was very familiar, the shadows under the eyes and in the deep hollows of his cheeks and the slight yellow tinge to his skin. He was almost bald, a tuft of hair on the very top of his head combed back and the hair at the sides of his head slicked into what might have been a curly ponytail or mullet. Pale from a hat always worn to cover it. His lips were unusually pouty, which suggested to me that he might have been missing teeth.

'Didn't I see this guy on *Cleo Bachelor of the Year*?'

'Desperate times.'

'What do we know about Super Creep?'

'The usual history of small-time aggressions,' Eden sighed, slipped a stapled sheet of police reports in front of me. 'Mostly drunken and drug related. Three sexual assaults and no convictions recorded, all withdrawn before trial.'

'This is sounding like a good tip.' I flipped through the report swiftly. 'Except for the fact that he's been a fucking angel for five years now. What? He found god?'

'Came into money. Daddy died and left him the farm.'

'What did he say when we pulled him in?'

'Nothing. He hasn't been pulled. No one at the farm has been questioned at all. Best hope is that none of them know we're even looking.'

'Why?'

'There are approximately eighty people involved in the day-to-day running of Jackie's farm. It doesn't look like much but it's big business. His costs are low and profits are high. He sells specialty organic meat and other produce to major supermarket chains all over the West. He also makes a lot of cash from housing horses. There are two separate camps of workers with caravans where up to five people live at a time. Here and here.' Eden slipped an aerial map from the folder and pointed to two clusters of white blocks in a huge brown wasteland. 'People come, and people go. Jackie takes anyone and he's notorious for it. Runaways go there either to work on the farm or to hook up with the farm workers and share their beds. He's given a new start to plenty of violent criminals, people on the run, labourers looking for money on the side. It's a living breathing community of deadbeats. It's not as simple as just locking Jackie up, no matter how good he looks for it. All these girls seem to have stayed at Jackie's place long enough to give it as a stable address to their parents. But there's nothing to suggest Jackie himself even knew who Ashley and Keely were, that they were on the property. If we string Jackie up and he's not the killer the whole camp'll know before we have time to put up the fences.'

'Okay,' I sighed. 'So we bring them all in. All eighty.'

'You ever tried catching eighty cockroaches at once with your bare hands?'

'You sound like you have a better plan.'

'Captain James wants to send me in undercover,' she said.

The steaks arrived and I stared at mine. Eden shifted to the other bench and began hers. It was rare. She noticed me watching her.

'I'll be fine, Frank.'

'What if you have to sleep with someone?'

'That's your first concern? Of course it's your first concern. It's all you think about.'

'You've never been undercover. I have. You have to do things to keep your identity. Things you don't want to do.'

'I'm sure it was traumatic for you.'

'Eden.'

'I won't be sleeping with anyone.'

'What the hell am I doing while you're in there? Standing outside the fence holding my dick?'

'You'll head the surveillance team.'

'Oh, okay. Parked in a van outside the fence holding my dick.'

'Frank.'

'I don't like this,' I said. 'Why you and not me? I'd be a lot safer in there than you.'

'Why?' she asked.

I was about to tell her that it was because I was a man, but she gave me that look, the hunter's glare, and it halted the words in my mouth. Watching her neatly slice her meat in the soft gold light of the bar, I'd succumbed to her camouflage. Her thin silky fingers, the way that now and then she tucked a wave of inky hair behind her ear, revealing the sparkle of a modest diamond. It was all bullshit. She held my gaze for a second or so, showing me the emptiness buried deep in her pupils, and I remembered that I was in the company of something very foreign.

I cleared my throat. 'You might be right.'

'You get your meeting over early tomorrow morning and I'll get working with the team on an alias. We'll meet at, say, ten?'

'When are you thinking of entering?'

'Tomorrow night.'

'This is all happening very fast.'

'Spoken like a true commitment-phobe.'

I ordered another scotch and she finished her steak. I wasn't very hungry. She reached over and stole a chip from my plate with the swift, seamless actions of a bird. We small-talked for a while and then she checked the time on her phone like she had somewhere to be. Early in our partnership Eden and I had silently established that despite our opposing sexes and the usual social rules we didn't kiss or hug hello or goodbye. In fact, I rarely touched her. When she left that night though, she gave my forearm a couple of little pats and smiled.

I sat with my scotch for a long time wondering what that meant.

Eden liked driving at night. Hades had driven her and her brother around in the dark, through the city with the windows down, in their younger years when they refused to sleep. He would drive around Kings Cross and point out places he had lived and describe people he knew, winding the car down the hill to Woolloomooloo past the humming navy boats, then on through the city to look at the display windows at David Jones. She liked the shudder of wind through the car and the people creeping along the streets, some dancing and falling, drunk, some strolling arm in arm. She liked the way the city throbbed and glowed like an egg sac nestled in a black cave, huge and minuscule at once, writhing with ill-formed life.

Tonight she began the ritual by taking a packet of cigarettes from the glove box and lighting one, hanging her elbow out the window. She didn't smoke, didn't hang her elbow out the window of the car usually, but this brought a little of Eric back to her. And lately she didn't feel as though she could continue the night games without him.

She turned up the radio and let her speed drift down ten under the limit, started preparing her mind for what was to come. *Do you remember?* Eric would ask her. *Do you remember that night?* Eden wondered sometimes if half the reason she and Eric had let the need control them was to preserve the rage, the fear, the fragmented memories of the night their parents were murdered. Over the years, some memories had died, but now and then something new came to her – her and Eric crying together in the boot of the car, the tape muffling their helpless sounds, or words on the wind, pleading, as they were dragged from the house. Gunfire. Maybe Eric had been chasing these memories through all those years of killing, trying to get as much out of that night as he could, as if somehow he could return to it by living it in its most vivid form. Change it. Do something. Warn them. Eden knew that was impossible, but she liked to think about it sometimes. Dream about the woman she might have been if Hades had not saved her, if she had not been reborn a killer. She might have been an artist, she thought. But there was art indeed in what she did now, so she supposed it wasn't all that bad.

She pulled up outside Vinh Lim's apartment block and sat looking at the gold squares of light above her for a long time. Life – buzzing around in little boxes aligned carefully towards the sky, people laughing and watching television and cooking dinner and going to bed, blue-and-white light flickering on chipping vermiculite ceilings. Students, most of them, like Vinh. She let her eyes rise floor by floor to Vinh's balcony, to the banana lounge where he spent his Sunday afternoons oiling his stocky hairless body and sunbaking, calling other drug dealers on the phone. Because, yes, Vinh was a student, and like most students he had figured out a way to do as little work as possible for maximum returns. But unlike his neighbours, this wasn't through a combination of cash work and government benefits, a little petty theft or kinky massage services – Vinh's family serviced much of Kensington, Kingsford, Rosebery and Alexandria with ecstasy. Eden had been watching him for a couple of months, intrigued initially by Vinh's deadly reputation and the combination of this power with his strange obsession.

The first time Eden had been inside Vinh's apartment she came across the obsession accidentally. Vinh had been way down her wishlist of potential night-time playmates – she had bigger and badder targets for her cravings than him – but she'd been passing through and decided to do a little inventory, find out if Mr Lim was worth her time. If he'd be any fun. The living room, small kitchen and guest bathroom were all minimalist, clean, stylish. Chrome, black glass, red velvet. She had wandered into the bedroom and found a huge painting of a Japanese dragon hanging over the bed, inset with mirrors, the ferocity in its design impossible to ignore. Eden had pulled her gloves on and toured at leisure, picking up things, examining them, getting a feel for Vinh. She opened his laptop and went through its video and image files. Nothing interesting. Her instinct had told her, the first time she had laid eyes on Vinh, that he was worthy of a spot higher on her wishlist. That there was more to him. She didn't know what. She and Eric had only ever been interested in other hunters as their prey, and Vinh was just a convenience killer who snuffed out lives to feed his business. In order to fulfil the ritual, in order to bring back the memories, in order to play the game as it had to be played and finally satisfy that bloodthirsty urge inside her, Vinh had to be badder than this. He had to be a true prize. Eden went to the door to the spare bedroom and tried it. The door was locked. She smiled.

The door took a couple of minutes. Eric was the one good with mechanical things – locks, bolts, small machines, gadgets, engines. When she got it open, Eden was confronted first by the eyes in the dark. She switched on the light and looked around.

Stuffed animals. Hundreds of them. There were ponies and monkeys and piglets and bears, the whimsical characters of Japanese cartoons, horned and speckled and scaled, staring at her from the floor, shelves, bed, crowded around the little desk. There were laughing animals and crying animals, sleeping animals, staring animals, there were kittens and puppies and baby dragons. Eden closed the door quietly and stood in the centre of the room, in the midst of them, the main attraction in a packed stadium of stares. She reached out, plucked up a sock monkey and held it in her hands.

Most of the animals were infants of their species. Most of them had grossly oversized innocent eyes. Most of them were undeniably female, a distinction made merely by a pair of pigtails, a set of eyelashes, a little tutu velcro-strapped around a fluffy waist. Some of them had been altered, their mouths or crotches slit open and narrow fabric tubes inserted, then re-stitched. Eden let her eyes wander to the computer in the corner of the room, the toys sitting there. The favourites. She went to the computer and switched it on, knowing even before it began to power up what she was about to find.

Now, two weeks later, Eden sat looking up at Vinh's window and remembering the army of toys, the things she had seen on the screen, the way the light played about the faces of the toys behind her, the way the small screams through the speakers seemed to come from among them. She decided she would line some of them up around her on the shelves and windowsill of Vinh's bedroom as she worked on him, let their big buggy eyes watch. The lights beyond Vinh's balcony doors flickered on. Eden got out of the car.

It was always loud in the house of Bear and Caesar. It took a couple of days for Heinrich to get used to it. At night the women danced, sang, giggled, played, and the men wrestled with them and drank. Men came to the door and knocked and hollered – they always seemed happy to see Caesar and a little afraid of Bear, who spent most of his time at the front door, talking quietly and smoking. Heinrich couldn't sleep for the nightmares about the French Man and for Sunday kicking him in her sleep, so he wandered the house and watched and listened. Everyone seemed to want to feed him as soon as they saw him. He'd never eaten so well in his life. The women, some of them naked all night long and some of them clad in tiny underpants and corsets, patted his head and kissed him and brought him bags of sweets. His first year there, Heinrich ate with panic and hoarded some of what he received under the bed and in his cupboard in case he got no more, in case some day Bear took him by the collar and put him out on the street as quickly as he had welcomed him in. Heinrich knew never to get comfortable, no matter how comfortable life became. The Winter Days were only a memory away – and somehow he knew they had ended years of safety.

During the day while all the women were asleep on couches and beds and mattresses wedged together all over the house, the men workers came. They were skinny and dry and dark-eyed creatures, sorting cash into bags, organising it into packages and tying it with string, talking quietly and swearing. These men ignored Heinrich. He followed Bear around and tried to make sense of the conversations he heard. As much as he tried, he could never predict when the Silence would come over Bear. One minute he would be talking softly, gently, slowly, and then Caesar would give him a look and he would grab someone by the neck and drag them out of the house. Heinrich watched the violence with fascination. Bear's face was calm, his lips slightly parted, his eyes downcast, watching as his hands crunched bones and spattered blood up onto his cheeks.

Some nights Bear took Heinrich down the garden path and into the greenhouse, where they sat on wooden stools next to each other at the huge wooden table and worked. They potted tiny seedlings for hours and hours together, saying nothing, pinching the little white lives into the rich black soil and lining them up in trays. Sometimes Bear talked and talked and Heinrich listened. The big man got out his heavy, glossy books and pointed out plants he was growing. Heinrich learned their Latin names and when he got them wrong Bear made him say them over and over. Heinrich read long passages aloud and the big man sat and listened, helping when he stumbled over words. Sometimes they sat together and read other books – mechanical manuals and sports magazines and books of poetry. They dived into books about Greek mythology in the summer and Heinrich tried to follow their strange, winding tales, to remember names and gods of things.

Their most important work was harvesting the plants. Some of it was marijuana, which was fairly easy to dry, chop and package and could be done with careless hands. But Bear's special plants, the plants no one but him was allowed to touch, took a lot of training to handle correctly. All of them were deadly. They harvested cassava root for concentrated cyanide, Abrus precatorius for abrin poison, Ageratina altissima for milk poison. Heinrich didn't know what Bear did with the hundreds of tiny bottles of deadly potions but he loved the exacting art of dissecting the root bulbs, milking the seeds, boiling Cerbera odollam down into a dry powder and mixing it into spices. It was very crafty, and the hours seemed to fly with the big man beside him telling stories of cattle dying from ingesting this plant and an ancient king feeding that seed to his court to eliminate his enemies. Bear knew a thousand stories. In the early days, when Heinrich's hand and wrist were still strained from the killing of the French Man, the boy merely watched and marvelled at how such huge coarse fingers could reap such meticulous work. As the weeks passed, Bear began to give him assignments. Later he often left his apprentice alone to work while he smoked and chatted in the garden.

The only thing Heinrich didn't like about the house of Caesar and Bear was the girl named Sunday, who was always within arm's reach. She would wander in the garden behind the house, pouting and sighing and yelling abuse at them. But Bear never gave in, never let her so much as watch their business in the greenhouse. He said that a woman with Sunday's kind of temper let loose with the means to kill could bring the very world to its knees.

Heinrich didn't know what that meant, nor did he really consider Sunday a woman, but he followed Bear's rules and didn't tell Sunday anything about their lessons, even the ones that weren't about the plants. At night when he tried to sleep, curled at the very edge of the thin mattress they shared and desperately gripping his corner of the blankets, she was constantly whispering, half teasing him and half pleading for some crumb of information on Bear and what he'd talked about that night. Heinrich didn't like Sunday, but sometimes he felt sorry for her. Most nights she cried in her sleep, called out for her mother, and he did his best to ignore it, but it didn't do much for his chances of rest.

Whenever Bear and Heinrich would go on a 'trip', Sunday would want to come along. Today was no different. Bear was there, standing over the bed the two children shared, before the sun had risen, as he had done dozens of times before, his enormous frame outlined in the pale silver of the dawn waking outside the windows. Heinrich jolted awake and was hit with the heavy, comforting smell of warm bodies. Milky skin and sweat and hundreds of soft exhalations. Sunday sat up beside him and rubbed her eyes.

'Let's,' Bear said, cocking his head. Heinrich nodded and rolled out of bed as the big man disappeared.

'Tell him to take me,' Sunday said.

'No.'

'I'm coming.' She grabbed her dress, a yellow-and-white floral frock that was far too big for her, and wriggled into it. Heinrich tugged on his shirt. 'I'll be ready in just five seconds.'

'No,' Heinrich repeated. 'It's too scary for you. You're only a girl.'

'I'm ten times braver than you are.'

'Forget about it.'

'I'm coming.'

'No, you're not.'

'Will you guys shut the hell up?' someone yelled from the shadows. Groans and the creaking of bedsprings. Sunday slapped his arm. It stung.

'Yeah, Heinrich. Shut up.'

Bear passed the doorway, eclipsing it for an instant. Heinrich ran after him. Sunday weaved her hand with his, squeezed his fingers.

'Come on,' she begged.

'Sunday, get back to bed before I clobber you,' Bear grunted.

They walked out to the car. The unmown grass at the front of the house was wet with dew. The moon hung, a white eye, over the terrace rooftops of Darlinghurst. The car door opening was like a gunshot in the crisp silence.

The man and the boy drove off, leaving the girl standing on the lawn. Bear lit a cigarette, steering with his knees.

'Women,' he said.

They drove to a house in Surry Hills. It was a small brick hovel set back from the street and hidden at the front by unflowering bottlebrushes and weeds as tall as Heinrich's shoulders. A colony of ants had taken up residence on the concrete stairs leading to the lopsided porch. Heinrich jumped over them. Bear stood at the door for a moment or two, listening, and then looked down from his great height at the small boy at his side.

'Got your whomping stick?' Bear asked. Heinrich lifted the short wooden club Bear had made him from the lower half of a piano leg and waved it in the air. The man nodded and listened again. He seemed to make some decision, took a step back and kicked in the door.

Bear didn't usually carry a gun. He said they made him nervous. When they entered the little house the Bear Man simply stood in the doorway to the living room with his hands by his side and hollered. There were people everywhere, men mostly, sleeping on blankets on the floor and curled up on the sagging couch. A woman began screaming, gripping her hair. Her robe had fallen open and her breasts oozed out like deflated balloons. Heinrich felt his heart pumping in his neck.

'Samuel Pritchard!' Bear yelled.

'Oh Jesus, Bear, please. I was coming round today,' said a wide-eyed, skinny man in the corner of the room. The man reminded

Heinrich of a frill-necked lizard. His shoulders were all bone and skin, his jaw wide and flat and flapping with desperation.

'Today is here,' Bear said. 'I want Caesar's money.'

'I was going to come today and talk to Caesar, Bear, I swear to god . . .'

'Caesar's done talking. Pay me.'

'I swear to god!'

'Pay . . . me . . .'

'Bear, please!'

Bear looked down at Heinrich. The boy had been waiting for the look. He took his whomping stick to the nearest window and lifted it high over his shoulder. The window exploded in a shower of glass. The woman screamed again and another man got to his feet.

'Hey! This is my house!'

'Pay me, Samuel,' Bear said.

'I can't pay today. Bear, please listen to me?'

Bear nodded to the boy again. He went to another window and obliterated it. The glorious, glittery, smashy noises awakened something in the boy. He felt his limbs twitching. It was hard to breathe. He giggled a little, felt rage burning behind his eyes.

'Pay me,' Bear said.

'Now wait just a minute! He doesn't own this place – get him out of here!'

'Help!' the woman screamed. 'Help!'

'I can't . . . I don't have . . .'

Bear nodded at the boy. He went to a wall hutch that was littered with dirty plates, cups, mugs. A pink china cat stood there, licking its lanky paw. Heinrich smashed everything, whomping and whomping, glass and porcelain chips spraying on his shoulders and neck and hair. He shut his eyes tight and whomped. Fragments of china scattered at his feet. Shelves came down with a crash. He laughed, and the sound was unfamiliar to him. It was a guttural sound, like a cough.

'You're next, Sam,' Bear said.

'I don't have anything to give you, Bear. I don't have anything!'

'One last chance.'

'Please, just . . .'

Bear nodded at the boy and the Silence came over him. It was a warm and soft enveloping silence, like a hug – although it had been years since anyone had hugged the boy. The boy floated in it, his head lolling and eyes rolling, drifting on a summery wind. He was breathing in and out, and the whomping stick was rising and falling, and that was all he knew. He liked the heat it created in his shoulders and chest, the muscles constricting and pulling his arms into action. Doing their natural work. The thing that broke the Silence was Bear's hand gathering up a handful of his shirt back and dragging him into the present.

The air was suddenly cold in his lungs, cold as ice, and he was heading towards the door of the house, and dozens of people were staring at him from the couch, the walls, the stairs, the street outside.

'Did I do good, Bear?' the boy gasped. The whomping stick was wet with blood black as ink.

'Maybe too good, little soldier,' Bear said. 'Man can't pay us if he's dead.'

They went to the car, got in, and the big man tore away from the kerb. He looked down at the boy, who was rubbing his hand up and down the whomping stick, taking in the blood. A couple of streets away from Samuel Pritchard's place Bear stopped the car. He lit a cigarette and sat smoking it quickly.

'Boy,' he said after a time. Heinrich laid the whomping stick on his thighs and looked up at the big man beside him. 'Boy, I want to ask you a question. And it's important, okay? You're not in trouble, I just, I want to know. You know?'

'Sure, Bear.' Heinrich shrugged.

'Before that night when I found you,' Bear said, looking at the windscreen. 'That night when the French Man came. Did you . . .? Have you ever killed anyone before?'

Heinrich settled in his seat, looked at the dashboard. Later at the house Bear would tell the men that he'd thought the boy might be trying to remember something, that his face had become twisted, that he'd reached up and touched the blood spattered on his cheek.

Heinrich was remembering. He could remember some things, but not all. The Night of Fire and Screaming flashed around him, yellow and white, and he saw again the faces of the man and the woman in the windows. He remembered tears on his face – could feel them with the fingers of one hand. In the other hand he felt a small paper box, shook it inside the dream and felt the matchsticks rattle.

Bear watched the boy as he sat dreaming and told the men later that before the child seemed to come to himself, he muttered some words gently.

'I was only playing,' the boy said.

It was sunset before Eden got to the road. Or Eadie, as she would now be known. Only the gold of a forgotten day lit the horizon, but the dirt beneath her feet was still warm. As she trudged along, huge brown lizards drinking the warmth slid away warily from the sound of her into the long grass. The pack on her back had been messily stuffed with clothes and felt lopsided, and high into the rib bones in her back a drink bottle or deodorant can protruded, rubbing up and down. She'd walked for five kilometres in the setting sun and a healthy stink was beginning to rise from her, which was good. It would all add to the story of the lonely woman feeling lost.

Frank had stopped, stared, and then started laughing when he saw her undercover get-up that morning. The team had shopped at the local op shop, buying flannelette shirts and cotton singlets, faded jeans, cargo pants, and some of the female staff had gone for a jog in the station gym wearing the collection to produce a bag of unwashed, scrappy clothes. A make-up artist had been hired to bleach her long black hair badly, leaving a good four or five centimetres of regrowth, and she'd dried the ends until they frayed and split. Her eyelashes were taken down a couple of shades to dull Eden's dark, exotic look, her eyebrows were dyed, her long perfect nails were clipped off and she was encouraged to chew a couple so they wouldn't look so deliberate.

Eden didn't mind this treatment. She was thinking about the kind of person Eadie Lea would be. She stood in her thongs and shorts and her moth-bitten singlet and let them admire their work while her mind wandered. Finally, they swapped her BlackBerry for an old scratched-up Nokia, gave her a used wallet with her new identity cards and receipts and coffee vouchers, bought her a packet of Winnie Blues and a lighter. They told her she had been born again.

When she was about to leave, Captain James asked if she was going to give Frank a goodbye hug. It would be a while before she would see him again. The team, nervous and fearful around her at the best of times, paused with measured awkwardness at the idea. Frank didn't look overly enthused either. When she wrapped an arm around his neck he squeezed her close, tighter than she might have imagined, and laughed a little in her ear.

'We'll be watching,' he said.

She supposed Frank was watching now as she walked, but she couldn't know that for certain. Over the coming week, there would be no way of telling when he was watching and when he wasn't – there would be no earpieces, no radio or phone contact, no secret meetings the way there were in the movies. Eden was equipped with five different cameras. She wore one as a short pendant around her neck, a pinhole device disguised in a patterned teardrop made from silver. The other four – hidden in a tin drink bottle, in a deodorant can, a book, a pair of sunglasses – were to be set up somewhere in her new life. On Friday morning she'd get the train back into the city under the pretence of attending to some business and change all the batteries. Until then, she was on her own. Completely. She wouldn't know if she was doing well, if she'd uncovered something connected to the missing girls, if she was heading down the wrong road. She'd only know when she met the team on Friday.

Eden walked, her head down, and thought. There was a lot of pressure on her. If she just kept up the act, she supposed, things would follow their proper course in time.

She reached the gates of Jackie Rye's farm just as the skin on the sides of her feet gave up and white-and-pink blisters emerged. Eden hadn't owned any thongs in her other life. She bent down, took the thongs off and hooked them on her fingers, walking carefully on the rocky clay.

Almost as soon as she breached the rickety wooden boundary three huge mix-breed dogs bounded towards her, emerging on the horizon as wavering shapes hovering above the land with their speed. They surrounded her, a rabble of howling, growling mongrels, dancing in the dirt. She walked on. At the crest of a soft hill she came into the view of a group of men standing by an open-bed ute. Big men. They watched, emotionless, as she approached, saying nothing, like hairy mannequins unposed and hung with filthy rags. They were near a shed with a leaning bar that was lined with brown beer bottles.

Eadie approached and stopped.

'Jackie here?'

One of the men flicked his head towards a group of caravans clustered at the bottom of the hill. Another dog joined the three berating her, this one a small white terrier with paws thick with mud. Eadie nodded and walked on. The men's eyes followed her.

Lamps were already lit and moths and mosquitoes were gathering in the gloomy light. When she reached the first caravan she listened but there was no sound. Eadie heard laughter from the next van. She stood outside it for a minute or so and tried to think about the sort of things normal people said and did, the way they looked at each other and the way they moved. Because that was what frightened her most in the end – acting normal, constructing Eadie Lea as a believable human and the kind of person who would fit in around Jackie and his friends. She knew she came off a little strange in real life, because she was different, because her true nature, the killer, the monster, was rarely far from the surface of her being.

Eadie stood in the dark outside Jackie Rye's caravan and listened to *The Simpsons* playing on a television inside, people laughing and talking, and forks scraping on cheap china plates. She breathed, then reached forward, knocked and pulled open the screen door.

The room was full of smoke. That was the first thing that hit her – lots of people wedged into the half-dark, smoking cigarettes, which created a coiling ceiling blanket in hues of royal blue and sunflower yellow lit by the television in the corner. Her eyes wandered over two creatures sharing a tiny crushed-velvet foam couch by the kitchen bench, one lying in the lap of the other, hairy and wrack-thin and pig-eyed in a way that left them sexless to the casual observer. Eadie noticed other sets of eyes in the dark, bodies stretched on the floor in the space between the couch and the wall, crammed in and around a plastic deck chair in a corner, lying on the bunk bed in the tiny annex bedroom. The last pair of eyes she found was that of Jackie Rye, who was sitting in a green velvet recliner by the sink, looking back at her through the smoke he exhaled.

Jackie gave Eadie the impression of an emaciated king, the way he was lounging with one leg up over the arm of the chair and the other flopped on the floor, leaving his tiny worn shorts gaping open, the darkness in the thigh holes blessedly impenetrable. Everything about him suggested dark hair and wet skin, spent bodily needs and unwashed crevices. His saggy upper lip stretched as she made eye contact and he lifted and adjusted the sweat-stained cap on his head.

'What's this? A visitor?'

'Jackie?'

'Who's asking?'

'I'm Eadie.' Eadie shifted her weight from one foot to the other, scratched her scalp. 'Some guys sent me down here looking for you?'

'You found me,' Jackie said. 'You must be after a bed.'

'Yeah.'

'Well, baby, this ain't no fucking hotel.'

Everyone in the room laughed. The impression was alarming. Nine or ten sets of almost identical hacking laughter, forced laughter, going off like two-stroke motors all around her. Eadie held her ground. The laughter drained away slowly and Jackie let it go completely before he began again, relishing, it seemed, every minute chuckle. Eadie got the impression that people around there laughed at Jackie's jokes a lot.

'Alright, everybody get out.'

They left, one by one, uncurling themselves, rolling, sliding, extracting limbs that had been wedged between milk crates, out from under shelves, from between the limbs of others. Eadie stood aside and watched them go. On their way out, one of the sexless twins stopped and stared and licked his or her teeth as he or she looked over Eadie's backpack, even reaching out once and grabbing the bag and shaking it to hear if it rattled. They all smelled. That was the thing about these kinds of people, even soap and water couldn't combat the endless stink of their lives – sheets that never saw a washing machine, animals that sweated on couches and pillows, sex that was had haphazardly up against things, the reek ignored, blended in, absorbed. The rabble slinked away into the dark. Eadie thought she was alone with Jackie until a tiny voice called from the dark beside his recliner and she saw the shape of a young girl sitting there.

'You're pretty, aye,' the girl said. Eadie followed the words very closely in her mind with the exact same thought about the girl, so for a moment she felt as though her thoughts had been laid bare and was frightened. The girl was very pretty, swimming somewhere in that glorious period between puberty and late teens, everything about her milky and soft, with an impish pointy nose that she probably hated and elf ears that curved forward a little too much, the big round eyes of a newborn rabbit. She was wearing what looked like a cotton shift in royal blue, braless and pantyless, flushed from the heat.

'Thanks.' Eadie cleared her throat.

'Siddown,' Jackie said. Eadie shifted some sheets and pillows aside and sat on the couch where the twins had been. It was damp. 'How'd you hear about this place?'

'I been staying with some girls I know in Wauchope. I was in Cronulla before that with my husband. I'm just trying to get away for a bit, maybe get some money behind me before going up north. I'm kind of . . . laying low, you know?'

'Laying low? From him?'

'Yeah.'

'Punching on, were ya?'

'Little bit.'

'Got any sprogs?'

'Nup.'

'Lucky.'

'Yeah.'

Jackie thought for a while, sat staring at her. He sucked in that flappy lip and chewed it, let his eyes wander until they settled on her breasts. Eadie scratched her upper arm, covering them, then let her arm fall. Seconds passed.

'Well look, it's pretty crowded round here right now.'

'Aww please, Jackie, let her stay,' the girl whined suddenly. The small man reached out and shoved her head the way a man might shove away a dog.

'No one fucken asked you.'

'I'm a hard worker. I've done some track work in the city. I'm best with horses but I can do other things. I learn fast.'

'Most of the girls here don't work that way,' Jackie said.

Eadie could suddenly feel Frank watching, his presence in the room like a heat hanging about her shoulders and the back of her neck. She reached up unconsciously and fondled the pendant camera, remembered what it was and dropped it.

'My girlfriends told me sometimes you make an exception.'

'Hey,' Jackie laughed, throwing open his hands. 'Doesn't bother me how you make your living. But you decide you're gonna work for me and then you start sharing that pussy around, you understand those boys who employ you gotta pay me for the labour I'm losing. You either work for me on whatever I put you to, whether it's horses or whatever I got going, or you work for them boys and they pay me for the privilege. Either way, I get your labour or your rent. Most likely, you won't get a day into straight work before one of these boys puts you in his bed. Toey fuckers from arsehole to breakfast time round here. But I find out you're freelancing that tight round arse and I'm not getting what's owed and I'll have you out on it before you can spit.'

'I'm good for my word.'

'Word's as good as shit round here.'

The girl leaped from where she was crouched, seemingly in one bound, onto the couch beside Eadie. She was all arms and hands and cold fingers, hugging and molesting Eadie's hair and neck in a flurry of affection. Eadie felt sick.

'Oh, I can't wait for us to be friends,' the girl said, gathering Eadie's ponytail and curling it around her fingers. 'Jackie baby, can she live here with us?'

'No. I got enough mess here as it is. Take her to the empty van near Pea's, and tell Pea to take her out in the morning. And don't you fucken come back till my show's over. Sick of your noise.'

Eadie tried to pick up her bag but the girl had it. *The Biggest Loser*'s opening credits had begun and Jackie turned up the volume until it was painful. It was a relief to be out in the night, despite the heat, which met Eadie's face like a hot breath.

'I'm Skylar,' the girl said, letting her hand trail down Eadie's arm and into her hand. 'I'll show you everything.'

I wasn't really expecting to find anything the next night when I set out for Utulla to catch Hades' watcher. I spent the night before and all that day near Rye's Farm, cooped up in a van parked behind a bottle shop in Camden with a tall, gangly ginger bloke named Juno, one of those 100-per-cent gingers so speckled and spotty and orange all over he was fascinating to look at. Hipster glasses with thick black frames and an unkempt flame-orange beard. Juno fit into the van the way a spider might fit into a straw, all joints and thin limbs tucked in towards his centre, whiskery fingers clicking and tapping, sensing vibrations in the string and things near to his grasp.

It was clear to me within minutes that Juno was new to our station and had never done much for the force other than tech work. For one thing, he was constantly going on about how 'hot' Eden was, even in her feral down-and-out camouflage. He talked about all the gear littered around the van, the cameras and monitors and radios and laptops, like they were his impressive and successful friends. I got sick of his jabbering midway through the night and wandered into the bottle shop just for something to do. The Jack Daniel's pre-mixers I accidentally bought were from the back of the fridge and painfully, gloriously cold in the summer night. All we were doing was watching Eden sleep anyway, in her unnaturally still and silent and beautiful way. I got out of there before Juno started sketching her in charcoal.

Juno was useful for the techy little iPad-looking thing he lent me, a flat-panel computer no bigger than my palm that had an infrared display and could work via satellite. I planned to use it to catch the watcher. He gave me instructions in about ten thousand words more than were necessary, so I was pretty confident I'd be alright.

It was weird driving the company car on a job without Eden. I turned the radio up for company and then turned it back down because the advertising made me frustrated. I wondered if all this restlessness might have been a strange kind of longing now that Eden was away and nowhere that she could hassle me and intrude in my life. I kind of liked her hassling. Eden being away meant that I was thinking about her, trying to fill the empty spot in the car with some vision of her and what she'd do and say and think as we drove along. This was awful because it meant I was thinking about Eden all on my own, without prompting, my thoughts just naturally turned that way, curious. I didn't want to be the kind of cop who thought about his female partner when she wasn't around, whether it was romantic or not. It's a sure sign of weakness – and weakness leads to addiction.

At the entrance to the wide dirt road that led to the Utulla tip I veered off and hid the car on the edge of an embankment.

I was only half-glad to be met with the angry scream of a million cicadas because it might mask my approach – but might in turn mask my target's retreat. I stripped down to my black singlet and cargo pants and made sure my boots were laced tight. I knew there was probably lantana in the bush around the tip, but as long as it wasn't waist-high I figured I'd be alright. I tucked some small binoculars, a 9mm, the tracking device, my mobile phone and a pair of handcuffs into the various pockets of my oversized pants.

Without much of a plan I started walking towards the tip. Eden was really the one who organised our operations. She would think about things for long quiet hours, sleep on it if she had to, draw maps and calculate approaches and write up contingencies. I like to wing it most of the time, which probably isn't the best approach, but it used to serve me well when I worked over in North Sydney with my former partner. Sometimes just turning up somewhere and hanging around, chatting to local store owners or ordering a coffee and reading the paper in the general vicinity of wrongdoing can throw up some useful clues. I'm one of those guys who turns up to a blind date early and sits at the bar, waits for her to get to the table and sit, to see if she's nervous, what her legs are like. Back in the days when people would set me up on blind dates, that is. These days no one bothers. I don't have enough class.

Hades had seen his stalker once with his own eyes, in a car on the road to the tip, but the other times had simply 'felt' that someone was hanging around. I wanted to know how easy it was to see Hades in his shack from the road. I wanted to know what it took to sit out there for lonely hours watching, just how dedicated this guy would have to be, what he hoped to see while he watched.

I had a sweat going before I got far. I stuck to the mud tracks in the road to muffle the sound of my boots and now and then glanced up at the stars, which were blazing like pinholes of lightning between the dense canopies of the trees that lined the road. There was no moon to speak of and now and then animals rustled and scampered in the blackness around me. It was nice out there. I could see the appeal. I usually think of bushwalking as an itchy and arduous, annoying activity, but at night it feels very natural, something I could do often. Some of it is knowing I'm the most powerful creature out there. A natural predator. The animals fled at the sound of my breath.

Things seem farther in the dark. I reached the end of the road, where Hades had seen the car, in about twenty minutes. I smelled the tip well before I saw it. My hair was slick with sweat and the singlet clung to my stomach. The tip's orange sodium lamps cut perfect cone shapes into the dark, illuminating what was beneath them and nothing else. Moths ducked and dived in their rays. I crouched by the gates and took out my binoculars, had a look at Hades' shack. I could see the kitchen quite clearly, but there was no Hades. A slice of curtain or something, bright green. I watched. As my eyes adjusted I picked out the knitting-needle rabbit and the peach tree at the back. In time Hades walked into the kitchen, sat where I assumed he always sat at the table facing the door and read his newspaper. It was the briefest flash of stern face, grey hair, collar. Then he was gone.

I let the binoculars drop and thought for a while. What was the point of all this? The experience of seeing Hades there had been exhilarating, I had to admit that. It was a cheap thrill though. He didn't know I was there, and that gave me a little zing in a very simple, ironic way. After a second or two the thrill wore off, because he was just a scary old crim no different to plenty of scary old crims I'd come across in my career. There was nothing personal in it. Whoever was after Hades was feeding his curiosity – because it needed feeding to endure the sweat, the patience, the physical discomfort required to stalk the old man out there all alone in the bush. It was fury, that fuel. A sad or romantic or hurt one. Real fury burns low and strong, sometimes for years, but the explosion potential is always there. I knew this from years of looking down at the mangled bodies of unfaithful lovers, abusive fathers, overly successful sisters, those who had ignored a quiet fury for too long, until it got out of control, until it turned and came back to bite them.

I felt Hades' nervousness then. He'd been right to act quickly.

I set myself another hour to wander in the bush. There were animal tracks everywhere, smooth and bare between the dry forest bedding, and each time I crept up on some beast in the dark it retreated from me violently, sending chills through my stomach. I've never been afraid of walking around at night – I was big even in my teenage years and was usually the one instigating pub fights in my twenties rather than being picked on. I've never been mugged or stalked or hunted, so I suppose nothing much has happened to encourage a fear of the dark. I walked into a spider web once as I wandered and calmly backed out of it, more to avoid the annoyance of getting my fingers tangled up in it than any real fear.

In time I came across an old shack and walked up onto the porch to have a look. Inside were two bare desks and empty bookshelves, a couple of couches covered with sheets. The place looked clean and cosy. I wondered if this had been some kind of teenagers' retreat in Eden and Eric's old days there. I tried the door. It was locked. Above the porch steps hung a hand-carved fairy wind-chime, its slender body intricately chiselled from beechwood and strung with a collection of mismatched bells that tinkled when I reached up and touched it. I turned the fairy in my hands and noticed a single word, 'Eden', carved into one of her dragonfly wings.

I sat on the porch and pulled out the device Juno had given me, set it on my knee and waited for it to power up. The thing worked like a GPS, gave me a colourful layout of the land constructed by Google Maps and a blue ball telling me where I was. The highway out to the Utulla tip loaded, along with the dirt track and the tip grounds illustrated in a pleasant stone grey. The map adjusted as it found my position and the blue ball began to radiate waves on the screen. I stood and walked a few paces, watching the ball to get my bearings. There was even a little compass feature that turned the map around. I smiled. I was thoroughly alone in the shapeless green wonderland of the bush around the tip.

But right in the middle of the Utulla tip a red dot was glowing. I tapped the screen and a bubble emerged with some data and a phone number. The device was triangulating Hades' phone. Right. Now, all I had to do was see who else was around.

To the north, just off the highway, was another red dot. It was stationary. I tapped the dot and found the number for the mobile phone my device was detecting. I hit the arrow alongside the number and a web page opened. John's Tyre Lot. Of course. I'd seen it on my way in. John probably left the phone at the office when he was not there to keep clients from bothering him. I wandered and played with the device. Two more businesses up on the road were blinking their presence. I shifted the map around and looked out to the east. Nothing. I walked along the barbed-wire fence separating the bushland from the tip and fiddled with the device's settings. West, nothing. South, nothing. It was kind of fun, watching my progress on the screen, an insignificant blue bubble rolling along the earth, surrounded by a few other idle blobs and, as I widened the map, dozens and then hundreds of others. A little electronic ant farm. I found my car on the map, another red bubble, giving off a signal. My mobile. I stopped walking and chewed my lip. Then I slid my hand into my pocket. My mobile was there.

I started walking faster and, as I did, whoever was giving off the red bubble at my car seemed to sense this new awareness and began to move. I shoved the tracking device into my pocket and ran.

The return journey is always faster, because you know how far you've come. Once again I had no real strategy. I'd never worked as a private investigator, so when I began to formulate plans in my mind I kept running into roadblocks posed by the loss of my police power. Pulling my gun, even carrying it, in this situation was probably inappropriate. The handcuffs were useless too, unless I got myself into some real trouble. I didn't see much advantage in the idea of putting the watcher on the ground and asking him what the hell he thought he was doing. I decided it would probably be best to simply follow the watcher and see if I could find out who he was. Surely someone with this kind of grudge against Hades would be known to him.

I hit a rhythm and was back at my car within minutes. I was surprised how easily my body took to the exercise, almost as though it had been longing for some kind of exertion and was buzzing with a strange joy at having secured it. Everything was ticking – my temples, my scalp, my jugular, my thighs.

There was no sign of the watcher. I pulled out the device and looked for him. The red dot was moving steadily towards the east, winding a diagonal path back up through the bush to the highway. My car had spooked him. I tapped the bubble and a window emerged, but the number was replaced by a series of dots. I didn't have time to think what that meant. I pocketed the device and took off at a quiet jog, up on my toes, following the sheen of smooth clay on the road. The embankment was steep. The thin fingers of bracken clawed at my bare arms. I stopped, held my breath, listened. I couldn't tell if the sounds I heard were footsteps or my own breath. Ahead through the trees glowed the orange lights of the highway. Something passed before them. I stood still. The voices of the cicadas fell and there was a strange warm silence, as though they could feel what was coming.

I was aware of the watcher's presence behind me and to my right, half a second before he swung at my head. I ducked and his fist glanced off my ear. In those first frenzied seconds I remember thinking how rude that was, how cowardly to try and clock me without even saying hello. But that was just the adrenalin and the shock talking, slowing my thoughts. I spun and ducked and threw myself at his legs. He was all taut limbs and rock-hard fingers and pointy elbows in the dark. We wrestled awkwardly, teeth glancing off skin, and bones jolting painfully with more accidental luck than real strategy. It was pure chance that my gun slid out of my back pocket and the light from the highway hit it just right so that from where he was he saw it and I didn't. Before I could even tap into all that hidden horror still left over from being shot by Eric and nearly losing my life on the job, the man in the dark lifted the gun above his shoulder and clubbed me in the face with it. I sprawled in the wet earth.

'One guard dog ain't enough, uh, bro?' The man laughed. He dropped the gun beside my head and stepped over me.

It was light by the time I got off my arse. I don't know how long I sat on the embankment in the dark with my face in one hand and my gun in the other, blood running between my fingers and down my wrist, trying to come to full consciousness. Some part of me knew that it was dangerous sitting there, that the watcher might return now that he knew how easy it was to flatten me. Whenever I tried to get up I swayed, and I wasn't game to lie down in case I passed out. So I just sat there like a child breathing and thinking about what I should do next. I even considered calling Hades and asking him to come see if I was alright. I dismissed that idea pretty quickly. A lot of it was probably the drugs and not sleeping right, plus coming down from the adrenalin high of realising the red ball on the screen wasn't my own. The rest of it was the sheer brute force of the blow to the face. He'd got me good.

I went back to the car and took out a notepad. I wrote down everything I could remember about the watcher in the dark. Tall. Wiry. All bones. What felt like short, hard hair in a shaven afro. A sort of Aboriginal-sounding inflection to the end of his phrase. *One guard dog ain't enough, uh, bro?* Then I put the notepad away and drove in to work.

I woke up at around five in the afternoon, the grossly clean bedroom full of pink light, my phone vibrating under my shoulder. I'd come home around 2PM and just lay down on the edge of the bed for a minute, my hands on my chest, my face up towards the window. Sweat. My mouth like sun-baked sand.

I took the call with my notepad on my knee and my pen moving slow, crookedly. I was getting old. Once upon a time I could get in a good punch-up and carry on for days like a kid with grazed knees, never slowing, the pain becoming part of every moment until suddenly it was gone, as though it had never been. I used to like it sometimes, the ache, the memories, the wounds provoked.

Gina at the station gave me three names living in the Sydney metro area that matched the partial print from my gun. From them, I picked the guy who was identified as Indigenous Australian on his criminal record, short wiry hair, bony, previous assault charge. Gina was good for squeezing things through the lab that should have been placed in the queue, things that didn't necessarily need to be written down in the log book or explained to bosses. Some women, you just have to give them a look. They're the kind of women who had good fathers. I sat for a minute and thought about sleep, staring at the name on the paper, the man who'd hit me.

The watcher. Adam White.

I'm coming for you, Adam, I thought.

Eadie slept little. She'd lived in places like Jackie's farm before, when she was growing up at the tip and for a couple of months during her specialist training – city-limit places where the air was thinner and colder than it should have been and carried sounds for miles. A cough would reach her as she stood at the window looking out at the yellow lights, even though her caravan was away from the clusters of others. It was up against a fence, nestled in overgrown weeds and grass that for all manner of creatures probably acted as ladders up to the badly sealed window in the filthy kitchenette. The cough could have come from anywhere. There was laughter out there too, and the lowing of cows in the first light hours.

Inside the caravan things crawled and crept and shuffled about. Eadie lay in the damp sheets as the sun was rising, watching some elongated grasshopper-like insect wander across the chipboard ceiling, feelers out exploring, touching mould spots and lumps of dried toilet paper hurled there. Cigarette-stain clouds spread out before it like burned wastelands. She wondered if it could fly. She didn't want to crush it but would if it pushed its luck.

She heard the girl, Skylar, coming at a sprint across the barren dirt. Sounded like she jumped on the fold-out stairs. Eadie was tying up her hair.

'Breakfast is on and you're gonna miss it.'

'Yeah yeah,' Eadie called.

The girl came bumbling in, child on Christmas morning. Dust-covered pink Uggies and a denim miniskirt. Eadie hadn't realised how oddly shaped she was, short and nimble but somehow layered with pale milk baby fat on her thighs and above her breasts. Cellulite under the skirt. Bad diet begun long ago. Something to grope in the dark. The peachy face and rabbit eyes were beaming with curiosity beneath layers of unnecessary make-up. Eadie imagined Jackie spooning the girl in his grey-stained bed and sighed.

'Heard from the ex?'

She was straight to the drama, this one. Probably addicted to it since birth.

'No.'

'Rude.'

'It's a bit of a rude business.' Eadie shrugged. She pulled on a denim jacket and stood looking at her chewed nails. The girl was going through her things unabashedly, taking the sunnies from the counter and trying them on like a bored kid in Daddy's big office. Eadie took the glasses.

'Do you want this?' Eadie held up the deodorant can with the camera embedded in its base. 'Gives me a rash.'

The girl took the canister, smelled its tip.

'Mmm, yum. Thanks.' She bounced on the bed. 'So what happened with your ex? Tell me everything. Was he sleeping around? My ex was. Some short slut from his work. Fat, too. I mean I'm short but I ain't fat. This bitch was like your reflection in a car door. Fucken wide.'

'Cushion for the pushin',' Eadie said.

'Yeah, man. I mean, honey, you gonna trade in? *Upgrade,* for fucksake.'

Eadie smiled. A girl child talking about exes like a seasoned housewife from the North Shore. She couldn't pull it off. Couldn't know how ridiculous she sounded.

'Men are idiots.'

'So?' The girl pulled her leg up, exposing floral undies in the hollow of the skirt, settling in for a deep'n'meaningful. Truth or dare.

'Oh, you know,' Eadie said. Shrugged. Sighed. 'Let's go get this breakfast.'

'Oh.'

'It's too early for this. Really. Trust me. It's a pathetic story, hardly the sort of intrigue you're imagining.'

'The what?'

'Never mind.'

'Alright then.' Skylar jumped up and pulled down her skirt, seemed to want to do a little dance but, because of the limited space, settled for an enthusiastic stamp of her boots like a soldier marking time. 'Sorry, I talk too much. I'm just excited, you know? It's been ages since I've had a mate out here.'

'You do talk too much,' Eadie said. She held open the door. 'But that's alright. You can do the talking for the both of us. You can be the company rep.'

'The company rep.' Skylar laughed too hard, mouth open, teeth like a sheep, some missing in the back. 'Yeah, that's me.'

The meal sheds were little more than a pair of flimsy aluminium carports touching unevenly in the middle. They were concreted into the barren earth, surrounded by dry white dog faeces. The dogs rushed out to welcome them as they headed across the plain, a three-legged kelpie, some half-dingoes and a collection of scruffy rat-dogs. The frustrated barking of the hungry and kicked, the unnamed, arthritic, flea-ravaged. Several heads turned as she approached. The groups were oddly segregated by sex. Some women in moth-chewed Kmart jumpers and Ugg boots were smoking around a wooden picnic table, a two-litre Coke bottle swaying between hands. In the group of men Eadie recognised the androgynous twins from the night before, one staring at her, heavy browed, the other picking its nose. Blue smoke leaked from the men's table. Skylar grabbed a paper plate and passed one to Eadie. She loaded it with a pair of black chalk-like sausages and reached for the bread.

Plenty of eyes on her. None of them Jackie's. She wondered where he was. A plastic kettle stood at the end of the table, a box of coffee sachets, tea bags, sugar packets lumped together in a Tupperware container. All of them McDonald's brand. Someone had done a smash and grab at the local.

Eadie turned to ask Skylar if she wanted a coffee and found a rock-hard male chest where the girl's face had been. Eadie looked up into a leathered face, jewel eyes peeking from beneath a scarecrow fringe of sun-scorched blond. Trucker cap, high-vis. Eadie took it all in and went back to her coffee.

'You're new,' he said.

'I am.'

'You're hot.' The big man hooked a finger around her ponytail, let the blonde hair slither through. 'Wanna date?'

'I'm here as a labourer.'

'You're funny.'

'No, really,' Eadie sighed.

'What's your name?'

'Does it matter?'

'Does to me.'

'Eadie.'

'Eadie. Cute. Greedy Eadie, stealing all my sugar packets. Keeping those fine round titties for the horses and the pigs. What a fucking tease.'

Eadie didn't smile. She slapped the sugar packets in her hand to loosen the old grains. The man reached around her to take the Tupperware container. They were wedged between two fold-out tables, nowhere to go, no move to make but submission or outright refusal. Eadie ignored the cock against her hip. The casual brush of her ponytail as he righted himself.

'Pass the milk?'

Eadie slid the jug over. His hand grabbed at it, her fingers, entrapped them in his own. She shook him off. Laughter from behind her at the men's table.

'You didn't ask my name. How rude.'

Eadie let out a sigh, staring at the kettle, waiting for it to re-boil. She worried a nail with her teeth.

'It's Nick.'

'Good on you.'

'Let's think of some things that rhyme with Nick.'

'Let's not.' Eadie poured. Watched the water fall on the old coffee without encouraging the black grounds to mix at all, water on dirt, black, heavy. She thought of her new espresso machine at home, the five grand she paid for it, the manual it'd come with and the chapters explaining how to get the perfect crema, how to make sure the press didn't scorch the powder. The smell of it. Eadie scraped at the coffee with her plastic spoon.

'Let's just have coffee and get to work.'

'What a bitch of a thing to say.' Nick licked his lips. 'I'm only playing games. I give you a compliment and you just brush it off. Who are you?'

'I'm someone who doesn't like games.' Eadie smiled, turned around, found herself almost pressed against him. The heat of his body enveloped her. Too much Lynx, not enough soap. He smiled back and reached for the kettle. His hard groin pressed against her. She bore it without stiffening, without letting her eyes leave his own. He took the kettle and stood back, poured the water. She thought of thrusting her hand up, knocking the cup into his face. It was almost as if he was tempting her to. His eyes through the steam. Challenging.

'Well, you come tell me when you want to learn how to play,' he grinned. 'Greedy Eadie.'

Approaching the table where Skylar had settled was very much like the first day of high school. At least she'd had Eric to walk her onto the barren grounds of Utulla High and see that she got to the right classroom, but when recess came around she'd been alone in the jungle for the first time, and the loss was aching. She remembered the groups of children sitting hunchbacked against the wind, making mounds of wrappers and apple cores and orange skins in the centre of circles like witches swapping runes, laughing, throwing things, trading and comparing cards. Some of them kissing, lounging about, boys' heads on girls' stomachs, fingernails inspecting skin. Boys wrestling, kicking each other, pulling down tree branches. Eden was aware of being a misfit from the first moment, as she stood beside the door to the classroom, trying to find a slot. She'd watched for a while and then gone back inside where her teacher was sorting piles of assignments on her desk. An adult. Someone like Hades who would look down at her, guide her with a steady hand on her shoulder, frown at things that confronted her and stand in the way of things that frightened her. Just to be in the presence of an adult had been a relief, like coming inside from the rain – warm, sheltered. She had crept to the back of the room and sat there a good ten minutes, watching the sorting and the sighing before Mrs Daniels noticed her and ushered her back outside into the turmoil.

'It's important to fit in, Eden,' the teacher had said. 'Here, let me find you a buddy.'

Eadie supposed that Skylar was her buddy now, even though the girl hardly seemed at ease with the others at the table, sitting at arm's length on the end of the bench, eating a sausage with her fingers. Eadie toyed with the camera pendant. Frank was there too, she supposed, though she couldn't hear him, the way he broke into any kind of tension with a joke, a look, a comment he knew was stupid but necessary, taking the self-deprecation in exchange for the comfort of others. Eadie sat next to Skylar in the cigarette smoke and sipped her coffee. One of the girls was illustrating an argument, standing with one leg up on the bench on the other side, waving her arms.

'I said you can have him. You fucking take him, ya mongrel.'

'Mongrel bitch,' someone confirmed.

'You know what she's like. Ain't the first time. Ain't be the last. Fucking lunch-cutter.'

'What pacifically did she say'd gone on?'

'Aw, just that she'd been there watching a fucking DVD. Thinks I came down in the last rain. I did so much for that bitch. I gave her everything.'

'So what then? Did ya have a go?'

'Did I have a go.'

Laughter. The plastic bottle was passed around, but not to Eadie. She watched it, smelling the bourbon. She perked up a little, listened to the retelling of the story about the fight. This, at least, was something she understood. Violence. Brutality. The blessed surrender to the animal instinct and the primal relief when the prey was vanquished. Skylar offered her a cigarette and she took it, lit it in cupped palms. The wind was carrying desert heat across the farm, already baking the morning. Soon Uggs would be replaced by thongs, sun for shade. A fly, in her hair, waved away, back again on her temple. The dogs at their feet, snapping, growling at each other.

When Eden had joined her first station, Redfern Metro, she'd known the rules about being new in a house full of aggression and constantly challenged pride. She had said nothing for the first three months. Not where she'd been, what she'd done, what she hoped to get out of the work or what she thought of the area. She took paperwork that was dumped on her desk without asking where it had come from, who should be doing it, who it was for. She did it, stacked it, left it for whoever had dumped it to pick up. On her lunch breaks she sat at the edge of the group and listened, nodded or shook her head when she was addressed. It was important to fit in, and you only fit in with cops when you have shown them your respect – quietly, subordinately. It hadn't been the same for the recruit who joined with her, Matt or Dave or some other ordinary name, who was full of excitement and enthusiasm and clichéd cop jokes. Matt was still a walker when Eden was bumped up to highway patrol, the first ticket out – the warm car and the takeaway parking lot meetings. Matt the walker going by, sideways glance, the walker that no one wanted to walk with.

Eadie sat on the edge of the bench with Skylar for a good ten minutes before the conversation ebbed. Eyes on her. She flicked the ash from her cigarette onto the ground, watched it fall.

'Is this Nick's new root?'

'No,' Skylar said. 'Eadie's working with Pea.'

'Jesus, you've got your priorities screwed up, girl,' someone laughed. 'Nick's free. I'd rather be bent over Nick than a pile of horse shit.'

'What's her name?'

'Eadie,' Skylar answered.

'I weren't talking to you.'

'Eadie,' Eadie said, glancing up.

'Girl, you'll change ya mind, or Nick'll change it for ya. Ashley's been gone what, two weeks now? Man's got to be toey as fuck. Two weeks is ten years in a man's world.'

'Toey as, mate,' someone agreed.

Ashley, the missing girl. Eadie tried to keep her expressions neutral, disinterested.

'Yeah, maybe,' Eadie said. She tapped her cigarette out on the edge of the table and put the butt in a paint can in the centre of the table, the cauldron. A woman approached, short and round all over, shoulders sloping to fat-coated arms and hands, calves that would never fit boots. She was wearing ex-army coveralls, the epaulettes and name bar torn off with only the crest remaining. Her black curls were tucked behind her ears and under glasses with taped frames. A face like a bronze moon, downturned, creased with hard years.

Everyone looked. Fell into silence.

'This her?' The woman flicked her dimpled chin at Eadie.

'Sure is.' Skylar leaped up, standing upright like a soldier presenting a prisoner to a commandant. Eadie swung off the bench and rose to her full height, a good forty-five centimetres above the stocky Pea.

'Well, let's go.' She gave Eadie a look up and down and spat in the dirt. 'Ain't got all fucking morning.'

Heinrich looked forward to the dogfights every month, sitting on the back porch and watching the men wrestle the animals and train them on mutts lured in from the city wilds – the spray of blood and the howls and squeals. Somehow he knew that what he was watching was wrong, but there was some thrill in containing the excitement as he watched, suppressing the desire to get up from where he sat, howl with the dogs, growl and cheer and gather up the blood, rub it warm between his fingers. It made his face hot. His secret joy. He'd get as close as he could to watch the beasts tumble and dance and snap in the chicken-wire ring before someone noticed him and pushed him away. One time they'd let him tie the rope harnesses for the bulls, loop the slobbering, panting beasts and attach the truck tyres they dragged around and around the yard, building muscle, each dog like a miniature ox within weeks – massed, veined.

Sunday would stay inside during the training sessions, refusing to look out the windows, squealing and covering her ears at the sounds. She had watched once when John Boy and Uncle Mick had cut a new dog, clipped his ears off neatly with a pair of shears, making an uncatchable monster of it. It's better for the animal, John Boy explained as he heated the shears with a cigarette lighter. They get cut off or they get ripped off in a roll. Uncle Mick stood nearby with a fat white terrier struggling between his legs, filing teeth. Sunday turned grey and threw her guts up in the garden. Everyone laughed.

On fight night it was Heinrich's job to run back and forth between the car and the pick-ups, because Bear was the escort, the encourager, the showman. The more people they could bring to the event, the happier Caesar would be. Although he wasn't the happiest of men usually, as far as Heinrich could tell, sitting at the back of the bar on Abercrombie Street, smoking, talking to people who came and leaned close, putting their ear near his mouth to catch his secrets, then run away. Most of the time Heinrich couldn't tell the difference between Caesar's happiness and his everyday grumpiness. The old Captain just sat in the back of Bear's car and watched the city rolling by, smoked, eyed the window-washers, bored, as they approached the front of the vehicle, realised he was there, retreated. People ran from Caesar a lot. Heinrich had only seen him really laugh once, when he had snuck down the stairs to the laundry-room one night to try to find Bear. The lights in the greenhouse were off and the big man's bed in the back room was empty and cold. He'd peeped through the crack in the laundry-room door and seen Bear standing in the corner with his arms folded, looking at something on the huge folding table in the centre of the tiny room. Heinrich gripped the doorknob in terror at the sound of Caesar's laughing – it was so sudden and unfamiliar, and punctuated here and there by a crunchy, crackling sound that was like footsteps on wet gravel.

'You have to get away from this for a while to appreciate how good it really is,' Caesar was saying. His hand appeared, the long handle of a pair of bolt cutters. There was blood all over everything.

The fingers. The cutters. The cement. Something screamed. 'It should never feel like work. Each one is special.'

On the fight nights, Bear would pull up outside a big house with all the lights lit in the wet front garden, the back door of a restaurant surrounded by cats and bags of rubbish, an apartment block where kids his age darted along the musty carpeted hall. Heinrich's job was to dart into the apartment blocks, houses, buildings, knock on the doors, thrust out his chest and say, 'Good evening, sir. Your ride is here.' Sometimes the men he talked to peered out their doors, saw Bear in the car and nodded knowingly. They'd grab their coats and follow the boy out. Sometimes they came out without their coats, leaned on the passenger side window and squinted into the darkness of the vehicle.

'Who's in?'

'Ricky's got a couple of good rollers. Going to play Sharky's big brute from December.'

'What happened to Old Mark?'

'Two broken legs.' Bear didn't look at Heinrich. 'Rug accident, I heard.'

'Treacherous, those rugs. The Persians, I hear.'

'Won't have them in my place.'

Laughter. The men toss their coats into Heinrich's arms. Or they'd wave the big man away with promises for next month. Heinrich would clamber back into the front seat as the car rolled away, asphalt moving beneath his feet. By the time the sun set, the pick-ups were finished and they headed back to Abercrombie Street into the crowd that lined the pavement. Bear didn't need to push his way through. People parted for him. Heinrich struggled forward before the sea of legs and hips and skirts and feet closed on him. Caesar was at the basement door, talking to Uncle Mick about the dogs.

'That it?'

'Yeah.'

To Bear, 'That prick. Fishburn.'

'Had a quick look. Not home. Boy went round the back. Nothing. Stuff's still there.'

Caesar glanced down at Heinrich. The boy chipped paint from the doorframe with a fingernail.

'Send your little offsider round there tomorrow. Pass on my disappointment and get what's outstanding.'

Bear nodded and thumped the boy's shoulder. Caesar glanced again at the boy, creased his brow slightly, the faintest twitch of furry grey eyebrow.

The big man led him downstairs. The noise was rushing up from below as Heinrich descended into the dark, it was going past his ears and spiralling upwards – stomping feet and cheering and laughter and the smashing of glass. He could hear screaming. The birds. There were mixed fights before the dogs – cocks and sometimes a ferret, a pair of teenagers with a rivalry of some sort. There was no music while the fight was on. It drowned out the cracking of bones and the splatter of blood and the smack of flesh on the concrete. But now and then between bouts someone struck up a guitar, trying to soak up some of the money going around.

Heinrich could barely see anything from the floor of the basement. He was swamped by backsides and elbows, a forest of them. As Bear shifted forward, he grabbed onto his coat, allowing himself to be pulled through. It was getting to be a shameful thing to do, something that only Heinrich noticed – the constant need to scramble between people or have a path cleared for him. A couple of nights earlier he'd been moping around the greenhouse, scrubbing pots with barely any enthusiasm. Bear had had enough.

'The hell's got your goat?'

'How old am I?' the boy asked. Bear looked at him through his huge glasses, dazzling in the light of a candle over the tiny saplings in his hands.

'I dunno. Twelve? Thirteen? Bout eight when you turned up probably.'

'How old's Sunday?'

'Bout the same.'

'She's taller than me by miles.'

'Heaven forbid.'

'I'm gonna end up taller than her, right?'

The old Bear had laughed, turning back to his work.

'There's no telling.'

'I can't be short.'

'There's worse things to be.'

'Bear.'

'Look.' The big man turned, hung a huge arm over the back of the chair. 'Being short's not the end of the fucking world. A woman don't mind if you're short, long as you can fight, you got money or you're great in the sack. Work hard enough and you can get to all three, even. Alright?'

'Yeah. Alright.'

'Now shut up and get back to work.'

By the time Heinrich made his way to the front of the crowd the pit was empty but for two men half-heartedly sweeping feathers and bits of flesh from one end of the concrete ring into a heap at the other where the mess would lie with the shit and blood and piss of losing dogs, parts of other birds, a lump of shirt ripped from one of the teens. The winner's owner climbed out of the pit with his bird under his arm, its feet struggling, wet and black. A couple of dogs were next. Heinrich watched the money pass hands all around him, names and notes scribbled on notepads buried in palms, men shouting across the pit and holding up fingers.

Two cages were lowered into the pit. The dogs were snapping, throwing themselves at the wire. Heinrich saw Sunday on the other side of the ring, talking to two men. One whispered in her ear, bent low, smiling. She was laughing in an odd, heavy way. Lopsided. She was still wearing that yellow dress but now it was higher than it used to be on her long gold legs and was caught up in a black wool jumper. She was barefoot on the beer-soaked floor. She was always barefoot. She hooted at the dogs, cheered. Bear's hand fell on the boy's shoulder and he jerked at the feel of the man's beard on his cheek.

'Listen here.'

'Yeah?'

'I'm gonna say this once, and you don't repeat it. See that man up there with Caesar? Don't look just yet. Guy in the leather jacket. Blond. You don't go anywhere near him, you understand?'

'Huh?'

'Don't go near him. Don't talk to him, don't look at him. Don't go anywhere with him, even if he tells you it's okay with me. Get me, boy?'

'Why?'

'You know not to say "why" to me.'

'Alright. Alright.'

'Good man.' The Bear squeezed his shoulder, thumped him too hard, made him wobble. Heinrich felt a strange shift in his stomach, a flush in his cheeks. Bear never spoke like that, like he felt something. Heinrich wasn't sure that Bear felt anything about anything much.

He snuck a look across the pit to where Caesar was standing on the stairs with a thick-headed blond man in a brown leather jacket. The two were talking, holding short glasses, looking at the crowd. Heinrich didn't see anything especially threatening or interesting about the forbidden man. There was white and grey in his temples, smile lines cutting deep into the corners of his eyes. The man put his hand on his hip. A revolver. A cop. Heinrich tugged at Bear's sleeve.

'He a cop?'

Bear gave him a look. Heinrich scratched his neck and turned back to the fight. He knew there were cops in the crowd. There were cops who passed things to Caesar sometimes, met him in the early hours in uniform, rode in the back of the car in plain clothes. Heinrich wasn't afraid of cops. He knew to be polite to them, take their coats and hats when they arrived at the house, send the women to them straight away, bring them drinks. You don't talk nothing but the weather, Bear had said. Sunny day, isn't it? Cold out there, isn't it? Warming up, isn't it? That's it. Get me? Heinrich wondered why this cop was different. But he didn't wonder long. The cage doors were lifted and the dogs began to dance.

There was always a clear favourite. It was usually size, but tonight it was attitude – one of the dogs was obviously more afraid, and the fearful one is the one who fights harder, considers that his life is in this, that he doesn't want to die. A dog that isn't quiet and trembling before the door goes up, piss running down its back legs, bashing its head on the cage walls in terror at the sound of the other animal, isn't a dog worth betting on. An animal barking and howling and making noise when it's about to fight doesn't have the potential for the flipping point when fear transforms into rage. The one that makes the noise, makes the threats, gives a performance – that's the one distracted, the one that doesn't believe he can be taken down. The raging beast tonight was the smaller one, a caramel mix with a black snout, waxed up all over to make it hard to pin, two perfect pink scars where they'd clipped it long ago, a tail docked from birth. It wasn't a new fighter and didn't move like one. The other, some kind of charcoal thoroughbred, certainly stolen, came out of the cage and was immediately driven back against it. Glances snatched from the corners of eyes, puffed chests, exposed gums, bouncing strides and thrusts of legs, and then the lunge, the roll, the frantic scratch of claws with no grip on wet cement as one backed the other into the corner, scrambled out, rushed up against another wall. The crowd was howling. There were squeals. First blood in three seconds. Nothing to grip but prancing legs.

Heinrich looked across the pit at the man he was forbidden to speak to, shouting in Caesar's bent ear. Sunday was nowhere. The boy glanced back to see the thoroughbred's right front foot stripped of meat to the pink bone, flapping flesh, hopping. It was pretty much half-over in a minute. A limping finish. Smart bets were being paid already. The mutt got the big fellow's throat and swung back and forth. Wet, squelching bites, the happy mumbled growling of a mouth washed with blood. Heinrich put his hands in his pockets and looked up at Bear. The big man was smiling, shifting notes from one hand to the other.

'Here you go, short stuff,' he said, flapping a note in the boy's face. 'Don't lose it all in one pop.'

Heinrich grinned and pressed back into the crowd. Elbows and arses. He pushed, pulled, squirmed, shuffled his feet waiting on the wet floor. A penny buried in grime. He reached down and scooped it up. Uncle Mick was there on the corner, arguing, pointing into the pit. He took plenty of tugging to bring around.

'Where's Sunday?' Heinrich asked.

'No idea. Care less.'

'Take my punt on the next one?'

'Oh, Jesus. Yes, alright.'

The man snatched Heinrich's note and stuffed it into his pocket. Two more dogs were being lowered into the pit. Heinrich had a quick look. Breathed the thick air. He searched for Caesar and the forbidden man. They were gone. Bear was talking to someone in the crowd.

'Hurry up, dickhead.'

'Sorry.' Heinrich chewed his lip. 'Alright. The black one.'

'Which?'

'Black.'

'All in?'

'Yeah.'

Uncle Mick nodded and folded his arms. Heinrich heard a familiar voice behind him. Caesar was drawing on his cigarette, the dogs in the cages forgotten, his eyes on the faces in the crowd. The forbidden man. The cop looked down at Heinrich. The boy turned back to the pit, straightened his jacket, cleared his throat.

'This Bear's sidekick?'

'Yeah.'

'Who's he belong to?'

'Search me.' Heinrich turned for a second, saw Caesar shrug. 'Care less. Bear's always bringing in stray cats. Been doing it for years.'

'Stray cats.' The cop laughed. Heinrich looked up at him. 'Stray cat, are you, boy?'

Heinrich chewed his lip. A smile danced on Caesar's thin scarred lips.

'That where the nigger girl came from?'

'Yeah, and others. I don't know why he does it. Half the time he raises them up and they go wild on him. Break his bones.'

'They don't bother you.'

'Now and then they bother me,' Caesar glanced down at the boy. Heinrich dropped his eyes. 'Mostly he keeps them out of my way.'

'I don't know how you stand it,' the cop said. 'I hate cats. You know how to get rid of unwanted cats?' the cop asked the boy. The boy shrugged. 'You feed 'em to the dogs.'

The push was so unexpected, so light, that Heinrich hardly felt it. He reached up and touched the cop's hands as they touched his chest and they felt gentle, warm even. He hadn't known how close he was to the edge. There wasn't time to make a sound before he hit the bottom of the pit. And then the air was out of him, his elbow split inside the jacket and leaking, his vision vibrating. The crowd was screaming. The dog in the cage nearest to him in his ear, the sound making his eardrum pulse, too loud to be anything but a physical sensation, a punching of noise. Heinrich rolled. Blood and feathers on his palms. He wasn't sure what of it was his, if he'd hurt himself this badly. All he knew was that he couldn't move as fast as he should have been able to, that a weight had fallen over him and his limbs weren't responding in time with his thoughts. Bear was on the edge of the pit, his arm outstretched.

'Here,' the Bear said. 'Come here. Get up.'

Heinrich looked back at Caesar and the cop. Caesar was smiling. The cop was smiling. Caesar nodded to the man holding the rope that released the door of the black dog's cage. The man paused, looked at the boy, looked at Caesar.

'Get up, Heinrich!'

Heinrich got to his feet, only to feel the weight of the dog slam into his legs. The concrete floor rushed up at him. His hands splayed out, rolled him, gripped limply at wet fur. He didn't feel the bite. All he felt was the hot breath and the wetness, the pressure on his forearm, his shoulder, the back of his neck, as he rolled.

'No!'

'Don't you dare,' Caesar shouted, pointing his gun finger at Bear, a hundred miles above Heinrich in the tumbling, lamplit world. 'Don't you fucking dare!'

Howling from the men above him, bottles thrown into the pit, popping and exploding and spraying off the walls. Heinrich glimpsed money changing hands through the blood in his eyes. He struggled into the corner, closed his fists, finally the bones and flesh responding. He struck out wildly, turned, struck out again, a hammer of blows. The second cage door lifted. Heinrich felt his legs shaking, refusing to lift him.

And then the Silence came. Everything responding now. His fingers unclenched, gripped, dug, held on. He took the grey dog down with his hands, lay on it, gouged at the eyes, raked and heard snarls coming out of himself or the beast – or both, he didn't know. The other dog had his calf, tugging, and Heinrich could do nothing about it. The grey dog threw him off, came around, blind, rose up on its hind legs, danced. Heinrich blocked it with a forearm, knocked against teeth as hard as stone. His shoe was off. The boy grabbed it, beat at the beast with it. He punched, felt the rock teeth again against his knuckles, cracking and wedging a rough, warm tongue. He lost the shoe. Reached out. Grabbed glass. Mashed it in the eyes.

The dog rolled, scampered off. He twisted and threw himself at the black one, the big one, the one he had picked as a winner for its depthless eyes and its restless feet and the piss all over him. The boy swung his leg over it, almost went too far, wound an arm around a neck thicker than his own waist. He hugged it. The legs scratched his own. The boy sat up and squeezed. He had a moment to look around. Bear and Caesar and the forbidden man, watching, expressionless, their hands by their sides, pillars of a pier standing strong against an angry ocean of men. The boy realised he was growling but he couldn't hear the sound. The Silence had it. The dog was slipping. He dug his nails in. Twisting, slipping from his grasp.

Heinrich leaned forward, gripped the mouth, gums, teeth. Gripped the open holes where the ears had been. Pushed one way, then jerked the other. Felt the snap, the rush of warm air.

The boy dropped the limp dog and stood. Out of the sea of people, Bear landed and grabbed the shoulder of his jacket. There was nowhere else to hold the boy as his knees went from beneath him. His arms were ribbons.

I found Adam White at the Courthouse Hotel out the back of Newtown, right on sunset, a position his landlady at the end of the street told me was his standard for the hour and the day. The hotel was on a corner two streets back from the hip wonderland of King Street, a catwalk already being strutted by office workers on the way home to their damp Ikea-furnished pads above the bookshops and online daters searching for each other in the light rain, phones out like guns.

The main hall of the hotel was wallpapered with news sheets from twenty years ago and hung with Christmas lights. It was instantly dark, the air thick with expired beer. I glanced around the U-shaped bar. Nothing but red noses and eyes. Outside, uneven bricks hedged with grass led to a sprawling garden boxed in by lacquered bamboo. White was sitting hunched on a stool at the outdoor bar under an umbrella, nursing half a beer. I walked up, nodded at the bartender and tapped White on the shoulder. I gave him a second to turn, then punched him square in the face.

It's never good form to punch a man from behind. It's not right, either, to insult him with a glancing blow. I smacked him hard and felt the impact ripple up my arm, crack my knuckles for me. The sound was wet, unexpected, accompanied by a little breathy yowl. It was good. I hoped it was as good for him.

White stumbled off the stool but didn't go down like I had. His glass danced off the counter and spread out on the bricks at our feet. The bartender dropped the tray he was holding soundlessly on the rubber mat.

'Whoa!'

'It's alright.' I held up a hand. White recovered quickly, wiping at the bloodless graze on his left cheekbone with the back of his hand. I brushed his skin off my knuckles. He took me in for a few slow seconds. The cut on my face and the bruising seemed to get his bearings back. Then he began to laugh.

'What took ya so long?'

I kicked the base of his shattered glass against the bar and signalled the bartender to pour White another.

The young man behind the bar didn't look like the violent type. Tattoos and piercings and oddly shaved hair, things that decades ago might have meant he was dangerous, were diluted by a backpack full of books under the bottles behind the counter. University type. They thought violence was the language of the weak and tattoos were soul writing on skin. I probably agreed about the violence, to a certain degree, but I also knew that when a man gives you a good thump you do him the courtesy of matching his gesture. Never talk above someone you need something from.

I ordered a scotch on ice and the bartender reluctantly put the glasses up. When I'd paid he just about ran inside to tell his manager. There were a couple of other patrons in the garden, barely interested now that White had failed to swing back.

He laughed again as he took his drink and nodded towards a picnic table set in the back corner under another umbrella.

'Damn,' he said as he sat down across from me. 'Got you good, didn't I?'

'Not classy, using a tool,' I said.

'Hey, you brought it with you, bro.'

He laughed and held the beer glass against his eye. It was already swelling shut. He was as I imagined him from what I'd heard and felt in the dark – tall, lithe, smooth, a weird boyishness to his smile contradicting the greying in his short dark curls. The clothes had the same odd effect of juvenility and age, an oversized denim jacket with intentional fraying on the cuffs over a pair of navy trousers that hung too low in the crotch and were pulled up too high at the waist with a cracked leather belt. I wondered what he did for a living, dressed like that. He looked like he'd be at home behind the counter of the local Vinnie's. Not the Newtown one. The Marrickville one.

'Adam White. Congratulations. You've been discovered, which is fairly obviously what you intended all along.' I made a little half-bow. 'My job is to tell Hades Archer who you are and what the hell you want. The old man said nothing about where you'll be when he hears the news. Now I feel like I'll have earned my money if I can tell him what your fucking problem is. What you do after I leave here is up to you. I don't care.'

'I'm not running off just because the old man knows my name,' White shrugged. 'And I don't have to tell you shit, boy. My fucking problem is with the old man. Nobody on my side asked you.'

'You're playing a dangerous game if you want my opinion, mate.'

I shrugged, sipped my drink. He was considering me quietly, casually, the way a man considers the rolling of waves onto the shore, how this thing works, why it never stops, what it means. Dreamy. I was confused by the calm.

'Just tell me what you want. You might even get it.'

'What I want is a conclusion,' White said. Left a lingering poetic silence. I folded my arms. 'You know about conclusions, right? Being a cop and all? Things happen, meaningful things, and they have to happen for the world to keep turning. People lie and cheat and steal from each other. People murder each other. But you, you know, you understand, right? These things need to be equalised. The scales need to be balanced. You know what I mean, don't you, bro?'

'I didn't come here for a philosophy lecture.'

'I know. You came here for an explanation. I'm providing it, bro.'

He put his palms out. He was oddly well spoken for someone so badly dressed, someone who peppered his conversations with 'bro' and 'aye'. I sighed to signal my boredom and leaned back on my bench, scratched my chest. He watched. I made a 'get on with it' gesture.

'Ask Hades what he knows about a girl named Sunday,' White said. He rested his forearms on the table and clasped his hands. 'Ask her how she died. Turn on those sniffer-dog senses of yours and see if you can detect any guilty twitches.'

'Sunday?' I asked. 'Sunday who?'

'Her surname was White. Sharon Elizabeth White. But everybody called her Sunday.'

'So you reckon Hades knocked your sister off?'

'My aunt.'

'And when was this?'

'Around about 1979.'

I laughed. Maybe it was the wrong thing to do, but I couldn't help myself. I laughed and laughed.

'Oh dear. Oh god, that's funny.'

'Laugh it up, bro.'

'Are you serious?' I squinted through tears.

'I'm deadly serious.'

'You're on some vigilante mission to avenge your aunt's death?' I snickered. 'Who are you? Batman?'

He sipped his beer.

'Look, mate,' I said. 'You're kidding yourself. I mean, I get it. Hades Archer is a bad, bad man. I can't imagine some of the things he's done over the years. If he did knock your aunt off, in 1979, for god's sake, chances are he's so old and so used to knocking people off that he doesn't even remember doing it. And even if he does, even if I rattle it out of his ancient, decaying mind with a bit of new-age hypno-past-regressive therapy, and the old crocodile happily tells me, *yeah, sure, I remember that bitch, I put her black arse in a petrol drum and dumped her in a creek*, I can't imagine what you think you're going to do about it. You threaten Hades hard enough and he'll come after you. And he doesn't look to me like the kind of guy who negotiates.'

'I don't care what he does or what he says. I'm going to haunt that man until he tells me what he did to Sunday. I want to know.'

'What the hell do you care what he did to your aunt? You couldn't have even known her. How old are you?'

'My mother loved her.' The man became suddenly fierce, leaned over the table so that I could smell the beer on him. 'You understand that? My mother loved her.'

I gave the man a moment. His breathing had elevated so suddenly that he was now out of breath as though he had run around the block. He'd done well to keep the rage down while I laughed at him. It wasn't something I saw often as a cop. A bit of self-control. A bit of covert emotion. I was beginning to think Adam White was a good match for Hades.

'You got a mother?' he said.

'I had one.'

'And a dad too?'

'Most people do.'

'What were they like?' he asked, putting his elbows on the table. 'What were you like as a son?'

'Let's not do a diagnostic on my childhood. Please. I'm right on the edge here.'

'My mother spent her whole fucking life looking for Sunday White,' Adam said. 'It was her purpose. It was her calling. She'd never had a moment of happiness in her life until she found that woman. When you've never had any kind of family, you walk out into life without any kind of plan, without any kind of fallback. You grow up without really knowing what love is, how to take it or how to give it. Imagine a kid raised in the wilderness. In the desert. Imagine what it's like to grow up without love, because that's what it was like, bro, growing up with the reformers. When she's an adult wandering in this kind of crazy loveless wasteland of a city she finds her own sister, her own blood, and suddenly she knows what love is. Hades Archer took Sunday away from my mother and she never got that trust back again. Not even when she had her own kids. When she had me. It was never the same. Something was taken from her and I had to watch that finally eat up everything she ever was.'

'This is all very deep and I'm sure very moving.' I cleared my throat. 'Well, it would be, for someone other than me.'

'I think you understand better than you know, bro,' he smiled. 'You're a cop, which means your dad was a fucking prick.'

I chewed my lip, shook it off.

'Let's just cut the sermon and be straight with each other, Adam. You're going to get yourself killed for some nothing justice mission.' I leaned forward, looked in his eyes. 'They're never even going to find your bones.'

'Here's the thing, bro.' White opened his hands again. 'My family might have been happy to accept what happened to Sunday last generation, when they were too timid and sick and powerless to do anything about it. My uncle was a drunk. Drank himself to death in the early eighties. My mother was raised in homes. Institutions. I never found out the kind of things they did to her, but she grew up pretty familiar with terror. She wasn't the kind of person to answer back, to question things, to seek satisfaction. And when she died, she didn't even have the words to write out what she really felt, what she'd really needed all along. She just blew her brains out. Bang. The pain denied. And you know what? I feel good for her. I feel good that she's at peace. But she left me here, and I've got to be selfish. I've got to feel right about it all. I'm not happy to let the old dog lie. I demand satisfaction, always. Always, bro.'

'You talk a lot.' I drained my drink. 'I don't have a notepad, so I'll just sum this up as I'll present it to the old man. What you're basically saying is you blame your mother's shitty life and your own on an aunt getting tangled up with the wrong crowd decades ago. You're going to piss the old man off until he admits what he did and says he's sorry, like some fucking girly schoolyard catfight. You know what, bro? Your mother should have sought some fucking counselling. And you know what else? I think you're bored. The motivation behind your vendetta is really thin, mate. If you can't figure out what to do with your life, go get a hobby. Take up dance classes.'

'I have a hobby, bro. It's setting things right. Making people accountable.'

'You're not Batman. You're not. There's one Batman, my friend, and he's not you. This is not Gotham City. You will not be satisfied by this. You're going to end up a missing person and they're going to put your file at the bottom of the pile like they did with your fucking aunt.'

He sniggered over his drink. I sighed again.

'I'm trying to help you, boy. You hang around that tip long enough and you'll become a permanent fixture, I guarantee it.'

'Oh, please.' White smiled, made begging gestures with his hands. 'Please tell him to come after me. I film everything I do out there. Handycam. Wireless feed. I'd love for that old man to get fed up one night and come down the hill and shoot me. I'd just love it.'

'You're filming? Oh, this is just priceless.'

'Everything. Everything, bro. Who goes in. Who comes out. The old man reading his newspaper hour after hour, night after night. He needs a hobby, you ask me.'

'They got a name for what you're doing, Adam.'

'So tell him to charge me.' White shrugged. 'Make me hand

over the tapes.'

I scratched the back of my neck. My face hurt. White's left eye was barely a slit now and it was beginning to weep. He dabbed at it with the back of his slender hand. I thought for a while, turning my glass on the tabletop. There was no telling what was on those tapes. Or who. I didn't think they'd lead to any direct legal danger for Hades – he had connections high up in the police force and the tapes would go from the front desk to the incinerator before anyone even knew they were there. But if they ended up on a journalist's desk . . . or on the internet. None of this would reflect badly on me, of course. I had no stake in keeping Hades out of jail. Except that his going to jail would be cataclysmic for Eden, making her dangerously unpredictable about what she would do to punish those responsible. Which would include me. I wondered if White knew what he was seeing out there, knew how very valuable those tapes were. I could only hope he was doing it as an insurance policy in case anything did happen. At the least he had to be aware that Hades was being visited by unsavoury characters. I wondered whether he had any evidence of unsavoury goings-on.

'What would be a satisfying conclusion to you? Huh? What would settle accounts with the Justice League?'

'Knowing what happened. Being able to bury my aunt with respect and dignity.'

'That seems simple enough.'

'You'd think so, wouldn't you?'

'Why not?'

'Because he says he didn't do it.'

I rubbed my eyes. They were heavy. Aching.

'When was this?'

'A month ago. To my mother. Just before she shot herself. She had one last stab at the truth and the old man denied her. Didn't even offer her a place to sit down. She'd driven six hours.'

'And what?' I said. 'Hades is supposed to believe that if he admits to what he's done and gives up her remains you'll just toddle off, all fair and square?'

'He'd better hope.'

I got up, swung my leg over the bench.

'Stop going out there, Adam.'

'Why would I, now that I have company?'

I walked away, heard his laughter as I reached the door of the pub.

Eadie began her day in the stables. The maintenance required in this place seemed minor at first as she began at one end of the building, scraping the wet hay and manure into a wheelbarrow, transporting the muck to a skip at the end of the concrete lot, returning, doing it again. Her shovel moved swiftly and the lifting, twisting, hurling, the pressure on her knees – it all felt good. Eadie liked to work out. Liked to feel her heart beating in her neck. To be breathless. She cleared one stall down to the bare concrete, her lungs full of the earthy, grassy smell of the beast, now and then the acidic ammonia of the animal's urine at the back of her throat. She swept the stall out until there was only thin mud at the bottom and then put the pressure hose on to it. Her boots were too big and rubbing holes through her socks into her feet, but she didn't mind. She liked being dirty and sore. Knew she would earn sleep. She led the animal back into the stall and stood while it snuffled in her palm with its warm velvet nose, black eyes wary, blinking wire eyelashes. Animals didn't mind her. She'd always wondered at that, given what she was deep down inside.

She moved to the next stall and led the horse out into the sun, ducked when it tried to nuzzle the side of her head, roughly, a kind of loving head butt. Sweat began to tickle at her temples. She wiped hay dust onto her cheeks and forehead. Being dirty reminded her of home.

She had always been a homebody at the tip. Eric was the adventurer, wandering off into the labyrinth of trash and coming back at night with bits of things he wanted to show her, pieces of broken jewellery and toy guns and little wooden boxes with rusted hinges. She liked to be around Hades when she was little, bringing him coffee in bed and letting the smell of it bring him out of his restless, snoring slumber, sitting with her legs under the blanket while he drank it in silence, watching his face come back to its regular shape. It was probably a year before she stopped being afraid of him. Even learning what he did for a living endeared him to her. The first time she snuck down to the backlots and watched him heaving the body of some fallen drug lord into the compacted trash, she was awed at his care and delicacy. The way his tired arms lay the shoulders of the man down gently, how he crossed the hands over the chest. It was people that Hades disposed of, not things. Once it had been her destiny to be laid down by him like that, her face passive and sleepful as the nylon sheet came over her, the rubber after that. Her deep, acid-filled grave. She liked Hades more the more she spied on his night-time doings.

The adult Eadie was spraying out the fifth horse stall when the woman named Pea returned. She was covered in filth too. Pea's instructions that morning had been shot out from her thin lips briefly and loudly, so Eadie straightened up when the woman arrived and expected more of the same. The squat figure leaned on the rails and watched her work for a while. It was uncomfortable. Where Pea stood there was no way Eadie couldn't hit her with the back spray. She didn't know whether to go on or stop. The gaze was lowered, critical, the lips ever-so-slightly snarled. Eadie stopped the compressor with her foot.

'Lunch,' the woman said. Eadie nodded and followed her out to the sink to wash her hands. That earned a frown. She wiped her hands dry on her filthy jeans, supposed that might make up for the insult of hygiene.

She walked through the stable doors to the back area. There were other animal workers there, all of them men, sitting on milk crates or the bare earth, smoking, drinking coffee laced with bourbon. A milk crate piled up with sandwiches, ham and cheese, tomato and cheese, pickles and cheese, Vegemite and cheese. Eadie glanced quickly around for Nick. He wasn't there. Neither was Skylar. She took a milk crate close to Pea, but not too close, and nabbed the first sandwich she could reach. She flipped her sunglasses down, knowing it was better to have two cameras recording the stubbled faces and scarred hands, profiles that would be checked for violence, kidnapping, drug charges. Eadie looked around quickly but took nothing in. It was Jackie she wanted to spend time with. Skylar would be her ticket into his company.

'You know, I ain't never seen a stable mucked out so slow,' Pea said suddenly. 'You never done this shit before?'

A couple of the workers nearby sniggered. Conversations drained away. Eadie coughed. The sun was belting through the cheap sunglasses.

'Didn't realise we were on a clock.'

'We're always on a clock. Life's a fucking clock.'

'I'll speed up then.' Eadie shrugged.

Pea imitated the shrug, looked around. The men laughed.

'The hell you doing down here?'

Eadie leaned back, chewed her sandwich thoroughly before she spoke.

'What, on the farm?'

'No. The stables.'

'Working,' Eadie said.

'Working?'

'Yeah.'

'You working or you wasting my time until you decide which dick you gonna sit on up there at the breakfast sheds?'

More laughter. One of the older men swigged a beer, yellow light dancing off it from above.

'Come on. Lay off, Pea,' someone said.

'I'm not planning on sitting on any dicks, all due respect,' Eadie said.

'What's the matter? You a fucking dyke or something?' Indignant.

'Actually, yeah.'

There was a group inhalation, a few groans of excitement. Eadie felt the air change. She'd let the words tumble off her lips thoughtlessly, but as they hit the ears around her she understood it to be the right move. She couldn't let the chess pieces shift around her for too long without making a challenge or two. Lying was easy. She almost felt gratified by it. It had been a little while since she'd played any really entertaining lying games. They'd been Eric's specialty. The first lie was always the best, made her cheeks feel hot, her hair stand on end.

'I heard you were married,' Pea snorted.

'I was.'

'And now you've decided muff-diving is your game.'

'It's not really a decision,' Eadie said. 'Or a game.'

'Imagine that,' Pea mused. 'Imagine you come home from work one day and your wife is horizontal with another chick.'

'It wasn't like that,' Eadie said.

'What the hell's wrong with you? You hate men or something? Plenty of men here. You hate them, do you?'

'No. I don't.'

'Plenty of girls here,' one of the younger men said. 'If, you know, you want to do a reenactment of that night.'

Laughter, Pea's the hardest.

'Alright, leave her alone now Pea,' an older man said, getting up from his milk crate. He pointed to the two women in turn, the beer in his hand swinging. 'You, put ya back into it. And you, find some other feathers to ruffle.'

The men left slowly, laughing, chattering quietly to each other about the new gossip. By nightfall it would be all over the farm. Pea looked at Eadie appreciatively, as though she'd won something. Eadie wasn't sure exactly what. She was looking forward to lying again. To seeing what else would come out of her under a little squeeze. It was like a dance. The pressure, the pace, the motion, caused snap thinking, a move, the righting of balance. She reached forward and took a water bottle from the Esky at the centre of the gathering and stood with it.

'They're not gonna like that around here,' Pea said. Her tone had changed.

'I ain't got time for what they like,' Eadie said as she went back into the stables. 'Clock's ticking.'

I came up on the van fast, the Jack Daniel's pre-mixer bottles in my fingers, and thumped on the door with my foot. I heard a yelp from within. The ginger spider. Juno rolled open the door and glared out at me from beneath a beanie pulled too low over flaming blond eyebrows.

'Get your hand off it.'

'Arsehole,' he said, watching me get in. 'Arsehole.'

'Here, take this and shut up.'

I handed him the second Jack Daniel's and crawled into the space beside him. The whole van smelled like teenage body odour, mildly sexual, full of unfulfilled dreams. There were fast-food wrappers everywhere, orange plastic cheese and a stack of crime novels knocked over by his feet, some fantasy titles with dragons on the cover, a couple of Anne Rices.

'You know, you're supposed to be watching.'

'I watch.'

'What are you getting?'

Juno took a notepad from the ledge before him, handed it to me. I don't know why. It was unreadable. There were some good sketches of birds, and some naked ladies with black wings.

'There are a few nasties getting around,' he said. 'Nicholas Hart, couple of previous charges for assault, assault with a deadly, arson and a sexual assault that didn't stick.'

Juno fiddled with a laptop wedged between the monitors. Cleared dirt out of the corner of his eyes, yawned, drew up a still from one of Eden's cameras of a lanky blond man in a cap.

'Gave Eden a good rub at breakfast this morning. He's on parole so we could snatch him up any time, but I'd like to see a bit more of him first.'

'Okay,' I shifted closer, touched Juno's knee with my own, shifted back again. 'Who else?'

'There's Penelope Goodman.' He double-clicked on another still. A plump woman in coveralls.

'What's her deal?'

'Just a couple of domestic violences way back, but she's such a bitch I thought she warranted mention.'

'That it so far?'

Juno picked his long teeth with a fingernail, nodded. The exhaustion was radiating off him now as his eyes wandered over the monitors.

'No Jackie?'

'No. No Jackie yet.'

'When?'

'Eden's pretty chummy with his current screw. Might be her ticket in. Gave the girl the deodorant can camera, which was clever, except the girl put it on the bathroom sink backwards so we've only got audio from that one.' He pointed to a blank monitor, the shadow of a can against a tiled wall.

'Anything interesting?'

'Some mildly interesting telephone conversations by Rye. Mainly drug deals though. Nothing about the missing girls. I emailed the files away for a transcript.'

'Well, we're in. I guess we just wait.'

'So is Eden gay?'

I didn't even register the question at first. I'd found a sleeping Eden on one of the monitors, her body turned towards the camera, a slender arm hanging over the edge of the bed. I understood what drove Juno to watch, hour after hour. She looked like a Botticelli. Sleep took all the hard edges off her.

'Is she what?'

'Gay.'

'What?' I turned back.

'She told a bunch of workers today she was down there shovelling shit because she's gay. She's not sleeping with anyone at the farm because she's gay. Is she gay?'

I laughed. 'She's not sleeping with anyone because she's a cop.'

Juno shrugged. 'Yeah. I know.'

'Does it matter if she's gay or not?' I couldn't keep the humour out of my voice.

'No.' He shrugged again. I started laughing and couldn't stop. He looked like he wanted to punch me but I outranked him by about two decades of gruelling cop work. So the best he could do was pout and scratch the back of his bony white neck.

'Shit, give me a break. You live someone's life for two days fucking straight and you get to wonder about them, that's all. I'm just curious. There's nothing wrong with being curious.'

'I get it.' I wiped my eyes, gave his shoulder a slap. 'I get it. She's a beautiful woman. Just don't fall in love with her.

Don't even think about it. She's not your type. At all. Okay? Not even close.'

The young man didn't seem to know what to think of my assessment. We both watched Eden on the screen for a while. Shadows passed over her face, gave her a black mask – reminded me of the look she'd given me back in the city before she shipped out to undercover, the way her entire being could change before you when emotion crossed it. Yes, the outside of Eden was very attractive. Like a beautiful poisonous flower. But the truth was that she was no one's type. Gay or straight or somewhere in between. I hadn't considered what her preference was from the moment I learned what she and Eric had done. What I was sure she still did. I had the feeling sexual partners would be fleeting things for Eden if there were any on her radar at all. It was dangerous to be close to her. As dangerous for them as it was for Eden. I was way too close as it was.

The gay card was a good move. I sat thinking about it as Juno dozed with his head against the van wall and his hairy spider arms folded. I couldn't see the ferals on the farm being very supportive of such a contemporary admission. It would grate on female sensibilities out there in the grassy badlands. The men might not be so hard on her because she was a beautiful lesbian and would fall into fantasy category and not be an offence to their masculinity. In any case, the admission would stir up trouble, bring out a few true colours, drop a few masks. I wondered if she'd planned on it. It would certainly make for interesting viewing.

I sucked the Jack Daniel's dry and was about to go out for another when Juno's voice stopped me.

'What was that?'

I looked back at the screen.

'What?'

Juno was leaning forward, nose up, like he was trying to smell the monitor at the same time as he watched it, intently. He let his head drop, grabbed the mouse, did some things. Zoomed in. Zoomed back out again. Sat back in his chair, unsatisfied.

'What was it?'

'Thought I saw something move in her caravan.' He tapped the screen with a speckled finger. 'Here.'

I looked. Saw nothing. The image wasn't great but there was nothing moving on it. I widened my eyes, slitted them, blinked. Nothing.

'A shadow,' I said.

'Maybe.'

'Probably a gay pride march.'

'There.' He stabbed the screen. 'Look.'

I looked. The door of Eden's caravan was ajar. The camera gave us a view of Eden tilted downwards from her head, the camera probably on the bedside table, arm, elbow, the end of the bed lost in darkness. Beyond, lit by light from what was probably the kitchenette window, the caravan door. It was swinging open slowly. I felt my stomach clench, fall.

'Shit.'

'We got back-up on standby?'

'Yeah,' I glanced at him. 'Response time's about five minutes. But just, just wait a second. Let me see who it is.'

A figure slid into the van. Stooped below the sagging fibro roof. The figure seemed to sway. Put a long hand out, steadied himself against the slatted bathroom door.

A pylon of a man, all lean, square construction, symmetry, the solidity of something built slowly from the ground up. Deceptively strong. I knew his type. The skinny junkie thief you try to pin whose core body strength seems to come from nowhere, flips you over despite your bulk.

'Christ almighty, it's Nick Hart. We need to call this in.' Juno grabbed my arm. I could feel his nails through my shirt.

'Hang on.'

'He's going to hurt her.' He was almost shouting.

'Just wait.' I pulled his fingers off me. 'I know what I'm doing.'

Nick was at the end of the bed, looking down at her. Eden hadn't moved. Her breathing was low and deep. Mouth open. Women hate it when you see them sleeping with their mouths open. Like there's something about that image that could ruin all the hard work they put into the rest of their appearance – the lips parted, unarranged, vulnerable. She'd probably had the roughest workday in years. She wasn't the shit-shovelling kind.

Juno was panting. He grabbed his phone from the counter.

'We need to –'

'You blow this operation without my approval and I'll kill you.'

'Your partner is in danger,' he wailed.

'I know.'

'He's –'

'I know!'

Nick Hart, the shadow in the dark, was touching himself. Trailing his fingers down the bulge in the front of his jeans. A sudden grab, squeeze. He stood there for what seemed like an eternity. My heart was thumping. I silently pleaded for Eden to wake. She didn't. She was dead. Beaten bones. I reached for my phone. Held it. Didn't dial.

Nick kneeled on the bed softly, eased his weight down. Put a hand down by her waist. Even if she woke now all he had to do was fall on her. A hand reached for her face, hovered over it, didn't touch. I heard noises on the monitor outside the caravan, laughter, whispers, crackling. I took the lock off my phone. Poised my finger to dial. My eyes on her face.

Eden rolled. Something in her hand. Something big. It swung up, over, just as Nick dropped on top of her, met the side of his head on the way down like a police baton meeting a kneecap. A half-thump, half-crack, followed by a grunt. He fell sideways instead of down. She was on top of him, the long handle of the frypan she'd used across the front of his throat. She put a knee in the pan itself and both hands on the end of the handle and leaned down. Her mere weight. Crushing. Juno and I had our mouths open now.

They stayed like that, the two figures, for maybe a minute. I could tell she was really strangling him. When you strangle someone completely, shut off the airway all the way, they don't make a sound, not those loud grasping choking noises you hear in movies. It's a silent death. Every few seconds the click of grinding teeth. But that's it. Strangely peaceful for the person doing it. Juno stirred first, grabbed at his phone again.

'She's going to –'

Eden's voice came over the monitor. Her nose was touching Nick's. Breathing air by his breathless lips.

'You should be so lucky.'

She let him go.

Juno actually stood up in the van, bent in half, eyes locked on the screen. He dropped his phone and grabbed his beanie with both hands.

'Jesus Christ!'

I hadn't realised I'd been holding my breath. I exhaled, filled my lungs, panted as I watched Nick Hart crawl out of Eden's caravan. She darted over to the bed, grabbed the camera, wrenched back the curtains and showed us the landscape outside. Grey earth lit from nowhere like the surface of the moon. Nick Hart fell into a circle of men who were laughing, cheering, trying to bring him to his feet.

'Check up on these guys,' Eden said. She sounded calm. Unrattled. 'I'll find out their names tomorrow.'

Juno was looking at me. I licked my lips and nodded at the laptop. He understood. Rolled the film back, took a screenshot of the men in Nick Hart's posse.

'Well, hopefully you get it now,' I said, pulling open the van door again. 'Not your type, mate. Not at all.'

At first Heinrich wasn't sure whether or not he'd done well on the Night of Teeth and Tearing. As he lay in the cold morning hours trying to remember, trying not to sleep, he wasn't exactly sure what had happened at all. He knew he ended up in the dog pit and everyone was staring at him, pointing, howling, throwing things, and he'd killed the two animals, prize beasts. Uncle Mick would probably hate him for that. He wasn't sure exactly how he'd done it, how he'd ended up putting down the enormous weight of the black one from where it lay limp in his arms like a sack of fat. The one thing he was sure of, the one thing that remained at the forefront of his mind, was the soft but swift push from the forbidden man, the police officer standing with Caesar. They'd pushed him in. Why?

He only hoped Bear would tell him.

Heinrich lay unable to move. He guessed the sun was rising beyond the curtains. He didn't know where Sunday was. She hadn't slept in his bed for a month. Sometime during the morning he fell into a hot sort of daze and thought she was there, stroking his hair, which was a very un-Sunday-like thing to do. But whenever he spoke to her she didn't answer, and when he opened his eyes she'd disappeared. He'd lain listening to Bear wander about the house in a restless, lumbering way from the moment they got back from Doc's. Heinrich had been to Doc's place plenty of times before but

135

had never been the patient. He awoke in the single lock-up garage somewhere in Paddington around midnight, he guessed, stretched out on a ping pong table and covered in blankets and sheets. Plenty of people were there. Some of them held him down as he squirmed, covering themselves in his blood. A girl was crying, holding a towel around his neck, almost choking him.

'It's all off,' she'd wailed, looked at the ceiling. 'It's all off. God. There's bones. God!'

'Shut up. Hold him and shut up.'

Someone put a vodka bottle near Heinrich's lips and he drank greedily for a second before Bear appeared out of the bright gold light and knocked it away.

'None of that. He feels it. Every bit of it.'

He started saying sorry, over and over, but no one listened. He looked for Uncle Mick, hoping he could hear the sorries, but couldn't see him, too much light. Someone put a rag in his mouth, pulled it down by either ear, locked his head to the table. It tasted of salt. Then there was fire. Slow, poking, stitching, knotting fire.

Bear walking in the dark, back and forth, back and forth, the kitchen to the front door to the back door, across the veranda. Heinrich dozed to the rhythm of it, jolted at the sound of neater hard-shoed footsteps meeting those of the heavy soft Bear.

'Don't start,' Caesar's low milky voice.

'I can't even. I can't even speak.'

'You've been like this for a long time, Bear. Your head stuck on the little things. The pick-ups. The rat boy. The nigger girl. The angry housewives who buy your potions and lotions to knock off their angry hubbies. You need to get your head out of your arse, my friend. The baby games are over. The boy, Jesus. That was just a bit of fun. Thomas has his mind on bigger things and he's going to lead us to bigger things.'

'I cannot have that man around me.'

'You put a price on that? Because having him around is going to change things for us. There's only so much you can do with guys and dolls, making loans and breaking bones. It's about to start raining gold in this town and you're under an umbrella counting pennies.'

'Get away from me.'

'Bear, I need you with me on this.'

'Get away from me.'

Bear came into the bedroom as the first white light was leaking from beneath the curtains, stirring the men and women on the mattresses. Heinrich had closed his eyes a couple of times but had felt hot breath on his face, dog's breath, and snapped them open. Bear pushed him into a sitting position and pulled his legs around, started gathering his trousers around his feet. Everything hurt.

'Bear.'

'You get up, you get dressed, you get moving. No matter what happens. Every day, understand? No one ever sees you hurt.'

'Bear.' The boy's face was wet.

'Come on.' The big man pulled him to his feet, wrenched his shirt down over his head and tugged his bandaged arms through. He pulled an extra cardigan on before his usual denim jacket, wrenched it across in the front, Heinrich's eyes on Bear's huge fingers as they worked the tiny plastic buttons.

'We make like this never happened, boy. Understand?'

'Why?'

'Because you'll write your reputation today.'

'Why did they –'

'Nothing happened. Get it?' The big man wiped the boy's face, hard – a pawing, took the sweat and the tears and the dried blood. Pushed down his crazy hair. Turned him and thumped him on the back. They walked out into the kitchen. People were waking everywhere. Men standing in the kitchenette, drinking coffee, sharing cigarettes. They looked down at Heinrich. One turned, glanced at Bear.

'Well, look at that. It's Dogboy.'

'He made it, huh? Well, whatta ya know?'

One of the girls slipped into the kitchen and touched Heinrich on his hair. The boy felt the world sway. Felt himself trembling beneath the clothes. They were heavy today, heavier than usual. Dragging at his useless arms.

'Toast, baby?'

Heinrich felt sick.

No. Please, no.

'Yes please,' he said.

Nothing happened. Get it?

Heinrich sat at the counter while the girl made the toast, sprinkled it with cheese, grilled it. The men watched him. Bear handed him a glass of milk and he swallowed three or four times before putting it to his lips. He thought of cold things, of still things, tried to make like a block of ice. Bear watched him over his shoulder, a look he only had when Heinrich was working with the really dangerous seeds, the oils, the things that could kill him if he breathed too hard, slipped, forgot, didn't wash his hands properly with the brush and the other chemicals. More people came into the dining room, leaned on the big table, murmured to each other. Heinrich ate the toast. It tasted like rocks.

'What's that boy's name?'

'Heinrich.'

'Heinrich the Hound Hunter, ay?'

'What a tough little scrap.'

'Let's see the wounds.'

'What wounds?' Bear said. No humour in his voice, but people chuckled anyway. Heinrich finished the toast and climbed off the stool, steadied himself against the counter for a second. Everyone was looking at him. He didn't know why. He went to Bear, brushed the crumbs off his jacket, looked up the great height to the man's hairy face.

'We going out, or what?' Heinrich asked.

Everyone laughed. Bear smiled.

It was a good sleep. I got home and sank a quarter bottle of scotch or so, splashing it around like it was water and I'd been running in the heat, then popped three Endone and showered, leaning my head against the wall, thinking. Worrying, a little, about Eden. I knew I didn't have to worry about Eden but I did anyway. Got to convincing myself, as I did sometimes, that she was a woman like other women I'd known, who needed guidance and protection, who was likely to do silly things if left alone too long. My mother had been that kind of woman and I suppose that's how I got the idea. You didn't call her for a couple of weeks and she'd turn up on your doorstep with triple O already dialled on the clunky mobile she could barely use, thinking you were dead in there. I was her only kid, so I suppose if I'd had siblings she might have spread the worry around or we might have palmed her off to each other the way brothers and sisters do. I'd almost had a sister but she'd been lost to cot death early, so early no one had even named her. All the worry in the world can't prevent some things. She'd have been thirty now. I still thought about her sometimes, imagined myself calling her. *Hey, you. Coffee?* Forming her idea of the perfect man. Getting it wrong. Beating up deadshits who messed her around, because she chose them, because I was her idea of the perfect man. An angry cycle.

I woke up with the cat on my neck, sprawled across from shoulder to shoulder like a great woollen scarf, heavy enough to wake me, make me catch my breath. It yowled indignantly when I shoved it off. I knew cats could kill babies lying on them like that. Cot death. Cat death. Could they kill cops in their forties who drank too much? I lay looking at the creature a little warily for a moment. Pretty little killer. Like Eden. I don't know why I kept it, what piece of Martina I hoped could be preserved by a lazy, angry, smelly thing that whined all the time and had probably forgotten she ever existed.

I wanted to see Hades but I didn't have the time, so I called while I laced my boots, the phone wedged in my ear. He was up. Old people are always up.

'You owe me ten grand.'

'That was swift.' His voice, gruff, grating on years of whisky and cold air. A sandpaper throat that hadn't spoken a loving word in decades, maybe never.

'I don't really have the time to be otherwise.'

'Eden?'

'Doing what she does.'

'You tell her to come out to me when she gets off.'

'Yes, Dad.'

'So.'

'Did you kill a girl named Sharon Elizabeth White?'

Dead silence. I listened to it. Tried to fathom what would come next. If it was a cough, he did it. Crims always cough to break the air, come down an octave without looking like they meant to. If he was angry, or pretended he didn't know what

I was talking about, he might have done it too. Maybe I was underestimating him. Hades was old and had done a lot of things, and no one had ever been able to say for sure which ones he did and which ones he didn't. I straightened up and held the phone against my ear.

'This again,' he said finally.

'Seems so.'

'No, I didn't kill Sunday.'

'Well, you've got a problem then, haven't you?'

'Who is it? Her sister?'

'Sister necked herself.' I patted the cat. 'Nephew's on the case. Adam White, badly dressed, hell of a right-arm swing.'

'It never ends, you know.'

'I can imagine.'

'You want to solve my problem for me?' The old man set his coffee mug down. I heard it clunk on his kitchen table.

'No, I don't. I really don't.'

'You find Sunday's killer and I'll give you a hundred grand.'

I stopped patting the cat. It frowned at me and head-butted my arm, walked around the back of me, climbed onto my lap.

'That'll make for interesting conversation with my accountant.'

'Get an ABN. Register yourself as a private investigator. I'll pay through my lawyer. Anonymous, unless the case is ever investigated. Which it won't be.'

'I can't just –'

'Don't spend it too quickly in your mind. I don't see you getting it. Nobody ever found Sunday.'

I felt cold. The way he said it, like there was a Sunday to be found somewhere, he was sure of it, cold bones lying in dry earth somewhere forgotten, probably built over now, a shopping centre, a cinema full of hipsters texting and throwing popcorn at each other, groping in the dark. No one ever found Sunday. *I don't do this shit for fun, boy-o.*

'I'll come out there this evening,' I said. He hung up. I shook myself all over, decided to put thoughts of Hades and his dirty money out of my head for the moment. The eager cat got under my feet as I headed out into the kitchen to feed it. Soft toes squished under mine. It hissed and skittered away from me.

I wanted to make sure I wasn't late to a meeting with the families of the missing girls. They'd agreed to get together at Keely's mother's house, but I'd seen footage of them fighting about the girls on the news and knew nerves were already frayed. I sat in traffic and beeped and sweated and swore at people who couldn't help me, crunched Endone and tried unsuccessfully to find a radio station not saturated with advertising. White noise. I phoned headquarters half an hour before the meet time and told them to warn the families there was a wait ahead and to break out the cigarettes.

I parked outside the Manning house in Narellan and noticed a few men were following my advice, standing on the pebbled concrete steps peppering the garden with orange butts and ignoring each other. I could hear female voices raised inside the newish semi as I approached. If not for the number on the mailbox, there would have been no distinguishing this place from hundreds of other rental townhouses lining the street. They all shared the same neutral tones – apricot cream, pastel pink, ivory rose. Hardy plants that would withstand the blazing treeless summer sprayed from garden beds in black and red spikes. Dogs barked. The whole estate looked like it had gone up overnight. There was still chain-link fencing scattered about on bare-earth street corners, waiting to be picked up by labour hire boys. The street was probably owned by some crooked Asian crime lord living on the harbour on the north side near the bridge. I'd seen these sprawling addresses in asset lists during years-long drug prosecutions. Numbers 8, 9, 10, 400, 401 Possum Avenue confiscated, pending trial.

I walked up to the house thinking about the girls. This was the last place her family had seen Keely before she headed to Bankstown to grind out some cash in the sex trade. What she usually did was sink into the body-perfumed sheets of the upstairs bedroom until 12PM every day, when *Dr Phil* woke her, then off to the shops for cigarettes and frozen lasagne – a cycle with its own biology. The pretty lazy girl with the curly hair. One of the men on the doorstep jutted his chin at me. Same curls. A brother? I'd wondered if there would be press hanging around the front of the missing girls' houses, but by the look of these two I could understand why there weren't. These were the kind of guys who'd chase you off the lawn with cricket bats given half the chance.

'Getting hot in there,' he said.

'Sounds like it. Sorry. Traffic.'

I offered my hand but he didn't take it – held the screen door open instead. Maltese terriers crowded at my feet, three of them, the haggard panting of animals fed too much and locked inside with dope smoke all day.

Right inside the door an icy tension was announced almost poetically by a misplaced air conditioner wedged on the wall over the coat rack, blasting out arctic mist. I led my brigade of dogs into a small living–dining room. Venetian blinds, some missing, blocking off a view of the yard. Yellow clouds on the ceiling. The reek of smoke. Everyone turned and looked at me. The only sound was the consistent peal of budgerigars in a cage hanging from the edge of the window over the oven in the open kitchen. The bottom of the cage was misshapen and covered in spaghetti sauce splatter. The birds panicked as I neared and flapped around the cage, spraying seed husks and feathers out of the bars.

'Frank Bennett.' I offered a hand to the nearest woman, a big hulk of curly-haired suburban mother I assumed to be Keely's mother. Tit tatts. Her whole arm seemed to take the tremor of my contact like a seismic monitor made from cellulite.

'About time you got here.'

'Let up, would you, for Christ's sake,' another mother said from across the room. The Kidds. About five of them, crowded around one of the overstuffed faux-suede recliners. Mother, father, confused pre-teens, all of them thin-faced and angular. I picked out the Benfields across the chessboard from them, holding down the opposite recliner, Mum and Dad only. The thin rodent-like Kidds and the fat-speckled, curly Mannings. The Benfields distinguished themselves by being economically superior to the others, at least I assumed, given the disdain with which they observed their surroundings. Mrs Benfield brushed at her forearms like they were picking up toxic dust. The only two people in the room who seemed to be getting on were a pair of toddlers sitting on the shag-pile rug in front of the television, trying to swallow bits of Lego.

'I'm really sorry about the time.' I cleared my throat, tried to face them all, couldn't help putting my back to someone. 'Really sorry. I understand you're all frustrated. And you're right if you're thinking you're probably going to spend the next couple of hours repeating to me everything you already told my case workers over in Parramatta. I'm the principal on your case, however, and I've got to see you all together. So I'm going to try to make this as painless and as meaningful as I can.'

I was very careful to get my 'ful' and 'less' in the right spots. There was a moment of silence in which they all made sure. Then everyone tried to talk at once. No one invited me to sit down. So I went to the couch in front of the toddlers and sat anyway. One of the babies began fooling with my shoelaces.

'Mr Bennett, was it?' said Mrs Benfield, still scratching her arms. She was making me feel itchy. Someone thrust a coffee into my hand, spilt it on my fingers, on the throw over the couch.

'Hi, yes.'

'We had a principal on our daughter's case already. What happened to Detective Ellis?'

'When we conclusively connected your daughter's case with those of the other missing girls, the file shifted out of Missing Persons and over to me and my partner. I'm sitting down with Detective Ellis and Detective Costa this afternoon to get a briefing.'

'Who's your partner?' asked someone behind me.

'Eden Archer. You might have seen her on the news. The surgeon case.'

'Ellie who?'

'Eden.'

'What kinda stupid name is Eden?' The father, Michael Kidd, a mountain of a man.

'Who gives a fuck what her name is? Where *is* she?' One of the brothers, accusatory, shrugged thin shoulders connected to crossed arms.

'She's operating on this case in another capacity right now.'

'The fuck does that mean?'

'She's off,' I turned my head, gave him my profile, 'doing other shit. This is a one-man job.'

'A one-man job. You hear that? Three young girls missing and they send us one fucking guy.'

'There are plenty of people working on the case right now.' I rubbed my eyes. 'But sitting here with you for a briefing is a one-man job.'

'I'm writing to *A Current Affair* about this.'

'Mr Kidd, I understand you're upset –'

'So, the cases are connected.' The Benfield father seized the floor with an expression like he'd smelled something foul, like something rotting inside him was giving off fumes up the back of his throat. Rage. 'They're connected through Jackie Rye, aren't they?'

'Right now Mr Rye is a person of interest. There are a number of persons of interest being monitored closely at present.' I slurped my coffee, wondering what I'd find at the bottom if I ever got there. It tasted of margarine.

'You arrested him?'

'No.'

'The fuck not?' One of the Kidds.

'Look,' I held up a hand, 'I know what you want right now is action. Arrests. You have to understand that sometimes making an arrest straight away can be the worst thing you can do, no matter how obvious it is who you should be after. Your case is being handled with the utmost tactical consideration. I can't tell you how, but people are on this with everything they've got, and some very dangerous shit is going down for members of my team. Trying to pull apart the investigation is a natural reaction, and I totally get it, but it's a waste of time. Everything that can be done is being done.'

The crowd considered this for a second or two. The babies at my feet babbled and sang in their strange, jarring way. The one with the shoelace fascination, a Manning by the curls, grabbed my fingers and pulled herself up by them. I sat and let her tug at my hands like the reins of a horse, jostling, investigating the buttons on the cuffs of my shirt. The baby's trust seemed to win me over to the watchers. Their attention left me and turned on each other.

'Someone should be taking these lot aside and talking to them about how long they've known Jackie Rye,' the Manning father snapped. He stabbed a finger at the Kidds. 'I haven't heard a single thing yet about your relationship with that man. Your daughter introduced our daughter to him. You *knew* he was trouble and you let my daughter – and your own – go out there.'

'Erin was the one who knew Jackie. We met him once.'

'Didn't you buy a car from out there?'

'Yeah?'

'Wasn't that two years ago? Don't you also buy goey off him? Haven't you bought goey off him in the last six months?'

'This has nothing to do with anything.' The Kidd father was burring up, shoulders back, chest out like a gorilla trying to ward off a rival, nipples jutting at his damp T-shirt. 'Stop thinking you're some kind of fucking Sherlock Holmes. This fuckwit's been spreading shit around the entire town about us and how we raised our kid.' The man waved across the room, glanced at me, as though I was supposed to agree based solely on the Manning father's face, his shoes, the way he stood.

'Oh fuck off.'

'You fuck off.'

'I don't have to spread any shit about your mob, mate. You do it just fine yourselves.'

'Our daughter is missing too, you moron.'

'Is she? Is she, or is she out there somewhere with him? She and Jackie are probably selling my daughter's bones. Erin could have talked Keely into anything, she was such a manipulative little slut.'

The Kidd father was up, halfway across the room before he found himself tangled in the arms of one of his sons. I sat back and watched, making notes on the pad on my knee. This was what I'd wanted, after all – for them to forget I was there, to talk about smack and stolen cars and who knew who and didn't want to implicate themselves. The women were sneering at each other now, about boyfriends stolen and skirts worn too short and a birthday party ruined by a drunken confession. The babies seemed used to all the turmoil. One stood by my knee, trying to take the pen from my fingers. I reached up and patted down the infant's blond hair, tried to pick if it was a boy or girl in its shabby grey tracksuit.

The Benfields were watching the argument quietly, tears running down the mother's cheeks. She was watching the faces of those around her like she was trying to imagine how they could have appealed to her baby, how she could have felt at home among this type. I'd seen the look before on the mothers of junkie girls whose murders and overdoses and hotel balcony swan dives I'd investigated back in North Sydney, girls who had been sold, used, discarded like used fast-food wrappers. Some mothers have bad girls and they know it. But they're always shocked when they see the kind of friends she kept, the bed she died in, the state she'd let her body get into when the clothes were stripped away and she was laid out on a morgue table – meat made of a person you created, a person whose safety you obsessed over once. You ignore these things when you have a bad child. You get blinded by your own love.

I kept listening, sipping my bad coffee. It took a good twenty minutes and about ten pages of notepad for everyone to work up a sweat, a couple of women to storm out, a few death threats to be fired back and forth. I didn't take much notice of the death threats. Bogans will chuck one your way the moment you look at them crooked. The girls will text you death threats. Describe the way they'll do it, how they plan to get off. Very rarely had I ever seen a death threat by a dope-smoking, dole-collecting nobody carried out in all its proposed intricacies. People like this killed each other in a drunken, angry snap over a barbecue on a Saturday football night, chips spilled every-where, glasses broken, no time for threats, for thinking, for planning. It was all very boring. The urban-sprawl homicide beat was an easy beat. Dave-o stabbed Johnno. Oh no.

In the lull between arguments, I gathered more information about the girls. Ashley Benfield was the one who didn't fit – hadn't been born, at least, into the kind of life that encouraged recklessness like the other two. The babies at my feet weren't so lucky, were already accustomed to chaos, crisis, hollering

151

and frightened tears, the way the men talked over the women and called them things, put them in their place like unruly children. Keely Manning had grown up much like my murdered girlfriend Martina – a grimy face in a loud brood, each distinguished only by whether or not her particular crimes for that day would interrupt dinner. Martina told me that she enjoyed the sensation of being bad, liked to be hated because when she was hated she was being noticed, being heard. I wondered if this was why Keely sought the arms of strangers because, besides the money, for once she was the focus of someone's attention even if only for a few minutes, someone's desire, someone's only one. From what her sister told me, something had been missing in Erin almost from the beginning. She never slept. Constantly swirled through violent emotions, even as a child. Would strangle her siblings until they turned blue in the face and then seconds later want their affection.

But Ashley. Ashley was different. I listened to her parents while the crowd around us sniped at each other. Ashley had been everything her mother ever wanted. An artist. An academic. A perfect little angel. The Benfields had plenty of photographs of the little girl performing in dance classes, receiving awards on the assembly stage, adding bicarb of soda to a model volcano to make it erupt pink foam for a science fair. She was gentle, they said. Giving. The mother wanted to get into an elaborate story about the teenage Ashley and her work with the elderly but the father told her softly there wasn't time. Was I looking for Ashley now because she had tired of that perfect life? Had someone come along and convinced the girl, as so many bad-boy figures do, that everything her parents had put into her had been to benefit themselves only?

I didn't have any kids. I'd come close. But I had no idea what kind of trouble teenage girls could be. Runaways were not my department. All I got to see were the girls who had been found too late and the bad boys with their masks off, crying their eyes out in piss-stained jail cells. I looked at the pictures of bright-eyed Ashley and wondered what she'd been thinking.

The meeting taught me little about Rye and what had made the girls head out to his farm. But I said my goodbyes at least knowing a little more about who I was looking for. I stepped out onto the porch where the boys were standing and stopped, flipped my notebook shut, waited for something before I left, some nugget of gold waiting to be uncovered, glimmering in the dark. Maybe it was instinct, or the angry dog look I'd copped from the Manning boy when I'd arrived, but he offered me a cigarette and I took it because I knew he was standing on the nugget I wanted, grinding it thoughtfully in the dirt with his shoe.

'Got email?' he asked. He looked inside. I glanced in after him, blew smoke respectfully over my shoulder.

'Yeah.'

'Might email you something.'

I gave him my card. He examined it as he spoke. There was a great nasty ulcer just inside his mouth. One of those ones that makes it hard to eat.

'I'll email you something I don't want going no further than your inbox.'

I was going to tell him I couldn't guarantee that, but he pulled open the screen door, took his cigarette from his mouth and walked inside. I lifted my eyes and got a cop-hating goodbye stare that burned me all the way to the car.

Jackie Rye was at breakfast when Eadie arrived. She'd slept badly again, the scratchers and crawlers and wandering things that lived inside her caravan somehow sensing the tension in her body and increasing the volume of their night orchestra. She woke sometime in the middle of the night to the feeling of the camera's black eye watching her like an owl and some long-legged thing crawling in her hair. She pulled it out, whatever it was, and hurled it towards the darkness at the end of the bed. Made a promise to herself to block the drains, try to tape the windows. When Skylar thumped on her door at sunrise she felt pain in the act of waking, a dread so real and deep it made her bones ache.

Jackie's presence at the edge of the men's table made it all worthwhile. He was talking to Nick. Everyone turned when she approached. By now her news had passed on every set of lips. Some laughs. Some scowls. Some assessments based on the new information. Suddenly her long, manly gait meant something. The squareness of her shoulders and her rare smiles. How could they have missed it? Eadie put toast on. Skylar went for the eggs lying hard and dry in a dirty corner of the grill.

'People been saying things,' the girl said. Eadie hadn't heard her usual scared-cat sprint to the door that morning. The girl's lips were restless, being chewed.

'I imagine they have.'

'Is it true?'

'Jesus, Skye,' Eadie laughed. The girl looked up, relieved. 'It's not terminal cancer. They didn't just announce the end of the world.'

'Some people think so, though. Things like that.' Skylar shrugged helplessly. 'It's like, city stuff. City people are like that. Not out here.'

'People are like that. City people. Country people. People on fucking islands in the middle of the Pacific. People on snowy mountains. Eskimos. Around here, they *move* to the city. But before they move, they walk among you.' Eadie wiggled her fingers in the girl's face. She cringed away.

'There ain't no fucking gay Eskimos.'

'How many Eskimos you met?'

'Jesus.'

'It's not a big deal.'

'S'pose.' Skylar sucked air in the side of her cheek, made a click sound like she was trying to attract a horse. 'Don't really care that much myself, to be honest, I'm just telling you how it is. I'm more worried about who's gonna win *MasterChef*. You watch it? Watch *MasterChef*?' Her elbow in Eadie's ribs, high, bruising.

'No.'

'Tonight we're watching it at yours then.' She nodded to confirm her decision. 'Jackie hates it. I'll bring chips.'

She tottered off to the women's tables. Eadie set the kettle to boil. The morning was already heating and the dogs that had taken up their places in the shade of the fold-out tables were being harassed by flies gathered on the humps of their backs and behind their ears. Sucking at scratch wounds. Eadie imagined the police raiding this place, when she had finally pinned down whoever was responsible for the missing girls, black-clad officers knocking over these tables, kicking dirt in these snarling faces, throwing open caravan doors and rifling through possessions, making piles of them in the sun. Because that was what they would do when it was over, secure the killer and make everyone else's lives a misery simply for being there, for being in the company of a monster, whoever it was. Some youth worker would get Skylar off in a corner and listen to her cry and ask when she and Jackie had first had sexual intercourse, assess whether charges needed to be pursued. Someone would probably round up the dogs and send them off to a vet. She watched them squirming as she stood at the table waiting for the kettle, watched the flies walking in the blood. She didn't feel bad.

Eadie didn't notice the men leaving the table until they were all around her, scraping char off the barbecue, opening cupboards, slamming them, emptying the tiny bar fridge of butter, sauce, bowls of onion. Round two. Eadie stiffened as Nick passed behind her. She felt his breath on her neck.

'Look at this. It's Rye Farm's newest hand,' Jackie said, leaning on the edge of the barbecue as the men went to work around her, his thin arms folded. 'How's the working life, Eadie?'

'Fine, Jackie, thanks.' Eadie poured the sugar. Grabbed for the kettle. It was gone. Nick adding to it, meeting her eyes over the sink, through the fine steam. She'd got his left cheekbone with the frypan, right where the flesh was at its thinnest on the bottom rim of the eye socket. It would have hurt.

The handle hadn't left a mark, but she'd likely crushed something in there, left it rubbing, angry, hard to swallow. The feel of hands around her throat was not unknown to Eadie. Once or twice she'd found herself in sticky situations with playmates, and the first thing a man tended to go for was a woman's throat. The vulnerability of it, soft and round and critical to life, how it fitted in fingers. A good throttling was more painful than it looked. There were capillaries burst in the corners of his eyes.

'Bet the hard work's helping you rest easy,' Jackie said.

'Sure is. Slept like a lamb.'

'Everything nice and . . .' the small man licked his flappy lips, glanced at Nick, 'secure over there in your van?'

'More now than it was,' Eadie said.

'Good. Good. You never know what creepy-crawlies might come wandering in at night.'

Jackie squinted at the sun, seemed to want to say something more, to be putting the words together in a row in his head, selecting the best one, like a man choosing the pig that would be slaughtered that day from the dozens of wide-eyed squealers waiting in the stalls. She watched him and felt Nick at the end of the table, tapping his fingers on the plastic surface, watching the water bubble up around the temperature gauge. Someone passed behind Eadie, dragged a table into line with the one she stood by, bent down and began unscrewing the struts to dismantle it.

'I'm glad you're feeling happy here,' Jackie was saying. 'Glad you feel like you fit in. I'm not sure everyone feels that way. I'm sure some people around here feel like you're a . . . square peg, I guess they call it.'

'Nothing wrong with being a bit square, Jackie.' Eadie shrugged off her jacket and folded it in her arms, over her breasts. A loving bundle of denim. She felt a muscle tighten in the corner of her left eye, the only thing in her body that reacted to the tension in her mind. Eadie was good at looking placid. She was hardly ever placid. Life's most dangerous moments were hidden in the calm like spiders tunnelled into the moist, green earth.

The kettle clicked. Boiling point. Eadie heard a clunk behind her, felt the earth shudder under her feet as the table-top slid onto its side and she was stalled like a horse between the table at her hips and the table at her backside. She met Nick's eyes as he tipped the kettle, knocked it good and hard from the side, no room for error, flushing the tabletop with scalding water. Eadie dropped her denim jacket on the table in the half a second it took for the burning water to reach her, pressed it with her hands, made an instant dam. The water rushed around the jacket and fell at the sides of her body. She felt it splashing on her ankles, the burn of tiny droplets that would do hardly any of the damage the full kettle would have done to her stomach, her hips, her thighs, her crotch. The men around her sent up a yowl of apparent surprise. The women nearby turned, stepped off the benches they leaned on, curious.

Nick's eyes. The cold eyes of an insect.

'Ho!' Jackie laughed, clapped his hands. 'Look at that. The reaction time of a coiled spring. That coulda been really nasty.'

'Jesus, Nick,' someone said. 'Watch what you're doing.'

'Clumsy fucker.'

'You'll have to be quicker next time,' Jackie laughed, folding his arms, watching Nick's face. The tall man said nothing.

Someone slapped Eadie's shoulder in appreciation. She fought the impulse to grab the hand and crush it in her fingers. Eadie took the soaked jacket, still hot to the touch, and slid out from the trap between the two tables, wrung it onto the dirt. Skylar came bounding towards her.

'Man! What happened?'

'Just an accident. Someone trying to give me a bath.' Eadie shook the jacket off, walked over and hung it on a string connecting the two carports. People at the barbecue were laughing. Jackie demonstrated what happened to the women, the rush of water with his loose hands, those hands tightening around an imaginary bundle. Jackie grinned and winked at Eadie as she walked away towards the stables. The muscles of her legs were stiff, the dogs an angry entourage, snapping at her hands.

People called him the Dogboy of Darlinghurst and stopped calling him Heinrich altogether. Everyone except Sunday, that is, who never liked to be caught doing what everybody else was doing. For a couple of years it was the Bear and his Dog who arrived at the back doors of suburban houses in the early morning hours to whisper in kitchens with women about what this poison would do or that one, how long it would take husbands or bosses or mistresses to start coughing or choking or turning blue, what those moments would be like for the ones who had to watch and explain. It was the Bear and his Dog on Sunday mornings on the front doors of terraces in Redfern and Chippendale with the whomping stick and the list of names, Bear and Dog on the logs down by the pier in Woolloomooloo watching the navy boats and eating Harry's pies, Bear and Dog picking a path through crowded bars to the back booths to talk to dark-eyed foreign men about the girls at the house. The Night of Teeth and Tearing always seemed to come up during these meetings, when everyone stopped leaning forward over the table and sat back in their seats and sighed, their glasses empty and cigarettes smoking in the glass ashtray. Heinrich would sit, folding coasters into squares, with one arse cheek off the booth because that's all that would fit beside Bear. The eyes would fall on him in the lull of words and someone would say, 'Hey, isn't that the dog-killer?' Bear liked to tell the story, to rub Heinrich's head with his oven-mitt hand until his hair was all messed up.

He did this even when Heinrich was fifteen, or what he guessed was about fifteen, when his shoulders spread out and his knuckles developed calluses and his nose had been broken enough times that no one took pity on him when it happened. Heinrich had noticed that – the slow disappearing of pity, and care and affection, particularly from the women, the gradual change in those creatures who once only wanted to put clothes on him and now only seemed to want to take them off. Heinrich was just warming up to the idea of letting these giggling, whispering, lip-licking beings have their way one of these days – pop his shirt buttons off all the way down and see what they might do after that – when Bear pulled him aside in the hall and told him not to shit in his own nest, whatever that meant.

And even though he was the Dogboy of Darlinghurst, even though he had done something no one had ever seen before and then pretended it hadn't happened at all, which seemed to be the thing to do to get anyone to look you in the eye, the boy was always landed with tasks given to someone who hadn't accomplished anything. Bear would tell him that these were the things he needed to do to make sure he kept his feet on the ground. Heinrich was still the runner on fight nights and he was still kept away from the dog training. He still had to read to Bear in the greenhouse, even though he was pretty good at it by now and even liked reading in his own time. And he was still responsible for all the cleaning work that went on back there, sweeping out the dirt and hosing the floors and watering the seedlings and labelling the bottles, every single goddamn one. Heinrich was still the carrier of messages, the keeper of keys, the filler of glasses, the protector of coats and hats. But he didn't mind. It meant he never missed anything.

It seemed to be Bear's mission that Heinrich never missed anything either. That for every meeting and every fight and every trip and every conversation in the street Heinrich was there with his ears turned on and his eyes open. Over the years the boy began to understand just how much of a hold Caesar had on every person he came into contact with, from the girls at the house who couldn't leave because they had no families and no money and couldn't read, to the junkies wandering Darlinghurst Road who couldn't go too far because Caesar was the only one who could get them what they needed even when they couldn't pay for it up-front. You couldn't even get out of his grasp by killing yourself because Caesar got to know everyone you'd ever loved before he gave you a penny, so that when you couldn't pay he could hold them all in his hands like mice as they tried to claw and squirm their way out of his big fingers. When you came to Caesar you left with a stain, even if you didn't know it yet, a tiny ink spot on your cuff or your palm or your shoe, something that would grow and spread overnight, a cancer dancing over skin. He could hook you with a glance, a word. Caesar Steel. Suddenly you were in. So deep in, you couldn't feel the bottom beneath your feet.

And his reach went everywhere, no matter how low down you tried to crawl into the dark, no matter how high you climbed or who you dragged in front of you. Caesar sent the Dog and the Bear to clamber through the hatches of navy ships to pick up bags of guns, to talk to men in bunks and engine rooms, to stand on the bridge and look at the city and talk to angry men in white. He sent them into warehouses to walk through streets and alleys of machinery parts, cameras, televisions, blenders, costumes, leather jackets, fur coats, shoes. Through back-alley doorways they walked into clubs to empty safes while moustached men cried into their hands. Bear would sit in the car with the boy and his list, rubbing his hands to keep them warm, the wharfies trudging the gravel wastelands around the car towards the steel-grey water, their lunch boxes swinging and shoulders hunched against the wind.

'Know where these came from?' Bear asked, holding up one of the cameras, turning the thing in his hands. Heinrich always felt a little sick around cameras but couldn't exactly remember why. Lips shut. Nothing happened.

'Where, Bear?'

'Vietnam. Bet you can't tell me where that is.'

'Sticking out the side of Cambodia.'

'Sure is. Crazy shit going on over there right now. Boys killing boys your age. Younger. Going mad and hacking them up like fish.'

'Doesn't sound any good, Bear.'

'No good at all, boy. We got eight thousand boxes here, six cameras a box. How many is that, young scholar?'

'Bout forty-eight thousand, I reckon.'

'I reckon too. Never miss a thing, Heinrich. Never let anyone give you a job unless you know what it is, what they're going to make from it, and whether or not you're getting yours, fair and square. Someone tells you they've got a hundred gold necklaces, you count them. Someone tells you they've paid the dealer, you call up and check. Someone tells you a guy's dead, you call his mother and ask when the funeral was. Always watching, always listening, always checking. You get it?'

'Got it.'

There were rare times when Heinrich missed things and it was only ever when the forbidden man was involved. Heinrich had learned that his name was Savet and that he was a detective sergeant, but nothing more. When Detective Sergeant Savet arrived at the house Caesar would look at the boy the way that a man looks at a collarless

164

dog wandering in his yard, trying to decide if it deserved brutality or could afford to be ignored. Heinrich would wander away, find girls to tease. Bear always got angry when Savet was around. Afterwards he'd want to drive for hours, not going anywhere, just staring out the windscreen and lighting a cigarette off the end of the cigarette that had come before. When Heinrich would ask what was going on, Bear wouldn't answer. It wasn't often that Bear didn't answer something. He had answered so many questions when Heinrich was little, even tried to tackle things he couldn't know – like where had Heinrich come from, what had happened to the people in the burning house in his mind.

'They were probably good people,' Bear would say. 'One of them was probably short.'

From what Heinrich could tell, all Savet wanted to talk to Bear and Caesar about was boats and planes and maps of Vietnam. Heinrich didn't know if the man had been in the war or what. He walked with a limp and had the same hard-edged look that Heinrich had seen in boys coming back from Nam, the sideways glance and quick turn of someone who had been crept up on a few times too many and couldn't sleep properly because of it.

The thing that worried Heinrich most about Detective Sergeant Thomas Savet was that he was sure the cop had the Silence in him. Once he watched Savet being run off by Bear when Caesar wasn't at the house, and though Heinrich had seen Bear run plenty of people off – men looking for loans who already had pieces of their bodies missing for not paying last time or girls who'd cleaned out the safes before they scampered away into the night – this was different. Savet had stood on the path at the bottom of the steps and looked up at Bear as the big man yelled and threatened and his face had been placid, calm, unhearing. Heinrich wasn't close enough, but had he been he was sure he would have seen pictures moving in the policeman's murky eyes. Bad things happening behind black glass.

'You really hate that guy,' Heinrich said afterwards as Bear stood panting on the porch looking at the empty street.

'Warmonger. Filthy . . . greedy troublemaker.'

'Why's he keep hanging round here?'

Bear grunted, kicked a cat off the porch that had been whining and wandering around his feet.

'You know that Kingsley kid that went missing? In the papers?'

'No.'

'Neutral Bay kid. Rich. Volleyball.'

'Oh yeah, yeah.'

'He solved that.' Bear pointed to where Savet had been standing. 'They're telling us this lazy ignorant fool solved that.'

Bear looked at the boy as though the very fact that Detective Sergeant Savet had solved a murder made something very clear but, as often happened in his life, Heinrich found himself on the very edge of understanding without really knowing what was going on. He didn't like the feeling. He was more comfortable following directions, staying out of the way, keeping his head down. Heinrich opened his mouth to offer something, some half-committed line that would assure Bear that he wasn't an idiot but not reveal the crushing emptiness in his knowledge. But before he could do it Bear walked inside the house and slammed the door.

I got home about three in the afternoon and was walking up the stairs to my apartment when I got a whiff of some perfume ahead of me, something light and expensive and European. When I looked up the shrink was standing there with her arms folded, leaning against my door. I stopped walking and dropped my hand, let the keys jangle against my hip.

'What have I done now?' I said. 'Go away.'

'You're such a charmer, Detective Bennett.'

She was all baby blue today, a T-shirt that crumpled up towards her hips and curved nicely around her taut biceps, tiny blue studs shaped like flowers in her ears. Grey skinny jeans that she could pull off without looking sag-bottomed. Cashmere boots with round toes. I got up close to unlock the door and was struck by how small and freckly she was, like a little hairless leopard.

'I don't have to play doctors with you anymore you know, Stone.'

'I'm not here to play doctors with you,' she said, slapping a bunch of files against my chest. 'I've been trying to call you so that you can take these back. They're originals. I'd have paid to have them sent but it's not my responsibility.'

'Oh and you were just in the neighbourhood, so you thought, you know,' I shrugged, gave a flourish.

'I really was just in the neighbourhood. My mother lives two streets back.'

'I'm a cop. I can tell when people are lying. Especially women.'

'Oh yeah?'

'Yeah. Confess, Stone. You've been up all night outside my windows watching me shower. Taking photos. Sticking them in a scrapbook.'

'You're so weird.'

I took the papers, held open the door for her. The cat trotted towards us, meowing like a needy wife interrogating me about where I'd been and who I'd been with. It always did that. It was kind of nice.

'I didn't know you were a cat man, Frank.'

'I'm not a cat man.' I nodded at the animal. 'It's a man cat. Coffee? Tea?'

'Coffee.' She dumped her handbag beside the door like she lived there. I frowned and began herding beer bottles off the sink. Wondered if I had any milk. If it was any good. I opened the fridge and exhaled.

'How are you?'

'I'm fine,' I told the fridge.

'Busy?'

'Yep.'

'I've been following the missing girls in the papers,' she said, perching on the arm of my grey Ikea couch. 'Not much movement there.'

'Oh, there's movement,' I said. 'You just can't see it.'

168

We talked about the case for a little bit. Kept it vague. How the families must feel. Similar cases. Guys she'd treated who came away fucked up from finding teens tied up in basements, guys who'd chased traffickers out of the country and through the jungle. I forgot to switch the kettle on, remembered. She laughed at me. I glanced around and felt a little less embarrassed about my single-man hovel now that Eden had taken care of it for me. The cleaners had made it look considered, put pictures on the walls and arranged things on shelves. I was happy to take the credit. I'd never been a man with any style.

The cat was whining, looking at me, pawing at my trousers.

'So, all this work, Frank,' Stone sighed.

'Yeah?'

'I was hoping it'd keep you all squared away. But it's not, though, is it? If we're really honest with ourselves.'

I looked over. She was examining an empty packet of Endone she seemed to have plucked from between the couch cushions. I went and took it from her and slipped it into the bin.

'Did you manage to take a look at this place before you started psychoanalysing my colour scheme?' I asked. I motioned to the room. 'Noticed how fucking immaculate it is? It's like a showroom in here. It must be exhausting to be so critical all the time.'

'Your cat's starving.'

'It's not starving.' I snatched the box of cat food from the top of the fridge, tried not to trip over the animal as it wove desperately between my feet. 'I fed it yesterday.'

Dr Stone was watching me as I fed the cat, rinsed its water out, patted it a little as it crunched the biscuits. My face felt hot.

'Do you feel like I'm attacking you?'

'I feel like you're trying to decide what disorder I have from how I tie my shoelaces,' I said. 'What is it? Bipolar?'

'Are you trying to undercut my credibility in order to defend yourself?' she smiled.

'I'm not defending myself in my own house,' I shrugged. I scratched the cat's rump. Its back leg twitched in pleasure.

'What's the cat's name, Frank?' she asked. I looked at her.

'Greycat.'

'Is it a boy or a girl?'

I straightened. Tried to glance down.

'Don't look at it. Tell me. Is it a boy or a girl?'

I licked my teeth. Dr Stone cocked her head slightly.

'What's your point?' I asked.

'That's not your cat, is it?'

'It's mine now.'

'Is that Martina's cat?'

'No. It's mine.'

'Why have you got Martina's cat, Frank?' I could tell she wanted to squint or frown, to let some of the raw confusion flooding through her mind show in her face. But I was sure they told you not to do that in shrink school, not to make the fish fuckers and kiddie fiddlers and sleepless war vets and guys who couldn't get over the violent deaths of women they barely knew know you thought they were weird. So her face remained still and open and understanding, and in a way that was worse, made me feel like an even bigger loser or psycho or addict or whatever her diagnosis would turn up. So I turned back to the coffee I'd failed to make and tossed the grounds out into the sink, rinsed a mug and set it on the counter.

'Got any other plans, Stone, or was ruining my afternoon it?'

'No, this was it,' she said.

I nodded and looked out the window until she was gone.

Hades was standing on the steps to his shack, leaning on his cane, as I arrived. I'd hoped to be in and out of his place before nightfall but the sun was setting as I clambered up the drive. Some new creature was in the process of being assembled on the knoll in front of the house, a long-snouted thing made from hundreds of birdcages. Tiny doors opening everywhere, different types of chain hanging between them suspending objects – a bright red toaster heart, a ball of cracked and splintered wine glasses tied together with wire for a brain, the snaking intestines made of washing-machine tubes and suspension springs. Hades lifted a hand against the pink light over the tip. A stray dog emerged from around the corner of the shack and glanced at me before loping down the hill.

We said nothing to each other. When we got inside he handed me a beer from the fridge while I laid my papers out on the table.

'I've had one afternoon on this, so don't expect wonders.'

'I rarely expect wonders,' he said.

I'd been at my local library since Dr Stone left my apartment, fighting off retirees trying to accost the research specialist for their ancestry scrapbooks so that the skinny young woman would help me trawl through online archives. I'm not sure if she knew it was police work, and I certainly didn't tell her it was, but there have been times in my life when people have been able to pick my occupation just from the way I look at and talk to them. I think she might have got the gist of my purpose from it. Copishness isn't something I cultivate or something I particularly like to think I have. I remember as a young man thinking all my father's cop friends were dick-heads, the way they stood with their chests out and their eyes down and their words intentionally edging around whatever it was they really wanted to say. Afraid to laugh, ever ready to take things the wrong way or question motives or cut down jokes – so cynical you could almost smell it coming off them. Every now and then a little of that edged into me and people knew what I was. I hated it.

I sat down and shifted a black-and-white photograph over to Hades. A dark-skinned child of one or two sitting on a wooden stool in nothing but a pair of cotton pants, pulling at her feet and looking away. Someone had labelled the photo-graph in blue ink, identifying it with a serial number.

'Sharon Elizabeth White,' I said, unfolding the file that the photograph belonged to. Printouts of scans from the National Archives. 'Removed from the care of Donna Anna White by the Victorian Children's Protection Society in August 1956. Report cites vagrancy and alcoholism on the part of the mother. Only child at the time but two others would follow. Both would also be removed – Lynda in care until adulthood and Scott deceased at seven, traffic accident. Sharon's father unknown, father of the other two a steelworker. Mother illiterate, unemployed. Removal wasn't easy, it seems. Lots of trouble caused in the community. Lots of similar removals. A small riot.' I pushed a folder towards Hades. It was thin. Handwritten, full of medical notes. Hades was looking at the photograph, frowning. His glasses were on the sink.

'Someone pissed off the local constabulary,' I said.

'They would do that.' Hades nodded. 'Go in and clear out whole towns. Night raids. Keep everyone in check with the idea that they might get them back if they kept their noses clean. Sunday never talked about it but I knew it would have been something like that.'

'Well, she's in foster homes until five,' I said, flipping the edges of the other folders. 'A good kid, but a very slow learner. Basically non-verbal. Then she takes off one morning from school. Gone walkabout. For a while police thought she might have been abducted, but she's filed officially as "Absconded from care" and that seems to be the end of it. Probably presumed a relative took her and closed the case.'

'A beach.' Hades smirked a little, sipped his beer. I waited. He didn't continue. He seemed to be dreaming, looking at the photograph.

'What?'

'Bear found her on a beach. On a Sunday morning.'

I lifted more photographs from the files, shuffled through them. Laid one out before him. A group of people standing on the porch of a large house, lots of women smiling and laughing, some shadowy-eyed low-lives with big dogs on chains. The girl who was found on a Sunday was there at the edge, looking at her fingernails when the photograph was taken. I pointed to the big man at the back, in the shadows by the door, a hairy colossus.

'Michael "Bear" Harwitz?'

'That's the one.'

I held the photograph up to my nose, squinted. I'd heard things about Bear Harwitz and Alec 'Caesar' Steel from the sixties, old academy stories that were probably so removed from truth as to be completely useless to my investigation. Gun fights and towns terrorised and cocaine parties and prostitutes slain in their beds. Hades took the photograph from my hand, having waited long enough. I watched his face. He didn't seem particularly upset about any of it. I imagined he'd never seen any of those photographs before. He finished his beer and caught my eye, set the photograph down.

'What else?'

'Nothing else at this point. A few drug arrests. Twelve. Fifteen. Seventeen. Eighteen. That's it. That's the mark she made on the world.'

'That's the mark she made on the public record.'

'Who was she to you?'

'She was the love of my life,' the old man said. I waited. He folded up the papers before him and put them neatly out of his way. He clasped his hands and looked at my eyes. Concrete and steel and storm clouds in his eyes, the grey of hard times weathered in silence. He reminded me of my father – when that thought came to me I shook it physically out of my head, looked away. This was not my father. This was a killer and a king. He didn't know the word 'love'.

'You kill her, Hades?'

'No.'

'I've heard plenty of smack talk about you, old man.'

'Like what?'

'Like you bit some guy's thumb off in a bar fight.'

He laughed, hung his head back.

'I've been in some good scraps, but not that good. The thumb is connected to the hand by about a million complex, intertwining muscles. Its tendons go as far back as the wrist. You can't just bite it off. It's not a fucking breadstick.'

'I heard you know a lot about bodies. How they work. How to dispose of them.'

'There's a shovel out on the porch there, boy, and a torch in the cupboard. Go ahead. Go treasure hunting, if that's your idea of a good evening. Plenty have before. I ought to start charging for it as a tourist activity. I'm going to sit here and have another beer.'

'You're pretty good with the denials,' I sighed. 'But you know that I know about Eden.'

'Careful now.'

'I'm a police officer. I look at the facts. I look at the rumours, even if you say they're not true. You can't be surprised that you're my first suspect.'

'I'm not surprised. I'm just waiting for you to get your arse into gear and move on from me. I didn't kill Sunday. I told you that. I loved her. I'm as keen to know what happened to her as that stupid boy out there on the road.'

'Then why am I sitting here? Why is Adam White so sure he's got you?'

'Because she was on her way to see me when she disappeared. It looks bad.'

I waited while he cracked another stubby.

'She was supposed to meet me,' Hades said, shifting back on his chair, moving old bones around. 'At Central Station. Platform Two. Right outside the ticket booths. Nine o'clock, I said, because she never got up early. She spent the night before at a hotel called Jeremy's. I sent a note, and she got the note. I waited and she didn't come. Something happened to her. She'd packed her things. She was ready to go. And then she was gone, all the stuff still sitting there.'

'What happened to her?'

'I don't know.'

'Any guesses?'

'Anything could've happened to Sunday. Trouble loved her. She'd always been like that. She was working on and off for a cat house in Crest Avenue when she disappeared but she hadn't been there long. Bounced around a lot. Pissed people off.'

'So you don't know who nabbed her.' I sat back too and hung my elbow over the back of the chair. 'No idea?'

'Plenty of people didn't like me. I'd just shaken everything up. Scorned some people pretty bad,' he sighed, shrugged. 'But then, plenty of people didn't like her.'

'What would be your guess then? Your people or hers?'

'I told you. I don't know.'

'No clue.'

'If I had a fucking clue I wouldn't have some idiot on my road watching me take a piss and some smart-arse cop boy sitting interrogating me in my own kitchen.' He flung an arm towards the door, towards me. 'I'd have brought White up here the moment he showed interest, sat him down and described how good it had felt to slowly and carefully carve the wet, beating heart out of the chest of the man who touched her. If I had any fucking clue who killed Sunday you'd have known about it, because it would've been in the papers, what I did to the killer.'

I finished my beer. A bunch of clocks were ticking in the other room, part of some collection, going off like the twittering of tiny mechanical birds. I only noticed it in the dead silence left behind by his words. I dragged the group photo towards me and pointed at Caesar Steel.

'Caesar?' I asked.

'I looked into it. Over and over. He and his people were accounted for.'

'I thought you were his people.'

'Not always.'

'Who did you account for and how did you account for them?'

'Caesar was ... incapacitated the night Sunday went missing,' the old man said, raising his eyebrows. 'That's all I'm prepared to say about that.'

It didn't surprise me how easily Hades slipped from client into defendant mode. I nodded my appreciation. There was no real reason for me to pressure him further. Pushing Hades Archer past uncomfortable was just about the stupidest thing anyone could do.

'Who else?'

'His major lieutenants were with him, so I knew where they all were. Tom Savet was at a policeman's ball at the city all night receiving awards.'

'Tom Savet?'

'He was very close to Caesar at the time.'

'So if you had to guess, you wouldn't say whatever happened to Sunday was something personal?'

'Look, in my time, you wanted to do something personal, you let everyone know what it was. No point in knocking off someone's bird without sending them something. A finger. An eye. Leaving her somewhere. Telling the papers and splashing it about town. That was how you did things in those days.

None of this drive-by punk shit. None of this, this shoot 'em up hooligan crap. You set examples back then. You spoke to people's faces.'

I sighed. The old man folded his arms on the table, looked at the windows, the night.

'Caesar and I . . . We had trouble at the time. Big trouble. If it had been anyone meaningful it would have been him. Him or one of his men. But I told you. I looked into it. I looked into it for years. It wasn't them.'

'It's going to be difficult to find out what happened if it was just some angry john or a deal gone bad or something.'

'You'd remember killing Sunday,' he said. 'She wasn't any ordinary girl. People still remember her. She was . . . different. Wild.'

'Whoever killed her might be dead.'

'They'd wanna hope.'

'Alright.' I nodded. 'Well. You keep your head down until we chat again. I'll work on this as much as I can but I've got to watch out for Eden as well. Don't cause any trouble. Don't go inviting any guests. And don't, whatever you do, go down there thinking you're going to talk to the guy. You slip up once and it's on tape.'

'Tape?' Hades sat upright in his chair.

'He's filming you.'

The old man's face hardened. I hadn't thought it could get any more menacing, but it did. I felt my stomach drop.

'This is harassment. This is stalking.'

'I know it is.'

Hades' eyes drifted away from me. I could almost see his old clockwork mind ticking away, devising painful scenarios.

'Don't do anything. Not yet.'

'You better move fast, copper,' the old man said.

I packed the papers back into the folders. I was going to take the last photograph, the picture of the child Sunday sitting on a stool, but Hades' elbow was on it so I left it where it was and told myself I'd get another copy. I left him there with it in the shack. The sun was red over the trash mountains as I walked to my car, angry and giving no glow as the night folded around it.

Waiting outside Eden's apartment, Juno was like a teen in the queue for a rock concert. It'd been awhile since I had been to one, and I was sure people his age didn't carry on the way we used to while they waited for Lady Gaga to come out of an egg or Kanye to get his clothes off, or whatever the hell the attraction was. But I recognised the shuffling feet, restless eyes, anguished sigh towards the heavens every now and then. Taking his backpack off, unzipping and staring into it, putting it back on. When Eden emerged from the elevator he stopped in his tracks and folded his hands into his pockets, dropped his head. She looked tired. Her eyes flicked to me and there was some of that raw animal rage you see in people who've had their civility worn down to glass, all the emotion bare underneath.

'What is he doing here?'

'He's the tech,' I shrugged. 'We gotta have him.'

'I thought we were just talking tactics.'

'We are. There are things he might have noticed that you didn't though. He's been on the surveillance a lot longer than I have. I've been slack.'

Eden narrowed her eyes at the boy, seemed to measure him with a glance. She unlocked her door with exaggerated movements. I stood looking at the black hair creeping into the bad dye job, the way it turned from midnight to brown to burnt orange to sunflower yellow over a matter of centimetres. Like a sunrise. I could see the tendons moving in her white neck.

She flicked the gold halogens on. The apartment was as I remembered it, like some weird kind of gallery hotel, somewhere you could pay to sleep among the art. No signs of humanness about it – no T-shirt lying on the couch or pair of knickers on the floor or empty coffee mug forgotten, stains on the bottom. Everything was sterile, tucked away, folded up, shelved. Furniture-store neat. It was probably a good thing. I didn't know what Juno would do if he caught sight of a pair of Eden's knickers. He stood looking around with his mouth open until I bopped him in the chest and he came to himself.

Eden hung her bag on a hook by the door, punched a code into the alarm system, tossed her keys into a bowl on the kitchen counter. Coming home. Her shoulders dropped from where they'd been, rock-hard, five centimetres higher than usual. She turned to us, pulling off her jacket.

'You, watch him.' She nodded at me, and then Juno. 'You, order dinner.'

Juno snapped to attention.

'What, uh, what should I get?'

'I don't care.' Eden walked towards the hall under the loft stairs. Juno looked at me helplessly.

'Not Japanese,' I said.

'What, so, anything? Anything, just not Japanese?'

'Anything,' I said.

'*Anything?*'

'Just order the fucking food.' I put my stuff on the floor by the coffee table. 'And don't touch. She'll kill you.'

Juno went out onto the balcony, panting, curling the orange ringlets behind his ears around his fingers. I set up the laptop and wandered into the kitchen. I selected a bottle of wine from the rack and grabbed some glasses from the immaculately arranged cupboards. Out of curiosity I opened a few for a peek. She had the stainless-steel knife set of a professional chef and all her cutlery was polished to within an inch of its life. All the mug handles were facing the same way and her foodstuffs were from weird organic stores I'd never heard of. Sicko.

I poured the wine, took a sip, listened to the shower running down the hall. I heard it finish, a door open and close, and headed down there. The hall was warm from steam. There were two doors, both closed.

'Eden, I need to use your loo.'

'Go ahead,' she shouted.

I was sure her voice came from the door on the right. But when I opened the one on the left, I caught a glimpse of a big room, red curtains, a stiffly made bed. And Eden standing with her side to me, a towel around her hair.

'Frank!'

'Oh god. Oh god! I'm sorry.' I slammed the door and started laughing, still holding on to the handle. 'I'm sorry. I thought this was the bathroom.'

The doorknob twisted in my fingers and she wrenched it open. She was now wearing a black satin robe.

'What the hell is wrong with you?'

'I'm really sorry.' I stood there laughing, unable to stop. She was looking at my eyes like a wet, angry tiger. 'Honest mistake, really. I couldn't hear which room you . . . and . . .'

'Stop laughing, use the bathroom, and then fuck off out of my hallway.'

'I just have to stand here a minute.' I closed my eyes and drew a deep breath, expanded my chest. 'I just have to recover from the single greatest joy of my young life.'

She slammed the door in my face. I was still chuckling in the bathroom. I'd seen Eden in her underwear once before and the effect had been just as thrilling, like catching a glimpse of a rare butterfly, so swift and glorious it's gone before your eyes can really settle on it. We'd been upgrading our riot training together down in Jervis Bay at a fire grounds, and she was behind a curtain stripping off clothes saturated in tear gas. Back then I hadn't seen the bright-pink birthmark that looked like a prancing horse on her ribs, so perfectly shaped it was almost like a tattoo. The only blemish on an otherwise marble-sculpted frame.

I spent most of my time trying to be a mature, restrained, well-rounded almost-middle-aged man but the sight had set off something really juvenile in me – not helped by her obvious annoyance. I went back to the living room, where Juno was sitting rigidly on the couch, setting up his laptop.

'I just saw Eden in the nick,' I said.

'You *what*?'

'The nick. The nuddie. Nekkid. Starkers. Bare-arsed like the day she was born.'

Juno's mouth was hanging open.

'No way.'

'Way.'

'I bet she's hard, man.'

'Like a stone.'

'She's gonna kill you.'

'She's gonna kill me,' I agreed.

Eden came out of the hall drying her hair in a towel, wearing pale jeans and a long grey shirt.

'You guys quite finished?' she asked, hanging the towel on the back of one of the kitchen stools. 'You want to call the papers?'

'No, we're good,' I smiled. 'That's a really pretty birthmark in a really pretty place though.'

'One more word about it and I'll slap your face off.'

'I know you will.' I shook my head like I was clearing water from my ears. 'Alright, let's work.'

Eden took the wine I'd poured her and sipped it long and slow like she hadn't had any in years. She gave me a filthy look. She wedged herself into the corner of the couch and put her feet up next to my leg. Her toenails were perfect pink squares but she had a scar on her left foot about eight centimetres long and white as porcelain. I'd glimpsed other scars on her ribs. I wondered where she'd got them, then came to the natural conclusion and stopped myself from wondering. It was easy to forget what Eden was. Now and then I liked to pretend she was just a strange and beautiful woman and that her social awkwardness was nothing to worry about. That she wasn't, in fact, something that I spent most of my day hunting and most of my night dreaming about hunting. The fox to my hound.

'There are a couple of people out there who worry me,' she began, cupping the wine with her hands. 'Nick's and Jackie's natural tendency towards violence makes them stick out among the pack. There is genuine malice everywhere though. No one has a problem joining in. I don't know how we're going to separate suspects if everyone's willing to egg each other on.'

'That was a clever move by the way,' Juno piped up. He grabbed his wine glass and tried to hide behind it. 'The gay thing. Everybody's a little more aggressive now.'

'Thanks,' Eden said. Her voice was flat.

'And, and this morning,' Juno swallowed. 'Man, that was swift.'

'What happened this morning?'

'Forget about it, Frank. Jesus. Move on.' Eden waved at my computer.

'Well, I have something that might put a nail in it.' I leaned forward and drew up my email. 'Got this from Keely's brother. Says he found it on his sister's phone and moved it to his before Persons took it.'

'Why'd he do that?' Juno asked.

'People do weird things when someone's missing,' I said. I started playing the video, turned up the sound. It was scratchy.

A mattress in a small dark caravan, barely visible against the green mesh of bad lighting, the pillows stripped and a sheet heaped at the side. A body curled, arms bound behind her at the wrists and elbows, making her shoulderblades meet painfully in the middle. A mop of curly hair, dark, maybe black. She turned, moaned, looked at the ceiling. A slice of white breast, pointy as an elbow. A body moved before the camera, threw something into the corner of the room. Jackie. Another figure in the mirror beside the bed, leaning against the doorframe, arms folded. Jackie climbed onto the bed. Boxers only. White legs from a distinct line high up on his thighs. One of those men who always wore short shorts so he was ready to go at any second.

'Oh god,' Juno put his wine glass down, covered his mouth with his hands. 'Oh. Oh no.'

Eden was watching passively. She sipped her wine. Juno got up after a few seconds and faced the balcony doors.

'That's Nick?' Eden pointed to the man in the doorway as the figures moved on the bed.

'Yeah.'

'Who's this, then? Keely? She's got the curls.'

'I thought so at first but there's no tramp stamp.' I pointed to the back of the girl on the screen, milk-white in the dark. 'Keely's got a big tribal across the top of her arse.'

'This some girl we don't know about, then?'

'Could be.'

Juno was covering his ears and shaking his head. I stopped the video a couple of times, looked at the shapes in the dark, tried to see if there was anyone else in the mirror, in the hall behind him. The footage was terrible. It had probably been shot and downloaded in a couple of formats, moved from computer to phone to computer, downsized and then upsized.

'This singles Nick and Jackie out from the others,' I said.

'Is this enough for an arrest?' Juno said, taking his fingers down from his ears carefully, in case the video started up again.

'No.'

'Why not? That's . . . that's rape.'

'It's a non-consensual-looking sex scenario,' I shrugged. 'There's nothing to say it's not role play.'

'I'll bet the girl will say it's not role play. That's . . . that's sick, man. It's sick.'

'Well,' I said, 'you find her for me, Juno, and we'll ask her, huh?'

'Who is this guy?' Eden asked me, jutted her chin at Juno. 'Are you out of the academy or what?'

'He's a civilian.'

'How do you get to do what you do?' Eden was squinting. 'You're not even signed on.'

'I've got a pretty unique skill set.' Juno sat down, gulped his wine, coughed. 'They had me break into some mob computers on a contract basis last year, Captain Renalds in Drug Squad. I told them I could do surveillance. They offered me a sign on but . . . I want to go to the academy in November. Do it properly.'

'You're going to the academy?' I grinned. 'You're softer than camembert cheese.'

'Some things I just don't like.' Juno's face flushed a painful pink. He gulped more wine. 'Jesus. It's not every day you see something like . . . like that.'

'Would you not drink that wine like that,' Eden snapped. 'It's a fucking Armagh.'

'Sometimes you do see shit like this every day, Juno. Sometimes you see worse. You learn to switch off.'

'I don't want to switch off.'

'Then look for another job,' Eden said.

'Give him a break.' I grabbed Juno's neck, shook his head for him. Something about him made me want to grit my teeth. 'He's only a boy. He's got a big heart. A big, orange heart.'

'Why don't you get your boy to start proving his worth on this video then? I want to know who that girl is and whether or not she's still alive.'

I shifted the laptop over to Juno and he began clicking away.

'I gave Skylar the deodorant can camera,' Eden said, leaning over me to frown at the boy. 'What did you pick up on that?'

'Nothing much,' Juno sighed. 'Nick doesn't visit Jackie in the cabin a lot. It's mainly a TV room for everyone else in the park, and Jackie and Skylar's love nest.'

'Have you been watching a bit of Discovery Channel action, Juno?' I snorted.

'I can't watch them,' he sighed again, louder. 'The camera's still turned around. She hasn't used the deodorant.'

'What do they talk about?'

'They fight a lot. They're either fighting or talking about how in love they are.'

'The mean–sweet cycle,' Eden said.

'What?'

'They abuse you 90 per cent of the time, shower you with affection 10 per cent of the time. Classic abuser behaviour. You hang in for the 10 per cent because it's kind of a reward for all your hard work.'

'Boring,' I yawned. 'Sounds easier to be single.'

'Not for these girls. They're afraid of being alone. No self-confidence.'

We sat watching Juno work on the video. He felt our gaze, writhed.

'I just don't get why the brother would hide this video,' Juno said. 'It's sick.'

'There's no telling,' I shrugged. 'Might have thought it was Keely and didn't want a bunch of cops watching her. I've seen it before. Family hides the victim's past, even to the detriment of the case. Add a little old-world culture into the mix and finding anything on your missing person can be like getting blood from a stone. Me no speak English. While five minutes ago they were talking it just fine.'

Juno clicked away, minimising things, drawing up other programs. He seemed to have the weight of the case on his shoulders. I remembered being that age and half-involved in what few big cases the department let me see, feeling like my chest was being stood on with anxiety for the victims and hatred for the perps. If we found a body it would hit Juno hard.

I put an arm over the back of the couch and Eden glanced at it beside her, irritated.

'Your dad wants to see you,' I murmured.

'How's all that going?'

'Fine. A little trip down memory lane required.'

'Is that what this is all about?' She reached over and poked the graze on my face, the yellow bruise fading now, almost gone. It was rare to be touched by her.

'Ow. Yes.'

'How is he?'

'He's alright.'

'How're you?'

'Don't start on me. How're you?'

'Oh, you know. It's a hard place.' She sipped her wine, rolled it in her mouth. 'Lots of pricks out there. They get bored. Start picking on each other. Nothing I haven't seen before. It's high-school dynamics. Cliques. Alliances. Fringe dwellers.'

'And you're on the fringe?'

'Me and the girl. She might be next. I worry about her. She's not bright. She's like a happy rabbit, bouncing around, looking very much like prey.'

'Someone's idea of tasty. You managed to get a proper look around yet?'

'Not yet. A couple of restless souls about at night.'

'Oh yes, I saw that. We both saw that. You've got a good swing there.'

'Shoulda been a cricketer.'

'So where from here?'

'I want to get into the kill sheds. Out the back, into the grasslands. Sunday night maybe. They have a bonfire on Saturdays. I'd have stayed if I didn't need the batteries changed. No one seems to be bothered that I'm coming and going – they think I'm sorting out my divorce and looking for a better job, and they're happy at the idea that I might leave. The girl, though. She thinks I'm off having some big adventure. I don't want her to try to tag along. Next time there's a bonfire I'd like to stay,' she said.

'You thought about checking the pig pens for samples? Sending some bloods back? I saw a documentary on this guy in the States, this pig farmer.'

'These pigs are pretty domestic,' she said. 'He sells them to Coles. It's not the way I'd operate. A stupid move if you ask me, feeding your victims to pigs. The thing sits there with your evidence inside it waiting for someone to come along, trip on a finger bone in the mud. Stupid.'

I sat watching her face. She was casting a critical eye over Juno as he worked. I wondered what she did with her bodies. I wondered where the six men I knew she and Eric had killed had ended up, if they might be found some day, if I might live to see Eden arrested for what she truly was. A beautiful taker of lives. I only half-wanted to know why she did it.

At what point had she and Eric decided that they would follow through on their dark fantasies of personally issued justice. I knew something had happened for Eden and her brother to have targeted a specific group of men, all linked by lives of crime, all working-class Sydneysiders with histories of violence. She'd wanted to kill Jason Beck, the organ thief, but I beat her to it. Did she carry on the dark life now that Eric was gone? Had her underworld father taught her how to do it?

The doorbell rang and Eden buzzed the delivery girl up. She brought bags of steaming curry-smelling boxes to the table.

'What is this?' I said as Eden unpacked the bags, lifted lids on dishes laden with vegetables I didn't recognise. Nothing smelled familiar.

'Ethiopian.' Juno ducked his head.

'Ethiopian?'

'You said I should order anything.'

'You get told you can order anything and *Ethiopian* is the first thing that comes to mind?'

'It's alright.' Eden gathered some hot flatbread out of a paper bag. 'You'll like it. Here. Have some of that. Mix it with that.'

Juno let a long breath out of his body as Eden started dishing out the food. I saw his chest deflate and his tiny stomach bulge. There was sweat in the ringlet curls on his temples. I sat staring at him.

'*Ethiopian?*'

'Give him a break,' Eden laughed. 'He's only a boy.'

On the night that his world ended, Heinrich was on watch. Watch was Heinrich's most hated of all jobs. It was because he learned nothing from it, and Bear told him he must always be learning if he wanted to have a good life. When he attended Bear's meetings or barged into the houses of men who owed Caesar or rounded up gamblers for the fights, even when he chased whores into the back alleys of the Cross and cornered them and wrung a little information about their johns out of them, he always learned something. How to make a girl cry. How to duck a good swing. What a broken bone sounded like. How to make someone agree to something that was entirely bad for them, and do so in a way that made them happy, made them laugh and slap your back and order you drinks.

But once a week on watch nights, Heinrich was alone on the porch of the house in Darlinghurst and he was not allowed to read by the light of a candle, so he learned nothing. He would sit on the old leather couch there with one hand on a cat or a dog, and he would stare at the street, the abandoned lot across the road, the wire fencing, the townhouses beyond that, the pub on the corner – watch it all descend into the late hours. He would sit and stare and think about people in the house behind him, the girls and the stupid things they fought over, Uncle Mick and his dogs and which one would win next month, the men who came and stayed some nights and their wives turning up and screaming and throwing things at them. He would think about Bear somewhere out the back in the greenhouse soaking beans, making ricin, the big man singing to himself as he only did when he thought he was alone, which he frequently did – Heinrich was easy to forget. Heinrich would sigh and groan and shift around, gather rocks from the pathway and toss them at things, wrestle whatever animal had decided to be his companion and annoy it until it left. Watch nights were long nights. The moon shrunk slowly against the burnt-orange sky, saying goodbye, leaving him to rot.

When he spotted the figure walking towards the house from the pub, Heinrich got up from the couch and stood on the steps. Most of the human traffic from that place left from the front door and split over Smart Street, but this person seemed to have come from the back, wound down the small hill to the wooden fence and crept along the gardens there. When the light of a street lamp fell on her, Heinrich felt a mixture of anger and relief surge through him. It was a sickening feeling. He turned, walked back up on to the porch and pretended to be distracted by the cotton strings hanging from the splits in the couch. Sunday wasn't dressed for the weather, but she hardly ever was. She never seemed to be cold. The cold got into Heinrich's bones, reminded him of the Winter Days. It could make him annoyed for weeks, grind his patience down to nothing. She came up onto the porch and hoisted herself onto the wooden rail.

'Long time no see, boy.'

'Where the hell have you been?' Heinrich gave her a look-over, from her head right down to her feet, the way Bear had taught him to do when he wanted someone to feel small. 'It's been weeks. Don't you live here anymore?'

'I don't live anywhere, man. You know that.'

'You sure seem to live here when it suits you. Bet you're here to raid the cupboards. Take my blankets. Take whatever cash you can scrape outta the bottom of my pockets.'

'I never scrape no cash off you. It's all you can do to give it to me.'

'What a lie.'

'You know you love me,' she laughed, came and sat beside him. She smelled like wine and flowers tonight. Heinrich felt disturbed by it somehow, deep in his gut, the sourness not all bad the way it should have been, but a little nicely dirty like a good night had by all. She smelled like a party. Like rooms full of people, sour breath, laughter, sweat. Her eyes glittered in the dark, too big for her head. Her hair was everywhere. Heinrich decided to stop looking at her. She scratched around in her little cloth bag and lit a joint.

'Gimme that.' He took it from her, dragged half of it up in pure spite.

'How's Bear?'

'Busy.'

'The big Shark?'

Sunday had always called Caesar the Shark. His teeth frightened her, even when she was a girl, the way he laughed his phoney angry laugh with his head snapped back and they all showed, right to the rear of the deep pink hole, rows of them, white and pointed, bone crunchers. She'd whispered to Heinrich at night about it in those early days. He'd shushed her and told her to get off him and go to sleep.

'Won't be back tonight. Where you been?'

'Fine.'

'I said where, not how.' Heinrich gave her back the joint, watched the way her lips gathered around it, wet like rose petals. 'I look for you everywhere I go.'

'That's kind of nice.'

'It's not nice. I don't know what you're doing. When you'll be back. If you'll ever be back. Why you ain't here with me.'

'What am I gonna do here waiting for you, boy?' she snorted, smoke rushing from her nose. 'Drink tea in the kitchen? Sweep the greenhouse? Read penny mysteries? I ain't your wife. I'm your sister, mister.'

'You're supposed to be waiting for when we get enough cash to get outta here. Go up north where it's warm. Buy a bookshop, like we talked about.'

She laughed openly at that. The sound of it echoed in the street, a tinkle of glass carving the cold air. Heinrich felt his face grow hot.

'I'm always surprised when I come see you. It's always a shock.'

'What is, for chrissake?'

'How you can still be such a child when there's so much darkness around you.'

'I ain't no child.'

'Maybe what happened to you stopped you from growing,' she murmured, the joint glowing red against her long fingers. 'Maybe you froze in the fire. Someone's lost baby forever. Sometimes I wish I could go back to that time on the beach. Be the baby again. A wet and cold thing Bear gathered up. That was the last time he touched me, you know. There's something nice about being abandoned and then being saved. I try to do it whenever I can, but it's never the same.'

Her eyes scanned the street, caught a little of the moon as it bounced off the newly fallen rain. When they found his own they lingered there for only a moment before falling to his lips like she was afraid of what she might see in his face.

She was the one who moved. He couldn't make his limbs work. Her hands wound up into his hair and gripped it, and when he felt the pain it seemed to awaken him and he gave it back, pulled her to him, crushed her. He had to stop her once or twice. Her shaking, hard restless hands in his shirt, her breath in his mouth. She needed him, climbed onto him, pulled his neck. Forced herself against his chest, her lips on his ear. A noose of arms.

After a while, when they were both warm, he held her, rocked her slowly, let her hide her face against his neck. Not being able to see her in the dark as the moon left them didn't matter, though some part of him ached to put shapes and colours to the skin under his hands – where it stopped being soft and went hard, where it was tight and where it was dry and smooth like sun-warmed stone. He squeezed her ribs and felt the bones bend. The sounds she made were helpless things, whispers, pleas, a sudden cry of want, of fear when he tried to shift. He didn't want to sleep until she did, but she pulled the rug from the end of the couch up over them and curled her feet around his, and her kisses on the side of his face, on his neck, pulled him away from himself.

'Will you save me?' she whispered.

He opened his mouth to answer her and his face was flooded with light so hard and white it crushed the sound out of him. The porch lights above, the hall lights, all flicked on at once. There were men above him. Sunday was gone.

Heinrich's first instinct was to roll. He didn't know what was happening or who was above him in the black, the hoods. But he rolled, and the action saved him. The panels in the porch seemed to explode upwards in chips and fragments, getting in his eyes. He covered his head, the sound so loud he missed it, just a thundering in his ears and all around him. They passed over him and into the house.

More gunfire. Heinrich gripped the ground, breathed wood, coughed and tasted blood in his mouth. All his bones had locked at once. Unlocking them took frantic seconds. He crawled, one leg dragging and useless, threw himself through the front door.

Screaming. One of the girls running out into the kitchen and being cut down, dancing her way to the ground. Men rushing out, naked, falling. One of the men in black went to the open bedroom door and Heinrich watched his shoulders shudder as he pumped the room. People wailing, short, sharp. Silent. The next room, a spray. Heinrich pulled himself behind the armchair, heard shouting, Bear's bellow from across the house.

He tried to get up and bullets pocked the wall around him, through him, pulled the window down in a rain of glass. He cowered in it, pulled his head down against his chest. The blood on his chin, in his nose, seeping through his shirt. Was this dying? The world was turning hard and clicking back into place like a moving picture on a wheel, his body at the centre. The gunfire stopped and there was running, and the kitchen windows shook in their frames and glasses fell from the counters.

Heinrich dragged himself across the glass, got up, fell into the door-frame of the back room. Someone was coughing and crying like an infant in one of the other rooms, the sound rising upwards, hitting a gurgling pitch, breaking away and falling into silence. There was blood spray and holes all over the walls like black stars. The boy fell into the dark back room, crawled, climbed up the floor as it tilted up before him, a ramp, a ladder without rungs.

Bear was there, under his hands. Shuddering. Wet. Impossibly hot. Heinrich wrapped his arms around the thick heavy head, squeezed it, tried to lift it from the ground.

'Bear! Bear! Bear! Bear!'

He could see two white points glittering in the blackness. Heinrich pushed his face against the big man's face, felt the hair hard like wires. His fingers found the hole in the fat neck, tried to stem the gushing.

'Anigozanthos,' the big man coughed the words. 'Rufus. Ani . . . Ani . . . Ru . . .'

Heinrich howled. The sound came out of him without words, without sobs, just a noise like a siren that started in the pit of his guts and crept up louder and louder until it met the air, made his ears ache. A scream. The big man held him, limp fingers, weak arms around his middle.

'Oh, boy,' Bear said. 'Boy.'

Heinrich felt him die like a great mountain crumbling to the earth.

Every now and then Harry Ratchet took a moment to close his eyes and enjoy his space. He had been alone a long time now, and yet still, once a day at least, he would stand in the silence of his tiny caravan in Cronulla among the things that were his and solely his – his Ned Kelly memorabilia collection and the damp towels on the floor and the empty pizza boxes on the sink and the Jimmy Barnes records – and feel blissfully alone. There was barely floor space in this place, a few footholes in the dark between the door and the end of the bed and the television stand, a square of bathroom mat before the bathroom annex. But these were his for treading and no one else's. The shower cubicle he stood in, mere centimetres on all sides of his round and taut and hairy body where weak but blistering hot water fell, it was his. His space. It was all about space for Harry. A handspan of Harry Only Territory was something hard won, and he was determined to enjoy it.

Scarlett had no idea about space, which made Harry laugh now, because the woman had been obsessed with being close up and now she was probably as close as a body could be with some sweaty bull dyke over in Silverwater Women's. In the early days after Harry had found her, she an uptight career rabbit and he a lazy but presentable week-to-week hound,

Scarlett had been able to make a two hundred square-metre penthouse in Mosman feel crowded, following him around the huge balcony while he watched the yachts being tossed around, rubbing up against him. Her couch had been the length of his current lodgings and had cost more, but he'd fought for a centimetre of room on it. She'd have a room full of television identities and socialites and politicians spread out around her at one of her charity gigs, lights on her perfectly sculpted biceps, everyone's favourite weather girl, male models adjusting their trousers at the sight of her, and she'd cling to Harry's arm like she hadn't found him in the dark one afternoon on set, fumbling with wires, swigging Coke and itching in his uniform polo. He was her star. Her home. The rock she anchored to. Harry could hardly breathe but he liked the money, so he learned how to distract her and slip away, look at the sky, have a smoke without her jabbering at him.

After a year or so Harry got sick of ducking and diving away from Scarlett whenever he got the chance and started trying to train her, because the big Four-Oh had made him realise he was onto a good deal and starting again would be a hassle he couldn't be fucked with. She'd made the national news too, so he could give up the audio-rigging game. If it was going to be the long haul with Scarlett, Harry needed to straighten her out and show her who was boss. The first thing he did was take the money. The second thing was push her mother and her loudmouthed friends out of the picture with a few carefully placed ultimatums. Step three in his plan was positive reinforcement, the way you train little wide-eyed terriers with liver treats – be a good girl, a quiet girl, and I'll come home on time. I'll come home sober. I'll come home and cuddle you.

Everything had been snap, snap, snap, the way he wanted it. Sit! And she slammed that arse on the floor before he'd finished making the sound. Then one day she presented him with a white plastic strip with two blue lines and tears in her eyes and talk of names for it. And all his hard work had come down to nothing.

Trump card.

Plan B. His pup had gone wild. Nothing to do with a wild animal but put it down. He'd nudged her down a flight of stairs one afternoon before Christmas, when the thing inside her had started to take hold and ruin her body and her logic. Hadn't worked. A couple more knocks, a couple more quiet nudges, and she'd presented him with the perfect solution to his problem. A 9mm bullet, right in his guts. He lay in the hospital bed and watched her trial, chatted up the rehabilitation girl about it as he clambered along steel bars and walked himself up and down the wide halls with a walking frame – poor Harry, abused and misused husband just trying to learn how to love again. When they carried Scarlett off kicking and hollering on the evening news she'd once sparkled on, her regrowth showing and her eye make-up smudged in a way he knew she'd hate, he thought he was free.

He began claiming his space again in a little apartment in Eastlakes, steadily chewing through her cash on pretty horses and Blue label and little Asian women with perky tits. Then a couple of drably dressed social workers had knocked on his door and put a baby in his hands.

Another trump card.

Even from behind the razor wire she was still in his space, filling up the place like a bucket of water in a paper cup.

He took it inside, forgot it for days, lay in the bed in the other room and cried about it, cried louder than it did, because this was his space and he'd cry in it if he wanted to. He sat on the carpet in its room in those dark first days and watched it wriggling and screaming, the stink of its piss taking up the air. People brought him clothes and toys and bedding for it, so much stuff he had to pile it in corners like he was preparing for a winter, the kitchen cluttered with sour milk and coloured plastic and empty jars of muck. He stood in the shower with it, slept on the floor with it, sat in the car with it, beating the steering wheel, beating his head, beating the windows. He sat outside his ruined apartment with it at the top of the concrete stairs and watched it shuffling and inching around on the damp at his feet like a swollen, snotty grub, watched it edge towards the empty space before the five-flight fall, bulging backside waggling, worm toes squirming up and down. Harry stood, looked at the fall, the screen doors, dozens of them, most hiding angry Indians in leather jackets who would hardly know how to answer a phone let alone testify to his possible negligence as a father. Harry stood. Harry watched. Then Harry put his foot out, pressed against the soft, papered rump with his toes, gently-gently, softly-softly, until it tipped.

Harry stood now in his shower remembering his own screaming, because a man didn't scream unless he couldn't do otherwise, unless something had happened to destroy his very soul. He kept screaming and screaming when the ambulances arrived, screaming and screaming when the cops arrived, screaming and screaming when the two homicide detectives showed up. A lanky guy with dead eyes named Doyle and some black-haired vixen he couldn't remember the name of, distracted as he was by the way her jeans cupped her apple-shaped rump. He sat on the edge of the ambulance and watched that perfect posterior through tear-soaked hands as she wandered, calm and curious, through the tarpaulin barrier to where the thing lay dead, around the thing and the people chalking and photographing it, up the stairs, down the stairs, all around. The guy with the dead eyes came over to him and talked and made notes and gave condolences and numbers to call, but the dark apple-bottomed beauty just stood there, off and away from the crowd, looking up at the top of the stairs, looking down at where the thing lay. Harry was just starting to get a cold feeling about the way the woman was standing and looking and frowning and thinking when she disappeared and he felt safe again. Days turned into weeks. Grief counsellors came and went. The sun set and the evening news came on. Harry swelled, slowly opening like a wary flower, and filled up his space.

He towelled off now in his little caravan bathroom annex, stretched his limbs, ruffled his hair in the mirror, laughed to himself. Almost a year had passed, and still the thrill of a room empty but for him. He was smiling at the feel of it as he entered the caravan, but the smile disappeared when he found a woman sitting on the end of his bed with her hands between her knees, restful. He didn't recognise her as the apple-arsed stunner from the day the thing died until she stood, turned towards him, looked at him, set her feet apart on his crowded floor. She rolled her shoulders. He noticed the knife in her hand when she adjusted her grip, flicked the thing open so that it shone in the light from the bathroom.

'What the fuck is this?' He threw the towel around himself.

She glanced at his naked chest, belly, wrinkled her nose, sniffed the air. She flicked her chin towards the bathroom as she came towards him.

'You used soap in there, right?' she asked.

I made no appointment at Galaxy Fitness, Randwick. There's a certain joy in being able to walk into anywhere and stop things in their tracks in the name of the law, like Robo-Cop or one of those *Law & Order* hard-boiled eggs, pushing people aside, roping things off. The thrill never wears off, and mine is rarely a thrilling job, so when the opportunity arises I take advantage. There were a couple of middle-aged women at the counter chattering and filling out forms, their towels hanging over their shoulders, and a young man behind the counter who I'd have said was on 'roids from the sheer unnatural shape of him. All wads of muscle on probably tired bones and snaky veins, the sculpted eyebrows of someone who waxed weekly. I went straight to the young woman beside him, a tanned and toned Jack Russell of a creature, caramel-coloured, short and stringy. She smiled as I entered and I smiled back and it was on – train departed from Flirt Central. Sometimes it can be like that. Two people in a harmlessly flirty mood. It's something you can smell in the air.

'Morning.' I put my badge and a bunch of papers on the counter in front of the girl. 'Detective Frank Bennett, CID. I'm going to have to be really annoying and serve a warrant here today, if you don't mind.'

Everyone looked. The girl's smile dropped. Captain Eyebrows shouldered in beside Jack Russell.

'Morning. I'm the floor manager, Steven Kent. How can I help?'

'Good to meet you, Floor Manager Steven Kent.' I shook his hand. He squeezed too hard. 'Hoping to make this short and sweet. I'm on the tail of a missing person and need some questions answered.'

The girl was looking at my badge. The plastic one pinned to her sculpted chest read 'Clarinda: Customer Service'.

'Well, I hope I can be of some help.' Eyebrows puffed his chest out. 'Shall we go back to the staff office?'

'It's alright, mate, go ahead and see to these ladies.' I waved at the women at the counter, who bristled like birds disturbed. 'I'm sure young Clarinda here can help me.'

If Jack Russell girl had a tail she would have wagged it. Steve scowled, then laughed, hard.

'That's nice but Clarinda's hardly the person to talk to. I'm in charge here. I'd be the most qualified to help you get what you need.'

'Uh huh,' I said. 'That's also nice. But you're busy. I try not to interrupt busy people.'

'I can assure you –'

'Unfortunately, regardless of your being in charge, or the best person to get me what I need, a warrant of this type requires me to be overseen in the entirety of my operations here today by the person I serve it to.' I shrugged helplessly. 'Clarinda, honey, looks like you bit the bullet here.'

'But,' Steven the Floor Manager opened his mouth, shut it, opened it again, 'she hasn't signed anything.'

'She sighted my paper first.' I shrugged again, curled my lip at Clarinda. 'Sorry, Bub.'

'What's . . . what's this all about?' Steve squinted.

'Clarinda, have you got an office we can use with computer access?'

'I don't think –'

'She's got it, Steve,' I winked at him. 'Haven't you, Clarinda?'

Clarinda moved quickly, almost stumbled over her own feet. 'Yep, got it, Steve.'

Jack Russell girl came out from behind the counter with a set of keys. Steve swallowed, did some funny jerking thing with his neck.

'Yes, uh. Yeah, okay. Clarinda if you could help the detective with anything he needs. Clarinda will help you with anything you need, Detective.'

I slapped Steve on his iron-hard back as I passed. Clarinda led me to a room off the side of the free-weights section where tradies and retirees were squatting and staring themselves down in the wall of mirrors. Nearby I could hear an aerobics instructor shouting over some thumping bass music. The little room held a table and a laptop and a couple of desk chairs, some anatomy pictures. There was a set of scales in the corner and a measuring tape pinned to the wall.

'Jesus.' She sunk into the desk chair and crossed her legs, adjusted the bottom of her gym tights. 'You're going to get me sacked if you're not careful.'

'I can't help what the warrant says, young lady. That's the law.'

'That was all bullshit about the warrant. Wasn't it?'

'What an accusation.'

'Uh huh,' she smirked. Swung sideways back and forth in the desk chair like a bored kid in the computer room at school. 'So, what's the deal here? Are you looking for one of our members?'

'Well, I might be,' I said, sitting down in the other chair, pulling it close so she could smell me. 'I'm here on a real long shot and, yes, it'll involve looking at your member files. What we're looking for might take a while. So I hope Steve will forgive me for not wanting to spend the next couple of hours in here with him.'

'Oh, he's a pretty forgiving guy.' She smiled, played with the mouse on the desk beside her.

'Lucky.'

'I didn't catch your name out there in all the macho games.'

'Frank.'

'Well, Frank, thanks for getting me out of membership emails for a few hours.'

'My pleasure. You think our forgiving friend Steve would make us a couple of coffees?'

'He'll burst in here in a minute or so to see what we're up to,' she shrugged. 'So, I guess you could ask him. You'd be pushing it.'

'A bit protective of what goes on around his floor, is he?'

'Certainly is.'

'Floor manager. The pressure.'

'It's tough,' she sniggered.

'Alright, well, we haven't got all day to exchange pleasantries.' I set the folder on the table beside the laptop and extracted a series of photographs. 'This is the girl I'm looking for.'

Juno had done a great job on the footage the Manning boy had sent me. The extent of my technological skills is exhausted at checking emails and the odd Google search, so when he emailed me back the refined version of the video I was suitably impressed. All the green grain was gone, and the sound had been clarified down to individual breaths and wheezes, muttered words between the action. He'd even transcribed the few words said on the twelve-minute clip and sent a file of ten stills that best showed the girl's face. I made a note to myself to make sure Captain James knew how very useful the boy had been. He would be good across the departments, and there was no reason he couldn't be making solid money out of it to spend on ridiculous beanies and manscaping equipment and lambskin seat covers for his old-fashioned bikes.

'Oh my god.' Clarinda the customer service girl frowned at the photos. 'What is this?'

'It's no one's idea of a good time.'

I'd cropped the photos dramatically, but what was left wasn't exactly a family picnic album.

'You're looking for this girl?' She touched the girl's face, the duct tape. 'This is . . . Is she . . .?'

'It's from a video. We're not sure yet if it's fake, so don't freak out,' I told her. 'We see a few of these every now and then. People find them online, report them, identify people making them and passing them around. It's actually very common. Don't worry yourself too much about what might be going on – that's my job. You just focus on the girl.'

'How do you expect to find her? Do you know her name? Is she a member?'

'Well, see. I'm here because I've been looking at these pictures all night long and there are a few things I'd like to test my brain against.' I folded my arms, looked at the shots in turn.

'Okay.'

'We don't know this girl's name. We don't know anything about her. But she's pretty damn toned, don't you think?'

Clarinda looked at the photographs. There was no denying the girl in the photograph had amazing biceps and the kind of abs a man could comfortably stand on while waiting for a train. In one shot, where the girl in the photograph was down on her hands and knees, her right calf muscle was strained tight, showing the taut slope and ball of muscle you only get from hours of riding bikes. Clarinda took a while to look, before she began to nod slowly.

'Okay. So she works out. That's a clever thing to notice I guess.'

'I thought you might agree. Then there's this. See this here?' I lifted one of the pictures. The black shadow leaning against the wall was so small and fine I could only indicate it with the edge of my little finger. 'Is that one of your gym bags?'

Clarinda took the photograph from me. Held it close to her nose. Stretched her arms and frowned in the light.

'Jesus. This *is* a long shot. It kind of looks like a jacket to me.'

'Yeah, maybe. But at the start of the video one of the guys has it in his hand. One hand. And he sort of swings it. It hits the wall and falls in a heap. When you throw a jacket or a piece of clothing on the floor you sort of drop it, don't you? It's got no weight. This is like a . . . like a swing and then a thump and then a slide. What would you carry into a room and drop like that? A bag. A bag you'd been carrying for a while.'

'Um. Okay.' She didn't sound convinced.

'Maybe I'm being overly hopeful.'

'Maybe,' she sighed.

'It does look to me, after staring at it for a few hours, like one of those blue-and-black bags you've got hanging above the counter out there though. I see them everywhere. Uni kids carry them. You give one out to every new member, don't you?'

'I can't see the blue.' She looked at my eyes. 'Couldn't it just be any old backpack?'

'A very clever colleague I'm working with tells me that in pixelated form, whatever the hell that means, there's half a grade median tone difference between the top half of the bag, assuming it's a bag, and the bottom half of the bag – which might suggest that the top and bottom halves of the bag are different colours.' I took the picture back. Showed her. 'Your bags are blue on the top and black on the bottom. So it's possible, right?'

'It's possible.' She shrugged at the pictures. 'But shit, man, I don't know how the hell you get anything from this. It's all shadows to me.'

'Well, it's worth a try.'

'Yeah, I suppose it is.'

'So if we get that far, and we're right, we need a name. At one point in the tape that these images are from, one of the men in the room calls the girl "Shelly". So what I'm working on here are the extraordinarily fucking unpromising ideas that maybe the girl in the pictures is so amazingly toned because she spends a lot of time in gyms. Maybe that's her bag that the guy carried in and threw in the corner. Maybe it's a Galaxy Fitness bag, and maybe we can find a girl on your system whose name is Shelly or Michelle who has crazy curly black hair like this girl does.'

'What if it's Rochelle?'

'Don't rain on my parade, Clarinda.'

'God,' she laughed, rubbed her eyes, turned to the computer. 'I don't like your chances here, mate. Do you know how many tens of thousands of members we have, just in the Sydney region? Do you have any idea how many of those are going to be Michelles? There'll be hundreds.'

'Let's stay positive. Think big. Over the mountain. Go hard or go home. All that shit.'

'Right.' She started clicking. Checked me out from the corner of her eye to see if I was still smiling. I shifted closer and watched. She smelled like sweat. Not body odour, but sweat, woman sweat, the kind that gets into your sheets and leaves you thinking about her days after she's left your life. I hoped I didn't smell like scotch.

'Is all your work like this?'

'Sometimes it's worse.'

'Is she in trouble, this girl?' she asked, took a chance and looked right at me. 'Is it, like . . . Is it bad?'

'We'll see,' I said. 'If it's that bad you'll see it on the news. You might even see me there. Here. You can tell your friends you know that ugly copper on Channel Seven. Friends in high places. Celebrity connections. You could call me to prove it.' I took a card from my back pocket and tucked it into hers. I wasn't usually this obnoxious but the look on her face told me she didn't mind. She shook her head. Steven Kent the Floor Manager swung open the door without knocking. Clarinda was tapping away at the keys.

'How's the floor?' I asked.

'Fine, uh, good. Clarinda able to help you with what you need?'

212

'She's invaluable, just like the coffee you're about to make me, which is going to rescue my entire morning. Hot, white, and strong, just like me. And Clarinda . . .?' I pointed to the girl.

'Oh. Uh, black, Steve. Sorry.'

'Sorry, Steve,' I agreed.

Steve grumbled and disappeared.

'You're such a dick,' Clarinda the Jack Russell girl said. She gave me a cute scowl like she meant it. But I knew she didn't. She'd call.

Heinrich remembered small sections of what had happened after they dragged him away from Bear, but there were long dark stretches between them that were filled with blackness and wailing, the frantic whispering of those left behind after the Fall. He remembered lying in the back of a car, squashed between the bodies of two people, someone fumbling with rags at Heinrich's stomach, listening to them and the two people in the front as their words rose up and down against his ears, like the ocean through a window.

'We can't go in. We'll leave him out front.'

'We can't take him there at all. We need to get him out of the car. He makes it and Caesar hears we took him to Doc's we're all dead.'

'He's not going to make it.'

'Calm down, Sam. He's gonna bite it. I'm covered in his fucking blood. I'm fucking soaked in it.'

'What if he does make it?'

'He won't.'

'Christ Jesus. I'm scared. Why are we doing this?'

'Shut up.'

'Sam, his eyes are all rolled up.'

'Why are we doing this?'

'Because it's the right thing to do. Shut up! All of you shut up.'

The asphalt, hard against the side of his head and his shoulder, wet with rain or blood, he didn't know. Rolling onto his stomach, clawing to look, the lights of the car in the distance. Heinrich the Dogboy of Darlinghurst scraping his head against the tiny black stones because it was too heavy to lift, looking at the door as the light fell on him. Doc's form there thin enough to be eaten entirely by the light, a strip of black against the sun. Doc looking at him, breathing, breathing, grabbing his bag, running away into the street, down to the corner, towards the pub where other men would see him, say he was there, say he never helped the Dogboy when Caesar came knocking as he inevitably would. Heinrich hugging the ground. Gripping it with his nails against the pain. Bending his knees and trying to hold onto it as the earth thundered and shuddered and turned. All of him wet. His socks, wet. Thinking he would be alright if he just kept hold of the moment that Bear had left him, because if he could somehow know just how long it had been, just how far he had gone, maybe he could get back to that moment and change it, react faster, run into the back room before the shooters went there, call out, scream, fight, do something more than hide behind a chair, anything more, one thing to save them all, to save the man who had saved him. So he lay on the earth and kept his eyes open wide and breathed and tried to remember.

It's an hour or so since Bear died.

I'm three miles from the spot.

Heinrich held the bullet in his stomach and watched the moon creep across the sky. As the light began to grow, he dragged himself up until he was on his knees, began to crawl, used the moving cement at the side of the road like a ladder.

It's five hours or so since Bear died.

I'm three miles and a few yards from the spot.

He pushed the door to Doc's house open, blundered about, knocked things over, grabbed things he wasn't sure would help him, left blood dark brown and smeared like shit all over the jars and tables and cloths and walls. He packed it all in a bag, holding his guts in with one arm, dragging the lead weight of the supplies with the other, out into the street again, through the laneways, down the hill, to the warehouses lining the canal.

It's ten hours or so since Bear died.

I'm five, six, seven miles from the spot.

He rested in the dark and cold and grit of a warehouse floor, the coiled metal shavings and flat hard carcasses of dead rats and woodchips and screws that made a bed for him. No idea what was around him, five or six feet from the door that led to the seven miles that led to the spot where Bear had died, that spot he would return to, he promised to return to, to fix things, fix it all. He slept and lost count of the hours, cried at that, cried and howled at that. He hadn't cried, though, when he began to strip off his trousers to see to the hole there, because Bear wouldn't have liked a thing like that, tears shed over stupid things like blood and torn flesh. He twisted the cloth, bit it, fished around inside himself. When he pulled the bullet free and threaded the needle and pulled himself together and washed it all down it was like nothing had ever happened, and he felt good, because that was how it should have been, how Bear would have liked it. He pulled the bullet from his shoulder, but left the one in his guts, because it was lost in all the softness and slippery folds, a little tick buried deep inside him, refusing to let go.

He slept more. Lost more hours.

It's ten days since Bear died.

I'm seven, six, five, four miles from the spot.

Heinrich approached the house from the back alley, stood leaning against the wooden fence and avoiding the shape of it with his eyes. The tape that was around it fluttered in the wind at the edge of his vision, crisscrossed against the doors and windows. He focused instead on the ropes and chains lying in piles in the unmown grass outside the greenhouse until he found himself wondering what would happen to the dogs now that Uncle Mick was dead, because he would be dead, everyone who had been in that front room where the shooting began would be dead. He half-expected to see Sunday there, and then realised that Sunday was a dark hole in his mind that he couldn't bear to step into right now, to wonder how she got away before the shooting began, how she'd known, if she'd known at all.

Heinrich shook himself, let the solid walls of the greenhouse support him as he shuffled through the grass to the door, his heart breaking already as he looked through the glass at the pots over- turned and cracked and scattered, the dirt turned to mud, the tiny plants shrivelled and curling brown in the craters of footprints, tiny lives snuffed in their hundreds, a massacre on the edge of a massacre. He wobbled and wavered and dragged himself into the back room. The bigger pots here were knocked from their shelves too, trees overhanging, leaves curled and rolled and folded. The one he was looking for was still in its place among three or four others, too heavy, it seemed, to be easily shifted in the chaos. In it, the gnarled fingers of many red flowers, spiked kangaroo paws gripping at nothing in death.

Anigozanthos rufus.

Ani . . . Ani . . . Ru . . .

Oh, boy.

Boy.

Heinrich reached over, grabbed the kangaroo paw by its sticky trunk and pulled the pot towards him with all his strength. It tumbled, rolled, crashed. He lifted the board from beneath it with shaking fingers and then stopped, breathing, trying to maintain his balance. It was the leg that gave him the most trouble. Tired, as it was, from the walk. The sun was red and glittering through the glass ceiling. A fire in the city, beading sweat on the sloping panels. Heinrich reached into the cavity dug into the dirt beneath the panel and pulled up the bag.

It was heavy. Bear had been close to what he needed to leave for good.

It took all day and some of the night to find Michelle Wisdon. I got home from the gym around midday, slapped a couple of packets of Endone on the kitchen table, opened a bottle of red and started at the top of the list. It was lonely work. The cat made a circle of himself on the end of the couch, his nose an inch or so from his own arse, and stayed that way blinking at me resentfully now and then across the hours. At three or four I got up, fried a couple of sausages and microwaved some instant mash, plugged my phone in when it started getting low, put on some Chris Isaak, thought about Eden and how she knew everything all the time.

'Hello?'

'Hi. Is that Michelle?'

'Yes, it is.'

'Michelle, do you know a guy named Jackie Rye?'

'Who?'

'Never mind. Thanks.'

When Clarinda: Customer Service came over at about seven that evening I was barely able to move my shoulders. She straddled my back as I lay on the bed with the papers still calling, calling, calling – kneading my spine and neck and arms, making me groan. Her kisses behind my ears, folding the hard flesh forward, finding the warmth, exploring me. I went back to the kitchen table as she dressed, watched her walking around, bending over, making herself coffee, snapping off a row from a Cadbury's Snack block I had. I kissed her as she left, on the mouth, like I knew her. When she left she didn't look back. I wanted her to. I felt used.

Just after the clock struck nine I hit paydirt.

'Hello?'

'Hi. Is that Michelle?'

'Yes. Who's this?'

'Michelle, do you know a guy named Jackie Rye?'

Silence, a long one. And then a click.

Gotcha.

It was about eleven by the time I arrived at the excruciatingly lit supermarket in Paddington. I stood in the fruit and veg section for a few minutes molesting the avocados before I recognised her at the checkout, lethargically beeping items through for an expressionless Asian couple, the approach of midnight wearing on her shoulders, making them curve forward around her like the wings of an injured bird. The curly hair hadn't shown in her membership photo at Galaxy Fitness. It was only by chance that I happened to be looking particularly carefully at the screen as we trawled through the 174 Michelles in her age range and seen a single raven ringlet poking from behind her ear.

She had it out in all its glory now but seemed to be regretting it. She kept pushing it back as she gave change, looked for barcodes, turned things around in her strong hands. I left the avocados alone and walked to the cigarette counter. She came around to meet me with barely an upward glance. As she swung open the door to the cigarette-counter section I wondered if my phone call had rattled her. I didn't want to rattle her. Rattling women isn't really my style. But I'd stood around in the fruit and veg section long enough feeling bad about the damage I was about to cause and trying to think of ways around it. And I think, deep down inside, I knew there weren't any and the damage hadn't been my idea in the first place. So when she hit the counter and plastered on her pitiful check-out chick smile I put my badge on the counter and left my hands there so she would feel less threatened. I conjured up a pathetic smile of my own.

'Hi, Michelle,' I said. 'I'm Detective Frank Bennett.'

She was more shocked than I'd anticipated. My words hit her like a punch – and I'd never recovered from the life-altering experience of making the decision to hit a woman myself, so the effect on me was rather like a punch as well. I felt sick and breathless. She touched her lips first and then seemed to swallow something hard in her throat.

'Oh, no.'

'I'm sorry.'

'Christ.' She slid a hand up her forehead and into her curly crown, gripped hard. 'Christ.'

'I'm really very sorry.'

'I knew someone was coming and I didn't run.' She looked around. Her eyes were wet, ready for tears. 'I knew it.'

'I was going to speak to the manager first but I wanted to see what you wanted to do.' I followed her eyes to the manager, a squat Greek guy standing texting in the tampon aisle. 'What do you want to do? Do you want to come with me now?'

'I finish at midnight.' She looked at the register in front of her.

'Okay.'

'Don't tell the manager.'

'I won't.'

'I'll . . . I'll meet you out there. At the bus station.'

She pointed. I looked. Put my badge back in my pocket.

'Don't run off on me, Michelle. I'm not here to make trouble.'

'I won't.'

I walked out the glass doors to the bus shelter. Sat there with my hands in my coat, watching skater kids on the corner trying to jump off the kerb and flip their boards doing it, land, roll away. One kid did it successfully, once. The rest of them attempted possibly hundreds of times. Over and over. Roll, scrape, crunch. Roll, scrape, crunch. My brain ached. For a bunch of kids who looked like school bored them to within an inch of violence, they sure did enjoy monotony.

Michelle came out in a pink hoodie covered in monkey cartoons. It didn't suit her but was probably warm. She sat on the other end of the bus bench, just sat there waiting for me to talk while she traced the engravings in the painted wood with her fingernail. I blew the air out of my lungs and tried to pack away the guilt in my heart one small box at a time. My car was a few metres away.

'Want to go someplace?'

'I'd rather not get in a car with you.'

'I don't . . . I know it probably means nothing to you,' I leaned towards her over the bench, 'but you can trust me. I'm not interested in anything in the world right now beyond nailing

Jackie Rye and his shit-faced offsider for what they did to you and probably dozens of other girls.'

'Words are cheap.'

'They are, but they're all I've got right now. Well, not all I've got. I've got a work charge card. We could get something to eat. Anything you want. You hungry?'

'Why are you alone?' She looked at my eyes with her full hurt and I felt my throat constrict. 'Don't you guys work in pairs?'

'We do,' I said. 'My partner's in the field right now. She's a tough nut, like you. But I still worry about her. I'd like to bring her home from where she is as soon as I can. She's relying on me to get this thing moving.'

Michelle considered my words quietly, her hands in her pockets and her back hunched under a great invisible weight. In time she got up and walked begrudgingly to my car. Must have seen me looking at it. I got in and shifted all the take-away packets out of her side before I unlocked the door.

I knocked on Eden's door at 3AM. There was light on under it, and when she pulled it open she was fully dressed and her hair was perfect – apart from the horrendous dye job. I opened my mouth to ask why she was dressed and up at this ungodly hour and then closed it swiftly, slammed those thoughts away into drawers and bolted them closed.

'What an inappropriate time to visit.' She gave me the once-over.

'I try to be inappropriate as often as possible.'

'Is it pressing?'

'It's more throbbing than pressing.'

She shook her head and sighed, pushed open the door. I scooted in before it could close on me. There was soft piano music playing and another bottle of Armagh was on the coffee table, a quarter full, an empty glass beside it. I helped myself. She sunk onto the couch beside me and hung her arm over the back the way women do when they're flirting in bars with men. But Eden wasn't flirting with me. I wasn't sure she'd ever flirted with anyone. Women like Eden don't need to flirt. She could make filling out her tax return look erotic.

'I've just been to see Michelle Wisdon, the girl from the video.'

'Don't you ever sleep anymore?' she squinted.

'Eden, the correct response was "Holy shit, Frank, you found her already? How can that be? How did you do that? You're a wonder. You're a star. Look at your biceps".'

Eden looked at the ceiling.

'Yes, I sleep. But not right now. I found Michelle Wisdon and she's the girl from the video and I turned up at her work-place and got it out of her. All of it.'

'And how much was there?'

'Not much.'

'Uh huh.'

'She tried to play like it was a fakey at first.' I stretched my legs out. Put them on the coffee table. Eden bit her tongue. 'I brought her round. We got a couple of bags of Maccas and some Jimmy cans and went up to the top of Watsons Bay. Looked at the city. You can get a woman to tell you anything over Maccas and a beautiful view.'

'*Your* kind of woman.'

'She won't testify, but she was willing to tell me the video was non-consensual. She thinks Jackie got her with Xylazine. It's meant for cattle. Helps them endure castration. Says she was at one of those Saturday night bonfires they have there and everyone was laughing at how she couldn't put her words in a row. And she didn't know why, because she'd only had two drinks. Literally, two. Then Jackie and Nick grabbed her bag and took her off, told everyone they'd put her to bed. Everyone seemed to know.'

'That doesn't surprise me.'

'Everyone seemed to know and did nothing.'

'It's pretty brutal out there.' Eden took the wine back, put it to her lips. Didn't drink. Thought. I sat looking at her, begin-ning sentences in my mind, watching them trail off into the dark. Eventually I let the words tumble out.

'Are you alright out there?'

'Yes, Dad.'

'I don't like you being in the middle of something even you admit is brutal.'

'You don't like women being in precarious situations in general. It's one of your many old-world masculine hang-ups.'

'Maybe.'

'You can't protect me, Frank,' she said.

'I guess we agreed you don't really need it, do you?'

'No.'

'Do you feel sort of . . .' I struggled. Got half the words out and then lost the rest, squirmed under her eyes. 'Do you feel like you know Jackie and Nick? Do you feel like they . . . Is there like a kind of . . . an instinct . . . ? Do you have a type of instinct that . . .?'

'Don't wander into dangerous waters, Frank.'

'Sorry.' I looked away.

'We agreed we weren't going to talk like this.'

'We're not. We're not going to. I just. Sometimes I want to know. And sometimes I don't want to know. Most of the time, I don't want to know. But sometimes. I came here tonight and you're up.' The words were dropping off my lips. 'You're up and you're dressed and your hair is done and if I went downstairs and felt the hood of your car it'd be warm . . .'

'Don't.'

'It'd be warm. Wouldn't it?'

'Frank.'

'Sorry.' I drew a deep breath, let it fill me, get to my brain, blow out all the stupidity with its cleansing chill. What was I doing? What was this going to do other than push Eden away from me, push her back into the dark, into that shadowy place where she hid like a snake in a cave and considered what exactly it was that made her decide to keep me alive – a liability, a fool who every now and then couldn't stop words coming out of his mouth. She had to know that what she had on me wasn't anywhere near as powerful and compelling as what I had on her. The inquiry into my murder of killer Jason Beck was all but over, evidence inconclusive, and even if it was ever rehashed, even if it was ever dragged out of the dark and deep airtight container it had been placed in by my comrades in the force, I was well within the realms of pleading temporary insanity and getting off jail time. Beck had killed my girlfriend. I'd probably lose my career. Probably give in to being a total drunk and a fat, hopeless loser, the sag-belly at the bar leering at the eighteen-year-olds, claiming disability for a knee I'd busted up in touch footy as a kid. Eden had to know all that wasn't worth her terrible, terrible secret. And yet she kept me alive. Day after day she greeted me like a friend, as much as a woman like that can have friends in her life.

'So we find the bodies,' she said. 'We find Xylazine in their systems, we nail Jackie and Nick. Boom.'

'Sounds pretty simple.'

'It's never simple.'

'Tell me about it.'

'What was the Manning boy doing with this video? Did he get it from Jackie?'

'No. He got it from his sister. Seems my girl Michelle managed to break into Jackie's caravan and get it on DVD, then texted it to the Manning girl as a kind of warning. I think the aim was to circulate it among the girls. Get them out of there. But it never went any further. Keely Manning went missing.'

'Could be that Jackie was trying to stop the leak.'

'Could be.'

'Huh.' Eden sipped her wine. 'So the girls got into the boys' greatest hits collection and started jibber-jabbering among themselves, and the boys decided to clean up their mess.'

'Maybe.'

'So why isn't Jackie after Michelle?'

'He might be.'

'Maybe we could give him some help.'

'No.'

'She wouldn't have to know,' Eden said.

'I'd know.'

Eden looked at me. A silence stretched full of memories,

of imaginings of things I never got to see but had read about, fought to be allowed to read about, because they wouldn't let me see her. I winced, stretched to cover it.

'Did the girl say there are other tapes?' Eden asked.

'A couple of others, but she didn't see who they were.'

'And these tapes are in his caravan?'

'Probably not now that he's got the little bunny rabbit living with him.'

'Did she say they were for personal use? Or is he selling them?'

'She didn't know, but Juno wasn't able to find any copies of the tape on the internet. Would have been a dumb move, now that the girls are missing. I'd say they're just for personal use. Trophies of conquests.'

'Could be that the other tapes are in Nick's van. Could be that the two of them started out with rape scenarios and then stepped it up with Erin, Ashley and Keely. We might have tapes of what happened sitting there on the lot.'

'You better get snooping then, Super Sleuth.'

Eden sighed, cracked her neck.

'When you going back?' I asked.

'Today.' She looked at the clock on the wall in the kitchen. 'Soon.'

'Ahh, Juno should be pleased at the series return of the Adventures of Eden Archer.'

'Give me a break. You staying here?'

'No,' I rubbed my eyes. 'I need to get back to the cat.'

'Stay here.' She smirked, got up and grabbed a cashmere throw from the back of the couch. Tossed it at me as she walked away. 'Jesus. The fucking cat, of all things.'

Hades stood up and stretched his arms out wide, groaned as the muscles between his shoulderblades stretched. It had been years since he felt stressed. For most of his life he'd had an inward calm and calculation so well-developed that outwardly he often appeared nonchalant, that he rarely considered the possibility things wouldn't turn out exactly as he planned, on time, every time. In some ways, this kind of calm scared his workers much more than anger or threats or displays of violence ever could. Hades knew his people would follow the rules. Hades knew his people wouldn't ask questions. Hades knew his people would get their work done and his deadlines met. He knew this, because it was clear, had always been clear, that the consequences of not doing what Hades wanted weren't worth the risk. He was a peaceful man because he'd spent decades cultivating the quiet confidence of a lion warming its hindquarters in the sun, licking its paws, wondering at nothing, knowing things, being sure of things, having instincts. He slept easy. He smiled often. King of the Savannah.

Until lately.

Lately Hades wasn't sleeping easy. He wasn't smiling often. And that was because the old man knew that Adam White was out there watching him night after night. It was turning out to be such a cruel and perfect punishment that Hades was surprised he'd never used it himself. It was exhausting to be watched. It was belittling. It caused the old man to hear voices in his head. To writhe and squirm in his chair as muscles he never used anymore twisted tighter and tighter under the strain. The one between his shoulders was like a splinter, a shard of glass in his flesh.

I see you, old man.

I see you there.

Sitting. Drinking. Thinking. Sleeping.

Hades rolled his shoulders and breathed through his teeth. Imagining what he would do to Adam White once the young copper had exhausted his search brought a bit of light into his ancient heart. There would be people out there who knew Hades was being toyed with. Family of the boy, who were probably cheering him on, who were talking excitedly about the long-awaited avenging of Sunday's killing, people who were drooling to see his bones offered up to that cheeky little ghost. Hades would have to make an example of Adam White so that these people were aware they would be starting a collection of lost souls if they bothered him again. It would have to be something drawn out and humiliating, the way this was – something he would sit and watch, watch with relentless, pressing eyes, something that would make the boy feel naked. He would probably see to it that the boy was, in fact, naked. That always made things interesting.

Hades went to the kitchen counter, topped up his scotch glass, drained it. He glanced down the hall to check the front door was closed before he went into the bathroom to wash his hands – they felt sticky and he didn't know why. That was something that he'd begun to do. The minuscule bothers, the checking. Checking the alarms. Checking the windows. Checking the phone. Checking his watch. He'd started keeping a gun on his thigh as he sat at the kitchen table, a heavy and annoying thing that wanted to slide off his jeans and onto the floor. Hades decided to make a note of it, of all of it, the way it made him feel. Paranoid. He'd make Adam White feel paranoid for a while before he squished him. Make him feel like his skin was crawling.

Hades came back from the bathroom and found a man sitting in the chair by the hall. The breath caught in him, half in, half out, making him want to choke. He didn't choke, however. He stopped carefully, put his slippered feet side by side, let the breath out slowly and soundlessly and then picked his scotch glass up from where it sat, turned and began pouring a drink.

'You don't knock?'

'You know me, Hades,' the man said. 'Generally my manners are meticulous. Princely. My mother did an exceptional job of them. Generally I take pride in displaying them, these princely manners.'

'But you don't display them where they're not warranted, Mr Grey.'

'I do not.'

Hades didn't know what Mr Grey's real name was. He didn't even know when he started calling him Mr Grey, if it had been the man's idea or his own. It had probably been about the third or fourth time the man had come driving up the hill towards Hades' shack in his sleek grey Beemer, the third or fourth time he'd extracted himself gracefully from the heated leather seats, the third or fourth time he'd offered the steel-hard hand that betrayed the softness and luxury and excess the rest of him seemed to want to make clear. Like most of Hades' clients, Mr Grey was not what he appeared. The princely mannered, perfectly sculpted, hand-woven male beauty he was pretending to be was really a very messy man. Mr Grey liked to peel skin. He liked to rip at organs with his fingernails. He liked to eat raw and red and throbbing parts. The first time he'd had a peek at Mr Grey's handiwork as he prised apart the expertly wrapped package the man had brought him, Hades had been shocked at just how aggressively messy Mr Grey could be. Hades had thought to himself as he waved the Beemer off that Mr Grey was probably someone he should try particularly hard not to annoy. Though the dark-eyed stallion in the expensive grey suit was looking pleasantly at him right now, the pistol in his lap loose in his fingers and pointed at the floor like an afterthought, there was no doubt in Hades' mind that Mr Grey was annoyed. Hades sat down and sipped the scotch. Mr Grey's eyes followed him, took in the gun on the table where Hades had set it, now useless.

'You gonna let me explain?'

'I'd love for you to explain, Hades.'

'You tell me what you saw, and I'll know where to begin.'

'I saw a man standing in the bush out there by the side of the road,' Mr Grey said.

'Uh huh,' Hades said.

'My senses tingling, my curiosity piqued, I gave closer inspection, and on closer inspection I saw a man standing in the bush out there by the side of the road *filming*. Filming *you*.

And when he'd finished filming *you*, he filmed *me* driving up here to your lodgings.'

'It's not a good look, is it?'

'It certainly isn't, old buddy.'

Hades sighed. Mr Grey tapped his index finger on the side of the gun, counting seconds. It was a nice gun. A handsome thing covered in filigree and unnecessary little polished screws. Fitting for a man like Mr Grey with his flawless skin and glossy nails. Not something Hades could have pulled off. He knew he looked good with a bat. That was about it.

'I knew it was only a matter of time before it started affecting the business.' The old man rubbed his eyes. 'I thought I'd have more time, though.'

'This has been going on for some time?'

'Couple of weeks.'

'And what is the purpose of this jaunty little occupation?'

'To piss me off.'

Mr Grey cocked his head slightly. The clean lines of him, the jaw cut with glass and the bones in his neck made Hades think of a Doberman. Hades wondered if there was a correlation between cannibalism and nice cheekbones, eating raw meat and looking like a dog.

'Seems to be working,' Mr Grey said.

'It is.'

'This is going to be bad for business, Hades. Very bad for business.'

'No shit.'

'It's going to be bad for your business and mine.'

'No it's not.' Hades drank the scotch. 'He's not interested in you lot. He's interested in me.'

'And you can guarantee that?'

'Lifetime.'

Mr Grey kept tapping. Tapping the gun like he was sending Morse code. He looked at the kitchen windows. It was the first time since he emerged from the bathroom that Hades got out from under the cannibal's gaze. He rolled his shoulders again, tried to stretch out that twisted muscle but the thing was buried deep inside him and it would take weeks to unwind it, to feel normal again.

'Why don't I just do my favourite waste disposal technician a favour and settle this score right now?' Mr Grey jutted his perfect chin towards the window.

'I'd rather you didn't.'

'Why?'

'Because.'

'Because?'

'Look, because the boy might be on to something. Okay?'

'You're allowing someone to threaten you, threaten me, threaten your very good name, because he might be on to something?'

'He wants an answer.' Hades sipped, swallowed. 'It happens to be a thing I've wanted to know myself for a long time, since back in the old days when a pompous little fuck like you would have gotten your neck snapped for walking into the kitchen of a man like me without knocking on the front door first. And I'm getting to thinking that if I play the game just long enough I might get that answer I've been waiting for. I might satisfy the both of us. I might return things to normal, so that I can go back to drinking my scotch in peace and you can go back to refining your princely manners.'

Mr Grey laughed. Sat back in the chair he hadn't been invited to sit in and laughed and laughed. Hades bit the side of his tongue and watched, and after a moment or two, just about as long as he thought he could take, the cannibal settled down.

'Okay,' Mr Grey sniffed. He wiped his eye with a pale blue handkerchief he tugged and whipped from his pocket like a stage magician. 'Alright.'

'Alright.'

'Well, you let me know when you get your answer, old buddy. You let me know when I can come a-knocking again.'

'It'll be soon. Don't you worry about that.'

The man called Mr Grey gave Hades a last look, a kind look, rocking the pretty gun off his index finger so that the aim swung up and down over the old man's walls. Then he left through the front door, pulling it closed behind him quietly.

When the cannibal was gone Hades stood and shattered his glass in the sink.

Victoria Krane had been running Icky's since her father died, and nothing had changed. She'd made sure of it. She had begun her life at Icky's in the back room, heralded into the world by her mother's swift and gurgling exit. Since then Icky's had been her universe, the kitchen her solar system of rotating pots and pans and cans and bottles, the tears and cracks and holes in the papered windows her stars. Her father's name wasn't Ichabod, but people called him Icky anyway, and naturally she followed along because he never corrected her – never looked at her much in fact since that red-stained night in the back room. It was a thing, they said, that had taken his attention away from the door and the men who lined there in the dark and cigarette smoke, and a thing like that was a hell of a thing, because Icky never left the door for no one. People told Victoria when she was older that on the night her mother died, the sound of her cat-wail first breath had drawn Icky from the front door for a good three or four minutes and she should be proud of that. He stood in the hall with the girls and looked in, took a cigarette from someone and lit it, made an account of the blood and the water and the rags and the heaving, sobbing, pleading doctor, and then he told everyone to get back to work. And got back to work himself.

Icky was always there, belonged there, at the door with his boot stuck out and his eyes on the guys and the skies. One brown boot keeping open or knocking shut the iron door on some foul-mouthed villain or another. Victoria had taken that worn brown boot off his foot when he died and put it there holding open the door, just before people started calling her Vicky. Funny thing it was, they said, that boot sitting there night after night, year after year. Vicky mourning Icky. The man who barely knew she was alive.

Vicky was standing at the door the night the boy arrived, though there wasn't a line of men in a cloud of smoke the way there had been when Icky was alive, and there weren't girls strutting from room to room down the hall, helping each other out when hands got tired or jaws got sore, bringing drinks to the fellows, selling smokes and telling jokes. Everything was quiet down there. No one had been tired out by the pair of quiet Chinamen who had arrived at sunset. There was no need for Vicky to stand at the door. But she was standing there because the truth was she didn't belong in the rooms beyond with the waiting girls, wouldn't fit among them as they curled on the beds and stretched on the floors, fiddled with each other, bitched and itched and poked at each other. Icky had always been above that type of thing and she was too, if she could help it. You lie down with the dogs, you get fleas, he'd say.

She was just about ready to lock the iron door and turn the red lamp out for the night and tell the girls to keep their racket down and go to sleep when the boy lurched up the path and into the rose circle of light. She let her hand fall from the brass handle that could keep her safe from him. And that's what she knew it was straightaway when she looked – a pretty brass deadlock handle that would keep him out. Because he had the look of a creature who should be kept out, all bent over and broken, an arm locked across his stomach and the other gripping the handle of a leather bag like it was keeping him standing up straight. Vicky looked into the hollows under his brow and stepped back, knocked into the door with her hip. She thought of the word 'Devil'. It just came to her like a voice. *A devil has come to your door, Vicky.*

'We're closing, mister.'

'No, you're not.'

He stood in the red light of the porch. The glow was hitting a million raindrops in his hair and on his cheeks and on the shoulders of his coat, making him look like he was dusted in fire. He was wearing a man's coat, far too big for him, and he had the squared shoulders and taut neck of a fugitive ready to pull a weapon – more of a spring pulled too tight than a man at all. Vicky glanced into the hall at the girls standing there. One of them caught her eye, knew without words what was needed.

'Should I get Mr Parsons?'

The boy seemed to know there was no Mr Parsons. But Vicky nodded anyway, shivered in her coat, pulled it around her to hide the things crawling under her skin.

'Perhaps you should, Amy,' she shouted.

'Let me in.'

'Maybe you're deaf. We're closed.'

The boy lifted his head and the light fell into his eyes, made them blaze pink like a rich girl's diamonds. Vicky felt something move in her stomach. Her hand was on her throat.

'I'm Heinrich. Bear's boy.'

'You,' Vicky was really shaking now. Her feet were shaking in her velvet boots. She'd heard people say you could shake in your boots but had never actually done it or seen it done. 'You ain't no Dogboy. The Dogboy's dead and so is the Bear.'

The boy stood there.

In time, Vicky's shaking hand raised with a will of its own and rested on the brass handle.

241

'Vick –' someone cried.

Vicky yanked open the iron door. She didn't know why she did it. It was like some kind of force had rushed up and over her – an anger, maybe, a horror, the same kind she'd felt when the men came running down the street two weeks earlier shouting that Caesar had cleaned house. Maybe it was a need to let in that hot, hurried, frightening wind, the way one lets in a breeze on a summer night, to feel again the electricity of change. She didn't think. Just let the change come in. Before she knew it the boy was inside with her.

In the white light Vicky could see his skin had gone a kind of navy-boat grey and the eyes were just as pink as they had been in the light of the door.

'Now you listen to me,' Vicky said, low, so the girls wouldn't hear. 'You ain't Bear's Dogboy. Not today, not tomorrow. I don't care what you say.'

'Right now I'm just someone's been too long on his feet,' the boy said. 'There some place we can go?'

She led him to the back room, where a life had been given and a life had been taken away. He sat on the edge of the bed and she stood by the closed door and watched him. She didn't feel safe to move from the cold hard wood. There's something safe about a door. Something as good as it might be bad, an in-ways and an out-ways, a beginning at the edge of an end. Vicky watched the boy enjoying the forgotten pleasure of the edge of a freshly made bed and adjusting the big man's coat around him. He smelled wretched. Like the loser of a fight. Didn't seem to be wearing much but trousers underneath the coat. His bare feet were black like he'd painted on shoes and the bones she could see were purple.

The boy brought the bag to the bed beside him and unzipped it. He started placing piles of cash bound with paper on the faded floral bedspread. He laid out one stack of cash as high and as wide as a shoebox. He started another, half the size. Then he made a pile of notes twice as big as the two first piles put together. Vicky Krane stood by the door and started feeling sick. Finally he picked out a stack about as thick as a workman's sandwich and put it on his knee.

The boy pointed to the first pile, and Vicky noticed that he was shaking too but he didn't look afraid.

'For the Les Girls, the Harpsichord, and Jenny's on Taylor Street, split three ways,' the boy said. 'I want them delivered in newspaper. Fresh newspaper. From the morning your girls deliver it. Tied with string.'

Vicky heard the girls whispering in the hall behind her. She shifted on her feet. The boy ignored her. He pointed at the second pile.

'For Chief Inspector Ronnie Redford, at the Watch House over near the Argyle. He'll be there on Sunday. Sunday night.' The boy coughed hard, wiped his palm politely on a handkerchief he took from his pocket. 'Senator Ted Lockett . . . He lives on Niall Street.'

Vicky could stand no more. She went to the bed and sat beside him and wrung her hands.

'And this one?'

The boy coughed.

'And this one?'

'For half of Icky's,' the Dogboy of Darlinghurst said, looking at her eyes for the first time. He breathed, turned away from her. Though he was turned she could see the grey skin of his temple bunch like nail-gripped sheets as he fought out the pain and won, briefly.

'Not half. Forty-nine per cent.'

'Forty-nine per cent.'

The Dogboy panted. Vicky licked her lips.

'We keep the name.'

'Of course,' he coughed, 'we do.'

Vicky stood and looked down at him. Watched him fumbling at the buttons of his coat, exposing cloth, reams of cloth underneath. She helped him get down to the last button, and the coughing finally stopped. He licked blood off the corner of his storm-coloured lip. She went to the door and he watched her go, fanning his damp face with the sandwich pile of notes.

'This here is for the girls,' he said as he tossed the stack to her. 'Tell them to be gentle with me.'

Eadie arrived back at the farm before the sun had risen. It was Sunday. As she made her way up the gravel drive, only the dogs greeted her, trying to shout her out of the place, stopping in their pursuit to scratch at their bellies, to roll in the dirt. The night before had been a big one for the few left behind at the farm. She could tell this from the burned things. A black washing machine drum filled with charred sticks in the breakfast area, a Coke bottle melted over the innards thrown in as the flames were dying, mutilated. There were cigarette butts everywhere and an electric toaster, toasted, lying on its side in the middle of a dirt patch. Out near where the pigs were kept the real bonfire was still smoking, sending a weak trail up just before the sprawling dry grasslands, as close to danger and death as a fire could be lit. The place smelled good to Eadie. It reminded her of summer at the tip, the way the smoke would come through from behind the mountains and conquer the sourness of the rotting meat and milk out there in the piles.

There was one other human moving on the farm and that was Pea. The movement was only to lift a cigarette to her lips as she watched Eadie walking through the gates. Her shoulders were hunched, bunching fat at her belly, her heavy breasts sitting like melons sagging on a shelf. There was no choice but to walk right by her, within six or seven metres. Eadie hitched her bag on her shoulder and nodded as she walked by.

'Morning,' she said.

Pea said nothing.

She saw what had been done to the van only as she rounded the corner of the long wooden fences. The spray-painted letters were red and as high as the tiny rounded windows rippling over the corrugated sides of the cabin.

DYKE BITCH.

Eadie took in the handiwork and then went over to the van and pulled open the door. The doorstep was wet and reeked of urine. They had pissed at the bottom of the door and flooded the carpet in the hall. The whole caravan reeked of it. She opened all the windows, stripped into her underwear and climbed into the bed. She was thinking of getting up again and drawing the curtains when she heard it, the pattering of Ugg boots across the dirt. The door burst open down the narrow hall.

A weight slammed into the bed. Eadie hid her face in the pillows.

'Pull the curtains before you get comfy.'

Skylar leaped from the bed again. It rocked and bounced.

'Someone prettied up your van.'

'They perfumed it as well. How nice.'

'You can come sleep with me and Jackie?'

'It's alright. The smell will go,' Eadie sighed.

'Where did you go? What did you do? Tell me everything.'

'Nowhere. Nothing. No.'

'Oh come on, Eadie, please!'

'You seem to think I live this wild crazy life on the knife-edge of danger and mystery. I went to a friend's place.

Ordered a pizza. Had a few joints. Watched a movie. It was all very tame.'

'You're lying.'

'I'm really not.' Eadie rolled over, faced the girl. The girl spasmed, kicked her legs.

'Stop lying to me. You're turning this caravan into a house of lies.'

'What do you reckon I did, if you know so bad?' Eadie laughed. Actually found herself laughing under the blankets like a teenager.

'You drove into the city, stayed in a flash hotel. Drank champagne. Dressed up. Went to a club. Danced on the stage. Raised the roof, baby, raised the fucking roof.'

'That's a good list. Is that what you'd do if you were me?' Eadie asked.

'Maybe.'

'You never stayed in a flash hotel? Danced on a stage? Raised the roof?'

'Maybe a couple of times.' Skylar rolled over, jutted her butt into Eadie's hips, forced a spoon.

'What's stopping you?'

'Oh, Jackie'd lose his shit if I went into the city. You know that.'

'Lose his shit, would he?'

'Yeah, man. He spent a lot of years doing that himself so he knows how bad it is.' She sniffed, wiped her nose on her hand. 'Lotsa bad people in the city. Rob you and mug you, kick your head in for no good fucking reason.'

'Why don't we go to the city?'

'I couldn't go with you,' Skylar snorted. 'You'd take me to some dyke club. Everyone'd think I'd been turned. They'd spray my van next. Piss on my nice carpet. I just vacuumed.'

'And you just do what people tell you, do you? I'd just make you kiss a girl. Make you cut all your hair off. Wear a flanno and wraparound sunnies. You'd be hypnotised.'

'Maybe.' Skylar rolled back over, nose to nose. Eadie could smell the girl's breath. Raspberry toothpaste. Kids' toothpaste. 'You think you can turn a person like that? Make them go over to the other side?'

'I don't think so, babe.'

'I heard about churches in America taking boys outta the clubs, putting them in vans, smacking the fag right outta them. It's true. It was on the news. Sometimes their parents take them to these places to get them fixed. Have, like, a full invention on them.'

'An intervention.'

'Yeah, man, one of those.'

'That's a shame.'

'What would you do if someone tried to beat it outta you?'

'Is that a threat?' Eadie rose up on her elbow, pulled the blankets back swiftly. 'Is that a fucking threat?'

It only took a push, hard and steady with the ball of her foot in Skylar's stomach. The girl grabbed, screamed, rolled, flopped into the space between the bed and the dressers. Breathless laughing, turning to snorts. Eadie pulled her legs back under the blankets and curled up again.

I got breakfast at an outdoor cafe in the Cross, keeping my eyes low over the bacon and egg roll, a little worried I might see someone I knew. I'd spent some of my younger years as a cop there on transfer nights, Mardi Gras and New Year's and Christmas Eve when the evening air would awaken under the setting sun, become electrified with impending trouble. Busting heads and throwing transvestites off their heels, pulling drunk girls apart and sending them sprawling in the wet with hands full of other girls' hair. It had been a fun time, but there had been regulars, a few low-level dealers who had taken my fatherly calm at ruining their businesses personally. It was back when I rarely heard my own first name. Loudmouth rich boys bleeding from a little old-fashioned heavy-handedness used to take down my badge number at least twice a night, threaten suits while their gay friends cried on the kerb. Before my shift I used to sit in the same cafe in uniform with rubber gloves tucked into my back pocket, eating chips without fear of love handles and taking bets with my offsiders on which prettied-up office girl wobbling in on her heels from the park would be first to claim that some boofhead had groped her in the toilets. Uptown girls in the strip joints, stupid girls trying to prove to their boyfriends they could stick out the sex-charged, masculinity-soaked atmosphere, that they were tough enough or modern enough or liberal enough or whatever the hell it was to clap and woot and cheer along, until they could stick it out no longer, until their crush copped a feel and they threw a tantrum and stalked out, mascara smeared, into the street again.

I used to have a good little side business in those days of ripping off the right kind of nobody dealers for a little smack every now and then. I'd sell it out in the suburbs to my neighbours, good people who only wanted something to make the backyard barbecue with the in-laws a little more bearable. This was when I lived with my first wife, when I didn't know she was pregnant yet, when I was sort of happy. As happy as I had been up until that point, I suppose, but when you're young you can fool yourself pretty easily into thinking you're happy. First time you have money, you're rich. First time you live alone, you're cool. First time you sell a neighbour a gram, their awe at what you do. You're a double agent, a fucking gangster.

I wondered about it for a while, how stupid I'd been. I ordered another coffee, waited for someone to come along. I wasn't exactly sure who I was waiting for, but I figured I'd know them when they arrived. I've always been that sort of cop – the waiter, the watcher, the folded-arms guy happy to let things unravel naturally rather than intervene before the trouble started. Squashing trouble before it gets interesting makes for a really boring job, so over the years I've learned to be a patient man, to entertain myself with possibilities before any possibilities present themselves.

In a little notebook on my knee, hidden from the eye of passing junkies just getting the itch after last night's satisfaction,

I doodled and made notes and underlined things I'd found out about Sunday White. Pulled little photocopied pictures of her out from where I'd stuck them between the pages, mugshots I'd managed to dig out of the Jane Doe files and more blurry group shots a librarian had found in the public records. About ten photographs of Sharon Elizabeth White existed in total. Her mark. Her mark on everyone but Hades, I reminded myself. I looked at her face. She looked like a fun girl. A fun and dangerous girl. Little smirk, like she knew I was looking for her and thought it was a game.

I put Sunday away after a while and thought about other woman-shaped bags of trouble I knew. I settled on Eden as the sun rose over me, cast its gaze on the empty public library, the clouded front windows of the injecting room. I worried about her, then didn't. That seemed to be how it was going to go from now on. Forgetting that Eden didn't need me to worry about her as a partner, the way I'd failed to worry about women partners before. Remembering again. The sensation was something like trying to tread on a step that wasn't there, the chest pain, the awkward landing.

Around ten a guy came and sat near me. His belly was hanging over his crotch in two distinct bulges side by side, as though he'd been stitched in the navel to keep the fat bundle from collapsing at his feet. Purple feet, ankles flaking, yellow toes. He fished in his pockets for a cigarette lighter, legs spread wide to accommodate the bulges, and after watching him for a minute or so I reached into my pocket and took out my own, tossed it onto the table in front of him with a clatter. I don't smoke anymore but I meet a lot of people who do. He grunted thanks, held the flame dangerously close to his grey beard.

A junkie girl shuffled into the little outdoor area with us, greasy black hair raked up into a bun above her pinched face, right on top of her head like a hairy cap. She held out a curled hand for change and started whining like a cat, lip snarled in discomfort.

'Yeah, yeah.' I cut the speech short and filled her hand with silver. The old man watched, looked after her as she dragged herself on.

'Wastin' your time,' he growled after a while.

'Ah well.'

'Gettin' scammed. Anyone feeds those lot gets scammed. Would have thought you'd know better than that, being a fucking heeler.'

I smirked. Half at his picking me for a cop, half at my own good fortune at finding someone in my first couple of hours of waiting who was street-smart and ancient enough to have been around when they still called cops blue heelers. Maybe this was the guy I had been waiting for.

'I gotta keep myself in business, haven't I?' I said. 'Spend money to make money.'

'She'll make you money. Maybe she'll make the council money when they use her for landfill.' The old man nodded after the junkie girl as she lurched too fast down the other side of the street, completing the circuit. 'Gonna put that straight in her arm like she's playing the slots.'

'What else is new?'

'Nothing. Nothing's new.' He eyed me for a while. I sat back and sipped the coffee.

'What is it then?' he asked. 'Those Lebs again? Those drive-by Lebs?'

'Nah.' I shifted my chair a little closer, not too close, because I didn't want to smell him and he didn't want to be seen with me. 'Cold case, actually. An old thing. From way back.'

'You're a bit fresh to be lookin' at old things from way back.'

'Maybe.'

The old guy snorted. Spat. The Asians running the cafe all frowned in unison.

'You might call this a private venture,' I said. 'A freelance job.'

'Freelance . . . private . . . bullshit. You jackos talk a lot of bullshit, y'know that?' he coughed. Didn't attempt to cover it.

'Maybe you can help me out.'

'Maybe you can go fuck a dog.'

'I'm trying to find someone who would've been around when Hades Archer was king of the castle.'

The old guy laughed, let his fat head loll to the side, raining skin flakes.

'You really are a fucking idiot. I thought you looked like one, but now I know for sure.'

'You could be right.'

The old man leaned close, hung a crusty arm over the stainless-steel table.

'No one on this street gonna talk to you about the Good Lord. You might be lucky if someone don't disappear you through a back door just for asking. Bet you didn't know they do magic shows here too. One minute you're poking the wrong eyes. The next minute . . .' He made a half-slurping, half-sucking noise. Plucked the air.

'What if I told them the Good Lord sent me?'

'You'd be telling a lie.'

I leaned on the table, causing it to rock back towards me on its uneven legs. We were both holding it down now. I could taste his rank breath. I'd been in homicide a long time. Smelled some things that made my eyes water. Rarely from the living.

'I'm trying to find Sharon White.'

The old man looked at me. Shrugged.

'Sunday.'

'Sunday?' He laughed, hacked, coughed, swallowed. Laughed again. 'Oh son, you'll kill me. You'll kill me dead.'

'I'm serious.'

'You musta been sent by Hades. Because ain't no one else ever believed that black bitch went anywhere worth looking, 'cept for Hades.'

'So you knew her, then?'

'Everybody knew her. She was the town cat.'

'Well, where'd she go, then?'

'Oh Jesus, that's funny. I can't believe. That's some funny shit. Fuck me dead.'

I took the lighter from between us. Put it in my pocket. The old man's yellow eyes were leaking into the creases at the corners.

'Thanks for your help.' I stood.

'Look, boy-o, Sunday fucked off some place up north. Years ago. Years and years and years ago.' He looked at me with pity, an old man's pity for youth and how they'll waste time. 'I hate to tell you, but you're on the tail of a wild goose you wouldn't want to catch. If she hasn't done away with herself simply by being a miserable little shit, she'll be up in Darwin with her Jigaboo people surrounded by sprogs and dogs. I just hope Mr Archer ain't paid you much to learn he loved a no-good mutt, because anyone coulda told him that. No one told him though. No one told him. Because you didn't tell Hades Archer nothing, not back then.'

The old man considered his own words, rapped the table-top with his knuckles as those words came back around from his mouth to his ears. I stood watching them have their effect. His smile sunk, slowly.

'Matter of fact, you don't tell Hades Archer that sort of thing nowadays neither,' he continued rapping, looked at the street, looked at me. 'You might try Pussy Cats. I don't know. I gotta go. I got people to see.'

He got up and started walking away on old bones. Before the Asians could chase him I waved to them, pulled out my wallet.

Pussy Cats smelled like pussycats, which was kind of poetic, I thought. It had that sort of wet, milky smell a cat gives a house, tainted sharply with the acid that comes out of them, something loved turned vile. Added to this cloud of invisible animal-variety reek was tap beer and disinfectant, toilets that were never clean, vomit undiscovered in the dark for days, chipboard rotting under the rain of a thousand toppled glasses. The crowd there, three men at the edge of the stage and a troupe of groggy Greek teens waiting to go into the private viewing rooms, were undoubtedly leftovers from the night before, leaning on the black walls, sagging in the plastic chairs.

The meathead at the door picked me for a copper as well and shut the gate between the reception and the rest of the bar before I could get in. He hit a buzzer to call his boss, stared me down, didn't say hello. I wandered on the checkerboard tiles, slapped my notebook in my palm and stared back. It took a long while for the boss to come down. There was no telling what he was trying to hide up there on the second floor. Guns. Drugs. Underage girls. Underage boys. Exotic animals. Bad cash. Boosted jewellery. Counterfeit joggers. I tried to make a mental list. It took too long. I was just about to bang on the desk when he popped out of a hidden panel behind it like a hairy cuckoo bird.

'How can I help, Detective . . .?'

'Bennett.'

'How can I help, Detective Benice?'

'I'm after a private word.'

'Got a warrant?'

'A warrant isn't warranted. It's just a private word.'

'Well, we're all about privates here, aren't we, Chase?' He looked at the meathead. The meathead didn't look back. 'Why don't you come upstairs?'

I followed him through the invisible panel. I bent. He didn't. I thought about Jackie Rye and just how many of the world's degenerates were undersize, narrow-shouldered, bobble-headed. He was well-dressed at least. The square shoulders of a very expensive suit brushed the walls of the tunnel ahead of me. We emerged into another foyer. The backpacker hotel next door. Ingenious. There were probably more tunnels for shuffling girls to and fro, shoving them into rooms rented by apparently legitimate guests from out of the country, rooms that couldn't be busted into using the same warrant issued to search the strip club. The system was common knowledge to cops, but nevertheless judges never issued warrants for private premises no matter what rumours there were of secret tunnels or magic doors. The trick had always been catching the rats before they fled.

'I should introduce myself,' the wiry old man said when we arrived in an upstairs bedroom. 'I'm Bobby Springs.'

'I'm well aware,' I said. I hadn't been. I sat in the wooden chair by the aluminium-foiled window. 'A friend of mine tells me you might be able to help me with some ancient history.'

Bobby adjusted the sleeves of his coat. They were too long. His face was so lined it hid the tension I knew was underneath it, a trepidation showing only in how often he licked his little teeth.

'I can't imagine what friend of mine might also be a friend of yours.'

'Well, friends are funny things.' I folded my arms. 'I'm trying to chase down a missing girl.'

'I thought this was only a private word. I'm very friendly with Metro Missing Persons. And they always bring a warrant to see my girls.'

'The girl I'm looking for isn't one of yours. She might have been one of yours, years ago, maybe. I don't know. All I know is you seem to be the guy to talk to about girls who go missing in the Cross.'

A woman came into the room without knocking. White-skinned and bruised on her thighs, a redhead who'd tried to make herself more appealing with a bad black dye job and only succeeded in making her red eyebrows stand out like thin strips of fire. She had a cold sore the size of a baked bean on her lip. She put a glass on the table next to me and one in Bobby's hand. Bobby didn't look at her.

'When are we talking about?'

'Late seventies.'

'So around the time your mama and your dadda knocked boots and made their own little man of the law? Why on earth would that interest you?'

'Let's not bring anyone's mother into this.'

'A bit of a blast from the past. Now I'm curious.'

'Good. Were you running girls back then?'

'I was running girls in the womb.'

'Remember one named Sunday White?'

Bobby thought for a long while, then laughed, slapped both his thighs. The girl sat on the edge of the bed and started braiding her hair.

'Who the hell is looking for Sunday?'

'Jesus,' I said. 'Everybody seems to know this bird. I'm having no trouble bringing her to people's minds.'

'Oh, she was a bit of a fixture I suppose. Iconic. A real sharp hustler. She was just everywhere, all the time – parties, bust-ups, big news on the street. Not that anyone particularly wanted her around, you know?' He thought fondly for a while, looking at the floor. 'If there was a spare lap she was in it, and it pissed people off, I guess. You always remember the ones who annoy you. Who wants her? Not the cops?'

'No.'

'Can't be Hades.'

'It's the finding that's important, not the looking.'

'Lord have mercy, that's a strange request. You know I never heard that girl called Sunday White. Didn't even know she had a last name.'

'Well I'm glad you remember her.' I sighed, released steam. 'Can we talk about where she went? I don't have all day to shoot the breeze, believe it or not.'

'I wouldn't have the faintest. Sunday wasn't one of mine.'

'Who did she belong to?'

'No one.' Bobby looked at me, waved a dismissive hand at the street. 'You might as well ask who the fucking moon belongs to. That's how Sunday was, like a moon. You look around. There she is. Where is she now? Oh, over there. Always somewhere. Drifting, drifting. Can't catch her. Close, but miles away.'

'Bit of a wild card.'

'You couldn't take her on,' he shrugged. 'I always thought it'd be nice. There was a good market for darkies who had a bit of pretty to them but you can't keep 'em, they're not the sort. Can't read a fucking watch. Go off for a fifteen-minute break and come back three weeks later expecting to be put right back on. Where were you? Oh, you know, walkabout. Walkabout my arse. It's the same now as it was then. You want a girl you know's going to be there when you wake up? Get yourself a Russian. Old-world Russian girls. They forget to make the bed when they're four years old and their daddies kick the shit out of them. That's why.'

'Good to know,' I said.

'It's all experience,' he sniffed and leaned back in his chair, sipped the drink. 'You make mistakes.'

'What happened to Sunday?'

'I had to guess, I'd say she took a hot shot and someone bagged her.'

'You wouldn't have heard about a thing like that?'

'It wouldn't have been breaking news.'

'What did you do with your rubbish back then?'

'Oh, Christ, Detective, how long's a piece of string?'

'Take a guess,' I said.

'You . . .' He sighed. Looked distant, eyes flickering over the wallpaper peeling beside me, head shaking slightly. 'You sent it out west with the truckies. You paid a cleaner. You fed the fish. You dug a hole. They were putting flash apartments up on the North Shore like they were walling off the coast against the fucking Japs. She'd be someone's concrete mix.'

I slapped my notebook on my thigh. Felt depressed. There was no way I was convincing North Shore Metro to start digging under the houses of millionaires.

'Girl like Sunday,' Bobby Springs shrugged. 'Man, it'd be a stretch to bother. You'd have tossed her out into the street.'

'Hmm,' I said. 'No one did, though. I've got no Jane Does that even come close.'

'Well,' Bobby shrugged. Seemed to want to say that was a good thing and then reconsidered it, found that he didn't actually feel that way or any way about it at all. He shrugged again and got up. He looked at the girl sitting on the bed, examining her split ends.

'Bridget here's gonna settle your bill.'

I got up. Bobby saluted me as he headed towards the door. He went through it, then leaned back, squinted at me.

'Think she had a little offsider named Kimmy or Jimmy or something. Some little short arse with a big mouth always talking. Might be able to point you somewhere.'

I was going to tell him thanks, but he disappeared. I headed after him to leave and Bridget the girl with the impressive cold sore put a hand on my chest.

'Oh, right, yeah.' I dug out my wallet.

'He said five.'

'Right.'

She smiled at me, tucked the notes into her back pocket. I knew she'd hold back a few notes but Bobby had probably factored that in. She put a finger into the gap between my shirt buttons and tickled the eagle on my chest. 'You in a rush to go?'

'Desperate rush.' I took her hand down, gave it a little squeeze, and slipped around her. 'But you be good, baby.'

'Never,' she laughed. I jogged down the dark stairs.

They took lots of breaks on Rye's Farm. Eadie liked it. There was something comforting in the monotony of her tasks – the shovelling, shovelling, shovelling, carrying, carrying, carrying – the way her breathing would synchronise to the task, come fast or slow as her limbs worked like the cogs in a clock. She could feel her body being lifted around midday, feel the gentle press of daylight shifting her over this invisible barrier, pushing her towards the slow tumble and fall of the night. She didn't have to think about anything. She was given tasks, she completed them and felt a zing of achievement – a stall empty of filth, gleaming wet in the white morning light, the horse led back into it and stamping gleefully on the gritty concrete. The happy munching, rotating of thick jaws. Pea gave Eadie instructions and she followed them. There were no decisions. She could see the appeal of this kind of work for someone who disliked pressure, deadlines, the weighing of options and outcomes. Risk and interaction. There was none of that here.

The breaks fuelled those tired hours, gave her mind coal to burn. Eadie kept her eye on the men and women who walked by her stalls, stopped to check the animals, led cows through for check-ups or borrowed bits of rope. A look. A sigh. The fiddling of fingers. Eadie began to make a catalogue of twitches.

She was in no way attached to the idea that Jackie and Nick were going to hand her the key one of these idle afternoons when they'd had enough of being her prey, so she kept the pendant camera trained on anyone who passed, made excuses to go out into the bays to record conversations, snippets, jargon, nicknames. She knew any of the girls or boys in Jackie's happy family could be the game-changer, the loose-lips, the Big One. They could put the hunters in a cage with no more than a long silence. She'd seen it happen plenty of times before.

Eadie knew that being a successful killer was mostly due to sophisticated acting skills. The same organisation, discipline and order required to make it in Hollywood. Most of the killers she'd found difficult to hunt – either for her night-time games or her day job – were such convincing actors that even the last seconds of their lives had made her question who the real person was behind the mask. It was important to fit in with everybody else. To laugh at the same time. To demonstrate loyalty and commitment and to be confused and disheartened at things like depravity, cruelty, violence.

It was the positive emotions that gave Eadie the most trouble. She found it difficult to express humour. Humour, she had decided, was somewhere between nastiness and tender-ness, but she wasn't sure which it was closer to. Sometimes she was outright cruel to Frank, and the crueller she was the harder he laughed. She didn't understand punchlines or gimmicks or impressions at all, why they were funny, what they meant about the person doing them.

Eadie understood what hunger was, but she'd never been good at sadness. There were so many different types of sadness. As a teenager she'd been forced to attend a sleep-over at the house of a girl in her science class. Hades had insisted that she find herself at least one friend before any more teachers approached him about her alienating behaviour. All the girls cried at a blue-lipped Kate Winslet letting Leonardo DiCaprio slide into the blackness of the ocean, a mixture of babbling rage and sorrow and regret pouring at the screen. Eadie had stared around her at the sea of faces in the sleeping bags, desperately struggling to understand. It was a film. The people weren't real. Was it normal to love people who weren't real?

Eadie knew the game was hard to play and that it couldn't be played forever. She needed her weekend to slip away, to let her mask fall, to release a little of her bloodlust on a deserving foe, Harry Ratchet. But whoever had killed the girls was here, on the farm, and they couldn't keep up the game forever. She was determined to catch the slip when it happened. A laugh hacked up too late. A tear faked or a crooked smile. So for that reason Eadie followed whenever Pea came and banged on the side of the shed she was working in, walked over the dirt towards the sunbaked picnic tables in the wake of the old woman's uneven squat frame. The first three or four breaks of the day were smokos only. She would quietly bum a couple of tokes from Skylar if she was around or sit peeling labels off the beer bottles while the others talked, picked at each other, laughed. Ramble on. Eadie would see and record it all.

There was an awful lot of reminiscing going on among the people on Rye's Farm, Eadie noticed, as though they were in the wake of some great party and all the guests of honour had packed up and left. There was a lot of talk about high school, the last great event in their lives, when no one had developed a habit and power was something seized through weight and strength alone – and not by money, elusive, unattainable money. Eadie would listen, cleaning under her fingernails with a corner of a plastic label, letting the pendant do the looking. Someone would get an iPhone going with music. Pearl Jam. Always Pearl Jam. Nothing really covered, nothing really changed, memories of parties rehashed and girls long gone analysed, dissected, re-created. The men would wander in the distance, silhouettes in the heat haze kicking the dirt, too simple and bent to fill a day with meetings like the women.

Today the topic seemed to be people who had come and who were gladly gone. Eadie edged onto the very end of the bench, one arse-cheek all that was needed, and started digging a hole in the dust with her boot, grinding the lumps of green manure falling from the grooves in her tread.

'. . . with a fucking beard,' someone was saying, words forced through dry laughter. 'A fucking blonde beard, real light, from here to here. Boys were calling her the Pirate.'

Everyone sniggering. Eadie wondered whether she should snigger along, then decided it was best to try to remain invisible. Pea sat down across from her and struggled with a lighter, fat hands quivering, the shakes.

'That foam hair removal shit is ten bucks a bottle. Fuck. There's no excuse. No fucking excuse.'

'Keely was blonde like that. Furry blonde arms.'

Eadie perked up, managed a glance at the speaker. A woman of many layers. Layers of stained clothing, Metallica T-shirt over singlet over neon-coloured Kmart sports bra. Chequered boxer shorts beneath denim shorts beneath layers of chain and leather and cotton holding things up, pulling things down. Eadie thought her name was Max or Maz or Mags or something like that. A name cut up and beat down and given to an undersized infant who grew into an oversized woman. Most of them had one-syllable names. Except, of course, for her. The outsider. The rug-muncher.

'Keely. Ooh. Ooh,' Maz gave a shudder, shook. Everyone laughed.

'Not your all-time fav, Maz.'

'I so regret not getting that girl's teeth,' Maz smiled ruefully. 'All I wanted was her fucking teeth. I just wanted to be able to say she never got away from me. At least not in one piece.'

'God, you're bad.'

'You're a bad bad girl.'

'What did she do?' Eadie asked. Everyone turned. Eadie shrugged and squinted in the light, tried to feign humility.

'She was an uppity little slut who never knew when to keep her mouth shut.' Maz leaned as she spoke, showing grey teeth. 'Not unlike some little blow-ins I've met of late.'

'Keely borrowed a few of Maz's things,' someone sniggered. 'Borrowed them fucking forever.'

'Slippery fingers. Nobody likes a slippery finger.'

'Well, maybe some people do.'

Everyone laughed. Eadie felt a nudge and only just managed to keep herself from falling off the edge of the bench.

'I shoulda borrowed a piece of that girl's brain while I had the chance. Borrowed it permanently.'

'I saw something on the news about her,' someone frowned. 'Like they're after her. The cops. They want to talk to her.'

Eadie cracked her knuckles quietly, one at a time. The speaker was a waif of a creature named Sally or Sal or Sam or something like it, one of the cleverer of the bunch, a rung above in the evolution sampler sitting around her. Eadie wasn't surprised Sal had watched the news. She had the intelligence to be interested in it. But if Eadie were lucky, Sal wouldn't be the type to watch regularly, wouldn't have put together the pieces and calculated that three of Jackie Rye's past residents were missing, ask why the police hadn't been sniffing around. Eadie had been banking on the residents of Rye's Farm being so transient that few of them would have been there at the same time as all three missing girls. It was better if no one knew the police were looking for the missing girls. Whoever was responsible might decide to burrow or bail before Eadie had managed to get hold of them.

'Keely was on the news?' Maz frowned.

'Yeah.'

'Why?'

'I think they said, like, she's missin' or somefink.'

Eadie wiped at a bead of sweat on her temple.

'Missing? Since when? Since she took off from here with my fucking DVDs?'

'I don't know. Didn't watch that close.'

'I hope she's dead.'

A moan of appreciation went up from the table, broke into laughs, the way some fireworks will rise and then crackle into shards of light.

'Aw, come on. No, you don't.'

'Yes, I do.'

'Not really though.'

'Don't tell me what I fucking mean.'

Eadie chewed her knuckles. There was no denying Sal had a few more biscuits in her packet than the other girls at the table, but that didn't count for much if her basic danger warning system was faulty. Eadie had been in the business of hunting humans since she was a child and she had seen bare-bone smarts paired with a sharp animal nature carry a person a long way. But Sal was wandering into dangerous territory, and only Eadie, it seemed, could see the water rippling. Warning Sal was impossible. She glanced at the breakfast sheds and saw Jackie and Nick there, hunched and smoking.

'I wonder if she's in trouble or someone's reported her gone.' Sal picked at the splintered tabletop, oblivious.

Maz had a bone and wasn't letting it go. 'I'm really fucking interested in how you think I'm some kind of dog no good for her word. Because I've never done nothing to make people think that. I always follow through.'

'Yeah, you know, but people talk sometimes.'

'You saying I'm all talk?'

'Jesus, you need to calm down a bit.' Sal squinted in the light.

'I mean what I say I mean.' Maz shrugged. 'They say they know where she is?'

'No. They just said they're looking. There was a mugshot. A description. A reward, maybe. I dun remember.'

'Dead. Dead in the ground.'

'Oh, Maz!'

'What?'

'Well what if she is dead? And you said you wished it?' Sal pleaded.

'Then I hope that. I hope that and worse. I hope some fucking piece of shit from out the back of fucking Bankstown put her in a van and gave her what she needed and then put her in the ground and gave the world what it needed.' Maz looked around for encouragement. The women laughed. Pea finally gave up on the lighter, threw it over her shoulder into the dirt and held her hand out to the girl beside her.

'No, you don't.'

'Oh my god. Somebody put a leash on this bitch, please,' Maz grinned, her face taught as nylon. 'I'm gonna cut sick in a minute.'

'Plenty of people steal shit,' Sally shrugged. 'You don't know what made her do it, maybe she, like, she had some kind of reason, you know, that nobody knew about . . .'

'You're stealing my good air right now, Sal,' Pea said, exhaling blue into the thin white air. 'You need to give it up before someone knocks your block off.'

An interesting move by Pea, Eadie thought. She'd got the impression so far that Pea enjoyed a good bullying session. No one was as they appeared. Sal herself had perked right up to her full height, the bones in her throat shifting up and down as she swallowed, apparently excited by the challenge of exerting her morality onto the group.

'You know sometimes you have to, like, give people the benefit of the doubt. People, you know. People can . . .' Sal was on the edge of something, Eadie could see. Something prophetic. Opinion changing. Something informed. But she didn't have the words. Hadn't been raised with the words. All she had in her mind were pictures of fairness and hard work and reward. Moving pictures, mental films she had made of a better world. 'Maybe, like, she. Maybe if you'd forgiven her, you . . .'

Eadie watched Maz attack Sal, and to prevent herself from being taken with the momentum of the attack when it began, to prevent herself from getting up, going for Maz, stopping the brutality and blowing her cover, she took pains to catalogue just how very many tiny gestures and surrenders and facilitations were needed in the other women at the table for Maz to be able to do what she did to Sal. Eadie counted, one, two, three, nothing moving but her eyes, as the woman between Maz and Sal swiftly got up and stepped back from the table, clearing the path. She watched as Pea leaned ever so slightly to her left, nudging Sal forward when she tried to lean back away from Maz's hands, watched as the three women on her own side of the table got up and moved around behind the fray, blocking Sal's exit.

Eadie let her eyes drift away as the beating progressed, to the horizon, to the stalking silhouettes in the heat haze, who stopped at the noise of the screaming, turned, looked, folded their arms, the way men will stop to appreciate a sunset, forearms supported by paunch, witnessing nature at its finest. She looked back and took in the blood, as everyone was, silently and without surprise, because you weren't surprised when justice happened – no, surprise would have been an insult. Eadie remained seated. Bent a little to watch Maz's boot going up and coming down. Thought about the science of blood coated in dust, how it formed little balls, why it didn't soak into the earth right away, how long it took for blood to do that. Eadie witnessed, and Eadie said nothing. She put her hands on the table as they dragged Sal away towards the hose by the stables and only looked down at them when she felt the heat of Pea's cigarette near her fingers. The old woman was watching too.

'Alright,' Pea sighed, flicking ash onto the blood-wet earth. 'Back to it.'

Heinrich went into a hole. That was what you did when you were dead, the fitting thing to do. He took the room that had once been Vicky's in the attic of the house filled with giggling and whispering girls and lay under the sloped ceiling in the dark. He hurt. He slept. He didn't function the way he used to function. In the time that passed after Bear's death, the hours, the days without light or sound, he began to learn how his new body would work, how much strength he would have left. He lay and thought about what was happening inside him, bones fusing back together from where they'd splintered apart, tissue strands reaching out and reuniting with torn brothers, blocked blood vessels shrinking and becoming clear and raging with redness again, with warmth. Smouldering ashes became a glow, grew smoky and hot and licked with flame. When once the girls came and lay on him, lifted him, held him, put their tongues and fingers into him, now he flipped and pinned them and showed them his strength, made them squeal and cry out.

Sometimes in the dark he thought about Sunday. Tried not to follow those dark paths down into the bottom of his soul where the Silence lived. It would endanger the people around him, those thoughts. The sleeping girls. Vicky with her quiet steps. The men who laughed and blundered about downstairs. No. He would save that for Sunday. He knew somehow she would come to him.

When the girls left him Heinrich used a stick that had belonged to Icky to make the distance between the bed and the table by the tiny window that looked out into the crowded lanes of Surry Hills. He pushed aside the papers and letters and notes Vicky had stacked there and waited for his coffee to come. He leaned his head on his knuckles and planned. At nine each night Vicky arrived for their meeting with her little brown glazed coffee set and her hair falling out of her tortoiseshell clip. Braless, waify, a whisper in the way she walked and a whisper in the way she greeted him – no lips, just brushes of fingers and nails. Heinrich didn't think Vicky gave her lips to anyone. He would look out the tiny window and talk. Vicky would take up a pen and write.

'Who's overseeing importations down there at the Point right now?'

'Ian Hereward. Brett's son.'

'Brett still alive?'

'No.'

'Junior got any naughty pleasures?'

'No,' Vicky would sigh, tap the name on her list, making inky dots on the lines like long, dramatic pauses in a script. 'Straight as an arrow. Doesn't even sip. They tell me you can't buy that one. Not with the Queen's gold.'

'Sometimes money's not the price.'

'Well, I don't know what to tell you, Boy. Money's all you got this early in the piece.'

Vicky always called him Boy, even though Heinrich guessed he was eighteen or nineteen now. The legend of what his childish hands had done to two snarling beasts would outlive him.

'Didn't his pretty sister marry some fucking loudmouthed wog?'

'Yeah. An art dealer.'

'Junior go to the wedding?'

'No.'

'He didn't go?'

'No.'

Heinrich sipped his coffee. It was thin and black. All his body could take. He was young and his body worked like that of an ancient. Whatever went in had trouble getting back out. Food. Water. Air. Thoughts into words. Luckily Vicky was one of those women who had been around enough of the right kind of men to need few if any explicit directions. She looked at Heinrich as he sipped his coffee, and after a second or two made a note in her book to send someone after the loudmouthed wog.

And that's how it went in those first couple of years, nothing but the gold light of the tiny windows. Heinrich sitting, talking quietly, Vicky making lists, pushing money and people around down there on the earth, a place Heinrich simply didn't go, happy enough as he was in his dark, deep hole.

'Who's the Father down there at St Margaret Mary's?'

'Where?'

'Randwick. Catholic.'

'I don't know.'

'Get to know.'

'Seen the light, have you?'

'I'd like to hear, not so much see,' Heinrich would say. 'Hear some confessions. Some secret sins.'

Out there, on the surface, Heinrich's money walked, passed, tumbled from hand to hand, bumped into other piles of money and multiplied, the way that rats will triple and triple again in narrow passageways filled with torn paper. It was gathered and presented in stacks on tables in backrooms and cardrooms and changing rooms. It arrived unexpectedly into groups of men in the shadows of crowded clubs, was passed in envelopes into confused and bloodstained hands, was tucked into coat pockets as lips brushed against the rims of strained ears.

'That thing. From last week. You're good to go.'

'Says who?'

'Nevermind.'

The 'Nevermind' emerged into the language of prostitutes, junkies, warlords, bikies, chemists selling unlabelled boxes from their back steps and truck drivers taking back routes through the bush, lying down on their bellies in the warm red earth, gasping as friends or brothers or old cellmates looped rope around their wrists. The 'Nevermind' trembled on the lips of theatre owners on George Street, just before the lights went down, just after the lights went up again by someone's suddenly empty back-row chair, program card on the carpet, spectacles fallen in the aisle. The 'Nevermind' was whispered in dreams. In cells. On ships rounding the headlands of Watsons Bay, plunging into the gathering arms of the harbour. Men in hats knocked on the doors of the homes of prison wardens, prosecutors, journalists, men who made their livings holding keys, slamming hammers, wielding pens like swords. An envelope passed. A wink in the light of the hall.

'Who's this from?'

'Nevermind.'

In the middle of bank robberies, a group of five became four and one comrade was suddenly tripped in the back lot before the gaping van, a foot on a heaving chest, the butt of a rifle lifted in the air.

'Sorry, bub. You need to go away for a while.'

'What? Why? Why?'

'Nevermind.'

Caesar was at dinner at Dominique's in Potts Point the last time anyone said Nevermind to him. He liked Dominique's. It was away from all the noise of the clubs on the Strip and the shouting of the spruikers, the degenerates who didn't have the class or the mindfulness to know they weren't to stop him walking no matter what, the girls dying for the prestige of having been between his sheets. Idiots. Fools. Caesar hadn't offered any mercy to a dribbling street-creeper in all his life and he hadn't had a whore in his sheets since he was a boy. His bed was a clean place. A sacred place. When he wanted a woman, he waited until he found something that had never known the touch of a man or something that wouldn't want his touch even if she knew what it was like. Someone's wife as payment. Someone's daughter. Some silly little girly on the run from Daddy's belt, some helpless creature looking for a break. Caesar broke them in. He didn't pay invites to classless creatures.

As he got older, he was beginning to feel the pull away from the crash and clutter and the sycophants, the brainless girls in their frilly dresses and draft-horse heels, the ones who would jump on his cock at the raise of an eyebrow. Those were the kinds of things that young men enjoyed. Gunfire and breaking glass.

Caesar retreated to Dominique's because they kept the lights and the music low, the place was always clean and his table always ready, tucked behind a wall of lit cabinets filled with cocktail glasses in the shapes of women and animals. It didn't really matter to Caesar who came along, who snuck into the seats, who wrestled with whom to put something to him while he ate – some grand plan worked out to within an inch of its life, some new avenue for his bloody river to wind down into the hands of the junkies. And though he despised them, resented them, was sickened by their simple travels between self-pity and self-gain, their itchy scratchy twitchy patchy existences chasing after the blessed release he'd been importing with Savet from Nam for years, it was these creatures, the junkies, who had made him what he was. In a way, Caesar hated them even more for his reliance on them, their bony quivering fingers snapping up his little white packets, their scraped-together coins and their crumpled notes and their pathetic belongings hocked to add to his gold pile. He hated the way they sold their bodies and their minds and their dignity for him, hated the way they failed over and over to expire into dust as they appeared to want to do, hated the exchanges that were needed to suck the money out of them, the time, the bargaining, the promises. If there had been some way to get what he wanted out of them without the exchange, Caesar was certain he'd be able to feel joy again. If he could just figure out a way of getting their life blood without having to touch or speak to them. He rested his chin on his knuckles. He sighed. Fucking junkies. He'd be locked to them forever.

'Caesar?' Someone broke him out of his musings. Caesar blinked. Savet had been sitting beside him only moments ago, shifting his prawns around his plate with his fork, and now some sallow-eyed fool was in his place, some soldier Caesar didn't know but who was probably running something important for him. Savet was the only man Caesar had ever known who would eat crisp cold prawns out of the tail with a fork. And even then he seemed to eat five or six and then give them up completely, like they weren't for him. He didn't understand it. The cop had moved down the table, was staring at his glass of whisky, plate full. Caesar felt annoyed. He gathered up another prawn from his pile and dabbed it in the sauce.

'What is it?'

'Tuesday's, um . . .' the soldier said. 'Tuesday's shipment, the one meant for the Punchbowl guys. The one that, um, was supposed to come in with, and, um – '

'Would you learn to put some fucking words together.'

'Well there's been a sort of, um, problem, and . . .'

'Say "um" once more and see what happens to you.'

'Sorry.' The young soldier scratched his neck, scratched it hard, left red marks. A few months off being one of Caesar's new clients. Caesar filled his mouth with prawns.

'Tuesday's shipment has been seized.'

'No it hasn't.' Caesar filled the gaps in his mouth with wine, swished, swallowed, sucked juice from between his teeth.

'It . . .' The soldier seemed to want to pepper the air with uncertainties again but instead just sat there gaping, mouth puckering like a fish. 'We got word from Billy down there on the wharf that the whole fucking thing's been, uh, uh, it's being held.'

Caesar looked around the table. There were six men and Savet, all of them talking except the copper with the restless fork. A young waitress brought a basket of bread to the table, set it within Caesar's reach. He grabbed a roll. The man to his right, some bulbous-nosed stock shifter-cum-hitman, grabbed one too.

'I'm not understanding you,' Caesar told the soldier. 'You're talking gibberish. Nothing has been seized. It's impossible.'

The soldier scratched his arms.

'Go back to Billy and tell him to stop feeding you lies.'

'Billy's in the clink,' the soldier trembled. 'Ronnie Redford came down there himself and just started gathering everybody up like sheep into a divvy van.'

The fat-nosed man to Caesar's right started coughing. Caesar looked over, frowned. Fatty looked apologetic. Spread a hand in the air.

'You've shocked my friend here into choking on his dinner with this despicable news,' Caesar told the soldier. He broke his bread and dabbed it in the sauce, munched it between his back teeth. 'I sincerely hope what you're telling me isn't true. But if it is, I want you to find out exactly how ten sets of eyes that were supposed to be turned away from my shipment all suddenly turned around at the same time. You might as well have moved the earth to get that shipment found.'

'Billy says he heard some guys talking about the seizure over in remand. Said somebody told somebody who told somebody else it'd been cooking for a while and there was more to come.'

'And where are all these excited little whisperings leading back to?'

'They didn't say. They just said nevermind.'

'Nevermind?' Caesar licked his lips. Glanced down the table at Savet. He wasn't looking.

The fat man was coughing again. Short, hard coughs, like he was trying to dislodge the bread from his windpipe. 'I'm hearing this more and more. This "nevermind". Someone knocks over my hock shop. Nevermind. Someone stirs up a couple of my girls. Nevermind. Someone seizes my fucking shipment. Nevermind.

'Nevermind. I mind, you little fuck. I don't know what's going on, but I'm really beginning to mind. And you better start paying attention to things that I mind. All of you. All of you little shits. What I mind should be all that's on your minds all the time, you understand me?'

Caesar grabbed hold of whatever he could get of the soldier, managed a collar and with it a bunch of warm, loose neck skin. Squeezed, felt the soldier tense with pain and try to go limp, to lessen the pain by letting Caesar pull him within biting distance.

'Someone says "nevermind" near me one more time and I'm going to snap. You understand? I'm going to snap, and they're going to be bagging whoever's near me when it's said.'

The fat man fell off his chair. Caesar let the soldier go.

The men around him stood up, but Caesar didn't need to. He could see the nameless man on the carpet beside him clearly enough, see the pink foam that poured up and began cascading down his suddenly blackening cheeks as though the whole thing had been set up just for him. A private show. He shifted upwards in his chair, threw a glance around the table. Watched. People were screaming. Caesar hadn't seen a man's face colour like that before. It was like his cheeks were being flooded with something just below the first layer of skin – black ink injected into the fluid there and creeping across the quivering mounds. The man kicked, hard, kicked again and then went still. Caesar looked at the men around him, the other diners uncertain whether to get up from their tables or not, hovering inches above their chairs.

Caesar pushed his chair back, got up slowly and reached down. He plucked the lump of crusty white bread from the fat man's gnarled hand and raised it to his nose. Smelled something. He didn't know what.

Something that wasn't bread.

I don't spend a lot of time in Glebe, but when I do I go to the AB Hotel. The food is served in obnoxiously large portions and the place is a big mess of levels and private function rooms and lounge areas. You can find the right type of music, lighting, space for whatever it is you're doing. On the ground floor, just inside the door, swollen-bellied tradies squint at the footy screens, while just a few steps above on the middle level first-daters huddle over chestnut tables for two, squeaking embarrassingly on the leather high-back chairs, watching the waitstaff. Higher up again there's a sort of confused mezzanine that sometimes hosts little interest clubs. On the top floor it's all neon-pink lights flooding heavy drapes, the tables pushed back for dancing, sick and dying tropical fish traversing the seven-metre-long bar-top tank.

I was in Glebe to pick up some papers from my contact in the archives – some maybes and probably nots from the unnamed mugshot categories, Jane Doe files and informant catalogues in my search for a Jimmy or a Kimmy connected to Sharon Elizabeth White. Sonya, a short woman who never wore make-up and was always in green, handed me three tattered, badly arranged manila folders and wished me luck. I promptly lost my hold on all the papers as soon as she was out of sight and had to gather them up from the asphalt before they were taken by the wind.

I sat at the bar sipping a glass of rum on ice and looked through the files. I'd already dug up everything there seemed to be in the official records on Sunday, but I'd learned from some old Department of Community Services records that Sunday's sister, Adam White's mother – the woman whose suicide had inspired her son to harass the most violent man in Sydney in search of retribution – was in the records too. Lynda White had been removed from the care of her mother in a similarly chaotic round-up of Aboriginal children to the one that had claimed Sunday. But the two sisters weren't united in the system – foster family shortages meant there wasn't a home with the racial reformists of Adelaide available for two little black girls. Sunday was sent to Sydney and Lynda remained in the southern state. According to a psychologist's report on Lynda accompanying some financial support she'd applied for in the eighties, she'd tracked down Sunday in the Cross when both girls were working in the sex industry in their late teens. What a reunion.

I fiddled with the stack of coasters nearby and stretched my neck, taking a break from the painfully faded transcript to look around the bar. Maybe I could find Kimmy or Jimmy through Lynda. Maybe they knew each other. Were arrested together. Anything. I sighed. My hunting quarry had tripled. I was now trying to follow the movements of three ghost girls vanished into the halls of time. I dropped the archive files and pulled out my phone.

Juno answered after one ring. I suppose he didn't have room to be more than an arm's length from the phone.

'How's the Naked Detective?'

'She's alright.'

'Working hard?'

'She does. Works really hard for someone who's not actually a farm worker. It's like she actually cares.'

'Well, I'm working hard, she's working hard. Don't you go exhausting yourself watching my partner's perfectly sculpted arse morning and night. Take a break now and then. Rest your eyes.'

'I guess I'll try.'

'Anything juicy?'

'A couple of things, I guess. Someone vandalised Eden's van. Pissed in it. Fairly classy. I don't have any cameras on who it was, exactly, and nothing was said about it in Jackie's van.' I could hear Juno moving things around, clicking. 'I ran a check on those guys who were hanging around the night Nick climbed into Eden's bed. Nothing spectacular. Just low-lifes. I get the feeling Eden's going to use the girl to cosy up to Rye. Not basing that on anything really other than the fact that she's making besties with the kid for no other apparent reason.'

'I'd love you to keep me updated on that.'

'This place is so full of fucking degenerates, I don't know how you're going to pin it on Jackie, man,' Juno said. 'This morning these bitches laid into one of the younger girls just for giving some lip. Some pretty conversational, non-aggressive lip, if you ask me. Nothing that deserved being bashed half to death and then hosed down for.'

'Bogans.'

'Yeah.'

'There's a big difference between mob justice and first degree, though,' I yawned.

Probably shouldn't have, given how upset and introspective Juno was sounding. 'What you witnessed was likely very routine, spurred by sudden passion, not really anything more than a passing thrill for those involved. Something to talk about. You completely do away with three whole human beings on the other hand. Well, that takes some planning. Commitment.'

'So in a way I guess we're not looking for the most outwardly violent.'

'Most likely we're looking for the exact opposite. I've got my money on the most organised. The most measured.'

A woman came to the bar and stood beside me. She picked up the coasters I'd been playing with and started arranging them in a fan shape on the woolly bar runner. I looked up as she tucked a curl of long black hair behind her ear and hailed the bartender from way down the room.

In her earlobes there were tiny red earrings.

Ladybugs with gold feet. Painted thickly with gloss.

'... I mean how long you gotta be doing this shit before you begin to think like that?' Juno was saying.

'It's not the length of time.' I coughed, thumped my chest. 'It's what happens to you.'

I hung up on Juno and put my phone away. Far away. Put it by the canister of straws. I gripped the bar and breathed, waited for the woman with the ladybug earrings to go away. The woman with the black hair. The tall, lanky woman with the dimpled smile and the bony wrists and the novelty earrings who wasn't Martina. No, because Martina was dead. In the ground. Under the dirt. Dead in the ground under the dirt because I hadn't been there when she needed me.

I took a packet of Endone from my back pocket and popped three. Crunched thoughtfully. Made it four.

'Right, mate?' The bartender flicked his beard at me.

'Yeah. Another.'

It was only about eight when Max Fara tapped on my shoulder. But I was already drunk. Badly drunk. Three drinks past cut-off point drunk, but I've got a pretty good drunk's poker face, and I know how to keep my mouth shut and shuffle the bartenders, so I didn't think I was that close to being turfed. I'd arrested Max Fara for a series of break-and-enters in my early days on the beat. So often had we encountered each other that we'd formed a sort of understanding that what happened between us wasn't personal, and that I didn't in fact go out of my way to come across him climbing in or out of windows all over Blacktown in his high school years. By the time I was getting ready to sit the detective's exam Max, or Mustafa as he was on his birth certificate, had begun treating our little interactions as a cat-and-mouse game. His father was some big government official over in Lebanon, so the thefts had been a game in the first place, one with little consequences besides the regular promises that Dad's bail contributions were well spent. Now he had someone to share the game with, and I didn't mind that much. He'd always been nice enough.

'Not you.'

'Sergeant Francis Bennett. Oh. My. God.' Max flashed a set of huge white expensive teeth at me.

'It's Detective Inspector now, dickhead.' I swallowed my rum.

'What are you doing here? You don't live here. Don't tell me all that pavement-pounding and crim-collaring has driven you to the drink?'

It was slightly alarming for Max to know where I didn't live. I pushed the alarm aside.

'There'd be something wrong with me if it hadn't. I'm just having a quiet drink and trying not to associate with any criminals. You know. The usual.'

'God, it's so weird to see you. So weird. Such a fucking blast from the past. You still a Westie?'

'No.'

'North Sydney?'

'Parramatta.'

'That's where the big HQ is, isn't it?'

'Been there once or twice, have you?'

'What you doing at HQ?'

'Homicide.'

Max submitted to laughter again. His bottom row of teeth were all gold, the centre four studded with small white diamonds. I wondered what Daddy thought about that. If he knew. The young man also seemed to be wearing some kind of razor tailored suit with a cummerbund. It had been years since I'd even seen a cummerbund in a shop window. I'd never worn one myself. I wanted to ask why he was wearing it but didn't get the chance.

'This explains why you look so shit. Hanging around stiffs all day. You're beginning to look like one. Look at your eyes.'

'Thanks.'

'You look tired, old mate.'

'You look like a penguin. What is all this?' I flipped his buttons.

'Just styling and profiling, Francis, like I always do.' He popped out his chest.

'Christ.'

'Let me get you something to perk you up.'

I scoffed. Began gathering up my papers.

'Nah, come on, please. Serious. Serious. You've always been good to me, Sergeant Bennett. I've always been such a stupid boy. An idiot. Those days are gone now, alright? Maybe I learned something. Maybe I changed. I remember where I came from though. What I've been through.'

'Oh yes, it's a hard life being the idle son of an absent millionaire. You should write a rap ballad about it.'

'You always softened it up for my father, even though I never asked you to. I never asked, did I?'

'I don't remember.'

I remembered something about him being sixteen and crying in the back of a divvy van, telling me he was going to get thrown out onto the street. Something like that. Maybe it had been someone else. Some other self-obsessed brat.

'Come on.' He swung an arm around my neck, dragged me into his Lynx cloud. 'There's a party going on and you're missing it.'

'What party?' I was letting myself be led now. Surrendering. Answering the call into the wild. It was so easy. So seamless. 'Where?'

I'd never been to a Lebanese wedding. The experience was something like walking onto the stage of a great opera at the moment of a battle or dramatic death. People were shoving against me, rushing forward, dancing or embracing with cries so deep and guttural or high and piercing they could have been anywhere on the spectrum of human emotions. The men reeked of cigar smoke and the women of expensive perfume. The food was laid out around the room like the walls of a great fortress – roasted, oiled, fried, bricks of cake, bread, meat. I must have been brushed by every texture of fabric in existence just getting into the room – scratchy gold-embroidered silks and rough leather and wool suits that cost more than my monthly rent. People were unafraid to touch each other, to touch me, dark-eyed beauties with skin drenched in glitter grabbing my fingers, wrenching me sideways, pulling my neck, insisting on a swing around.

Max put a drink into my hand. I must have been introduced to fifty people, ten of them in the dark courtyard area of the pub, under red lights, no one's eyes visible, a sea of devil masks. A man I didn't know, some cousin or brother or uncle, dabbed a little expensive something, a good and hard-hitting something into the webbing of my hand. Turning away, respectful gestures for disrespectful doings. My eyes watered. They always used to water. Louise, my first wife, used to call me a crybaby, back in the old days when I did this all the time. When I was out of control. On the edge. I groaned and looked at the lights, felt myself falling back in time.

I forgot all about Martina's ghost. Men yelled in my ears and I laughed, really laughed for the first time in a long time, got to crying, made people around me cry. Indulged a little in cop story-telling, once I'd deemed it safe. A few young Lebanese boys hiding from their mothers so they could stay out late perched on the bricks around the cigarette garden, trying to make like their older brothers, disguising their awe with quizzical frowns. Questions were fired at me, drinks shoved into my palm. A wind started in the palm trees above the courtyard, a whipping sound, and the boys looked up, howled with delight as a plastic bucket tumbled off the roof, spilling paintbrushes and rollers into the garden. A light rain. Everyone leaked back inside into the noise. I felt warm despite the wind. My hair was getting wet. Max put a hand on my shoulder, tried to get me inside, but I wanted to look at the stars, watch the black clouds eat them one by one.

It was some wonky-eyed teenage bartender who finally brought me in, practically dragged me, fed up with all the noise and mess the Lebanese function was making of the upper floor. I stood inside the door and brushed rain off the hair on my arms, felt great.

When I looked up and spotted her sitting there at the tables on the mezzanine area I felt even better. A surge of electricity between my shoulderblades like I'd been prodded forward by a cheeky angel, a cupid. She was sitting with some strange half-monkey with a heavy sloping brow that wasn't helped by a quiff turning into a mullet behind his ears, a denim jacket lined with orange faux fur. Dr Stone looked angry and he looked pleased with himself. Laughing at some joke he had just made. She turned her glass on the tabletop.

I strode forward and grabbed a chair from the empty set beside them, dragged it over, grinned down at her horrified face.

'Dr Stone, if this isn't the luckiest night of my life.'

'Oh Jesus,' she said, looked away.

'Mate, I'm Frank Bennett.' I offered my hand to the Neanderthal. He considered, pumped it half-heartedly. Wrinkled his big features.

'Curtis.'

'I'm sorry to interrupt. I just saw you from up there and I thought, *No, way. It isn't.* And then it was! It was you. How hilarious. You look beautiful, Stone. My god. I mean, what are you trying to do to us, ay?' I nudged Curtis. He swayed.

She was beautiful though. She was wearing something red. I couldn't tell if it was a dress or a long shirt but it was the colour of something freshly bleeding, full of life, and it made her freckles stand out like gold stars. The dress was textured with little upraised squares. I wanted to touch it. She was frowning at her wine glass. I watched her pick it up, scoop a bar fly off the surface with her finger, flick it onto the floor.

'Frank, you're drunk,' she sighed.

'No, I'm not.'

'We're sort of having a bit of a private moment here,' Curtis the man monkey said. 'Seems like the best time to catch up would be some other time.'

'Is this a date?'

'No. It's not.' Stone gave me some eyes that might have killed me had I not been so drunk.

'Well, actually it is,' Curtis said.

'Is it?'

'No.'

'He says it is.' I jerked a thumb at the ape.

'It isn't, Frank.'

'Is there some problem with him knowing that it is?' Curtis laughed once, like a cough.

'You'll just encourage him.'

'I'm easy to encourage,' I admitted.

'Mate, you're really starting to play with fire right now.'

'Hey, I'm just being friendly. Excuse me. We're old friends, Dr Stone and I.'

'This really . . .' Stone licked her lips, looked at me. 'You need to just . . .'

'Just tell him to fuck off.' Curtis flicked his chin at her. Looked at me. 'Mate, fuck off.'

'Whoa!' I faked being thrown back in my chair. 'Lordy! The new beau's got a temper.'

'Just settle down, the both of you. Frank, you're drunk. Now's not a good time.'

'You're right. I'll leave now so Captain Caveman here can apologise for using such foul language in your presence. On a first date and everything. What would your mother say, Imogen?'

'Is this guy one of your clients or something?'

'He's . . .' Imogen sighed.

'Alright, I'm going. I'm sorry. You look beautiful. Enjoy your date.'

'It's not a fucking date.'

'It *is* a date.' Curtis puffed his chest out. 'What the fuck, Imogen?'

'Maybe the problem with me knowing this is a date,' I paused on the edge of my chair, on the edge of my own hilarity, held my breath to stifle the laugh, 'is that she's dressed like a fucking fox and you're wearing a denim jacket with a fur trim.'

Curtis stared at me.

'I mean you should have looked in the front windows at her and binned that thing before she ever saw it, mate.'

'Wow.' The ape glared at Imogen. She licked her lips. Looked at me. At the ceiling. Then laughed, just once, the kind of laugh that cracks a taut face and seems half like pain. Then she swallowed it. Pushed at me so that I got out of the chair.

'Go away.'

'That jacket looks like someone killed a ginger cat.' I wobbled on the edge of my chair. 'And then stapled it to the eighties.'

Imogen lost control of her laughter. The Neanderthal got up. I got up. Let him push me. Wasn't really concerned about the ferocity of it, the desire he was communicating in it. *I'd like to hurt you. I like hurting people.* There were ten or fifteen young Lebanese men watching from the balcony of the third floor. Ready. So ready.

'Calm down, sunshine. I'm only having a laugh.'

'Fuck. Off.'

'Alright. I'm fucking off,' I saluted. 'Here I go. Fucking off now. Fucking off sequence initiated.'

'He one of your psycho clients or something?'

I didn't stick around to hear her answer. Went to the bar and ordered a scotch. Stood drinking it, laughing quietly to myself about the cat joke. Most jokes involving cats are pretty hilarious. Cats themselves can be outrageously funny. I felt a sudden wave of sadness pass over me, of longing for my cat, Martina's cat, annoying, food-obsessed, self-obsessed little jerk. Once or twice the thing had redeemed itself briefly by lying on my lap while I watched the footy, kneading me, loving me – if you could call that love, the biological instinct to cosy up to me in order to get what it wanted. I was distracted from my thoughts about cats by the Neanderthal brushing me roughly as he passed, heading out the doors. Imogen was close behind him, draining the end of her glass of wine, pulling on her long red coat.

'Hey,' I grabbed her when she got within reach, 'I'm sorry.'

'You should be.'

'What can I say?' I shrugged. 'What can I do?'

'Nothing. It's over. He's gone.'

'Jesus.'

'Look,' she sighed, her whole body in it, 'actually, without meaning to, you managed to rescue me from something really awful. I'd been trying to end it for an hour and a half but the guy likes the sound of his own voice.'

'Oh. Right.'

'Doesn't make you any less of an annoying fuck.'

'Yes, no, you're right, of course, annoying fuck. Sounds pretty accurate.'

'Frank.'

'So that *was* a date.'

'It was.'

'Where do you even find a half-monkey, half-man? I thought they had to grow those types in laboratories.'

'It was an online thing.' She smoothed down her hair. 'I'm not really in the mood for an exhaustive breakdown of it.'

'You? You date from the internet? *You?*'

'Yes. I date men I find on the internet.'

'*Why?*'

'It's almost like you're trying to make me angry.'

'Alright, I'll stop. I'm sorry, I'm drunk. I'm just drunk. Let me get you a cab.'

'I'm walking.'

'No, you're not, it's pissing with rain.'

'I live three blocks from here, and I have an umbrella. I won't die.'

'I'm walking you. Just to make sure. If you died I wouldn't have anyone to bully and judge me. Invade my life. Stalk me to my apartment.'

'You're not walking me anywhere.'

'Yes I am.'

'No, you're not,' she laughed.

'I'll put you under arrest.'

'Wouldn't you just love that.'

I grabbed her bicep and held it, gave it a squeeze. She rolled her eyes at me.

She was like a weather system, inexplicably predictable, something that once coming changed the air and brought electricity to the earth before she arrived, made things tremble. Eadie was starting to believe she knew that Skye was coming for her even before the girl herself had made the decision wherever she was on the property, and by the time she heard the patter of Ugg boots across the dirt she'd already be feeling that half-smile creep across her face. It was right on sunset and the girl's silhouette cut into the orange light, her boots as pink as the horizon. Eadie said nothing, continued tightening the shoelaces of her runners.

'What are you doing?' the girl said.

'Going for a bit of a run.'

'A run? Are you nuts? Haven't you worked all day?'

'Best time for a run.' Eadie squinted in the painted day, held a hand up against the glowing red ball caught in the girl's dry blonde hair. 'Loosen me up.'

'It's about to be dark. *Neighbours* is on in, like, twenty minutes.'

'It'll keep. It's only Thursday. The good stuff'll be tomorrow night.'

'I'll come with you.'

'I'm not walking. I'm running.'

'I can run.' A child's indignation. Hands on hips.

'Better hurry up then. I'm leaving today.'

The girl sprinted off, and Eadie pulled her heels into her backside, feeling the warmth of a day's labour pulse in her quads, groan in her back. Skye returned with nothing about her outfit changed but a pair of worn joggers – her denim skirt stained with motor grease on the right-hand hem, the pink singlet over the ill-fitting bra. Eadie guessed the girl would learn. She was a determined creature and talking her down only riled her up. Eadie watched her gathering her hair into a bun, not quite able to catch it all, leaving strands at the nape of her neck that if touched would make her shiver. It was all brown under there, the colour of mice, of people who weren't big-city, champagne-drinking babes.

'Go slow,' the child frowned.

'Go quick.'

'I'll die, Eadie. Go slow, will you?'

'Alright, Nanna.'

They set off towards the stables, between them, and passed the pigs, the croaking and groaning beasts already lying down to sleep. Eadie tasted them in the air. Skylar's face was rigid, the temples pulsating already, blood shocked at how fast it was moving and chemicals pouring through veins, trying to calm things down.

'Slow down.'

'We're crawling.'

'Just. Slow. Down.'

'Alright,' Eadie laughed.

They bounced through the back gates and found themselves in the bush. It was treacherous there. Recent rains had slicked the walking tracks with clay, left rocks disturbed, ready to shift under wayward feet. If the girl rolled an ankle, who would care for her, Eadie wondered. Would Jackie cook dinner if she couldn't get around their tiny kitchen? Would he change the DVD? Would he help her hop over to take a piss in the annex next to the bed? Eadie huffed, found a rhythm finally, a slow one but a good one, her fists loose in front of her, gripping air handles, pulling herself forward, dancing. Who did Skye think was going to care for her when she got old? Did the girl see herself and Jackie growing old together? Did she love the man at all? She talked about him with the restless awe of a teenager. His tatts. His bikie days. Did the long term factor into Skye's calculations at all, or was she playing it day by day?

'Hey! Slow down.'

Eadie laughed, slowed again. The girl came up beside her, gripping a stitch.

'I'm gonna. Die. Out here.'

'Chat to me. It'll take your mind off it.'

'I can't.'

'Yes you can. Open your mouth. Lift your head up. You run like an elephant.'

'I am. An elephant.'

'Do the boys come out here?'

'Yeah. Sometimes. They hunt. Roos.'

'Roo meat's good for you.'

'It's gross. Too tough.'

'They probably overcook it.' Eadie took a long breath, sucked in the moist air before it began to give way to the desert again. The trees thinned before them, revealing lantana, sand. 'They should watch more *MasterChef*.'

'Mostly they don't. Cook them. No one. Likes them much. And there's so much. Pig. Anyway.'

'So what do they do with them then? If they don't cook them?' Eadie frowned.

'They just.'

Eadie looked over. The girl was uncomfortable. Shrugged. Her breasts lifting, catching the red light with their film of sweat.

'They just kill them.'

'So it's just sport?'

'I guess. I don't know. I'm not allowed to go. Only the boys go.'

Eadie licked her lips, savoured the salt she tasted. She wasn't a betting woman, but she would wager money that Jackie and his team were doing more to the kangaroos out there than simply snuffing their lives out, triumphing over their bodies, collecting carcasses to hang on fences. A bunch of drunk men, a shed full of cutting, grinding, mashing, slicing implements, the dark barren land, and a bunch of helpless animals. It was a recipe for pain. For entertainment too brutal for a loud-mouthed, sensitive girl like Skylar.

'I'm gonna. I can't. Let's go back.'

'Keep going.' Eadie was shocked by the callousness in her voice. Softened it. 'You can do it. Keep talking. What's down there?'

'Cliffs.'

'Come on. Let's look.'

'I've seen them. They're boring.'

'Come on, I want to see.'

The trees thinned to brush, and then without warning a gaping crack in the earth, running in a curve out of eyesight.

A dry riverbed. Eadie turned and led Skye along its edge, ducking forward now and then to look into the dark below the reach of the light without slowing the pace.

'Let's stop.'

'No. Let's keep going. It's nice though.'

'Yeah sometimes. There's water. Down there.'

Eadie let the girl go ahead, jogged at barely a pace above walking, more bouncing than moving forward. She spied a lump of blackness on a rock ledge and doubled back, circled quickly before the girl could see, and squinted. Clothes. Burned and blackened. A pair of jeans maybe. Eadie felt her mouth grow dry, looked for some landmark that would remind her where she'd seen the discarded clothes. There were none. Just a line of bush. A sweep of desert. A fence etched into the mauve sky like the fine pencil lines of an artist. It was growing dark. Eadie chewed her lip, remembered the camera hanging in the pendant around her neck. So easy to forget. Something she'd forgotten a couple of times already, going into the bathroom annex, beginning to strip off.

'Burned clothes,' she said aloud, grabbed the pendant and held it near her lips. 'I'm seeing burned clothes on the riverbed east of the property. I don't see any landmarks to tell you where. I want these checked out.'

'I'm gonna stop if you don't catch up.'

Eadie caught the girl in a few strides and sprinted back through the wire fence onto Jackie's property. The kill sheds were ahead of her, already absorbing the dying light in their gaping doors. She ran to the front double doors, stopped and stretched her limbs. The girl came bobbing towards her, stopped and hobbled when she got within speaking distance.

'Let's never do that again.'

'Do it every day. It gets easier. I'll go with you,' Eadie smiled.

'Maybe. I want to lose weight. Jackie says I've got tuckshop arms.'

'You don't have tuckshop arms.'

'Yes I do.'

They walked into the sheds together. Stood in the fading light. Eadie could make out a long steel trough running the length of the sheds, a conveyer belt of hooks parallel to it, within a tall man's reach. Four large stalls, enough to hold twenty pigs each, were swept and hosed bare. These would be hard surfaces to keep clean. The first thing animals do when they see or hear their kind being slaughtered is shit themselves, attack the beasts around them. There'd be blood in the grout too deep to remove.

'They hang them here,' Skye pointed. 'Upside down. Gut them. This whole thing gets filled with guts. All the way to the end there. Guys stand here with their blades out. Sharp as a razor. Slash, slash, slash. From there, the bolt in the head, to there, the tagging line, it's about ten minutes. Jackie says sometimes they're still twitching.'

The girl gave a little wiggle, limp hands flapping.

'Gross,' Eadie said.

'Yeah, real gross.'

'You ever been in here when it's on?'

'Nuh.' Skye wrinkled her nose, stood huffing still with her hands on her hips. 'I couldn't do it. I like pigs. They're cute.'

'I'll bet you like bacon too, though.'

'Everybody likes bacon.'

Skye stood looking up at the hundreds of hooks, each pointing the same way and perfectly aligned like an infinite row of question marks. Then she shivered, and Eadie felt the same shiver run through her, though she couldn't understand why.

'Let's get outta here, man,' the girl said and grabbed Eadie's hand.

'Yeah.' Eadie felt the girl squeeze her fingers. 'Time for *Neighbours*.'

When Vicky knocked on the door to the attic room, she received no response. This didn't surprise her. Often Heinrich lost himself in his thoughts so completely that no amount of noise could bring him out of the complex network of plans being webbed together by tiny spiders in his mind, his eyes barely moving as they took in the sky beyond the window. She entered the darkened room and saw him sitting by the window, a figure shaped like a crone with the same sad, laboured movements, lost in his thick brown overcoat, fiddling with things on the table. Sometimes the boy didn't let any light into the attic room, but today a slice of sunset had snuck in and struck the side of his head pink, gold in his unwashed hair.

'There's a girl here for you,' Vicky said. She took a couple of steps forward and tried to see what the boy was doing. Another of his creations. After the first year in the room Heinrich had started building things, first from whatever he found lying around, paper folded dozens of different ways into the shapes of reindeer and dragons, fitted together to make intricate boxes that sprung open at the touch. Then he had started meddling with things the girls brought him, coils of copper that he wove into the intricate scales of a life-sized cobra. He strung beads together and pulled them impossibly tight, made colourful fish that from across the room looked like they would suddenly move, flitter through the air, dart beneath the desk. The girls marvelled at his work but it seemed to bring him no joy. Vicky had found a huntsman spider as big as her handbag made from twisted pieces of lead discarded on its side behind the door, a beautiful, terrifying thing the boy had spent a day constructing and then flung, forgotten, into the shadows.

'Heinrich?'

'What girl?'

'She's calling herself Sunday.'

The boy said nothing. Vicky tried to see what he was working on. It seemed to involve strips of wire being twisted around fragments of coloured glass. She leaned back into the hall and nodded to the girl, who came walking forward cautiously and took the door from Vicky's hand as though she feared it would slam shut on her. She was a beautiful thing. All square and taut, robotic almost, like the whirring, mixing, dancing things rich women were putting in their kitchens, shiny and full of joints. She tucked her hair behind her ear and went to the middle of the room, stood looking at the boy. Heinrich's eyes never left his work.

Sunday filled her lungs with air. Let it go as the older woman clicked the door closed silently behind her.

'I thought you were dead.'

'That was the plan.'

The boy looked old. His hands looked old as they pulled the wire, clipped the ends and placed the offcuts in a little bowl like shiny noodles. Sunday wanted to see his grey eyes but they were hidden, so she took a few steps closer and stopped when she saw the muscles in the boy's neck twitch. It hurt to be apart from him. She had been so used to touching him whenever they were together, from those years they slept together as children, his back rising and falling against her cheek, his ankle brushing hers. She was always a bad sleeper, his dark mirror, so there were many nights when she simply lay with his hand in her hand and watched his nostrils flaring as he snored. Annoying boy. Smelly boy. Bed hog. Her pillow partner.

'People been talking. This morning Caesar held a meeting with some of his top guys at Mickey Cousins' place down on the water.' Sunday picked at her nails. 'That Burgmann guy was there. The customs guy. Some others. They were all talking on the balcony and when they got up to leave Mickey's kid, the one they arrested last year, he goes and gets Caesar's coat from the back of the couch in the living room and hands it to him.'

Heinrich was examining a piece of glass in the light of the window, an almost perfect triangle of royal blue that threw a sky-blue beam onto the wall behind him. Filled the room for an instant with a piece of the ocean.

'So as he's handing over the coat the kid makes a noise, like a yelp, and he swears out loud, and he takes the coat back and pulls a thorn from the inside of the collar. Like a rose thorn. It's pricked his finger, made a little black dot, and it kills, he says, but no one cares. Caesar puts the coat on and goes to leave. He doesn't get down one stair. He doesn't get halfway out the door before the Cousins kid's dead on the floor like a stone.'

Heinrich lifted his eyes from the thing in his hands for an instant, looked at Sunday's face, just long enough to give her a flash of his cold, hard eyes.

'It wasn't a rose.'

'Caesar's going to figure out it's you.' Sunday felt a shiver run through her. Rubbed her arms. 'I figured out it was you pretty damn fast. Soon as people started saying they'd seen your ghost I knew you'd made it somehow. You were always like that. The little survivor.

You better stop with the near misses and do what you're planning to do, or he's gonna send someone round here.'

'I'm doing what I'm planning to do,' Heinrich said. 'And no one's coming round here.'

The finality of his words was like the slamming of a door, and she felt suddenly alone, looking at him. He finished what he was putting together, and when his hands let the sculpture stand on its own she saw in the fading light a small bird fashioned from glass in a hundred different shades of blue and green, the dark green of beer bottles and the pale sickly blue of church windows, the lime green of cottage doors and the royal blue of medicine jars. The tail feathers were daggers of a deep purple, the glass from where she couldn't guess. The thing's wings were spread and feathered with the sharpest splinters, so to look at it was to feel the ache of beauty but to touch it might have torn a careless hand to shreds. From across the room it looked as though he had flown in the window and landed before the boy, who gazed on it with disinterest, the way a man inspects a disappointing son.

'Why didn't you tell me you were alive?' She swallowed. Squeezed her fists to draw the hurt down from her throat so that she could speak. 'I've been alone.'

He was out of his chair before her eyes could follow him, but his hand on her throat was familiar, the way it crushed her windpipe made her remember that night on the couch, the way he'd wanted to squeeze her, to possess her, to bend her bones. Feel around for what was inside her, deep down, whether those deeply buried things beneath her flesh were secrets or lies. And that's what it had been, she supposed, back then – not lovemaking but an investigation of her body the way his eyes had been investigating her soul since the day the Bear brought him home, the boy

308

who trusted no one. She felt his breath on her face and the wall against the back of her head but she knew better than to raise her hands to his.

'You have no idea what alone is like,' he said. 'I was alone in that house when they found me. Surrounded by dead men and women and girls.'

'Caesar and Savet, they – '

'One minute you were there,' Heinrich snarled. She felt his spit on her face. 'In my arms. I had your body in my arms. And then I wake up and you're gone and they're coming down on me.'

'I didn't know.'

'Into the night like fucking smoke.'

'I didn't know!' she screamed, felt her throat flex against his stone hand. 'I didn't know. I loved that man. You know I loved Bear like my very own father. Don't you tell me that you don't.'

She was crying in his hands. He smelled like something trying to decide whether it was going to live or die, fresh blood and dead flesh and wet concrete. Something imprisoned. He loosened his fingers from around her neck.

'I ran from you because of what we did, I couldn't . . . I couldn't understand it. I wanted it but I was afraid of what loving you would do to you. I hurt everything that comes near me, Heinrich, and I needed to keep you from that.' She put her hands on his shoulders and she was relieved to feel the warmth of them beneath the old coat, the smooth flesh of his neck, the curls at the back of his ears. He stood rigid and she hung herself from him, pulled his face down into her hair. She could feel his heart beating against her cheek.

'You're going to start a fucking war,' she trembled.

'It was started a long time ago.'

'You can't get him back. Bear is gone now. You don't know what they can do to you. This is what they do, Heinrich. They were born to do this.'

He laughed suddenly. 'You can learn with the right teacher.'

'Come away with me. Let's go up north. Like we said when we were kids.'

'No. We're not kids anymore. Look at you. Look at what you've done to yourself.' He had her wrists in his hands, her impossibly thin wrists. He took her face and shoved her, tried to back away, but she yanked him to her and felt him break, that sharp intake of breath she'd heard a man give against her skin a hundred times, the surrender to the violence of an angry, hungry heart. He pushed her into the wood, pulled her hair, exposed her jaw to his mouth. She didn't fight.

I woke to the sensation of a tapping in the centre of my chest, the kind of insistent tapping and rubbing you get when a paramedic is trying to bring you back to consciousness. Dr Stone took my hand from my nuts and put a coffee mug into it. The heat brought me back. I was bent in a banana curve across her inappropriately stiff square couch, my boots hanging dangerously close to what looked like a vase stuffed with dead twigs and my head baking in the heat of a curvy glass lamp. She flipped the lamp off and I tried to move, felt everything creak like it was going to fall apart.

'Oh god,' I said. Breathed low and deep. 'Why? Why?'

'Yes,' I could hear her smile in the new dark. 'It's a good question.'

Her robed silhouette thrust open the curtains in front of the balcony. I covered my eyes.

'Stop. Go back to where you came from. Leave me here to die.'

'It's ten. The day's half over.'

I bent my head into my hand and felt dead inside. I twisted painfully, groped for my pills, found my pockets empty. The place was spotless and small, like she'd only half moved into it or like she recognised such a tiny space could easily get cluttered and crowded by the things she owned, so she chose not to own things – to just look at them instead. She walked in bare feet to the tiny kitchenette and retrieved her own coffee. I wondered if she was naked under the red satin. Her hair was out and tangled at the back. Restless sleeper. Maybe I'd snored. Probably I'd snored.

'Did we sleep together?'

She coughed and swallowed her coffee.

'No, Frank.'

'Why not?'

'Because that's the worst idea I've ever heard of in my life.' She looked at me, tried to stifle a smile. 'You're a train wreck.'

'I suppose.' I adjusted my shirt. It was misbuttoned and stank of cigar smoke. I tried to rebutton it and only made things worse.

'Your phone's been going off. Could be important.'

I picked my phone up from the coffee table. Juno had called me seven times. Imogen came to the couch next to me and pulled her bare legs up beside her. She didn't seem to mind that her feet were touching my butt. I was never going to get her, I decided. She was too together. And she was also right about me. Seeing the girl with the ladybug earrings the night before had derailed me a lot easier than normal people could be derailed, completely thrown sideways out of normal life and into oblivion. The night before it had been earrings but I had a feeling that now that it had been so easy to surrender, now that I felt that beautiful release, the next derailment would be even easier. A woman's laugh. Her smell. And wasn't Martina just my latest excuse in a lifetime of excuses to stop and throw away Frank Bennett, police officer, and get wild? Hurt people.

Break hearts. Damage myself. Was there something in me that liked to be this way? Something a little bit twisted? If I knew my old patterns right, eventually I'd stop waiting for triggers. I'd get into the routine of giving in.

Imogen Stone would be able to see things like that in your eyes. Smell it on your skin. I didn't know a way back from the knife edge. I didn't want her to show me either. See the failure in her eyes when I fell backwards after she'd spent so much time standing me soldier straight.

'There's a way back, Frank,' Imogen said, as though she'd been sitting there sipping her coffee and reading my mind. I hadn't touched mine. I picked it up and found my hand was shaking. It was good coffee. Black tar.

I got up and moved away from her, repelled by her easy morning beauty. Went to the desk by the balcony doors and started shifting things around there like a nosy jerk. Empty coffee mugs, the glossy expensive type you see in specialty tea shops. Dozens and dozens of manila folders stacked in a corner against the wall, spread out over the table top. Client files? I flipped one open.

'Oh ho! Look at this. The juicy, juicy commentary of Sydney's best nutcases.'

'Not exactly,' she said, curling her feet up underneath her. 'I don't bring my work home with me. Well, not usually. But you sort of followed me home.'

I looked at the papers in the folder under my fingers. Crime scene photographs. Photocopied notes. An autopsy report. I lifted the file and flipped through the pages.

'What's this?'

'Looks like the Beaumont children case from here.'

'You writing a book?'

'No,' she laughed, sipped her coffee. 'It's an embarrassing little hobby I have.'

'Evans,' I read through the spines of the files against the wall. 'Lillee. These are unsolved cases.'

'My name is Imogen Stone,' she sighed, a hand on her heart. 'And I am an armchair detective.'

'I can't believe this.'

'I don't know what's so hard to believe about it,' she said. 'I'm a cop psychologist. It's one of the lowest paid and least respected appointments in the field. Something must have drawn me here,' she shrugged. 'I like crime.'

'Look at you. Jesus. I don't know if this makes you more or less attractive.'

She came across the room and took the file from my hands, folded it shut and dropped it among the clutter, the other open files, the pencils and boxes of paperclips and muesli bar wrappers.

'I'm not some ageing true crime groupie. I provided a lead on the Emily Dooville case. Took me a year and a half. Earned me fifteen grand in reward money.'

'Ah ha. I thought those were dollar signs I saw gleaming in your eyes.'

'Jesse Deaver, here – that's up to a hundred grand. Imagine if I cracked that. Hello investment property.'

'What a little capitalist you are.' I smiled. She might have seen a weariness in it because she took up her coffee again and stood near me, not touching me, but warming me somehow with her very presence. I looked down at her and remembered what it felt like to be close to a woman, how it used to make me feel.

'You just have to do one job, Frank. That'll get you back to where you need to be. A bit of focus.'

'Focus.' I nodded.

'Be a cop. A good cop. Morning, afternoon, night. Stop being a man for a while and do your job. Your partner needs you. The families of those girls need you. The next girl in line, the one who's waiting to be the next body you dig up, she needs you. If you can manage to stop thinking about Martina for a while and start thinking about what's happening right now, I think you might be able to put yourself back on the tracks.'

I felt something stir in my chest. Some tightness, some desire, like the pull of magnets against my heart, making it beat in my throat, under my tongue. Funny how words can do that to you, make you shiver, make you feel like you're starving of air. Stone rubbed my hand briefly, the way a mother will encourage a wayward son, and I drank the coffee, felt it making connections in my brain.

'You might be right.'

'That's my job.'

'We should celebrate by sleeping with each other.'

'No, we shouldn't.'

'You're probably right.'

'Have a shower,' she said, taking my empty cup back to the kitchen. 'Then get the fuck out of my house.'

There was something about Eden. Some natural, beautiful thing. Watching her, Juno imagined, was like being privilege to the movements of a majestic and vicious creature in the wild lumbering around the lush gentle world with all its deadly capacity proudly contained, a thing that everyone knew was dangerous somehow, instinctively. Panthers, for example. Sleek. Soft. Curved, not needing to advertise their lethality with spikes or ridges or scales or splashes of colour. Eden was very much like a panther. She slept like a panther. With natural exhaustion. Still as a rock. The unbothered ease of the queen of the jungle. He liked to watch it. It made him feel excited and at peace all at once.

Eden going to sleep was one of his favourite things. She had a long wind-down procedure. Unlacing her boots seemed to take minutes. She'd unclip a pocket knife from her belt, an old and much-used thing it looked like, fold it open, examine it. She would arrange things by the bedside, the knife, her phone, a pencil and paper. She sometimes used the pencil and paper, but he couldn't figure out what she scribbled when she sat bolt upright in the early morning hours. Sometimes he thought it looked like names. Now and then she'd made a list and crossed them off one by one, her frantic breathing easing as she did, becoming the calm intake and exhale of sleep once more. In the mornings she always threw the lists away. She never mumbled or spoke in her sleep.

Sometimes Juno wondered whether Eden forgot about the cameras at night. But she never forgot in the morning when she disappeared into the bathroom, lifting the pendant over her head and setting it on the counter beside the sink. Beige ceiling squares inlaid in plastic, flowers of black mould like a meeting of spiders in the corners of the room. Juno had almost memorised their patterns.

Juno wondered if he was getting too close to Eden. He supposed that was a natural effect of surveillance work. Frank had warned him about it, said he'd spent two weeks watching a beautiful female drug dealer in his early days and had got himself all worked up about her. Small hot car. Hours alone. It had made the final arrest difficult. Impossible to follow the case in the paper after it left his hands. Afraid to know the sentence. Like she'd been a girlfriend. An ex-lover. In his mind they'd been together for years. In truth they'd spent a wordless car ride together to the station and that had been it. It had all been a dream.

'Nothing but your dick, the girl and as much junk food as you can cram in the passenger seat,' the cop had said, watching Eden on the screen with minimal interest. 'You start to think you know what they're thinking after a while. Start to put your thoughts into their head. Truth is you don't know a thing about them. You could watch her for the rest of your life. You don't know shit.'

That was what had set Juno off. The matter-of-fact way he'd said it, leaning back on the milk crate in the corner of the van, his legs spread and his eyes already lazy on the Jack Daniel's. *You don't know shit.* Said with the conviction of a man protecting his wife from the glare of a rival male, said with all the arrogance of a beast with a beauty on his arm he didn't, couldn't, appreciate. Frank was one of those hard cops who had spent too many years throwing his weight around to understand authentic interactions with other males any more. He had spent too long knowing that his role in the force automatically put him above every man in every room he ever entered, no matter their size, their intelligence, their capability, their history. He was one of those cops who used his badge to snag women. Juno could tell. Really, it was a weak way to live. Take the badge away and all you have left is a man with an ego problem. He wondered if Frank and Eden had ever gotten together in their time as partners. Small hot car. Hours alone. He doubted it. Eden was clever enough to see through shit like that.

Right now she was going through the boot-lacing proce-dure, strands of her bleached hair hanging in the lens of the camera, her wiry hands tugging the laces with unconscious fierceness like she was tying down a hog. She stood and Juno got one of his rare daily full-face shots of her as she tied her hair in the mirror, swept it into a bun at the nape of her neck, brushed her blinding white teeth for three and a half minutes like she did every day as though it was something she timed. Cleanliness was her thing. Organisation. Discipline. She'd be suffering out there beyond her natural environment. Juno sympathised. His cramped little van had become like a stinking cave, never long enough or wide enough to accommodate him, never sunny enough to dispel a strange dampness that covered everything. The blinking of the monitors and the humming of the machines was like the stirring of organs inside a creature that had swallowed him. It was good to feel that he shared something with Eden, even if it was only discomfort, a longing for home. Juno slapped his cheeks, cleared the burger cartons off the makeshift desk into a garbage bag near the door and tried to get a hold of himself.

Eden walked out into the daylight and turned towards the back fields. It was too early for work, for breakfast. Juno frowned. Maybe she was heading to the kill sheds to take samples while everyone was asleep. Eden's hands appeared on the screen. Three tiny evidence bottles, no bigger than toothpicks, that she examined quickly before putting them back in her pocket.

Frank had been wrong. Juno was inside her head. The evidence of it was everywhere. She was like his avatar, following his commands on the screen, her powerful body stalking across the landscape – part of it and yet somehow unbelonging. Juno got Eden. Men like Frank didn't get women like Eden.

Eden in the kill sheds. Gloves snapped on fast as lightning, a quick glance towards the doors, and then she began. She knew just where to go. The sorting tables. The slaughter line. The tools. If there was human blood here it would stand out among the pig blood like a fox on a bunny farm. One cell, one single cell, would add to the story. It would be near impossible for Rye and Hart to explain the girls' blood here. This was a man's space. Maybe blood from the missing girls found here wouldn't be enough to convict, but Eden was a hunter and she would hunt down whatever she could – a whisper here and a blood droplet there, clothes charred and burned and left on a cliff edge. She would find hairs and fibres and text messages left behind, sniff out the missing girls, gaining momentum like a hound running after a scent, closer and closer until she made her catch. That's how Eden lived and breathed. For the hunt. Juno knew it.

Eden capped the bottles and pocketed them. She left the kill sheds through the back doors and started heading into the bush. Juno watched. He crossed his legs, tried to tap into Eden's mind. She was probably going out to see if the burned clothes had been taken overnight. Of course they hadn't. Frank wasn't answering his fucking phone. He was probably drunk. Flashing his badge around.

Eden turned. Looked. Turned back around. Kept walking at an even pace.

'I'm being followed,' she said.

Juno sat up on his milk crate. Felt his muscles tense in unison, his whole body rock hard at once and then shivering with energy. There was no indication of his own terror in Eden's voice. Her feet kept the same rhythm, the camera on her chest looking forward into the wall of green before her.

'Nick Hart's following me,' Eden said, touching the pendant as though to make sure it was still there, making the microphone crackle in Juno's van. 'He's at about a hundred metres, following slow. Making no effort to conceal himself.'

'Oh god,' Juno said aloud. He grabbed for his phone, dialled Frank's number. It rang out. 'God.'

Eden kept walking. Her boots sometimes crunching on gravel and leaves, sometimes soundless on dirt. Her progress seemed achingly slow. She turned and Juno caught a glimpse of the tall lanky figure of Hart between the trees, following the same path through the undergrowth. He seemed no closer. A hundred metres or so. Within shouting distance. In eye-contact distance. And he was making eye contact. Juno could see that. Cold, expressionless, the eyes hollow across the morning shadows.

'He's not gaining,' Eden whispered. 'I'm not slowing.'

'Get out of there . . .' Juno cringed. 'Get out of there!'

She was heading deeper into the woods. Juno couldn't understand it. Paths forked in front of her frequently and each time she headed into the dark. The white morning light above her was disappearing. Juno cranked up the contrast on his laptop. She turned again and Juno caught the edge of Hart's shoulder between the trees, rounding a bend.

'Let's play, baby,' Eden whispered.

Juno felt his breath seize in his chest. His stomach was clenched. Eden stopped walking and turned around. He could hear her breath. It was slow and deep. A sleeper's breathing. This didn't rattle her. This was a game. Juno scrambled for his phone, dialled Frank again and listened to the phone ring out.

Nick Hart locked eyes with Eden for a moment, only a moment, before he heard the snap of her pocket knife as it slid open in her fingers. Hart smirked and Juno saw his whole body jolt with the laugh. The tall man followed the fork in front of him down the embankment and back towards the farm. Juno panted as Eden returned to her walk.

They tell you in the academy that if you're ever charged with being the leader of an exercise, sitting down is about the worst thing you can do to establish your authority. A straight-backed, upright stance and a steady gaze tell the other apes you're in charge apparently. By the time I left Imogen's apartment that morning, managed to wrestle the image of her out of my mind, listened to Juno's frantic dribbling updates and hit the station I was already ruined – and it was only midday. From there I'd briefed the captain, assembled a team, located where Juno thought Eden had spotted the evidence on an aerial map and then grabbed a quick kip in the downstairs change rooms to avoid collapsing at my desk in front of everyone. I probably looked like a drunk, and I knew I smelt like one, but there was no call for acting like one in front of the young and impressionable beat recruits shuffling in and out of the bull pit. It would be a decade and a half before any of them had any excuse to get this run-down.

Night had fallen by the time I got to Rye Farm. As the convoy of lights began heading up the highway towards me, I was sitting with my arms on my knees in front of my own car, trying to will myself to stand before any of my cronies saw any weakness. I was getting a good deal of clean thin country air into me, which should have given me some inspiration, I told myself. The police-issue flak jacket and cowboy guns didn't help my vertical thrust. Eventually I moaned at the stars, held my breath and dragged myself up by my bumper as the convoy switched off their lights and rumbled into a rough half-circle in front of me. I had a couple of beat cops for muscle work if any were needed, a couple of forensics specialists and a cadaver expert with a dog. Both of the forensics ghouls were women I'd seen around the office but never met – matching ponytails and serious faces, the type who read a lot and smiled a little. I introduced myself as we waited for the cadaver guy to unload his dog. One of them was Nicky, but I didn't catch the other's name. She mumbled it into her chest as she checked her gear. The hound was a shimmery caramel-coloured thing with a pink nose and against all expectations it dropped out of the cabin of the handler's truck, bounded over and hurled itself at me.

'Dog, I've got enough trouble standing upright without you.'

The beast shook itself, barked and tried to dance with me. I looked off towards the ridge over which the main body of Rye's Farm lay.

'Bones, get down.'

'You need to get this dog to shut up or you're going to blow this whole thing,' I told the dog's handler. He was a worried-looking guy, a brow creased prematurely from much disappointed frowning at unruly pups, I imagined. The thing was wearing a blue-and-white chequered police-pattern collar. I heaved a sigh.

'Sorry. Sorry. He's just excited. He's one of my best, really.'

'Really?'

'Really.'

'What the hell do you call this? Your dog's wearing a cop costume?'

'I got it at my kid's fete. Thought it was cute. Jesus. She is a cop. Sorry.'

'Dog's name is Bones?' Nicky the forensics ghoul asked.

'Yuh.'

'Bit morbid, isn't it?' she snorted, glanced at me. 'Like calling him . . . Detective Stab. Detective Strangle.'

'Detective Bludgeon,' her friend laughed. One jostled the other with her elbow. These girls were more fun than I thought.

'What is this? National Pick on the Dog Handler Day?'

'Alright, alright.' I took the map from my hip pocket. 'Take a look at this everyone, and we'll get going. I've got a bed calling me.'

I flattened the map out on my knee and spread it on someone's hood. I'd made a bunch of notes on it during Juno's call and now they were barely distinguishable from the mess of lines and ridges. I thanked my past self for having the foresight to highlight in pink. I pointed to the body of the farm.

'We're not even a kilometre out from this boundary fence, ladies and gentlemen, so the first thing I want to say is that everyone needs to keep their lights and voices down from now until we're back on the road. Minimal radio use. I want you two up there on the ridge looking out, both with a vantage point for our work out here in case we lose comms on the ground.'

The two beefcakes standing in as my lookouts nodded, hands in their pockets.

'What we're actually after is a pile of burned clothes or other cloth. But I want to run the dog the length of the riverbed and see if anything turns up. If it hits on anything subsurface we're to mark it on the GPS and leave it. We're on the edge of an undercover operation so we don't have the time or space for a proper dig around. It's in and out.'

The dog was licking its arse at my feet. I was swiftly losing faith in its natural genius.

'Are you guys close to an arrest here? Shouldn't grabbing any bodies be the main priority?'

I tried to think of a less appropriate time for this discussion and failed. I looked at my watch.

'It'll keep. Situation's rather complex.'

'It'll keep?' Nicky scoffed. Narrowed her eyes. 'This is what you guys do. You make our job harder so you don't have to file paperwork. What about the families?'

The dog handler stroked the dog awkwardly, avoiding human eye contact.

'It's not paperwork, honey.' I pointed to the ridge. 'My partner's up there and she needs me not to fuck up all her hard work by digging up a corpse right under the nose of her targets. Whoever this piece of shit's after next needs me to put him away and keep him there before he can do any more damage. The girl in the ground can wait, if there is one. Risking lives to avoid paperwork is not what I do, so I'm certain you weren't suggesting it.'

Things had gone downhill very swiftly. This is what happens when you come to work half-cocked, I thought. Frayed nerves. The forensics girl sighed and took out her torch. I straightened and sent the beat cops up the embankment. The truth was I was hoping we wouldn't find anything that could be a body. For the girls themselves, their families – and for Eden. Because what I was interested in was justice, not turning back time. If we found something, the countdown would be on to begin an excavation within the legal timeframe. We couldn't hold off if we had any reason to suspect someone might be buried on Rye's Farm. Eden would have to be extracted, and her work would be dismantled. Likely, at the stage we were at, Hart and Rye would get off. We'd be stuck with what we had forensically, which even then would be useless, because it could be argued by any half-witted defence lawyer that sexual or even violent relationships between the dead girls and Jackie and Nick were common knowledge, and they'd expected the forensics to show that. Rape, violence – it didn't prove murder. Very little proved murder. You could put people in the same room as the victim, on the same night, and not prove murder. Hollywood films teach people that finding the body is the end. Most of the time, it's just the beginning. If we dug now, the best we'd get would be rape if we could find other tapes of Hart and Rye's night-time games.

Once the beat cops had left, the forensics girls walked ahead, heads down and torches sweeping, probably discussing under their breath what garden variety of arsehole I was. Only the handler stuck by my side. Some men like to be picked on. It's familiar.

'So your partner's undercover up there?'

'She is.'

'How come you didn't go?'

'She wanted to.'

'Huh!'

'Yeah, women. Women and their ideas.'

The handler let the dog off the leash. He seemed to have established some sweeping motion with it across the riverbed and it followed, scooping the sides, nose down and snuffling, kicking up dust in the torchlight. I stopped and looked up at the stars, stretched my neck.

'Is it just me or did you work on that crazy doctor case?' the handler asked.

I bent my head and kept walking, kicking over stones.

'It's just you.'

'The one chopping up kids and selling their organs.'

'I know the one you mean. Wasn't me.'

'Dude looked just like you. Saw him on the news. I think I read somewhere one of the victims was his girlfriend. Shit like that you only see in movies.'

'Could we possibly focus on what we're doing here? This isn't a date.'

'Right.' The handler took it hard. Nodded ruefully. Might have imagined himself becoming my friend. Maybe this had been a date for him. A playdate with a human for a change, someone who wouldn't love him unconditionally, someone who couldn't be won with liver treats. 'Right.'

I felt bad. Missed Eden. I knew how to talk to her. Mostly I talked and she shot whatever I said out of the air like a slow pheasant. It was a system that worked.

I cleared my throat. 'It's a good-looking dog.'

'She's actually mine.'

'Use her to hunt cadavers in your spare time?'

'Yeah,' he laughed. 'Found me a roo skeleton in my backyard. Must be a hundred years old. Area's been built up since federation.'

Bones the Wonder Dog left the sweeping trail and sprinted ahead past the forensics girls in a blur of fur. Within seconds it was barking in the dark.

'Alright, shut it up.'

'Bones! Sccht! Sccht!'

The beat cops were following us overhead along the ridge line, hands on guns. The hand on the gun made me think they were probably new graduates. The late-night assignment certainly suggested it. They were probably hanging for us to find some bones so they could brag to their little brothers.

The dog had hit on what Eden had probably seen from the ridge line, a colourful patch of cloth half-submerged in sandy earth shifted in recent rains. The two forensics girls fell onto the evidence like scavengers, marking out a couple of square metres around the area, spraying luminol. We switched off our torches and they swept the area with little purple penlights, their words quick and barely audible. With the lights back on, they began excavating into evidence bags, dirt and all.

'Burned elsewhere and dumped,' one said.

'Yeah. Accelerant. Nylon here.'

'Probably lost any of the good stuff. Too much exposure.'

'We'll get a soil composite.'

The talk was almost cheerful. I suppose finding things in the dirt was what these girls had grown up doing. Examining things under microscopes their daddies had bought them for Christmas. Cutting things up in science class. It was probably like digging up treasure. They went about ten centimetres down. The clay was cut like dense cake and scooped in neat triangles. The dog had turned back to its arse again, now and then letting up to examine the air, almost frowning.

'Keep along the riverbed,' I said when the girls were finished. 'I want to go right to the end. There might be more.'

'Come on, Bones.' The handler clapped enthusiastically. 'Let's go, buddy.'

The dog looked at the handler, looked at me, seemed to assess its chances. Then it took off. It turned and bolted for the ridge line.

'Oh crap,' I managed before the handler was off after him. The dog loped up the ridge line and through the hands of the beat cop standing nearest to it before turning towards the trees. It was heading for the farm. I started running, struggling to unclip my flak jacket. I let it fall and hurled myself up the ridge, Eden and that ridiculous police dog collar on my mind.

Eden had decided she liked being around other killers. She always thought if she hadn't been a cop she might have liked to be a prison guard. She thought she might enjoy feeding them daily, watching them, keeping count of them as they slept like so many frustrated and dangerous pets. It wasn't anything that they did or said, but simply their potential that excited her. Some of the times that she and Eric had played their games she'd encouraged him to slow down, to simply *be* in the presence of their killer prize – killers almost always being their quarry. Sometimes she'd have liked to draw the deeds of their prey out of them, interrogation style, know exactly what their hands had done and to how many. How strong they were. How in command of the whispering need she knew all too well. Sometimes she wondered if this attraction to other killers might simply be a desire to be understood by another. Eric certainly understood where she had come from. What she was. But he'd never been big on sharing, enjoying, relishing in their play. It was all frenzy to him. Sometimes she had wondered if it really mattered to him who they killed, whether they deserved it or not.

Now she sat in a ring of people with killer potential. It felt like a treatment meeting, like someone might stand up at any moment and confess a long-held hideous desire, and the others might applaud. The sexless twins sat in the dirt nearby, one drawing pictures with a stick in the fine grains, now and then glaring, heavy-browed, at Eadie. Nick and Jackie were across from her on milk crates on the other side of the bonfire, like assessors, talking quietly between themselves. Not sharing. Eadie wanted them so desperately to share. Perhaps so she could take off her own mask, as she inevitably did, in those moments when her prey came to realise they were in the presence of one of their kind. Hello. Have we met before? Why, yes, we have.

Eadie watched as Nick leaned and fished in an Esky by his side, caught and popped a Tooheys New. She wondered if it had been this way for Michelle Wisdon before her night of terror – the gentle murmur of her friends and co-workers around the flames, the crackle and sparkle of the fire caressed by laughter. Dogs sleeping in the dirt. Milk crates full of brown bottles dusted with cigarette ash. The quiet of a storm not yet broken.

Pea sat among a group of women across the fire, glancing now and then at Eadie. The women were laughing. Pea was telling a story and her voice rose sharply as she threw Eadie a sideways glance.

'I'm starting to wonder if I shouldn't maybe start locking up the female horses,' she sneered. The women laughed. Eadie smirked and looked at her beer in what she hoped appeared to be submission.

Skylar approached from the direction of her and Jackie's van, moody. Eadie hadn't seen her all afternoon. She thought she saw the shadow of a bruise on the girl's left cheekbone as she rounded the fire, ignoring the men on the milk crates, but she couldn't be sure it wasn't the dance of unwashed hair.

The girl came and took a West Coast Cooler from the ice slush in an Esky near Eadie and then stood by demandingly.

'Hop down.' She flapped her hand. 'I want to braid your hair.'

'Your majesty.' Eadie slid off the milk crate and onto the dirt. The girl loosened her hair and began combing it with her chubby fingers. Eadie thought she heard a dog barking in the distance and turned. Skye pushed her head back into place.

'What's up your arse?'

'Jackie,' Skylar grunted.

'Care to elaborate?'

'What?

'What's wrong with you and Jackie?'

'He thinks he can fuck me like a fucking prostitute, that's what.'

'Oh dear,' Eadie laughed. 'No violins and satin sheets?'

'No.'

'Men, ay?'

'It's not like that. You know he used to be romantic, when we first met.' Skylar pulled at a knot in Eadie's hair, hooked her fingers in and yanked.

'I believe you. The violence is unnecessary.'

'We first met in the town. I was doing an apprenticeship in a salon there. I'd been saving for this for ages and I was two hundred bucks off.'

Skylar lifted her foot in her rubber thong and showed Eadie an intricate butterfly tattoo as big as a fist, surrounded by stars. The older woman nodded her appreciation.

'He put the money down straight off. We'd been talking maybe ten minutes. Just pulled it out of his pocket and said, "Here you go." We hadn't even been on a date or nothing.'

'Smooth operator.'

'Now everything's just . . . I'm just some pet. Some dog he's trained to do the washing up. He fucks me like he doesn't know me. Well, shit, man, I like a hug every now and then, you know? I like someone to say I love you.'

'I love you, Skye.'

'You're just saying that because I've got a fist full of your hair.'

'I got some dishes back at the van if it'll get you in the mood.'

'Shut up,' the girl laughed. 'Rug muncher.'

The braid was too tight, but Eadie didn't say anything. She didn't mind the feel of the girl's fingers in her hair.

Eden had rarely been touched in her life. Hades had been a physically distant father, something she trained him into almost from the beginning. There was something sickening about the sensation of being held. She was certain somehow it had come from the night she was ripped from her mother's arms, the night her parents were slaughtered by her kidnappers. Hugs made her feel like danger was approaching. Like goodbyes never escaped from dying lips. Since Eric died, since she had killed him, she'd decided to train herself to accept prolonged physical contact from others. Her brother hadn't liked people coming near her. She'd known that it would be a problem when Frank became her partner. His hungry eyes. His easy laugh. Perhaps it was something Eric had learned from that bloody night too, she didn't know. It had always been that he knew when interest was there, even before Eden did sometimes, and he was always there to stop it.

*

'What are you going to do, then?'

'About what?'

'About Jackie.'

'I'm gonna turn into a dyke and get a job in the city. Wear expensive clothes and drink wine.'

'You can drink wine now. I think I saw a goon bag hanging from the clothes line.'

'Good wine.' The girl nudged Eadie in the back with her knee. 'In restaurants.'

'You don't have to be gay to do all that.'

'Probably a woman would treat me better,' the girl said.

Eadie opened her mouth to reply, tried to think how to begin telling the girl that her life didn't have to be the way that it was, that maybe she didn't have the brains but she certainly had the soul to do what she wanted to do, which didn't sound very ambitious anyway. But her words were cut off when she heard the dog barking in the bush again. Skylar heard it too. The two looked towards the dark horizon. When they turned back there was an extra man in the reach of the fire's glow, advancing from the direction of the gates. Eadie felt the people rising from their seats around her as the man's pace quickened, all but Jackie, who had his back to the danger. The stranger reached down and plucked Jackie Rye from his milk crate.

Eadie felt herself being drawn forward. She knew the man, though they'd never met. She'd met eyes with him once through the glass of the station waiting room. It was Michael Kidd, the missing girl's father.

'Hey,' Skylar screamed. 'Hey!'

'I want to talk to you,' Michael growled. 'I want to have some fucking words with you, you little piece of shit.'

It surprised Eadie how small a man could look in the arms of another. Jackie might have command of the farm and everyone in it, but when he lost command of his own feet momentarily, as Michael Kidd yanked him into the air, all memories of that power were forgotten in an instant. Nick threw himself between the two men. People were joining them, trying to drag the pair apart.

'Where's my fucking daughter?'

'Mick, Mick, you're not thinking straight,' Jackie was saying, the words lost beneath Nick's furious snarls.

'I'm gonna kill you, you fat fuck.'

Nick threw himself forward, was hooked and pulled back.

'I want my kid. Where's my kid? What have you done with my fucking kid, Jackie?'

'What kid?' Jackie snarled. 'Mick – '

'What? What? What have you done with her?'

The big man was heaving as though on the edge of sickness, or tears. Gritted teeth. He lunged for Jackie again and arms got in his way.

'Just settle the fuck down and come talk with me. Come talk with me away from everyone else.'

'I'm not going anywhere with you, you piece of human trash. You've killed my fucking kid.'

At the edges of the gathering, men and women stood and stared, hands by their sides, looking to each other for explanation. There was none. None of these people, Eadie guessed, even knew Erin Kidd was missing. Who she was. That she had been here once, a grubby face among grubby faces, a hand that passed the bourbon bottle. She looked at Pea's group and saw

Sal, her mouth still swollen into a huge sagging grin, blinking confusedly at the others.

'Is that Keely's dad?'

'No,' someone said. 'Erin's.'

'Is Erin missing too?'

I ran. I used to run when I was a teenager, to pretend I was running from something and get all frantic and determined about it as I pounded suburban streets lit purple and gold by twilight. Used to dodge cars and kids on bikes and mothers talking on the footpaths in front of houses, wind my way out from the cramped streets to the Georges River and sit there on the bank as the night closed in. I was sort of a quiet kid. A wanderer. I liked the cold air in my lungs. But it's been years since I was that animalistic. Booze and beat-cop kebab dinners got a hold of me. Muscles I built then are long gone. As I pounded through the bush after the shadow of the cadaver dog I found I couldn't dodge anything – tree branches whipped at my face and arms, caught at my shins. The ground was uneven at best, uphill, and sometimes sheer bracken that thundered and crashed under my weight. My best bet was to catch the dog before it got out into the flat bare earth by the farm, because I knew if it got sight of other animals out there it would really go. Right now it was at a medium pace, stopping to snuffle just within shouting distance, galloping away when it saw me coming. I saw a glimmer of fire between the trees and grunted, shoving myself forward down an animal trail. I felt a splinter of pain in my left knee.

I'd gained on the beast by less than ten metres.

Without warning it stopped on the path ahead and looked back at me. I skidded to a halt, barely able to huff words.

'Stop. Bad. Dog. Bad dog. Come here.'

The dog stared. I caught its eyes at the right angle and they glowed green. I could hear my team crashing through the bush somewhere behind me. I stepped forward carefully, arms out in what I hoped was a friendly gesture of welcome. What came out of my mouth was not as friendly.

'Come here!' I snapped.

The farm's dogs barked and Bones' eyes widened. I threw myself forward and grabbed at the beast's legs, got hold of a back paw, a hard toe, and yanked it. The thing yelped, was out of my hands and staggering for a second. I fell forward and wrapped my arms around it. We were metres from the edge of the bush.

Skye was trembling when Eadie put her hand on the girl's arm, wrenching her attention away from the men as they turned and trudged towards the caravans. Her eyes were wild. For someone so accustomed to violence, that directed towards Jackie seemed to reach her tender core. Eadie wondered if the girl really loved the creep, if tearing herself away from this life would be more complicated than she first imagined. Eadie had never really been attached to anything or anyone that way. Her relationship with Eric was too complicated to be called love. She loved Hades, she guessed, but she couldn't be sure. She knew she would be upset if he died. Was that love?

'You alright?'

'That was scary,' the girl said. 'Where did he even come from?'

'No idea. I wish I knew what they were going to talk about though.'

'Same. Let's go spy.'

Spy. Always the curious child.

'You'll get us in trouble,' Eadie said, leading the girl towards the vans.

'It'll be alright if we don't get caught.'

They left the crowd at the fire and skirted around the back of the vans. Eadie almost tripped over Skylar as the girl hurled herself into the long grass beside the caravan and crawled forward on her forearms. Eadie, snuggling in beside her, put her hand in something damp and soft and imagined dog shit. A cloud of fruit flies swelled around her and she smelt organic rot. A peach.

The men's legs were within arm's reach. A cigarette fell and sparkled like a star.

'There are two other girls missing,' Michael Kidd was saying, 'And they've both been out here, and if you think – '

'Missing how? Are the cops onto it?'

'You bet they're fucking onto it. No one's heard from these kids. No calls, no bank account movements, no sightings, fucking nothing.'

'Who are the other two girls?'

'You know who the other two fucking girls are, you little – '

'Hey, back the fuck up, dickhead, or I'll go ya. I'll go ya before you know what your fucking name is,' Nick said through his teeth, his big feet shifting in the dirt.

'Who are the other two girls?' Jackie's voice was low, calm. Skylar was wiping her nose on the back of her wrist beside Eadie.

341

'There's a sex tape,' Michael said.

Silence. Eadie felt her pulse hammering in her neck.

'There's a sex tape of you two and some girl from Chatswood or some shit.'

'Mate, you don't know what the fuck you're talking about.'

'If you've done anything with my kid – '

'You better tell me who the other girls are or you'll be the one the cops are looking for.'

'Ashley Benfield. Keely Manning.'

'Ashley Benfield's in Freo.'

'What?'

What? Eadie thought. Skylar was brushing her hair roughly back from her face.

'The flies!' the girl whispered.

'Ashley Benfield's boyfriend ripped off the Liquorland on Green Point Road,' Jackie snorted indignantly. 'Jordon Brown. She'd been working there last year for a little while before she came here and she gave him the back door codes. The two of them ran off to Fremantle.'

'You're lying.'

'They snagged about thirty grand, from what I heard. Melbourne Cup Day. She was just kicking off a nice sugar habit so they've probably blown it all by now. Mate,' Jackie shrugged, 'you can believe whatever you fucking like. Ashley Benfield's in Freo and has been for months.'

Skye huffed hard through her nose to clear a fruit fly that had landed in her nostril. Eadie froze, and Nick's feet swiftly rounded the side of the caravan.

'Tha fuck is this?'

'Sorry! We're sorry. We just wanted to know what's going on.' Skylar put on her best whiny face, looked at Eadie for help. She said nothing.

Jackie and Mick emerged from the side of the van. Jackie spat at his feet, flicked his cigarette away.

'Having a good old stickybeak, are we, Eadie?'

Michael Kidd's brow dipped slightly at the sound of Eadie's undercover name. The big man's eyes examined her silhouette in the soft light of the distant fire. Eadie shielded her eyes, scratched her brow.

'We're sorry, Jackie,' Skylar howled.

'What did you say your name was?' Michael Kidd squinted at Eadie, and she fought the urge to bite the inside of her lip.

'Eadie.'

'Eadie,' the big man repeated. He licked his back teeth in thought. Nick frowned at the big man, then at Eadie.

'You two need to mind your own fucking business,' Jackie snapped at the girls. 'I didn't let you in here so you could eavesdrop on my fucking conversations, either of you.'

'I'm gonna go,' Michael said, backing away. 'I'm going.' The big man turned on his wide foot and walked away into the darkness. Nick Hart watched him go, then let his eyes drift back to Eadie, cold as an empty house.

'What was that all about?' Nick's eyes were locked on Eadie's. 'Do you know him?'

'No.'

'You sure?'

'Both of you get the fuck outta here.' Jackie waved his arm before Eadie could answer, fixing Skylar with a glare and a pointed finger as she tried to hide behind Eadie's arm. 'And don't you come back to the van tonight, you nosy little slag. I don't want to see your sneaky, deceiving fucking head.'

The two women turned and fled. Skye's hand drifted into Eadie's and squeezed her fingers, wet with terror.

'We're in big trouble,' she said.

'You said it,' Eadie agreed.

There was something about art that took Hades' mind away, put him in a place of swirling paints and flying sparks and woodchips, where there was no thought, only sensation. It was like he imagined exercise to be, though he'd never been any kind of athlete. He would begin a project, become a machine himself fixing and bolting and sawing and welding, oblivious to the labour he was putting his body through until he was left exhausted and filthy and sweat-drenched at the end of the day. He'd lock his workshop and shuffle up the hill towards the shack like an invalid. It would take a burn or a carelessly wielded hammer to bring him out of the warm, lofty place his work took him. And right now he was grateful for such an escape. It was four in the morning, and since midnight he had been tossing and turning in bed listening to the sounds of the tip, wondering which of them were animals, things rotting and falling over, the wind shuffling things around, and which was his stalker.

His current project was a four-metre-high Australian swan preparing to take flight, wings spread and long neck bent, made almost completely from polished copper pipes intricately interwoven and coiled and braided. It was a finicky job, a noisy job, and it shut him into a world away from Adam White.

The endless delicate puzzle made his old hands ache, gave him pain to focus on. Hades stood by the frame of the thing with his eyes glazed and his hands restlessly fusing pieces together to construct the head on his thick wooden workbench. He was happy, for a second or two.

The first lump of brick came through the glass panel of the workshop door. The sound of it split the thin bush air like an explosion. Hades fell off his stool and hit the ground. He held a hand up against the attack, whatever it was. Glass all around him. The old man didn't even see the projectile. He wondered if it was a gun blast.

Hades crawled to the nail cabinet and grabbed the Colt he kept there and pulled himself up by the edge of the workbench. His tools were everywhere. The second brick came through the east window and showered the tabletop there in glass, sprayed fragments all over his tools, his papers, his books. The sound was just as unexpected, just as deafening. Shards of pain prickled his chest and arms. Even with the first two blown out, Hades wasn't prepared for the last window to explode inwards, glass raining on his shoulders as he hunched against the impact. He ran to the workshop door and charged through it, expecting to find one of two things – an unhappy client with a gun trained on him or a bunch of kids fleeing into the dark. What he found was Adam White standing at the base of the hill, a video camera in his hands.

Hades knew immediately who he was looking at. The boy had Sunday's feral cat eyes, the same sly slouch to his shoulders as the humour of the situation rippled through him. The boy smiled and lifted the camera as Hades tried to catch his breath.

'You have no idea what you're doing, kid.'

'Oh, I don't know. I think I'm making a good go of it, bro.'

Hades lifted the pistol and pointed it at the boy's head. It had been years since he had felt such hard, heavy fury, the kind that sat between his temples like smouldering coals and made his eyes pulse. The old man had thought his raging days were over. *This is how you have a brain aneurism,* Hades thought. *This is how you give yourself a stroke.* The gun trembled in his calloused hand. Sweat was rolling down the back of his thick calves.

'Do it,' the boy said.

Hades didn't do it. Not right away. His trigger-happy days were gone, he knew that much. He knew what kind of a mess could be created with just a gentle, satisfying pull, an exhale of breath, a letting go of thoughts. It would be so easy. He reached into his pocket, the gun still wavering on the boy, and dialled one of only two numbers in the device with his thumb.

'Hades?'

'I'm holding a gun on your creepy little spider,' the old man trembled. 'You better tell me quick why I shouldn't just exterminate him right this second.'

'Jesus Christ, Heinrich,' Frank said.

'I said quick.' The old man clicked the hammer back into place. Adam White laughed, though Heinrich could see his body was shaking. This was a thrill. A terrifying, satisfying thrill. Something long planned, long worked for. Heinrich felt for the first time the dangerous nature of the boy before him.

'Just wait a second. Wait. He's got you on tape. Right now, he's taping you,' Frank said.

'I'll bury the tape with him.'

'Hades, listen to me,' Frank's words tumbled into each other, 'that camera he's holding is wireless.'

'I don't know what the fuck that means.'

'It means he's filming it there and it's recording somewhere else.'

'How is that even possible?'

'It's possible.'

Heinrich grunted with rage.

'Heinrich,' Frank's voice was calm, but trembling. 'If you shoot Adam White right now I can't help you get out of the mess you'll be in. And it'll be a big mess. You can take my word for it.'

'Is he putting a leash on you, Hades?' Adam White laughed, the zoom on the camera extending slowly like an accusatory finger. 'Is he getting his muzzle out?'

'Heinrich? Heinrich? Don't do anything stupid.'

'I'm being terrorised here. I have a right to defend myself.'

'Sure. Sure. You can tell them that in court.'

Hades thought. Dropped his aim.

'You better solve this thing the right way before I do it my own way, copper,' the old man snarled into the phone. 'There's only so long I'll play this stupid game.'

'I'm on it, Heinrich. I'm doing the best I can. I'm doing the best I can with the time I've got.'

Hades was hardly listening to the copper's placations. He was watching Adam White walk off into the black forest.

I knocked on Dr Imogen Stone's apartment door with my heart still hammering from Heinrich's phone call. Since 2AM I'd been sitting in my car in the street outside Camden trying to get my thoughts in order, the terror of almost losing a police dog into the middle of Eden's undercover operation leaving me jittery and uncertain. Juno had texted me some business about one of the missing girls' fathers barging into the farm and almost ruining everything all on his own, but I hadn't wanted to read it, to take it in yet. Then Heinrich had called and I'd driven straight to Stone's place. Maybe I was trying to use her to replace the Eden I needed right now, the grounded and practical and unshakeable Eden I'd come to rely on, the kind of woman who would kill her own brother just to make sure all her plans remained on an even keel. But even that was a fallacy, wasn't it? I had no idea how Eden operated. I couldn't possibly imagine what went on in that funnelweb mind. Maybe I would get a bullet in the brain when I became inconvenient, when I threatened her plans. *I'm sorry, Frank. You were warned.*

'Frank? Frank?'

I looked up and realised Imogen was standing in the doorway staring at me and I had to shake my head to clear my thoughts before I could answer her.

'Frank?' That robe again.

'Hi.'

'What the hell are you doing here?'

'You tell me and we'll both know, honey.'

'It's the middle of the night.'

'It's the middle of the morning, really.'

'What?'

'We're mere hours off bacon and eggs.'

Imogen shook her head, tried to get a hold on what I was saying.

'Have you slept?'

'No.'

'Get in here,' she scolded and held the door open. 'Jesus, this is the very definition of inappropriate.'

She pushed her hair behind her ears and went into the kitchen, took a bottle of milk from the fridge and drank from it, thought I couldn't see her. I heard the flip of a kettle switch and the kind of sigh you only give when someone you know is so beyond help they're beginning to undermine your faith in humankind. She came and sat next to me and rubbed her eyes, and I took one of her hands and held it in both of mine.

'I like you,' I said.

'I get the feeling I'd like you too if you weren't such a complete catastrophe,' she yawned. Squinted. Yawned again. 'I'll make the coffee. We need coffee.'

She went into the kitchen and started moving things around. Packet of some wanky espresso coffee from the freezer, the elastic band twanging. I fell asleep on the couch before she got back.

*

I got home around midday and went straight to the fridge, grabbed a beer and popped it on the counter. Didn't even look at the cat – no, because the cat was Martina, was an acknowledgement that she wasn't really gone from my life and that it was far too early to be even hanging around other women that even half meant anything to me. I stood by the fridge and looked out the window at the apartment block behind mine and told myself that the cat meant nothing, that I wasn't 'cheating' on Martina because Martina was gone now. Long gone, in the ground gone, deep and restful, the same place I had put the man who killed her, died with no thoughts of me on either of their minds. That train of thought didn't help. Wasn't Martina still alive for me, not only in her cat but in Imogen? Wasn't the major thing that had drawn me to Imogen all of that old-world survivalist intelligence wrapped up in beautiful golden skin, hidden behind dark knowing eyes? Imogen could get herself out of a dog cage and walk six kilometres in the dark only to run into and conquer her killer. Imogen could love me no matter how washed up and wrung out I was, how much potential I had to get worse, to completely surrender myself to this job. Was that going to be the criteria from now on? How much like Martina my partner could be?

Greycat was giving me a good shouting down. The thing that brought me out of my reverie was a claw penetrating my jeans high up on my right thigh, pretty close to some of my crucial bodily equipment. I shook the cat off and got out its biscuits, took them to the balcony with the beast in hot pursuit and poured them with a clatter into its bowl. The thing nudged its head into the stream of biscuits as I poured, scattered them onto the concrete. I really needed to spend more time with it.

'Just. Hey! Slow down, fatty.'

I sat in the old armchair I keep out there and looked at the traffic, thought about Hades' problem. My problem. Adam White wasn't going to leave Hades alone until I could find out who killed Sunday, and I was beginning to realise something like that was going to be virtually impossible. Cold cases this tricky needed a team – they were the type picked over by armchair detectives like Imogen for decades without being taken up seriously, the type written about in true crime books, used in the early papers of budding historians working on their PhDs. Usually it was child murders that made it out of the decades of darkness and towards some sort of resolution. They earned armchair detectives the most reward money. Next after children came well-to-do women. Then politicians and actors. People were still staying up all night over who really shot JFK. You could watch the event re-created digitally from ten thousand different angles. The problem was, no one cared about a black girl from the seventies who was no good to nobody, a girl with no real standing in the world, a girl probably only ever loved by a couple of people, one of them being Sydney's worst gangster. It was no surprise to me, thinking about it, that Adam White got his mind set on Hades being Sunday's killer. He'd probably been the only person on the earth who really minded if she lived or died.

Jimmy. Kimmy. Whoever this friend or co-worker of Sunday's was, she was probably my best bet at getting into Sunday's world. My brief search into Lynda's known associates hadn't turned up any Jimmy, Kimmy, Jenny, Kenny or anything close to the mark. Her best friend was a woman named Rachael Cricket, a dumpy character with a big grin who was in the mugshots with Lynda brandishing a long green tattoo of a cartoon bug in a top hat. The two had been arrested for shoplifting. That was all I knew. Finding Jimmy or Kimmy was the only way forward I could see, my only means of understanding what the White girls were up to back then, because I'm sure Hades, much as he loved Sunday, was hardly privy to half of it.

Women and their secret lives. Even the most forthcoming of women were a labyrinth of mysteries and histories, of things remembered and things noted and things cherished that couldn't possibly show on the surface of their world, things hidden without reason, simply because women were protective – hell, they needed to be. I got the feeling Imogen Stone had plenty of secrets, that I could spend years digging into her perfectly structured life uncovering pieces of her, vulnerable pieces, which she'd been trained all her life to protect. Martina too. But I didn't want to think about Martina again. I shook my head and cracked my neck. Drained the last of my second beer.

The cat was pouncing and flopping onto its side in the corner of the balcony, scrabbling with something, getting dust and hair clumps stuck in its thick fur. I got up and went over to rescue the creature caught in its clutches and pulled a fairly extensively chewed cricket from its teeth.

'You're disgusting,' I told the cat. I reached out and flicked the wretched insect off my palm into the air above the parking lot. I watched it sail into the garden below among the cigarette butts. It lay there, black in a sea of orange fellows. A cricket out of place.

I stared off my balcony and the realisation hit me like a punch.

Insects, *Caesar told himself*. They're all insects. *Crushable. Squash-able. To be trapped in jars and set aside on shelves, any of them he chose to pluck from their wriggling, twittering drove. There were endless varieties of them creeping and crawling all over the city, all over him, up and down the walls of Dominique's place where he sat brooding over his scotch at the head of the big private table. Most of the spiders were squatting fat and drooling, waiting to munch the worker ants and buzzing flies and dripping parasites who rushed through the door at him. They would leap up and tangle them up before they got too close, because Caesar hadn't wanted anyone too close to him lately, not with all the people who kept falling. Whoever this Nevermind was, his nemesis, he had some incredible power at his hands, and he was wielding it mercilessly.*

It was the fall of the boy with the rose thorn that had sent everyone packing. Caesar stood watching the kid writhe and spasm out his last kicks of life on the floor and knew he was watching his empire die, watching his own fall. No one wanted to be with him now. The dock workers with their bags of goodies had stopped coming. The people he sent after them never arrived, never returned. Doors his men knocked on went unanswered. Caesar needed to find out who was after him and quick, before his last few spiders fled the web.

It didn't help that he was deteriorating, becoming a shell of his former self. It had been difficult in recent weeks to let anything pass his lips – food or promises. A single hair bone in a fillet of fish left him coughing and spluttering and washing out his mouth. A girl he employed to taste all his food had keeled over in the candlelit foyer of the State Theatre in front of eighty people, cried bloody tears, chewed her own tongue in half. A profiterole. There'd been four men in the kitchen. Five waiters on the floor. A maître d' of sorts checking the platters as they went out, wiping the edges with a white linen cloth. Ten people. Caesar was sure if he rattled hard enough it might lead him to whoever was behind this torture. When Caesar stormed out to the car his driver, of all people, had pointed out that any one of the guests might have slipped something onto the tray as it was going by – the food was late, people were grabbing hungrily at the treats, elbows jutting and arms reaching over. Caesar had his guard pull the driver out into the street and give him a good taste of the concrete. He didn't need a driver's advice.

It didn't seem to be food alone that was a threat to him. The rose thorn in the coat proved that. He had started wearing the same set of clothes and boots and socks over and over, keeping them on a chair by his bedside. He checked the lining of his hat in the sunlight, brushed it out with a wire brush he kept by the door. One of the hussies who followed his party around had felt the point of a walking stick or an umbrella graze her calf as their party passed another outside the Hero of Waterloo. Nicked a hole in her stocking. She'd gone down when the light-pink scratch had gone black within the hour and she started coughing her guts up. She survived but lost the leg. Caesar hadn't even known it had happened. He'd been up the front of the pack with his lieutenants, making himself visible.

He stopped shaking hands with people. Stopped letting people come near him. He knew people had noticed the hollows in his cheeks, the weakness in his walk, the way he jumped when little street urchins rushed up to him, when people brushed his shoulders in the street. He didn't care. They could whisper all they wanted. If he ever heard it, he'd have them squashed.

Part of Caesar wondered whether all of this had something to do with Bear and the clean-out of the house in Darlinghurst. Bear had been some kind of potions and lotions magician, someone who could cook up quick, quiet deaths you could hold in the palm of your hand. Caesar looked into his drink, twirled it and watched the ice dance. Bear was dead. He knew that much. His men had told him that the big man had lolled on the ground like a whale while they pumped him full of lead.

He needed to keep his head. He couldn't be seen to be afraid of profiteroles and ghosts.

'Ghosts.' Caesar laughed to himself, looked up and saw Savet watching him. Savet was still by him. Savet was unafraid. Caesar sometimes wondered whether the wild-haired copper had ever felt fear, even knew what it was. He was an interesting man. He'd put together all the plots and plans and partnerships necessary to make the two of them wildly rich. He'd engineered a channel of goods from Nam that was so intricate, so genius, Caesar himself wasn't exactly sure how the whole thing worked. He was just the muscle. The front man. But he didn't mind that. Savet involved minimal people, had minimal labour costs, and flooded the streets with the product, which was selling at a dozen times what it was really worth. All Caesar had to do was smile and collect. The bikies were upset about it. The cops were devastated. The government was loving it, because most of their ground-level stamp-lickers were hooked on the stuff and having the most fun of their young colourless lives. Somehow Savet had managed to put a system in place that would probably go on long after Caesar was dead, had pioneered a smuggling, distribution and management system that generations of criminal overlords would replicate across time to come.

Yet, as Caesar sat looking at him, there didn't seem all that much genius to the man. His eyes weren't the calculating and manic eyes of a genius. They looked bored, in fact, unenthusiastic, resting in turn on the spiders around the table, the junkies shuffling and twitching in the doorway, the regular restaurant customers out in the public area through the tinted glass picking apart their beef wellingtons and licking their chops in the steam. At times Savet seemed more interested in his career in the police than his career on the street, which was bizarre to Caesar. The man had been kicking goals in the homicide department like some kind of budding superstar. They'd already added stripes to him, given him an office with a city window. He'd been in the paper, looking just as bored as he did now. True, Caesar had seen the younger man express enthusiasm a couple of times. His strangling games with the young whores. The way he toyed with the junkies, pushed them around, made them fight one another for cash, then sat and drank as they fish-hooked each other and knocked out teeth. But Savet's main goal seemed to be climbing the ranks of the police force. It wasn't his style, but Caesar could see merit in it. The power he could wield from those upper offices would make him unstoppable. He wouldn't need Caesar anymore. Might do his own house cleaning, in fact, put the older man out of his misery. But none of that would happen if the two of them picked up the wrong bread roll one of these days, drank the wrong glass of wine, slipped on a pair of boots and felt a prick in the bottom of their heel. Surely whoever it was who was after him was also a threat to

Savet. Caesar watched as the cop yawned. He envied the younger man's peace.

Dominique emerged from the kitchen with a tray of water glasses and began setting them among the food on the table, most of it near Caesar's end, piled on plates and untouched. Caesar felt the hair stand up on the back of his neck as she set a glass in front of him. Her eyes never lifted from it. He snatched her wrist. Everyone turned.

'What's this?'

'What?'

'I said – What. Is. This?' Caesar couldn't control the trembling in the hand that held up the glass for all to see, the water rippling dangerously close to the rim, to his fingers.

'Caesar –'

'Look at this glass.' Caesar turned and implored the nonchalant Savet. 'It's clearly pinker than the rest of them. There's a pink tinge to it. It's got something in it. Something pink! I can see it with my own goddamn eyes.'

'It's the light,' Savet said, flicked his chin lazily towards the shelves beside Caesar, those holding the cocktail glasses. 'It's those red candles there.'

'There's a pink stain in this fucking glass!' Caesar screamed. He twisted Dominique's wrist, forced the slender woman to bend down and down to save her fragile bones. She didn't make a sound. 'Don't tell me what I can and can't see.'

'Caesar please,' she wailed.

'Who put you up to this? Tell me who put you up to this!'

When she didn't answer the rage took hold of him. He put her head on the table and held it there, slammed the glass into the surface of the wood an inch from her nose and sprayed glass and water all over the both of them. Only a shard of the base and side remained in his fist, as big as a pocketknife. He pushed it into her cheek. Everyone was out of their seats. All but Savet. No one moved forward. No one would.

'I'll mark you forever if you don't tell me who did this, you sly little whore.'

'I didn't do anything. I didn't do anything.'

'You think you can kill me in my own place?' Caesar snarled, a thin stream of water and spittle leaking from his lower lip. 'Yes, you got your name on the door, you snide little bitch, but I made this place what it is. Without me you'd be out there sucking dicks with the rest of the degenerate scumbags in your line, like your mama before you, and her mama before her. You seem to have forgotten that I own this city. I own it, and I own you, and no manner of man is going to protect you from me no matter what you put in my fucking drink.'

The shard of glass had dug a hole in her cheek just from the force of his words, and it was only the clatter of a tray of glasses as one of the younger waitresses came out of the kitchen and saw what was happening that broke Caesar out of his stupor. He let Dominique out from under his forearms, watched her slither to the carpet at his feet. He barely heard Savet when he got slowly to his feet and spoke. The breath rushed in and out of his weakening frame so hard it sounded like the pounding of the surf.

'Everybody get out,' Savet said.

I stood outside the house in Ashfield and took phone calls, one after the other, hoping at some point to be able to stem the stream of information coming from Juno and the forensics team and get to the door hidden behind dozens of bags of rubbish and cardboard boxes, beyond the waist-high grass of the tiny lawn. Four underling detectives were heading to Perth to liaise with the department over there to see if there was anything to Jackie Rye's tale about Ashley Benfield taking off with her boyfriend. Captain James was threatening to take Eden out of the field if there was, because it seemed to him that a possible double homicide, with the potential for more, wasn't as critical as a triple. Eden's field play was worth three bodies, apparently, not two. Of course, the captain hadn't said as much in as many words. But it was clear. Everything Eden had done would be scrapped if Jackie turned out to be just another double killer and not the kind of glorious sicko serial job that made the department headlines.

I warned the captain that Eden was in a very delicate place and any disturbances to her work, including pulling her in for an interview to justify her position out there on the farm, as he'd recommended, would put her life in danger. She'd already been threatened by one of the victims' fathers turning up and almost making her in front of the very suspects we were interested in. I hadn't mentioned that Michael Kidd's recognition of Eden had been my fault, that I'd mentioned her name in front of the families out at Narellan, that he'd worked out that 'Eadie' had been ingeniously concocted out of 'Eden'. I wasn't sure I was even ready to admit that to myself yet.

When the forensics girl came on the line I moved into the shade of a tree to listen to her report. I knew it would be long. The sun was blazing on my shoulders, making my shirt stick to my ribs.

'There are two sets of female DNA present on a total of forty-two different items of clothing,' she began.

'Forty-two?' I scoffed. 'The stuff you picked up on the riverbed barely filled an evidence bag.'

'Fire is generally pretty good at reducing the size of items, Detective Bennett,' she sighed. 'Big pile of clothes, plus fire, equals small pile of clothes.'

'Alright. I'm the idiot. You're the scientist.'

'Uh huh.'

'I was just surprised.'

'Some of these items, like the bras for example, have been reduced to nothing but a portion of a strap. A hook, in one case. That's all we've got, but if we need to we can reconstruct from fibre analysis, find the brand, the size . . .'

'You're true wonders.'

'Luckily, some of the items are almost fully intact,' she continued. 'The pile was burned very carelessly, almost as an afterthought. One of the items interests us very much. There's back spray of blood on the rear of a cotton singlet. We don't have a report yet, because we're obviously rushing this through at an extraordinary pace – '

'I realise you are.'

'But on sight, a consultant said it's consistent with some blunt-force patterns he's seen. Someone gets hit hard enough and the skull-casing is split in the first blow. Flecks of blood travel upwards as the object comes back over the attacker's shoulder and then downwards as the attacker goes in for a second blow. The victim is usually down by the second blow so you just get this upwards-downwards pattern and nothing else. We've also got scissor marks on some of the items. Jeans.'

'Scissors? Not just some sort of blade?'

'No, the deliberate cuts of scissors, uneven and frequently changing direction. Upwards along stretched seams. The jeans were on someone when they were cut off.'

'Christ. Well. Good evidence of violence. Sexual element to it too. Might get us some more time in the field.'

'Uh huh,' the woman said again.

'Any idea who's been hit?'

'No. We don't have any names on our files. We're scientists. We're impartial. You'll have to wait for the report.'

'Yeah,' I sighed to myself. I'd known that and asked the question anyway. Looking like an idiot in front of this woman seemed to be a compulsion. 'Thanks for all your help, Nicky.'

It's a strange sensation to be glad that evidence has arisen suggesting someone has been hurt, that they're probably dead. Obviously it wasn't what I wanted. I had no malice towards those girls. I felt awful for their families. But from the moment Eden had sat me down and explained the situation, I'd known somehow that they were dead. It had happened, completely out of my hands, and I was more passionate about uncovering what had occurred than feeling unhappy that it had. I guess you lose your heart after a while in this kind of work. You don't give yourself permission to care like that, about everyone. If you did, if you kept it all inside you – each face, each voice, each sick and violent ending – you'd go mad. All I wanted to do was stop Rye and Hart from doing whatever they'd done to the three girls to someone else. Grieving for them was for their families.

As hungry as the new evidence had made me, I had to put that aside and think about Hades' case. Each time night approached he was getting closer and closer to killing Adam White. A man like Hades was only born with so much patience, and what little of it there was would have been worn down over the years. I wasn't sure if White had a death wish but he was sure playing the game like he did. He couldn't know that the fall of his dice would affect so many people – not only Hades but his daughter, and through her, me.

I'm not a religious man, but I walked towards Rachael Cricket's house with some kind of plea running through my mind, to whatever universal power was listening, that she could tell me something about what had happened to Sunday – that out of fear maybe, or love, she'd kept that secret all these years and was somehow willing to give it to me, a stranger, as unlikely as that seemed. I'd managed to track Rachael 'Jimminy' Cricket down fairly easily from her extensive dealings with Centrelink. Not Jimmy, or Kimmy, but Jimminy, named after the same ruefully wise little green sidekick of Pinocchio I'd watched as a kid on VHS. The green bug in the top hat tattooed on her arm. I hoped the nickname had been assigned to her for something she shared with the loveable Disney character, the faithful advisor, guide, conscience. Maybe she'd been there when Sunday went missing. Maybe she'd helped. Maybe she'd share some of her endless wisdom with me.

I was on the porch when I caught the first smell of what was inside the house. I couldn't get to the front door through the bags and boxes and rusting items piled up there. From the rust stains on the tiles beneath the windows, I could see this clutter had been there for some time. A troupe of dogs struck up a cacophony as I glanced in the window. I could see nothing but darkness beyond the heavy drapes. Flies tinked and bumped against the window, trying to find a way out.

'Don't be dead in there,' I murmured. I knocked on the window and one of the dogs started squealing with excitement.

'Rachael? Rachael Cricket?' I breathed deeply through my mouth to try to cope with the stench. 'I'm with the police.'

Nothing. I felt a lurch in my stomach. If Rachael was dead my only lead had dissolved, just like that. Failure. I rapped on the window again. The smell wasn't necessarily something dead, I reassured myself. I didn't get that telltale biological perfume the body gives off in the days after it expires, the gases that build up and swell in the stomach, the fluids that are released. This was rotting vegetables, dog faeces – human faeces maybe. I walked around the house and was hit with the reek of empty petrol jerry cans stacked in a pile as big as a car under the bathroom window, decorated here and there with a variety of hubcaps. Two sheds along the side of the house were stuffed full of hubcaps, in teetering stacks under the spiderwebbed ceilings, thousands of space-age pizzas dripping rust and grease.

I pulled some boxes and bags away from the back door. Drenched my socks in what I hoped was rainwater but knew wasn't.

'Rachael? Police. I'm coming in.'

I don't like things that crawl. I'm happy to admit that. Plenty of men don't like spiders, cockroaches, any half-squishy legged things you might encounter in a lush backyard garden. Things that come wriggling out of the soil. I'm a homicide detective. I've seen more maggots than most people have had handshakes. Men of my type just puff out our chests and clench our teeth and carry on bravely when faced with creepy-crawlies, because that's what you do when you're scared and you know you shouldn't be. But when I forced open the door of Rachael Cricket's kitchen I was faced with more crawlies in one room than I'd ever encountered together. And I was alone, so I indulged myself for a moment in letting my shoulders rise up near my ears, my hands come out from my sides, my lips draw back from my teeth and my eyes bulge from their sockets. Generally, to freak the fuck out as much as a man can standing quietly in one place.

What probably stole my attention first was a large glass salad bowl atop a pile of pots and plates and cups on the counter, a quarter full of orange grease and three-quarters full of large, black dead cockroaches. Here and there shiny survivors of the salad bowl massacre wobbled and shuffled over the piles on the floor, waist-high mounds of everything imaginable. Packets of plastic cutlery. Labelless cans. Papers. Bric-a-brac of every variety, assembled according to no scheme – not what room it might belong in, or how old it was, whether it was organic, plastic, chrome. A baby's rocker. A jar of thumbtacks. An empty fish tank still full of moss-covered pebbles and a wooden cross as long as my arm. More hubcaps, a box of waffle ice-cream cones chewed through by mice and sprinkled with their faeces. Here the flies were in their hundreds, most of them gathered around the windows and the microwave, some rushing over to examine me, my neck and forearms and ears, as I came in the door.

Be dead, I thought. *Don't be alive and living like this.* I drew a breath to call Rachael again, coughed, swept flies out of my eyes. I started wading through the rubbish, pushing bigger items out of my way, crunching others beneath my boots. There had been a path through it all at some point but the piles had collapsed. The hall was filled with books and newspapers to waist height, and then things lost their way with stuffed toys and plastic plants, a collection of umbrellas in their cloth cases that went for as far as I could see, rows of them like wrapped bodies lying in the dark waiting to be buried. A two-metre-high papier mâché flamingo that looked like it had come off an old mardi gras float fell as I passed and slid down my back, blocking the exit through the kitchen, if you could call it that. A wave of claustrophobia rushed over me. The dogs in the front room were going mad.

Rachael Cricket was sitting propped against a mass of yellowed pillows without cases in the far corner of the front room, barely illuminated by the glow from behind the drapes. She was a metre off the floor on a mound of items – cushions and boxes and plastic tubs, books and stuffed toys. For a moment I stood in the doorway and wondered if she was dead.

She looked it. Her skin was jaundiced, the way people get in the first couple of days, and her head lolled to one side. She was all layers – layers of skin folding and folding over each other around her arms and neck, two bony legs poking from beneath a grey blanket. The smell here was worse. I knew from the treacherous path to the kitchen that she was incapable of making a journey down there, and I'd only seen one bathroom off to the right on my way. I tried not to imagine what was in the green plastic bags tied and littered all around the room. There were packets of two-minute noodles here dumped in piles as high as the windowsill. No bowls.

The dogs broke free of the second front room and came crashing over the mounds of newspaper towards me. I picked one up as a gesture of goodwill and held it wriggling in my arms. Its fur was matted with dried hardened shit.

'Rachael, um,' I was suddenly lost. I felt strangely teary. I cleared my throat. 'I'm Detective Frank Bennett. I'm a police officer.'

Rachael said nothing. I jogged the dog up and down in my arms like a babe.

'I'm here about a girl named Sunday White. You used to be good friends with her, a long time ago? I got your name from a . . . a shoplifting case back in seventy-seven.'

Some reaction occurred, though it was difficult to measure from the doorway. It was mainly in her eyes, fixed pupils that suddenly reduced and then flared with what looked like terror.

'You knew Lynda. She was your friend's sister. Until recently, she's been trying to find out what happened to her sister. You probably don't know what happened to Sunday, or you would have told Lynda. But maybe you remember something now.

Something that could help me. Lynda thought it was Hades. But maybe there was someone else who was dangerous. Someone else you girls were afraid of.'

'Plishman,' Rachael said. Her mouth moved, and nothing else. The words came through black teeth and sagging lips. 'Plishman.'

'Yes, I'm a policeman.'

'Plishman.'

'You're not in trouble,' I said, patting the dog while the others snuffled and licked my boots. I needed to go back. Start at square one. 'Do you remember Lynda? Do you remember Sunday?'

'The plishman. The plish.' Rachael's eyes moved to me, locked on my face. 'The plishman.'

I squeezed the dog and felt sad in the doorway, watching as she frowned back at the window, said the word over and over, seemed to ponder what it meant. I said that I would go, but that I would call someone to come back and help her, help the dogs. The hardest part, strangely, was putting the dog back among the others, identical fluffy things that had once been white but were now different shades of brown and black and the rusting red of over-chewed limbs. I straightened and headed for the kitchen.

'Sabbet,' Rachael said. I stopped in the hall, cocked an ear to listen. 'The plishman, Sabbet.'

Eden had spent a long time finding the perfect apartment to call her sanctuary, and she was obsessively protective of it. Admitting people was always an ordeal. Although she wasn't stupid enough to keep trophies of her playtime in the night, she was well aware that she had unconsciously written the secret of what she was in her paintings, her sculptures, her notebooks full of sketches. They contained violence. Sadness. Much of what she explored in her art was how to capture those precious moments with her victims that she could treasure: here agony, here hopelessness, here rage. She enjoyed toying with raw emotions. Never were they so raw as when a victim knew death was coming, had accepted it, had nothing left to lose from submitting to it. It amused Eden that so many story-book victims were fierce and heroic at the end, defiant in the face of their reaper. No one was, in her extensive experience. But perhaps she had been playing too long with cowards.

With only eight hours to relish in her sanctuary, Eden wasn't going to waste it sleeping. She needed a battery change and to report in to the station. Rye had called a stop-work so the irrigation system could be fixed and it would be tight getting out and in again without being noticed. While she waited for Juno, she would burn off some of her frustration.

She hungered for making art the same way she hungered for the kill. She worked at the huge trunk of an ancient red eucalyptus she'd rescued from the clutches of someone she was sure had desired the wood for overpriced outdoor furniture. The trunk had been a well-oiled beauty tormented with black cancerous-looking knots. It had prompted her to dart out of the traffic on the M1 at Kogarah and outbid the other buyer at the counter. She'd been dying to try out a delicate little miniature chainsaw, suitable for wood artists and ice sculptors, but all she could think about as she curved out a figure from the wood was how nicely the device would go through bones.

She didn't hear her doorbell over the growl of the little thing but the flashing red bulb she'd installed above her door caught her eye, and she lifted up her goggles. She was sweating. She left the chainsaw running as she approached the door and pulled it open, hoping the rumble of the machine might diminish the need for any unnecessary conversation.

Juno. The computer nerd. Eden glanced behind him into the hall and didn't see Frank. She let her confusion show on her face. The guy looked intimidated by her dust-covered apron, the oversized gloves, the chainsaw humming away gently in her fist. She revved it a little to cut the gaze, get him talking. He cleared his throat and readjusted the leather satchel hanging from his shoulder.

'Got your batteries,' he said. Handed her a tiny package. She slipped it into the pocket of her apron and tried to close the door. His voice stopped her.

'Everything working correctly?'

'Seems to be.'

'Can you, um . . .' He glanced at the chainsaw. Eden followed his gaze. 'Do you mind?'

Eden switched the chainsaw off. Left it hanging from her arm, a menacing prosthesis.

'Did you, uh . . . I told Frank about Michael Kidd.'

'Frank and I have spoken.'

'Right, of course you have.' The boy nodded, an exaggerated bobbing, and scratched at the back of his neck. He really was very orange, Eden thought. Furred with it lightly, like a newborn pup. He was a marker for the difference in human genetic breeds, carrying with them colours and tinges and lengths and widths. The golden speckle on his arms. Cajun spice on milk. She found herself squinting, trying to get a better look at him.

'Is there anything else?' she said.

'Look . . .' The boy sighed. People only said 'look' when they'd reached the highest point of their discomfort, Eden mused. It was like a keystone of awkwardness. The point where the thermometer cracked.

'I've been . . . spending a lot of time with you lately. You know. Like, um. Frank said that when you, uh, you do a lot of surveillance you can sometimes get closer to people than you really are . . .' He was struggling now, looking everywhere but her face. Eden watched. Sort of enjoyed it. 'So yeah, you know, I get it. I get that over the last couple of weeks I've been spending more time with you than you have been with me, really. But, like, I've got to put it out there. I'd like to spend more time with you. Outside work. You know? And have you spend time with me.'

Eden squinted. Licked her lip. Tasted the microscopic layer of wood dust there, an ancient dead tree, something she understood better than most things, most people. It was times like this, tasting the long deceased soul of an unspeaking thing and looking at the jabbering wet mouth of a living, talking thing that Eden realised just how very far away she was from what she was supposed to be. She shut the door in Juno's face and walked back across the apartment to the stairs. Climbed them. Let the chainsaw roar.

Dr Stone had come to know my knock. I could tell from the smile she had playing about her lips when she opened the door. I slipped inside, into the dark, and let her lead me down the hall with her slender fingers. We fell into whispers in the kitchen, up against the bench, memorising the nooks and crannies of each other's necks and ears and shoulders with our mouths, our noses. She smelled like sleep, like the safety of freshly washed sheets. She lit a candle by a windowsill cluttered with tiny, overflowing pot plants and took two wine glasses from the back of the fridge. Hot night drinker.

'How's the case?'

'Not good.'

'This could go on for years. These late-night visits.'

'What a tragedy for you.'

She laughed. Bit my bottom lip lightly.

'What time is it?' I asked.

'No idea.'

'They want to take it off us. Hand it over to regional. They're saying one of the girls is hiding out in Perth. We've tried to confirm it. It's all nods so far. When they get hold of her it'll be swept off my desk. You'll never hear of it again.'

'Something tells me you won't let that happen.'

'No.'

'Eden?'

'No. No one wastes her time.'

'It'll come good.'

'It will. Something will happen. Some mistake,' I sighed. 'You never know how close you are until it's over. A phone call might do it. An overheard whisper. It's like those guys you see in movies trying to dig through the bottom of prison cells with a spoon. They don't know how deep they have to go. But they have no . . . There's nothing else to do. One day they make one last scrape. There it is. Precious earth.' I leaned back against the counter, drank the wine too fast. Convincing myself more than her.

I was always tired lately. Chasing one hangover with another. The truth was I was getting too old to be an alcoholic. I'd have to make like everyone else in my line of work and find a vice I could carry on for decades, something biologically economical. Planting evidence until I got the sack. Bitterness. Ruining family gatherings. Abusing young people in the street. I could take up jogging again maybe. Run for miles and miles until I slept like a baby.

'You're not trying to dig out of prison, Frank. At least you shouldn't be.'

'I'm digging up something.'

'But what are you burying at the same time?'

'I'll ask the questions and I'll construct the metaphors, thank you very much,' I pointed to my chest.

She smiled, ran her fingers up under my shirt, over my ribs. I let her pull it over my head. Run her nails up through my hair. I felt taken care of in her presence. Maybe it was the whole doctor thing. The certificates on her walls. The expensive waiting-room chic of the apartment. Maybe this was good. Maybe this was what I needed. Someone to take care of me, someone who I didn't need to feel responsible for. I'd failed Martina. It had been my job to watch over her, and I'd skipped out on my duty to chase Eden and her brother, maybe protect the world from them. I gave up the only woman I'd ever really loved to protect people I didn't know. That's how you know you're a cop, I suppose. Those people you don't know become your everything.

Imogen was pulling my belt off. I made myself forget about it all for a moment, scooped her off her naked feet and listened to her laugh against my neck.

It had been a day so long and so hot and so useless to the investigation that Eadie actually felt flattened, as though a great weight was lying on top of her in the bed and refused to give her more than the necessary inches to breathe. A day of being ridden like the horses she cared for – mostly by Pea, who somehow had an eye on every shortcut she tried to take, every stall she didn't clear fast enough, every beast under her care who looked unhappy. In truth, all of the animals were unhappy, and it had nothing to do with Eadie's care for them. They were waiting, all of them, for the weather to break, for the humidity to finally ease. Paint was running. Cows were moaning. Wood was seeping mould. The flies attacked everything, clung to eyelashes and clustered around sweating bellies, walked over food and the rims of beer bottles. Eadie lay in the dark and looked at the ceiling and thought about the missing girls' bones. She was at that reckless point now, that exhausted point, where she fantasised about going out in the dark and simply digging, anywhere, just so that she was doing something meaningful towards catching the men, giving closure to the families, stopping the same thing from happening again. It had been ten solid hours of horse shit and the old woman's watchful eyes. She hadn't had a chance to even lay eyes on Jackie. She'd seen plenty of Nick.

At sunset, when she returned to the caravan, he came from wherever he'd been working and took up a milk crate in the shade of the van at the edge of the nearest cluster, fifty metres or so from her door. He stared at her windows. She stared back at him through the lace, standing well back in the dark of the kitchen. Hours passed. She had dinner in the caravan, showered with her ears pricked and her knife on the counter by the camera pendant. She dressed and came back to the stalemate. Someone had given Nick a beer. He sat with his elbows on his knees, just watching.

Alright, arsehole, she thought. *Watch this.*

Eadie went into the tiny kitchenette, switched on her television and raised the volume. She drew the blind over the window, shut the doors to the bedroom and the hall, and then brought out the rusted toolbox under the kitchen sink. Rolling up the van's boat carpet, she prised up the edge of the internal door to the storage hatch beneath the van. There were two hatches – one leading to the generator and one that went to an old pop-out compartment accessible both from outside and inside the van. Eadie squeezed into the empty compartment, feeling spiderwebs collapse all around her in the corners of the rusting base as she descended into the dark. She took a dusty breath, pulled the hatch closed and felt in the dark for the latch holding the outside door at the back of the van.

Ten minutes, Eadie guessed, she was in the dark. The nuts on the inside of the hatch door were rusted and required plenty of spit and swearing. She got the top two undone and bent the door forward, then slid out into the long grass. She left the hatch hanging and crawled under the fence and into the field. Skirted the field back towards the farm.

There was no one near Nick's van. Everyone was over at Jackie's. It was *MasterChef* night. They would be gathered there in the darkness like they were the night she'd arrived, wretched laughing mouths and glowing eyes lit by the screen. Those strange ugly twins sitting with their legs intwined, mouths open, flashing lights on their wide flat faces. Eadie glanced about, then slipped into Nick's van. There was no possibility of switching on the lights. Her hands fell on dirty dishes and mugs and cups in the kitchen sink, fluttered to the curtains and then the blinds. Tiny cracks of orange light flooded the tiny space as she twisted the knob, opening the blinds. Her fingers were wet with sweat. Eadie squinted and came face to face with a poster of a large spread-legged blonde woman. Hundreds of other porn pictures ripped and clipped from magazines were stuck messily and overlapping on the kitchen cupboards. They seemed to consume the man's interest, those at the back turning hard and browning from sun exposure. Eadie opened the bedroom doors and glanced at the grey, sweat-stained sheets. A teddy bear slumped on its face in one corner, baby-girl pink and helpless looking. More magazines, underpants, dozens of crumpled tissues. Eadie frowned.

The DVD cupboard was by the bathroom annex – a tiny tower of shelves, neatly arranged cases. Cheaply made kids' cartoons, animated series starring foxes and birds and badgers and bears in classic fairy tales. *Sleeping Beauty. Cinderella. Little Red Riding Hood.* Eadie selected *Sleeping Beauty* and popped open the case. A disk labelled with marker: MICHELLE.

Eadie panted, remembered herself and checked the windows again. She popped open *Cinderella* and read the name. DANICA. Shoving the cases back into the shelves, she ripped out others, popped them open and slammed them closed. JOANNA. NONIE. STEPH. PENNY.

No Keely. No Erin. No Ashley. Eadie clenched her fists, shoved the cupboard door closed.

Eadie lay now in the early morning light and felt too tired to sleep.

When the soft knocking came she was on her feet before she knew what the noise was. Only the snuffling and whimpering behind the frosted glass told her there was no danger. She pulled open the door and Skylar came rushing in like a sweaty damp beast newly released from a trap. Eadie was momentarily blinded by lightning cracking above the treetops, distant but approaching fast.

'What's the matter with you?'

She switched on the rangehood light. The girl was drooling blood.

'I can't do this anymore,' she slobbered. 'I can't do this. I can't do this. I can't do this.'

Eadie's hands were prickling as she went to the freezer, animal rage. She popped the ice cubes from the frame and poured them into a tea towel.

'What was the blue about?' she asked.

'Ev-ery-thing,' Skylar sobbed. 'Everything. Is. Go-ing. Wrong.'

'Calm down and hold this on it.'

'I. Can't.'

'Stop talking. You're safe now. Just lie here and be quiet.'

The girl lay down on the left side of the bed, by the cameras.

Eden curled beside her. Didn't touch her. Thought probably she should. Human beings touched each other when one of them was sad, she knew, but something about it seemed dangerous to her. She couldn't care about the girl. Wouldn't. She hadn't cared about another being since her parents' death – besides Hades, and that caused her enough trouble. Caring for Skylar would mean giving something up. Giving everything up.

The girl was snuffling, letting tears and melted ice run down her neck. The bruise was deep in her cheek, probably rattling loose molars. A good side swipe. She'd been knocked about before, Eadie could see in the dim light from the kitchen. Something had split her brow long ago on the same side.

'What did you fight about?'

'Money. His ex. You.'

'Me?'

'He doesn't like you.'

'Most people don't.'

'I want to get out of here,' the girl said, her eyes on the door.

'We can make it happen.' Eadie folded her hands on her chest. 'Let's make a plan.'

'I don't want a plan.'

'Have you got any family out there?'

'I don't want to be with my family.' The girl looked at Eadie. Wet fierce eyes. 'I don't want to plan. I don't want to pack. I just want to go. I want to just . . . run. With you.'

The girl sat up. Eadie sat up with her.

'I can't take care of you,' Eadie said.

'We can take care of each other.'

'Girl, you've got the wrong idea.'

Skylar grabbed Eadie's cheeks, forced the kiss upon her. Salty with tears and shuddering with panicked breath. Eadie sat frozen and felt her mind closing, felt the shutters of her sanctuary coming up one at a time, automatically, an alert triggered and a defence mechanism activated. This was how it was with her, always, the slow shutting down of a machine with a hidden glitch, a thing destined to attempt again and again to get moving, to function as everything else functioned – but unable to, always unable to, because of that missing part. Eadie could almost feel it, the cog turning and getting jammed, the hook reaching and failing to catch. The closer something inched to her, the harder she faltered. She reached up gently and took the girl's hands down from her face.

'Girl,' she said again, 'you've got the wrong idea.'

Skylar looked at her eyes, fat tears rolling down her round cheeks. They lay down together in the gloom, back to back, and let the thunder roll them into an exhausted slumber.

It was storming outside, but the sound of it didn't reach Heinrich through the hollering of the crowd in the cellar, the stomping of feet and the whine of the violin. The only way he knew was the occasional slap of rain gusted against the tiny window of the keg room, the dim flash of lightning yellowed by scum on the glass. He had placed Vicky's powder mirror on top of two wine barrels, and he stood there adjusting the Windsor knot at his throat, the crisp white collar of the shirt she had brought him tight around his thick throat. He finished with the tie, pulled down his waistcoat and took the dark grey wool suit jacket from the chair by the door and slipped it on. He turned. Vicky was watching him from the corner of the room, her arms folded. She had helped him shave off the thick beard he'd grown in the attic. Heinrich felt somehow that she had taken on the years he had dropped in that simple gesture, that his preparations for the coming of his new life had taken something from her. He went to her and she kissed both his cheeks, as much to feel his new skin as to tell him goodbye. Heinrich stood in her arms and listened to the howling outside in the cellar, the roar of the crowd as one dog triumphed over another, as a life was lost to entertain the mass.

'You know where you're going?'

'Jeremy's, room six,' Vicky said.

'Tell her Central Station, platform two. Nine. Make her write it down. She forgets things. She's not to go out tonight. It'll be wild out there. It won't stay in the room for long.'

'Where will you be?'

'Nevermind.' Heinrich buttoned his coat.

'I suppose it might be dangerous to know a thing like that.'

'You'll have money enough for your own protection after I'm gone. I've left compensation with my belongings in the attic. Joe Harper's coming to see you on Monday.'

Vicky dropped her eyes, smoothed out her skirt.

'Why don't you stay?' she pleaded. 'This town will be yours. You'll have everything you ever dreamed of. Everything Bear ever wanted.'

'Bear didn't want this,' Heinrich said. He nodded towards the city through the grimy window, its wandering souls and lost children. 'No one good could want this.'

Vicky watched him go.

There are varying accounts of what happened in the cellar of the Abercrombie Hotel in Chippendale that night. Most who heard the story in the following weeks and months, as it was recounted in bars and clubs and smoking rooms and across kitchen tables, trusted what Dominique Patton had to say about it more than anyone else. Dominique had been standing in the front row, one of the only women among the crowd of spectators. She'd been proudly brandishing a stark white bandage on her left cheek where Caesar Steel had stuck a piece of glass into her only days before, so deep it had nicked her tongue. Some thought she came along not for the sport of the dogs in the pit but to show people what Caesar had done, but no one was surprised at it. And no one had the gall to lift an eyebrow at it because, although it had become a rare sight in a crowded place, Caesar himself was present. Across the pit, by the winding staircase, a slice of what had once been the upright, broad military hulk of Caesar stood shadowed by a group of equally dishevelled, thin-framed men staring into the pit, storm-cloud eyes following the blood as it was pooled in the corner by the attendant's mop. Later all would agree that Caesar looked lost, pressed by the great weight of some tremendous decision, watching all that he had built begin to lean, begin to slide, begin to falter, without accepting the inevitable crash. He was also afraid, Dominique could see. Tired and afraid. But no one could tell if these embellishments were Dominique's own. She was a beautiful woman before Caesar got to her, and the glass had made her ugly inside as well as out.

Three dogs had been lowered into the pit in cages when the young man walked out of the keg room at the back of the cellar. At first, all eyes were on the beasts. Odds were even, and money changed hands furiously, shuffling from fist to white-knuckled fist. The animals were all huge broad-shouldered things shaped more like bush pigs than canines, the result of being worked for months with tyres and lead weights, all of them riddled in their jet-black fur with the pink scars of beatings, cuttings, sharpenings. For two of them, tonight would be a welcome death. They snarled and thrust themselves against the doors of their separate cages, shaking their heads and howling above the rumble of the crowd. Feet started stamping all around Dominique, and she breathed in dog faeces and blood, the sweat of man and beast, spilt liquor so pungent it brought tears to the eyes. The young man in the dark grey suit pushed through the crowd beside her, and for a moment she looked at his eyes, and he looked at hers, unseeing. Her bones ached for a moment with terror, as did those of everyone around her as their eyes fell upon him, a ripple of horror through the bodies pressed around the pit. It wasn't only that most knew the face. The Dogboy of Darlinghurst. A dead boy, long forgotten, now a man. It wasn't the black pistol clutched loosely in his fingers. It was his eyes, the way they wandered calmly across the crowd and then settled on Caesar on the opposite side of the pit. They were hard, the eyes of a reaper.

The crowd fell quiet in one swift wave, as though a curtain had opened on a stage. Caesar seemed to be the last man in the room to see the boy. When he did, he showed no recognition. There was no terror, no rage. He watched the pistol rise in Heinrich's hand, swinging upwards at the end of a fully extended, powerful arm, and when the aim was levelled no words were said. It was as though he didn't believe it was going to happen this way. No one did. There was silence, then the blast and the flash.

Caesar fell into the pit, seemed to bounce sideways off the dog cage just below him and crumple in a pile of clothes and limp hands. The Dogboy stepped down onto a cage and then down onto the bare earth in his shining leather shoes. It seemed someone had given permission for the crowd to react, because everyone at once drew a breath, sucked the oxygen from the room, made it burn. Dominique felt sweat trickle down her neck. Caesar's handlers were gone, dissolved into the crowd.

The Dogboy's bullet had hit Caesar square in the front of his throat, blowing a hole in his windpipe the size of an eye, sprayed ruby-red blood up over his jaw and face, a spotted mask. Heinrich crouched over the older man, the pistol still in hand, and gently gathered the wet folds of shirt at Caesar's throat, lifted him slightly and set him down to wake him from the pain.

'You didn't think I was going to make it soft,' the Dogboy said when he had the old man's attention. 'It wasn't soft for Bear.'

Everyone heard the words, strained their minds at the same time as they flew with excitement to remember what was said, exactly what was said, so they could recall it through history. The silence in the room was church-like. Even the dogs had stopped their racket. Everyone listened as Caesar opened his bloody mouth and began to speak.

'He . . . Ee,' the old man said. He coughed, tried to control his huge rolling eyes, to focus them on the boy. 'Heh . . . Ee.'

Dominique thought it sounded very much like Caesar was trying to ask for help. Everyone did. The blood in the ancient warlord's throat consumed it. The Dogboy stood and looked down at the fallen man at his feet as he writhed and grasped at the wound. Then he turned, just like that, and stepped back up onto the dog cage, onto the concrete ledge where he'd appeared, back from the dead. Dominique was very close to him. She heard Syd Saville, the pub owner, speak to the boy as he paused there. The man handed Heinrich a handkerchief.

'What'd he say?' Saville asked.

Heinrich wiped his hands carefully and returned the cloth. He let his eyes wander briefly back to the man in the pit.

'He said "Hades",' the boy lied. 'He thinks he's already in hell.'

The boy disappeared into the crowd, and as he went, Syd Saville tucked the bloody handkerchief into his coat pocket. Tom Besset, one of the dog owners, yanked the chain connected to the front of his animal's cage and released the creature on Caesar. The dog finished Caesar in seconds. No one watched.

Someone shot Besset dead in the street later that night as he was trying to sell the now infamous beast. They never found out who.

I like to eat when I'm researching. It didn't bode well for me during my police exams. The weekend before finals I spent so much cash on Thai takeaway that my friends had to shout me at the graduation after-party and I nearly died during the last fitness test. I've always been an easy weight-gainer, but I seem to spread it over my shoulders and arms and thighs, so that I go from lean to beefy and not to pot-bellied or fat-faced, which I'm thankful for. I looked over what I'd brought to the table and thought Eden would probably have been happy that I was eating at all. The selection spread before me at the Police Evidence Archives Department in Chatswood was nightmarish stuff for most health nuts. An empty McDonald's sitting right across the street from the huge double doors was a trap I fell willingly into.

There was one other investigator in the records room when I arrived, and my fatty feast drew a scowl I cheerfully ignored. An attendant in the box watching a television set on top of a filing cabinet was seriously enjoying the company of a large desk fan. The rules at PEAD are that you're supposed to wear white gloves to flip through the records, but I forwent the rule and just napkined my fingers extra vigorously before flipping pages. More frowns from my research mate. He was older and interested in wartime financial stuff, from what I could see. Probably a retiree trying to get away from his wife. He was one of those men just waiting for something to piss them off every day, so I felt good for doing him a service.

I knew a bit about Tom Savet. Stuff I'd heard over the years in bored-cop small talk. He held the record for the shortest report-to-body murder investigation in the history of the Sydney Metro Homicide Department. He and another guy had been called to a house in Epping in the early sixties to look at a bloody bathroom and to help the old war vet who owned the place find his missing wife. Savet glanced around the scene for about five minutes, they said, and found a boot print on the kitchen floor. It was too big for the vet and had a heavy leftward lean. From this Savet deduced that a guy named Richard Kea, a known junkie and petty thief, had been responsible. Kea limped on his left leg from a kneecap he'd had knocked in for bad debts. Twenty-five minutes later, at Kea's basement apartment just three blocks away, Savet had squeezed a confession out of the guy with a pair of pointy-nose pliers. Eighteen minutes after that they had confirmation of a body in a pipe near Yarra Bay and Kea in the back of a paddy wagon. Wham, bam, initial report to bagged body in under an hour. Now that was some Sherlock Holmes shit right there.

Savet was a machine in homicide. He started his record streak by nailing Kea and then went on to mark himself as the top missing persons man in Sydney. The case that got him all the press was that of eight-year-old Elizabeth Kingsley from Neutral Bay. Lizzie Kingsley had been walking home from netball practice in the fading light of a winter evening, through the quiet suburban streets behind the beach, when she'd vanished into thin air. Reports of a red van in the area came up as a dodgy lead but distracted the public in the initial weeks of the investigation. Within twenty-four hours of being handed the case, Savet had turned Lizzie's bones up in a barrel of acid on the ground floor of a warehouse in Dubbo, of all places. The girl was a long way from home. They nailed a truck driver for the murder. After that, everything Savet touched turned to gold.

People ignored Savet's friendships with some of Sydney's nastiest personalities, including Alec 'Caesar' Steel when he was at the height of his reign of terror. Most people probably assumed Savet kept underworld connections to aid his uncanny instincts in digging up bones. They might have been right. I was determined to find out.

I looked over Savet's major case files. There were twenty-six in total. Lizzie Kingsley was his youngest. She looked up at me from the yellowed pages with her frizzy doll-haircut and chubby white cheeks, a netball clutched under her arm. Savet's work on the case was meticulous. I admired his organi-sation, his strict chronology and easy prose through interviews, underlining key phrases, posing questions to himself. The autopsy reports, scene diagrams and suspect lists were all there, numbered, catalogued. You're supposed to keep your records like this, so that someone can easily pick up where you left off if you're reassigned. His work made me think of my own, which at the best of times was spread throughout my car and littered around my kitchen bench-top, barely legible, half of it on the back of envelopes and crowded around the edges of electricity bills. Savet left no path unexplored, took nothing for granted and documented everything. He spoke to people who looked totally unrelated to the case, and from there he drew the most minute but often critical clues. Tom Savet was a textbook kind of guy. Maybe he'd been leaning on Caesar for some pocket money in the drug trade for a little while there, but there was no evidence of anything but a casual liaison, and when Caesar was gunned down by persons unknown in a cellar in Darlinghurst in the late seventies Savet didn't comment to the media, and he didn't attend the funeral. The man had never appeared even marginally in any internal investigations, even when the eighties brought a firestorm to every New South Wales policeman or policewoman who'd ever even brushed up against a bikie in the street. I doubted Savet had anything to do with Sunday White, whether the two had ever even met. But I wanted to look into every possible avenue before I started speculating about what was most likely Sunday's demise – her lifestyle.

I searched through the autopsy reports of each of Savet's victims. I read his notes on each closing interview, before the perpetrator was handed over to the court system. I read Savet's personnel record twice and spent the afternoon in the newspaper room reading up on the press coverage of his work.

I was beginning to lose interest in Savet. My motivation plummeted when I looked over at the television in the attendant's box and saw a frazzled and track-marked Ashley Benfield falling into the arms of her blubbering parents at Sydney airport. I checked my phone. The captain had called me four times and many of the numbers under his I recognised as press.

I got up to leave and began lumping photographs of victims into their respective files. My legs felt heavy from hours of sitting. I picked up a photograph from the floor and sat looking at it as I worked my legs under the table, trying to get rid of the ache in my hips and the pins and needles in my feet. The girl in the photograph was Bonnie Melich. Her boyfriend had bludgeoned her to death when he discovered she was cheating with her boss. Her body was discovered in a torched car in the bush near Botany, not far from the airport.

I looked at the girl in the photograph. She was a gorgeous olive-skinned creature, unusually tall, standing in the doorway of the Lord Nelson in the Rocks with a basket of roses in her slender arms. I knew the place well, had begun plenty of pub crawls there in my cadet years, with writing on my shirt and green paint in my hair. It was a good place for bucks nights too. You could make a lot of noise. The sandstone walls contained a good deal of raucus. I'd passed through that doorway where she stood hundreds of times. Could almost feel it around me as I looked at the girl. Smell the house-made beer. Bonnie Melich's head was almost touching the top of the doorframe though. Legs like stilts. I wondered how tall she was. I looked over at the autopsy report. Five nine – or around 175 centimetres in today's money. I looked at the girl in the photograph, then back at the autopsy report.

They'd moved the bonfire site out into the back fields to dispose of some of the bracken and branches brought down in the storm. It was going to be big. Something about a big fire was magnetic to people, exciting, dangerous, even though the men had lumped stones in a huge circle around the pit to contain it, to stop it wandering into the bush. As the sun sank low behind the caravans Eadie sat watching the men build the woodpile up and up until it towered above them, a strange sense of foreboding in her chest. She hadn't seen Skylar all day, had looked for her at Jackie's van and in the breakfast area, even down on the corner at the public phone that she frequented, constantly out of credit. She knew the girl would come to the fire. Everyone had at some point that afternoon, to load Eskys or spread out rugs, to admire the wood pile. The storm had been mostly wind and noise and all the kindling was still quite dry. Girls sunbaked in the warm fading light, their white bellies lolling on towels, passing oversized Coke bottles around a circle.

Skye came in the calm blue of twilight, Jackie at her side. The busted mouth gave her a worn and aged look. She hadn't bothered with her hair, and it hung greasy and long about her shoulders. She went over to Eadie and Jackie gave her a warning glance as she left.

The two women stood side by side watching the men squeezing newspaper into the base of the pyre.

'I feel like we need to talk,' Eadie said. Skylar didn't answer. Her eyes were on her feet. The girl wiped at her swollen eye and Eadie turned away, pretended not to notice.

'I can get you out of here. But you need to tell me how.'

'Let's go to your place,' Skylar said. Eadie chewed her lip. She wanted to keep an eye on Jackie and Nick in case they pulled anything at the bonfire. It would be crowded. Dark. Everyone would be distracted by the flames. Nick sat watching her from a milk crate, as though somehow knowing that she knew something was about to go down. But the girl looked on the edge. Eadie didn't want her running off into the bush to be alone, or hitching a ride into town. Whatever she was going to witness tonight, she would need to do it with Skylar by her side. The bush was pitch black, silhouetted against a red sky. Eadie put her arm around the girl and held her close.

'Come on,' she said. 'I think I've got some coolers back there.'

Juno stung. It was an all-body ache beginning in his brain and reaching right down into the pit of his bowels, flaring out at his fingertips like the licking of flames. He would grit his teeth and wince against the ache, but it was right there on time, always, whenever he remembered Eden Archer's door. He felt the wind of it on his face. The sudden shattering aloneness of the hall. Rejection, without so much as a word to soften the blow.

It wasn't like Juno had never been rejected before. He had, plenty of times. High school had been a half-decade-long rejection of his body and his soul, a slow and meticulous stock-take of all the ways in which he didn't fit with anyone who mattered, even the weird kids, the goths, the computer nerds and the drama geeks. He was far too ginger to ever fit in with the goths, but he'd always liked their dark side, their hatred. Juno called up that old familiar hatred now as he watched Eden on the screen sitting in the caravan with the girl, Skylar.

You don't fit in the police force, Juno.

You will never be the undercover, rigged up and risking your life for the good of man.

Nobody wants your help, Reject.

He should have caught this attitude off Frank long before Eden ever made it known to him. The way the older man talked about what Juno would begin to feel for Eden after all the hours of watching, how he didn't really know her, should never assume he did. Frank had him pegged, sorted out, stamped for disposal. Wasn't that the very reason he'd been hired to sit in a shitty van on the edge of nowhere for weeks at a time in the first place? To be Frank's eyes and ears while he went off waving his badge in people's faces and saving kittens from trees? Because no one normal deserved such a job. A robot's job. A loser's job.

Sit in the van away from all the normies, Juno, and let us know if you spot anything.

Juno had begun to think that Eden might be able to see that he didn't belong in the throwaway box. That, like her, he was different. He was valuable. Then the door had begun to swing shut, taking only seconds in real life but in Juno's mind hours from the moment he noticed her hand move. A slow rejection of his soul.

The girl was braiding Eden's hair as the older woman sat on the floor by the bed. Juno leaned back against the wall of the van, shook his head, tried to pry loose the emotion from his gaze. *You're watching an animal. She means nothing to you. She's just a cold and beautiful animal.*

Juno wrenched open the van and drank in the cold night air. He needed to look at the sky.

Eadie picked at the carpet beside her, her legs bent in the narrow space between the end of the bed and the wall of the bathroom annex. The girl's braid wasn't so tight this time. Her touch was almost gentle. Now and then the girl sipped from the West Coast Cooler at her side, her mouth making a seal on the glass rim and then popping when she drew a breath. At first, Eadie simply waited in the silence. The girl gathered strands from behind her ear, made her shiver. When words wouldn't come she cleared her throat.

'No man should ever lay his hand on you,' she said. No answer came. The girl took her hands from her hair. Eadie licked her lips and carried on.

'No man, no person, should ever tell you what you're worth. I've been alone a long time, and you need to know that being alone is not . . . It'll never . . .'

Eadie reached for the back of her neck, under her ear, where she felt a small but intense sting. She felt a lump, and then the carpet hard and scratchy under her nose as she slumped to the floor. She tried to right herself, exhaled in the dust. There was darkness.

*

The lights blasted into Hades' bedroom, through his eyes, into his skull. It was like a punch in the head. The cat rushed up over the bed, across his chest and into the crawl space behind the bedhead, claws scrambling on the floorboards. The old man rolled out of bed, steadied himself on the floor, blinked against the stark white light that filled the room. His first thought was lightning. It had all the power of lightning, but it didn't end, didn't fall back into the blessedness of dark. Then the horn began. He heard a guttural groan leave his mouth between his teeth. The horn came in one long deafening blast, then fell into a series of uneven hoots. Hades pulled open the drawer of his bedside table and reached into the darkness there.

Outside, the grey Commodore was pulled up to within inches of the knitting-needle rabbit, rigged with deer lights over its rusted frame. Adam White was leaning out the window, an elbow on the sill. Hades noted the white moon in the sky cast green in his damaged vision. He walked up to the driver's door, reached in and wrenched the man from his seat.

His fists were frail, arthritic and full of badly healed fractures decades old. But Hades still knew how to use them. The pain felt good. He lifted White by the collar of his shirt and punched him down again. *Try to put him into the ground*, Bear had always said. *Imagine you can bury him with your throw. Clench just before impact. Good. And again.* Bear had kept his promise, had taught him how to punch, stood over him while he gave it to a pimp with sticky fingers. But the big man had never been able to teach him when to stop. Hades felt the old tingles of the Silence at the edges of his being, like a warm body threatening to envelop him in its embrace. He stood and breathed, looked down at the camera strapped to the man's chest, a black eye watching him. He put a boot in the camera and felt it crunch under him, felt White's breath leave him as his ribcage deflated like a bone-ribbed balloon.

'Put that on your fucking wireless,' Hades snarled.

White was laughing. Hades took the pistol from his pocket and put it into the man's cheek so hard he felt the teeth beneath the blood-splattered flesh. He held him by the neck, pinned to the ground like a snake.

'I appreciate well-orchestrated mind games,' the old man said, breathing hard, trying to push back the Silence as it crept forward like a flood. 'Oh, I do. But after a time you show some respect and finish a man.'

'I know what you did, Hades.'

'You don't know shit.'

'I'm gonna haunt you,' White laughed, a loose tooth bending with his lip as he spoke. 'I'm gonna haunt you like her ghost. Like my mother's ghost.'

Hades saw that his hands were shaking, but he could not stop them. His right gripped the gun tighter and tighter, pulling down like a vice, and while his mind protested his fingers moved as though driven by some invisible force. He held White against the ground and looked at his eyes and saw Sunday there for the first time – her cheeky grin, the wildness there that had no explanation, that had no cure. Hades squeezed and squeezed, and at the same time his mind screamed out for his fingers to stop their pressure. There was sweat on the gun trigger. His skin slid.

Why did you leave me?

Why did you go?

Hades didn't hear the car. Or the cop's footsteps. He heard hurried breath first, then the crunch of gravel as the man slid

400

to a stop, and when he looked up he saw the eye of Frank's browning pistol in the blinding light off the side of the car. The cop held up a hand, palm out, fingers splayed. Hades had seen it before many times. The friendly hand. The dog eyes fixed on him, head bowed.

'Hades,' Frank said. 'Come on now, old mate.'

'Just in the nick of time, detective,' Adam laughed.

'Put the gun down nice and slow.'

'You had enough time to do your job, boy,' Hades said, his eyes burning in the deer lights. 'Now we do things my way.'

The trigger springs groaned.

'I found her,' Frank said, rushing forward, stopping himself after a couple of feet. 'Listen to me, Hades. I found her.'

The old man struggled to breathe. The trigger spring groaned again as he released his grip.

The first few moments were simply learning, learning which way was up and which was down, learning the nature of the restraints that bound her wrists and ankles, learning how to think again. She was calling back the voice in her head that told her what to do, and when it returned finally from out of the redness and the pain it told her not to panic. That was always good advice. Panic ruined everything, something she relied on as a hunter, something she enjoyed. Eadie opened her eyes, blinked while the blood and sweat that had run into them stung, cleared, finally subsided. She was upside down. Her head had fallen back and was looking downwards at her hands. She recognised almost immediately the concrete steel-rimmed trough that carried the pig entrails from the slaughter row down to the end of the kill house to be processed. Hard wet twine secured her wrists to a hook embedded in the trough. Above her, more twine secured her ankles to an iron rod, splaying her feet. Her whole body could be rotated, rolled along the line as different parts of her were cut away, lopped off and tossed into plastic crates. Eadie swallowed. She was missing one of her back teeth.

'This is what you call the ultimate hangover,' Pea said.

Eadie turned and took in the woman across her arm. She reminded her of a squat, round soldier. There was a double-barrelled shotgun pointed upwards and leaning on her shoulder, her other hand hanging loosely by her side. Skylar stood by, unreadable, her entire body dwarfed by the oversized plastic apron hanging from her neck and the sty-cleaning gloves on her hands. She was wearing denim workman's pants taken from the racks in the corner. She looked like the child she was. Eadie breathed, in and out, in and out, blinking in the pain. She had drugs in her system. Xylazine. Her head and face had been battered. She'd been dragged, she guessed, by the raw feeling of her lower back.

'Have you got any idea who this is?' Pea asked, jerking a thumb at Skylar. Eadie licked her swollen lips, tasted blood and dirt.

'Skye . . .' Eadie tried to find the girl's eyes. They were locked on the floor. 'Skye.'

'This is my fucking kid.'

'Look at me,' Eadie said. She coughed. 'Look. Skye.'

'People without kids don't understand. You try to do the best for them. Always. From the moment they're born. Skylar's got everything she needs here,' Pea said, casting her eyes around the enormous room. 'Everything she could ever want. She has food, and shelter, and a man who loves her. When he gets old and dies he'll leave her this place. She's set up here. She's got it all fucking sorted.'

Eadie panted as the woman approached her. Wondered if her ribs were broken. Her shirt was bunched against her armpits. It itched. How much pulling power did she have in her core right now? How much equilibrium would she have if she righted herself? She calculated the number of paces to the door. The distance her shout would reach. Where was the pendant camera? Probably caught and lifted off her head as she was dragged. Did that mean Juno had called Frank? Was Frank on his way? Eadie let her head hang back and looked at her wrists. They were bound tight, the skin bunched behind the twine. Bunched was good. She could shift the folds of skin under the twine one by one. With enough lubricant. With enough force.

'Pieces of shit like you come in and think you're offering her a better life,' Pea said. The fat woman crouched by her side, flipped the weapon in her arms. 'Try to play Mummy Bear where you're not wanted – or needed. Your own mother should have told you that sticking your nose in the wrong place will get it broken.'

Eadie had taken a few good knocks to the face, but being upside down somehow magnified the experience. She reeled from the butt of the gun and heard herself wail. It was the first time she'd wanted to cry in years. It wasn't emotion, no. Chemicals had flooded her brain, pounded into her face, made her want to draw up her lips and sob. A command was given and Skylar stepped into the trough. Eadie looked up at the girl's feet. Blood gushed up her cheek, into her hair, along her arm. She strained at the twine at her wrists.

'You don't have to, Skye. You don't. Have to.'

'You need to learn that your fantasies about the outside world are all bullshit, Skylar,' Pea said, tying the ribbon at the girl's waist, pulling the apron tight against her body. 'Your place is here. And the way you keep trying to follow these stray cats out the door is just getting them all killed. It's time to grow up. This is all you, Skye. This is all you, baby. You'd be dead out there without your man, without me, without a cent to your fucking name, no matter what you think you know about the world.'

Skye's legs were trembling. Eadie could see them beyond her own white fingers.

'What did you think you were going to do? Huh?' Pea snorted. 'Start again in the big bad city? Put on a suit and be an office girl? Drink martinis at lunch? You didn't even make it through high school, baby. You'd have failed before you opened your fucking mouth. People would know what you are, Skye.'

Skylar was trembling harder. Eadie struggled to breathe.

'You're not a friend to these girls, Skye. Look what you've done to them,' Pea murmured. 'We're not friendly people. We're bad people. And we belong here, with our own kind.'

'Skylar, listen!' Eadie screamed.

'Cut her pants off.'

Skye took a pair of scissors from the front pocket of the apron. She slid the blade into the waist of Eadie's jeans. The blade was warm. Eadie strained against the ties, shook her arm so that the blood ran down her wrist. Her skin was on fire.

'Cut her shirt off.'

'Skylar, I'm telling you to listen to me. Listen to me now. You're not bad. I know bad. I know bad. You can stop this now if you just listen to my voice.'

'Look at that body.' Pea's cold hand ran over her belly, her abdomen, her crumpled ribs. 'You probably like women looking at you, don't you, you dyke bitch? You probably worked hard on this body. Skye, start cutting here. We'll open her up first and get a good look inside.'

Skylar took a blade from the apron's pouch. A long filleting knife. Eadie knew it well. It was one of her favourites. Lean. Sharp. Good for going deep. She felt the pressure, then the tip pierced the skin, and then there was only heat. The blood ran up her neck into her hair. Dark as ink.

'I'm giving you a chance,' Eadie shuddered, looked down at Skylar's dead eyes. The girl's cheeks were wet with tears. 'Skylar, I'm giving you a chance to stop.'

Eadie inhaled as the knife went deeper, too deep. She pulled her wet hands loose from the twine. Eadie grabbed Skylar's ankles, yanked herself forward, twisted her head and bit down as hard as she could through denim, through skin, through flesh. Skylar gasped, began to scream, and the sound of it swelled up around Eadie. The knife clattered at her head. Eadie let go of Skylar's legs, reached and fumbled at the blade as the barrel of the shotgun came around to her face.

Juno looked at the monitors on the shelf in front of him, sipped the Heineken he'd bought from the liquor shop. All week he'd been parked in the lot behind the liquor shop and had not bought one item, had not taken one sip, hell – he hadn't even gone in for the free wine tastings they did on Friday afternoons. He'd sat there in the heat and the silence and the monotony completely sober except for a single fucking Jack Daniel's that hadn't even given him a buzz. It was enough. The beer was painfully cold, hit the back of his throat like a ball of nitrogen. He exhaled, bared his teeth. Eden's pendant camera was aimed at the ceiling again. She was taking a shower. The sunglasses camera was showing an empty bedroom, a blanket on the floor. Juno wondered if she was showering with the girl. If the frigid bitch had finally turned her. Probably. He stretched and settled back against the side of the van and looked at the speakers on the counter. Maybe he would put some tunes on.

Eadie arched her back and twisted, felt the heat of the blast against the side of her face and the spray of shrapnel simultaneously to the front as the shells ploughed through the trough inches from her head. She didn't open her eyes. She heard the telltale singing in her left ear of frequencies she would never hear again. The knife was in her fingers. She swung forward, reeled back, and then swung forward with all her might, crunching broken ribs, crushing torn flesh and punctured organs. She swiped at her ankle. One shot was all she could endure, all she had the strength for. One moment to take in the twine through the blood, to aim, careless of bone or skin or the iron brace, and slash for her life. The blade hit the twine. Cut. She fell, twisted, felt the twine rip.

Pea was reloading the weapon, fingers fumbling. Eadie managed to sit up, to draw a breath before Skylar's arms wound around her throat.

'Hurry, hurry! Jesus, Mum, hurry!' the girl screamed. Skylar's grip was weak.

Eadie twisted, rose up and drove the knife down into the tender flesh between the girl's neck and shoulder. Pea screamed. Skylar made no sound. Eadie scrambled over the top of the trough and fell in the dirt, her lungs squeezing out hoarse breaths.

'No, Skye, no, no, no. Please! Please!'

Pea pulled out the blade, grabbed at the girl's throat, tried to contain the blood. The girl kicked.

Eadie dragged herself towards the shotgun lying like a broomstick on the ground. She lay on her side and tried to fit the shells into the weapon with numb, sticky fingers. One would do. She held the gun and breathed. The older woman came to herself as the girl's legs stopped twitching. She turned on her heels, still crouching, and looked at Eadie where she lay.

'I gave her a chance,' Eadie said, and fired.

Hades sat in his chair at the kitchen table, silent, looking at the file I had put in his hands. My scrawled notes from a phone conversation with Nicky the forensics girl, after she'd finished abusing me for calling her so late at night. His breathing was still elevated from the brawl outside his house. Adam stood in the corner by the hall, his arms folded, staring at the sink. His face was a bloody mask, but he ignored it completely. The blood dripped from his jaw onto his shirt, a long series of red teardrops.

'Bonnie Melich went missing two days before Sunday disappeared. She was big. Six foot four. You can tell that from where she's standing there, in the photograph,' I said. I pointed at the photograph of the tall lean girl in the doorway of the Lord Nelson, the basket of roses on her arm. 'You count those sandstone bricks beside her, get out your measuring tape and there you go. Problem is, the body Detective Tom Savet turned up in the car in Botany a week later, the body which was supposed to be Bonnie Melich, was distinctly shorter. Five foot nine, or thereabouts. The autopsy report puts it down to shrinkage due to the extreme heat, the hardening of the bone fibres, the loss of cartilage. We can tell these things now – I mean, forensic scientists can. They can get it pretty exact, given her age, her approximate weight, the maximum temperature a body can get to in a motor vehicle.'

'Detective,' Hades said. One word. I cleared my throat, gave it a minute, felt my face grow hot.

'There's no way, scientifically, that Bonnie Melich was the body that Tom Savet found in that car.' I reached into my pocket and pulled out a small envelope the size of the palm of my hand. The label on the envelope had yellowed with the years. The handwriting on it was neat blue cursive. A forensics file number, and a name.

'Tom Savet was at a police function the night Sunday went missing,' Hades said. 'I checked. I checked a hundred times. He can't have been involved . . . He wasn't . . .' Hades murmured.

'They found this in a woman's coat. It was near the vehicle.'

I placed the envelope in Heinrich Archer's hand. He pulled a small slip of torn, yellowed notepad paper from it, unfolded it, smoothed out the creases over the stamped stationery header marked 'Jeremy's'.

One line of text in clumsy lettering, pencil.

Central Station, Platform 2, 9PM.

'Nine . . . Nine *pm*,' the old man said.

'Sunday thought you wanted her to stay in the hotel room until the following night, 9PM. So she was waiting there that morning, at the same time you were waiting for her at Central Station. Tom Savet, meanwhile, had a new case. He was looking for Bonnie Melich. He needed a body. He needed to keep up the charade of being Sydney Metro Homicide's fastest man.'

Adam White's breathing was hoarse. I could hear it from where I stood. I wiped sweat from my brow.

'You . . .' I cleared my throat. 'You thought Savet's big game was the drug scene. Caesar's connection in the cops. But it wasn't. His game was murder. He'd wait for a case, provide a body, and fill in the gaps. Twenty-six cases in all. They were all . . . Uh, Jesus. They were all unidentifiable. At least, with the technology you guys had back then. Burned. Buried. Boiled in acid. He was lazy and deadly and he wanted the power. The incredible power that would come to him in the following years. He needed someone that morning, and Sunday was . . . She was there. She was always underfoot. You said it yourself.'

Hades and White looked at each other. The old man ran a hand over his short hard hair.

'Why did you spend so long checking Savet's story?' I said. 'He wasn't a friend to you. Why didn't you just – '

'Because I was sad, alright?' Hades' teeth showed just for a second as he turned his profile to me, his eyes on the table. 'I was sure she'd run out on me. The more I checked the facts, the surer I was that Savet hadn't been there, the surer I was that . . .'

'That she'd left you.'

Hades put the note on the table in front of him, smoothed it out carefully, a relic to be treasured. His big hand covered it completely, as though hiding its awful truth across the years.

'After she was gone, I didn't care,' he said. 'I'd been so concerned with my own fucking . . . my pig-headed rage. Vengeance. Meaningless vengeance. I turned my back on her for a second, just a second, to do something for myself. For the man who'd saved me. And in that second . . . she was gone.'

Adam White was shaking his head slowly, ruefully. I barely heard my phone ringing beyond the pounding in my ears.

I pulled it out of my pocket and looked at it. Juno. I lifted it to my ear, anything to break the tension in the room.

'I'm busy.'

'Yeah, um, look. I'm just a bit worried about Eden.'

'Huh?'

'I just noticed . . . I just noticed she's off camera. Has been for maybe, like, an hour.'

'An hour?' My stomach plummeted. 'Which camera?'

I heard Juno inhale.

'All of them,' he said.

I shoved past Heinrich's chair and ran out the door.

Pea ran. Memories of the last few minutes collided and tripped over each other as her brain tried to catch up with the events in the kill shed, seemed to want to linger with sickening clarity over Skylar as she lay in the dirt, writhing, writhing, desperate eyes searching the encroaching darkness for her mother. The woman who was supposed to protect her. The visions rushed, slid, exploded, and there was Eadie under her hands, struggling for the knife with red wet fingers, the shotgun now useless, the blast batted away at the last second by something raw and animal and instinctual in Pea that still wanted her own survival even though she knew deep down inside that Skye was gone.

Skye was gone.

She stumbled to a stop beside the water tanks, kneeled and vomited in the dust. It seemed her body wanted to purge the visions from her, and when it was done she felt ruined, trembling as she looked at the huge bonfire blinking in the dark across the horse paddock, the bodies that passed before it, making it twinkle like a star. She heard music on the wind. Laughter. Pea gripped the earth and grass beneath her, tried to control the sobs that racked up from low in her heavy body.

She needed a plan. Couldn't make one here.

Pea found the wire fence that lined the horse paddock and inched her way along it, fists clenched on the wire and fumbling at the posts towards the gates. There, she knew, was one of Jackie's trucks. Wind-whipped grass cast pale in the light of the moon, howling along the plain towards her. She picked out the truck from the darkness and ran to it, wrenching open the driver's door and closing it behind her. Warm. Quiet. There was a canister of kerosene on the passenger seat, stinking, intended to fill the lamps in the stalls in the west corner of the farm. Pea rolled down the window, breathed in the night air and tried to calm her breathing. She gripped the wheel and bowed her head and shuddered long and hard with sobs, giving herself but mere seconds before she straightened in the seat.

At first she thought she had pulled a muscle in her back shifting upwards and back behind the wheel. Then she heard the voice of the one named Eadie and felt the girl extract the filleting knife from where it had plunged through the soft foam of the driver's seat and into her spine.

'I'm sure it's not all that bad,' the girl said.

Pea gasped, could draw no more than a quarter of a breath. Her legs were numb. She watched as the girl, now a ghoul with a bloody mask, climbed slowly and drunkenly from the cabin and shut the door behind her. She was wearing only work-man's pants, the bra, a vest of her own red, red blood. The hole in her belly gaped, inches deep, inches long, a vertical eye-shaped slit she ignored. Pea tried to lift her arms from where they had fallen in her lap. Somehow, the limbs refused the message, simply lay there on her thighs as though detached, someone else's arms. Eadie walked to the driver's side door, pulled it open, reached across Pea's body with strained, weak movements and poked the canister of kerosene gently with the tip of the knife until it pierced the plastic and sent the clear liquid gushing down the seats.

'I told Skye I know bad people.' Eadie straightened, slamming the driver's door shut. 'I know them, because I'm one of them. You made that girl what she was. In the end, even though her heart was telling her to stop, all she knew how to do was follow you. When you give birth to something, you should be held responsible for what it becomes.'

Eadie reached in the truck window and turned on the engine. Pea thought she should probably have been able to smell the kerosene, but for some reason, she couldn't. She could feel the fumes in her eyes, feel the tears they produced rolling down her cheeks. Eadie turned the wheel of the vehicle towards the bonfire in the distance, put it into drive and let off the handbrake. The truck began to roll. Eadie shuffled beside it, limping heavily, one arm clutching at the hole in her abdomen, the other extracting a packet of cigarettes from the pocket of her workman's pants. She put a smoke in her crooked jaw and struggled to light it against the wind. The ghoul she had become shuffled, shuffled, seemed to drag her leg behind her. Pea thought of the undead. She tried to scream, but no sound would come.

When the cigarette was half-smoked, the ghoul reached into the truck and jammed it between Pea's slack lips, where it burned, red, at the edge of her vision.

'Bye, Pea,' Eadie said, her voice haggard in the wind. 'Nice workin' with you.'

Pea closed her eyes and felt the cigarette falling, tried to force her lips to shut around it. They wouldn't. The truck kept rolling on, and the ghoul stopped following.

There was already a team assembled at the gates of Rye's Farm when I slid my car to a stop on the gravel drive. Ten men in flak jackets, with another truck on its way from the south. I'd spent the frantic drive from Hades' tip on the phone, so it seemed these men had arrived in only seconds, but I'd been assured weeks earlier they were all on standby for my call. In the distance I heard a chopper whomping, waiting for command. Captain James was on his way. The area commander, a dark-haired woman with small fierce eyes, strode towards me as I exited the car and strapped on my jacket. I was already drenched in sweat. I pulled my gun and loaded it as she briefed me.

'We've been told to lock the place down and wait for further instruction. The south section will be in place in five.'

'You've got the cordon, Chief,' I said. 'I'm going in for my partner.'

'I can't offer you backup at this minute.'

'I don't need it.'

My face seemed to get the message across. She took a step back and let me through. I jogged up the long gravel driveway into the dark. The wind was picking up and I smelled fire. The one thing they tell you to remember when you're closing on a hostile area is to keep your breathing regular. Focus. In, out. I found a wire fence and followed it along, past a clearing filled with junk and rusting car bodies, a barbecue area, a group of vans. No one was around. I crept along vans and popped into open spaces filled with dark.

I glanced up at the sky, saw bats trailing over the trees in the light of a distant fire. In a group of vans beyond a small breakfast area I came across a small wiry man just stumbling down the fold-out iron steps of an ancient Jayco, still zipping up his fly.

'Police! Hands up!'

Jackie just looked at me, his mouth hanging open. I rushed him and thumped his narrow shoulders into the door of the van. Put him on the ground like a doll.

This can't be it, I thought. *This can't be how it ends. Something's wrong.*

'Where's Eden?'

'Who?'

'Eden Archer.' I gave him a few good punches to the back of the skull, glanced about for backup. 'Eadie Lea, the blonde, you sick little fuck.'

'What's happening? What's happening? What?'

I lifted Rye and dropped his head on the bottom stair. Cuffed his limp body and moved on. The van was empty. In the dark behind the cluster, another fence.

Across the fields I spied a bonfire burning. Within seconds, a truck I hadn't even seen rolling through the dark of a paddock with its headlights off exploded, windows blazing orange squares hovering in the night. I ran along the fence line towards it. A chopper crossed overhead, flooding the paddock with light. At the bonfire, I could see more bodies moving, hear screaming dim and far away like the calling of night birds.

Under the cover of an awning made from dying trees I spied a figure walking towards me in the dark. The figure's hands hung by its sides, lolling. It was tottering, drunk. I raised my gun.

'Police!'

The figure kept walking. I moved forward, my aim fixed.

'Stop where you are or I'll fire.'

Eden was just moving her feet. When she stepped into the light of the moon I realised what she was draped in from neck to waist was not a lace shirt, as I'd first thought, but her own blood. She was crooked, her whole body slanted to the left and bowed forward. Her face was a mess, nose flattened, eyes black. I lowered the gun and rushed forward, skidded as a tall lean figure emerged from the dark behind her, a long arm wrapping around her neck.

'Hold up, copper,' Nick Hart said, pulling Eden upright. There was a little steak knife in his hand. Probably grabbed from the breakfast area. I lifted the gun and sprayed spit with rage.

'Drop it, shithead!'

'Just when you thought it was safe to have a couple of beers by the light of a nice fire. The fuzz comes in and fucks it all up,' Hart laughed. 'Typical.'

Eden reached into the pocket of her baggy, bloodstained pants, slid a long slender blade into the light. Hart grabbed her wrist, shook it. She was half gone. Her eyes lolled, found me hesitantly behind the gun.

'Listen to me, Hart,' I said. 'That's a police officer you've got in your hands there,' I inched forward as he inched back, dragging my partner with him.

'I was just starting to think that myself.'

'I'll shoot you dead right here, mate. I'll shoot you fucking dead.'

Nick laughed, and there was genuine triumph in it. To get him, I'd have to shoot Eden. She knew it too. Her eyes followed mine, rimmed in blood, her lips moving and words falling drunkenly off her lips.

'It's okay,' she said. 'It's okay, Frank.'

My hands were shaking. I didn't have the best aim even in the cool, sterile light of the shooting gallery. Frantic thoughts washed over me with unimaginable clarity, one after the other like deliberate calculations that had waited long enough to come to mind. I knew then, standing in the dark, that if I killed Eden Archer I'd be free of her. Of what she was. Of what she knew about me, and what I knew and desperately wanted to forget about her. This was the moment I'd been waiting for, my solution, my chance to put all the shattered pieces of my life back together after that morning in the church tower when everything I knew about my life had erupted under me. If I killed Eden now I'd be free of her devilish father and his landfill of horrors, of the memory of Martina that she carried with her everywhere like a perfume. Because, yes, Eden had been there. She'd seen me fall in love with Martina, seen me fall as far as a man can fall. She was the only piece that didn't fit in my recovery. The only thing stopping me from being whole again. Without Eden, maybe I could start over. If I killed her now, I could try to forget I'd ever known the monster that she really was.

Instead I dropped my gun. Nick laughed, shifted sideways, and as he did a bullet whipped past my ear, struck him in the jaw and sent him sailing backwards. I heard running footsteps behind me. Torchlight fell on my hands. I caught Eden as she started to fall.

'Oh no,' I heard myself pleading. 'No, no, no, please. Please god, don't do this. Eden? Eden? Eden!'

She was a dead weight in my arms. We slid to the ground as the officers swarmed around us. I wrapped my arms around her, lifted her and ran through them, back towards the gates.

Epilogue

Hades sat at his table. He had been sitting there all day. The newspaper lay by his gnarled hand, untouched, the front page dominated by a picture of the young cop, Frank, carrying his daughter. He couldn't think about that now. He couldn't process what had happened to Eden, what it would mean for her, what they would have to do next. He needed to finish his time with Sunday. To finally say goodbye. Hades' coffee cup stood on the sink-top, upside down, dry. In his left hand, he held an ancient photograph of a little girl sitting upright on an old wooden stool, looking off somewhere, unfocused.

That was how she was, always. Unfocused. Distant. A wild creature. That's how she had seemed to Bear the day he found her on the beach as he crouched in the dunes picking plants for his lethal potions – a panting, panicked creature running towards him over the sand, her hair whipping in the wind and her arms out, reaching. A child of the earth, risen from a crack in the mantel somewhere, hot as fire as she slammed into his body, scrambled up his back like a possum, gripped onto his neck, her fingernails claws. The boys who had been chasing her up the beach came to a stop at the bottom of the dunes, one of them swinging the lump of wood by his side, weighing up their options against the huge man on the sandhill. Bear had pulled the little girl off him with some difficulty when the boys turned and began to walk away. He found her barely conscious, wracked by days on the streets. He held her there in the new sunlight, sat down, tried to figure where she'd come from, what the hell she was doing there. He called her Sunday. His runaway. One of a number of children he rescued over the years. Strays. Wild things. Children of the wind.

There was nowhere to visit Sunday, and that might have been the hardest thing for Hades, sitting there looking at his hands. Her body, buried deep beneath the well-kept and flower-laden headstone of Bonnie Melich, would be exhumed for DNA testing, then handed back to White and his family. Buried, probably, where her people had come from, miles and miles from where the old man sat. He had seen White on the news already, railing at reporters about what he wanted done to retired detective Tom Savet, what it had meant to his family, his mother, to have lost Sunday, the one piece of joy the old woman had ever experienced in her cold and loveless life. The Melich family had been there too, stiff and non-committal, still emerging from the lull they'd been enjoying for decades and into a new nightmare, a new uncertainty, for their lost child. Hades had switched it off after a time. It was all noise to him.

Now, as she always was, Sunday would be just beyond his reach. A moon drifting, following, teasingly close. Hades wondered what had happened to Bonnie Melich, the girl in the pub doorway, whoever she had been. Hades wondered what had happened to all of Savet's case subjects, the little girls and boys, the old women, those lost souls he'd been too lazy to find. An inquiry would reveal it all, or kill Savet in the process. The young copper, Frank, told him that Savet was already locked down, extracted from his boutique retirement community in Woollahra and in custody at Silverwater. The young cop had made the call before he told Hades what he'd found. Smart. It would be harder to get at Savet now. Harder, but not impossible. Nothing was impossible for a man of Hades' history.

Hades closed his eyes, cracked his neck and set the photograph down on the tabletop. When he opened his eyes, the sharply cut figure of a man was walking down the short front hall towards him, his stride long, quiet, slow. Hades watched Mr Grey as the light hit his smooth high cheekbones, as they seemed to lift impossibly higher with his stark white, devilish grin. The manicured cannibal took up the chair across from Hades, sat down and hung an elbow over its back, the steel-coloured jacket hanging open, revealing its salmon silk lining. A shard of light from the kitchen window, red from the setting sun, glinted in the hitman's eyes. For a moment he was a youthful Satan, come to collect a soul.

'Greetings, old buddy,' Mr Grey said. 'I hear all your little rainclouds have begun to clear away.'

'Almost,' Hades said. He took the magnum from where it sat on his right thigh, lifted it and shot Mr Grey in the face.

The cannibal's skull exploded down the dark hallway. The old man stood, stretched, felt the clicking of bones between his shoulderblades. The pinched muscle there that had been bothering him for weeks seemed to loosen, to become warm. For a moment Hades felt young again.

Imogen stirred her coffee quietly, careful not to hit the edges of the cup with her spoon, though she knew nothing would wake Frank now. He was flopped on his chest on the bed in the same strange position he'd fallen into the day before, barely stopping to get his bloodstained clothes off. He hadn't spoken to her, but Imogen knew from the papers what had happened at the farm and the hospital afterwards. They said that Eden Archer was stable, but that she'd sustained terrible injuries fighting with the killers of two young prostitutes. The farm had been searched. Several arrests, including that of two men for a series of rapes. No remains of the girls had been uncovered, but on the news police choppers kept circling a large shed, and there was some hysteria surrounding Rye Farm organic pork supplies to various Coles supermarkets. Imogen went to her desk, spread the paper out before her and read the articles again, from the cover to the extensive middle spread to the editorial. The front-page picture had been captured by a paramedic using his smartphone. Frank with Eden in his arms, running on a gravel road, his mouth open, shouting. Imogen examined the panic in his face. The vulnerability. It was strangely attractive to see him like that. In action. On the run. Eden looked like a blood-drenched doll in his arms, her head fallen back, eyes closed and dreaming. She was naked to the waist, her small breasts cupped in a black push-up. The public would be eating up the grisly tale based on this picture alone. Imogen smoothed out the paper. She looked around for a pair of scissors, couldn't find one in the clutter. A moment like this was worth saving. Frank Bennett rescues the fallen heroine.

Imogen found the scissors and began to cut. As she clipped along the bottom of the photograph, she stopped. There was a rather unusual mark on Eden's ribs. A birthmark, almost electric pink in the image, shaped like a prancing pony. Imogen thought she might have heard people call that sort of mark a port stain. It was very pretty, crisply captured, distinct from the black blood that ran down her ribs. Just as Imogen noticed it, the mark seemed to dominate the entire picture. She put the scissors down. Felt strangely light-headed. She stared and stared at the mark, and then, as though her world had been spinning and had suddenly righted, reached out groggily and pulled a folder from the middle of the stack on her desk.

The Tanner children case. Imogen flipped open the files, pushed them frantically over the desk. She found the worn news stock image of the slaughtered Dr Tanner and his missing daughter, Morgan, at the beach. The respected scientist was stripped to the waist and hoisting a little dark-haired girl in a bikini into the sky. His big hands wrinkled the skin at her ribs but didn't go so high as the birthmark there, a pony, hooves reared, just under the child's armpit.

Imogen slowly put the two images side-by-side.

Acknowledgements

I'm indebted, as always, to those creative writing teachers who raised up the overly enthusiastic, frequently disturbing and constantly questioning young writer that I once was into the one I am today: Gary Crew, Ross Watkins, James Forsyth, Kim Wilkins, Ros Petelin and their colleagues. My academic supervisor, who has always been behind my career, Camilla Nelson, I thank you for your support and encouragement. I'll never be able to repay Gaby Naher and Bev Cousins for taking a chance on me, and for their ongoing commitment to my writerly dream. To Jess Malpass, my wonderful publicist, and her colleagues at Random House Australia, I owe too much.

As a writer who never found the quiet monotony of a home office conducive, I owe my thanks to bustling cafe workers who despite their traffic never disturbed me or hassled me for my table, regardless of how many coffees I didn't buy. It's difficult to find places with this kind of consideration, but Billy's at Maroubra Junction, Cafe on Parade at Maroubra and Marcelle on Macleay in Potts Point are a few. Thank you to a good number of online fans who never let me feel alone or unworthy.

Finally, to my wonderful partner, Tim – thank you for getting it. All of it. Me, the books, the murderous tinge to otherwise everyday discussions. You're a good man, and I'm glad I found you.

If you enjoyed *Eden*, read on for an extract from
the next instalment in the series by Candice Fox.

FALL

**If Detective Frank Bennett tries hard enough, he can
sometimes forget that Eden Archer, his partner in the
Homicide Department, is also a moonlighting serial
killer . . .**

Thankfully their latest case is proving a good distraction.
Someone is angry at Sydney's beautiful people – and the
results are anything but pretty. On the rain-soaked running
tracks of Sydney's parks, a predator is lurking, and it's not
long before night-time jogs become a race to stay alive.

While Frank and Eden chase shadows, a different kind of
danger grows closer to home. Frank's new girlfriend Imogen
Stone is fascinated by cold cases, and her latest project – the
disappearance of the two Tanner children more than twenty
years ago – is leading her straight to Eden's door.

And, as Frank knows all too well, asking too many questions
about Eden Archer can get you buried as deep as her past . . .

EBOOK AVAILABLE NOW

Prologue

Before the blood, before the screaming, the only sound that reached the car park of the Black Mutt Inn was the gentle murmur of the jukebox inside. It was set on autoplay, tumbling out a cheerful line-up of greatest pub hits one after another, but there was none of the growly sing-alongs of usual pubs, no thrusting of schooner glasses, no stomping of heels on the reeking carpet. The jukebox played in the stale emptiness of the building, and by the time it reached the car park it was no more than a ghoulish moan. It was windy out there and the stars were gone.

The Black Mutt Inn attracted bad men, and had been doing so for almost as long as anyone could remember, as though the ground beneath it had somehow hollowed a vent to hell, the men who frequented it drawn in by the familiar heat of home. Nightly, at least, a bone was broken on its shadowy back porch over some insult or breach or another, or a promise was made there beneath the moth-crowded lamps for some violence that would occur on another night. Sometimes a plot was hatched there – the corners of the inn's undecorated interior were very good for whispering, and the walls seemed to grow poisonous ideas like vines, spreading and creeping around minds and down necks and along legs to the rotting floorboards.

The staff at the Black Mutt saw nothing, said nothing, but they absorbed secrets and requests, their ears and palms always open, their lips always sealed. They were loyal to no one and this earned them respect.

On this night, Sunny Burke and Clara McKinnie entered the Black Mutt with their laptops and bags of chilli jerky and bright, suntanned smiles. The man behind the bar said nothing, saw nothing. He just served the drinks.

Sunny and Clara brought their smiles into the Black Mutt, and though their Macleans glimmer didn't reach any farther than the murky light above the door, the two carried this weak glow to the bar and set up shop there under the mirrors. Three men sat against the wall whispering, and another two stood at the pool tables watching the two travellers fresh from Byron, stamped with its optimism and cheap weed stink. Clara ordered a champagne and orange juice and downed it quickly, and Sunny nursed a James Squire and rubbed her legs.

Into the dim halo of light stepped a man from the pool tables, and from that very second, although the bleach-white smiles remained, things in the world of Sunny and Clara began to get very dark.

'G'day, mate,' the man said, thumping Sunny between the shoulder blades. The man was tall and square and roped with veins, and the two hands hanging from his extra-long arms looked all-encompassing. Sunny looked up, appreciated the density of the man's beard and smiled, swallowing envy.

'Hey.'

'Just down from Byron, are we?'

'We've been there a week,' Clara beamed.

'I can see, I can see.' The man brushed the backs of his fingers against the top of Clara's shoulder, a brief brotherly pat. 'Sun's had its way with you, beauty.'

'We're just on our way back to the big smoke,' Sunny said.

'If you ask me, you've just come from the big smoke,' the stranger jibed, and nudged Sunny in the ribs, hard. 'Tell me you've got some grass for sale. *Please* tell me.'

Sunny laughed. 'Sure, mate.' He glanced at the other figure in the shadows, the man by the table leaning on his cue. 'No problem.'

'I don't get up to Byron often enough. Me back's no good for the drive.'

Sunny nodded sympathetically. The stranger threw out a hand and Sunny gripped it, felt its concrete calluses against his palm. 'No probs, no probs. How much are you after?'

'Aw, we'll do all that later. Hamish is the name, mate. Can I invite you to a game?'

'Yeah! Shit, yeah. This is Clara. I'm Sunny.'

'Me mate over there's Braaaadley, but don't you worry about him. He don't talk much. Plays a rubbish game of pool, too, don't you, Brad? Ay? Wake up, shithead.' The man squawked back towards the pool table but roused nothing in his partner. 'Excuse me, miss, excuse me, but me old Bradley's prone to leaning on that pool cue till he drifts off and no amount of slapping can get him back, if you know what I mean.'

'Right,' she laughed.

'You want some jerky?' Sunny asked.

'Nah, mate, nah. I'm all good. Me chompers ain't no good, as well as me back. I'm falling apart at the seams here, mate.'

They racked the balls while Clara and the silent one watched, now and then letting their eyes drift to each other, the hairy man in the dark struggling beneath the weight of his frown, the young woman rocking awkwardly, swinging her hips, holding onto the cue. She finished her second champagne and wanted another, but the men were talking and laughing and making friends, and Sunny always had trouble making friends, so she didn't interrupt.

'How about a little wager, just to make things interesting?' Hamish asked.

'Yeah, sure.' Sunny puffed out his chest, ignoring a warning look from Clara. 'Where do you, I mean, what do you usually —?'

'Five bucks?'

'Five bucks?' Sunny laughed, coughed. 'Sure, mate, sounds great.'

They played. Clara was the most excitable, howling when she sunk the white ball, cheering when Sunny scored. There was plenty of kissing. Rubbing of backsides. The men in the booths watched them. The happy group at the table were cut off from the rest of the world by the cones of light that fell upon them.

'Very good, young sir,' Hamish said, offering his big hard hand again. 'How about another?'

'Twenty bucks this time,' Sunny said. 'You can pay me in labour, if you like. The van needs a wash.'

'Sunny!' Clara gasped.

'Listen to this guy, would you?' Hamish laughed. He squeezed the young woman on the shoulder, made Clara's face burn red. 'What a cocky little shit. You're lucky you're so goddamn beautiful, Sunny me old mate. No one's gonna knock that gorgeous block off no matter what you say.'

They laughed and played again. Hamish was hard on Bradley. The balls cracked and crashed and rolled in the pockets. Clara was good. She'd always been good. Her daddy had taught her the game young, bent over the felt, his hips pinning her against the side of the table. But she knew when to sacrifice a shot so that she didn't lean over too far and give Bradley a view of her breasts, her arse.

The man looked at her funny. Made her ache inside.

'One more?' Sunny said. The bar was empty now but for the bartender, who was motionless in the shadows. Sunny won, and won again.

'One more, little matey, and then it's off to bed with you. What say we make it interesting, huh? Everything you've won, you give me the chance to win it back. We go even. I lose, you take the notes right outta my hand, no hard feelings.'

'Mate,' Sunny drawled, 'you win this and I'll give you double what you owe me.'

'Sunny!'

'Oh ho. Just listen to this guy,' Hamish laughed.

'Sunny, no.'

'Cla,' the boy drew her close, 'they haven't won a game all night. It's fine. I'm just having a laugh.'

'Sunny –'

'Just shut up, would you?' Sunny snapped, giving her that look. 'I'm only having a bit of fucking fun.'

Clara shut up because she knew what men could do, and it began with that look. She watched the men shake hands, rack the balls. When the game began, it was all Clara could do to keep those lips shut as Hamish leaned down, took aim and began sinking balls.

The table was empty of Hamish's balls in less than two minutes. And then he sunk the black in a single shot. Sunny never got a turn.

'Mate,' Hamish said when it was done, straightening and leaning on his cue, the smile and the charm and the humour forgotten now, his eyes lazy as they wandered over Clara. 'Seems you owe me quite a bit of cash.'

In the car park, Bradley walked behind them, glancing now and then towards the Black Mutt, although no such careful eye was needed. Not here, not where a hidden hole drilled straight to hell warmed the air as it breezed across the asphalt and ruffled Clara's thick dark curls. Hamish's hand on the back of her neck was like a steel clamp. They approached the Kombi van, the only one in the lot. It was parked out in the middle of a huge barren wasteland so that the young couple would be safe from whatever might be lurking in the towering wall of dark woods when they returned. Clara put her hands out to stop Hamish slamming her into the side of the van and turned. Bradley had let a steel pipe slide down from where it was hidden high up inside his sleeve.

'Give me an inventory,' Hamish said.

'There's the CD player, some cash, and Clara has some jewellery,' Sunny was saying, fumbling with his keys. 'There's the weed, too. You can take it. Please, please, I'm asking you now not to hurt us.'

'You go ahead and ask whatever you like, you snotty-nosed little prick,' Hamish said. 'You bring out whatever you can from in there and we'll see if it's enough, and if it's not, I'll decide if anyone gets hurt.'

'Take them up to the ATM,' Bradley grunted. Clara jolted at the sound of the silent man's voice. She turned and found him staring at her, eyes pinpoints of light in the dark.

'Sunny,' Clara croaked, tried to ease words from her swollen throat. 'Sunny. Sunny!'

'Shut up and hurry up,' Hamish snarled.

'I'm going. Please. Please!' Sunny was pleading with anyone now. Clara heard the pleas continuing inside the van, heard the rattling of boxes and drawers. As soon as the boy was out of sight she felt the man with the concrete hands slip his fingers beneath her skirt. Hamish smiled at her with his big cracked teeth and pressed her into the van.

'All this excitement getting you wet, is it, baby?'

'Sunny! God! Please!'

'Your pretty boyfriend better come up with something very special, very soon, baby cakes, or I'm afraid you're footing the bill on this one.'

'How about this?' Sunny said as he emerged from the van, hands full, thrusting the items at Hamish. 'Will this do?'

The knife made Hamish stiffen, made his eyes widen slightly as they dropped to the items in Sunny's hands, which all fell away and clattered to the ground, revealing the leather handle they concealed, the leather handle attached to the long hunting blade that was now buried deep in Hamish's belly.

Sunny, as always, didn't give the man a moment to appreciate the surprise of the attack. He pulled the knife out of his
stomach and plunged it in again, pushed it upwards into the
tenderness of Hamish's diaphragm and felt the familiar clench
of shocked muscles. Clara slid away as the young man went
for a third blow, took her own knife, the one she kept flush
against her body between her breasts, and went for Bradley.
The hairy man backed away but Clara's aim was immaculate.
She set her feet, pulled back, breathed, swung and let go. The
knife embedded in Bradley's back with a thunk right between
the shoulder blades, and he fell and rolled like roadkill on the
tarmac.

She went to the silent man and pulled out the knife, wiping
it on the hem of her soft white skirt. Bradley was still alive,
and she was happy because it would be a long time until she
was finished with him. Clara liked to play, and though it wasn't
really Sunny's thing, she thought maybe because they were on
holiday he would indulge her just once with some games. She
turned and looked at him, Bradley still gurgling against the
asphalt under his cheek.

'Baby.' She turned on her sweet voice for her killer partner.
'What if we took this one home and –'

A whistle and a shlunk.

At first it seemed to Clara that Sunny had fallen, until she
felt the wet spray of his blood on her face. She tried to process
the noise she'd heard, the whistle and the shlunk, but none of
it made sense. She crawled, shaking, and with her hands tried
to piece back together the split halves of her boyfriend's skull,
grabbing at the bits of brain and meat sprayed across the asphalt
around him. There was no putting Sunny back together again.

She kneeled in the blood, both his and Hamish's, and tried to understand, little whimpers coming out of her like coughs. Hamish was sitting up beside the van, his hands still gripping at the knife wounds in his belly.

A whistle and a shlunk, and the top of his head came off. He slid to the ground.

Clara looked around at the tree line behind her, a hundred metres or so away, and then looked at the trees in front, the same distance, dark as ink and depthless. The silence rang, and under its terrifying weight she crawled, tried to get to her feet, heading towards the bar. Another whistle, another shlunk, and her foot was gone. Clara fell on her face and gripped at the stump of her leg. She didn't scream or cry out because there was only terror in her, and terror made no sound.

Clara lay and breathed, and then after some time began crawling again. She heard the sound of uneven footsteps, punctuated by a metallic clop, and looked up to see a figure coming towards her slowly, barely distinguishable against the dark of the trees from which it had emerged. The sounds kept coming out of Clara, the shuddering breaths through her lips, but through them the metallic clopping kept coming. A woman moved into the light of the van. Clara could see she was leaning on an enormous rifle, using the gun like a crutch.

The woman stepped quietly between the bodies of the men, and Clara lay in the blood and looked up at her. She thought, even as shock began to take her, about the woman's black hair, how it seemed to steal some blue out of the night and hold it, like the shimmer woven through the feather of a crow. The woman with the gun bent down, used the enormous weapon to lower herself into a crouch. Clara wondered what wounds she was carrying, what gave the other killer such trouble as she settled herself beside the dying girl.

Eden looked at the trees, the bar, finally at the girl on the ground.

'Just when you think you're the deadliest fish in the water,' Eden said to the girl.

Clara gasped. Her fingers fumbled at the wet stump where her foot had been. Eden sighed.

'I admire the game,' Eden said. 'I really do. It's clever. Two naïve little travellers just waiting to be picked on. You flounder around like you're just drowning in your own idiocy, and you see which predators come to investigate the splashing. Who could resist you? You're adorable. You lure them out into the deep, dark waters and then you surge up from below. Pull them down.'

Clara fell back against the asphalt, her mouth sucking at the cold night air, throat blocked by shock.

'If I was well, this would have been more personal,' Eden said, her leather-gloved hand gripping the rifle tight. 'But I haven't been at my best lately, so I'm afraid there's no time for play.'

Clara tried to speak, but she couldn't force words up through the whimpers. They came out of her like hiccups. The woman with the long dark hair rose up slowly, pushing the rifle into the ground, and when she'd risen fully she actioned the great thing with effort, once-strong hands betraying her as the bullet slid into the chamber.

'I'm the only shark in this tank,' Eden said.

The last gunshot could be heard inside the Black Mutt Inn. But no one listened to it.

The Victims of Crime support group of Surry Hills meets every fortnight. The only reason I started going is because my old friend from North Sydney Homicide, Anthony Charters, goes there. If I didn't have a friend there, I'd have never bowed to my girlfriend Imogen's demands that I get counselling for the 'stuff that has been going on with me' the last few months. That vague collections of terms, the 'stuff' and its propensity to 'go on with me', frequently came between the beautiful psychologist and me in our first few weeks of dating, when she realised she'd never seen me completely sober. She said she couldn't imagine me 'relaxed'. Privately, I argued I was a lot more relaxed than Imogen herself. Imogen takes an hour and a half to get ready in the morning, and the first time I farted near her she just about called the police. That, ladies and gentlemen, is not 'relaxed'.

But, you know. You don't tell them these things. They don't listen.

I'd started courting Dr Imogen Stone in the dangerous and electric place between my previous girlfriend being slaughtered by a serial killer and my partner detective almost getting herself disembowelled by a pair of outback monsters. Imogen liked me, but she was dealing with the psychological aftermath of both events. I was by all accounts an unpredictable, volatile and difficult-to-manage boyfriend. She couldn't count on me to turn up on time, say appropriate things when I met her friends, drive her places without her having to worry that I was about to career the car into the nearest telegraph pole. She couldn't be sure when I ducked out of the cinema that I wasn't going to knock back six painkillers in the glorious solitude of the men's room stall, or lose myself in thought and just wander off, turning up back at her apartment at midnight drunk and stinking. I was a bad beau, but I had potential, so she didn't give up on me. Ironically, I understand that the 'fixer-upper boyfriend' that I seemed to be is just about the perfect model for the worst type of man you can be attracted to – according to the psychology textbooks I'd perused in her office, it was the cute, broken bad boys who became abusers.

Nevertheless, Imogen took me on, and Imogen started nagging me to get help. So I started trudging with all the huffing melancholy of a teenager at church to a basement room of the Surry Hills police station every Sunday to sit under the fluorescent lights and listen to tales of horror and fear. It made Imogen happy. It made Anthony happy. I considered it my community service.

Somewhere, sometime, somebody set up a support group in a particular way and now all support groups are set up like that, whether you're trying to get over being sexually assaulted in a public toilet or you're addicted to crack. You've got the grey plastic fold-out tables pushed against one wall, the veneer pulling away from the corners and the top stained by the rims of coffee cups set down meaningfully, mid-conversation, to indicate concern. You've got the two large steel urns full of boiling water for coffee and tea, the ones that will, if you go anywhere near them, even so much as to fill in your name on the sign-in sheet, mercilessly burn some part of you. There's no avoiding the coffee-urn burn. To this you add a collection of uncomfortable plastic fold-out chairs forming a circle just tight enough to inspire that quiet kind of social terror made of things like accidental knee-touching, airborne germs and unavoidable eye contact. And voilà! You've got a support group.

There were fifteen chairs set out on the industrial grey carpet and Anthony was sitting in one when I arrived. I responded to his presence with a wave of paralysing nausea. Getting over a painkiller and alcohol addiction makes you respond to everything with nausea. You get nausea in the middle of sex. It lasts for months.

I'd worked with the bald-headed, cleft-chinned Detective Charters and his partner for about two weeks when my former partner committed suicide and the bigwigs were trying to find me someone else as a playmate. I'd have liked to have stayed with him. He was inspiring – not in the cheesy internet quote way, but in a real way, a way that gets you out of bed. He was somehow still enthusiastic about justice and the rule of law and collaring crims like it was a calling, even though his own seventeen-year-old son was in prison for five years for accidentally leaving a mate with brain damage from a one-punch hit at a New Year's Eve party. I figured if Anthony could get out of bed after that, I could get out of bed after Martina being killed (me allowing her to be killed) and Eden almost dying (me standing there doing nothing while Eden almost died). If Anthony could keep on keeping on after everything that had happened to him, maybe I could get over all the women I'd failed in my life, eventually. Maybe I could get over not doing anything about my father's long, slow emotional abuse of my mother. Not saving Martina. Not saving Eden. Not being there when my ex-wife had a stillborn child.

Anthony had been as powerless to save his own son. And yet here he was, smiling at me as I came to sit by his side. Maybe being powerless was okay.

When I'd asked him, Anthony put his unshakeable spirit down to the support groups. He attended one for drug addiction, one for victims of crime and one for anxiety. I thought I'd give it a whirl. It would shut Imogen up.

'Francis,' he said. I cradled my coffee and licked my scalded pinky.

'Anthony.'

'How's the comedown?'

'I think I'm past the shakes.' I held out my hand for him to see, flat in the air before us. My thumb was twitching slightly. 'I'd still murder you for a scotch, though, old mate.'

'I reckon scotch might be on your trigger words list, mate.'

'Probably. It's a big list.'

Some recovery groups don't let you say particular words, 'trigger words', because some members are getting over a level of addiction so great that even the sound of the name of their drug of choice can send them into a relapse spiral. Even if you're not an addict, but you're in a support group parallel to addiction groups such as Victims of Crime or After Domestic Violence or Incest Survivors, you have to acknowledge that some members of the group might also be enrolled in addiction groups, so for their benefit you don't say the words.

The first rule of Drug Recovery Group is that you do not talk about drugs at recovery group.

It sounded like a whole lot of bullshit to me. I wasn't sure all the tiptoeing around really helped anyone. I'd tested my trigger-happiness, said 'Endone' loudly and slowly alone in my car, like a little kid whispering a swearword at the back of class. I had not gone and started popping pills. But I was a rule-follower by nature, so I didn't say 'Endone' in or anywhere near the meetings I attended. I didn't say 'scotch', or 'bourbon', or 'cocaine', or 'ecstasy', or 'Valium', or 'oxy', all guilty pleasures of mine at some time over the previous months. I mentioned that I had a variety of 'drugs of choice' at my first meeting when I introduced myself, but I hadn't shared since.

In fact, I hadn't said anything. Imogen had told me to 'go' to the meetings. She hadn't told me to 'participate'.

People stopped milling around the treacherous urns when the facilitator, a hard-edged little blonde woman named Megan, came into the room with her large folder of notes and handouts. About twenty-five of her photocopied handouts were in the bottom of my car, boot-printed and crumpled, hidden in the undergrowth of a forest of takeaway containers and paper bags. Their titles peer at me from beneath old newspapers and cardboard boxes. *Six ways to beat negative thoughts. How to tell your friends you're in danger of self-harm. When 'no' means 'no'.* Sometime after the first meeting, I lost my eight-step grief diary. I hadn't even put my name on it. Diaries are for little girls.

When Megan was in place the people around me joined in the opening mantra in a badly timed monotone reminiscent of the obligatory and dispassionate 'good morning' we used to give Mrs Towers in the third grade.

'I am on my way to a place beyond vengeance, a place beyond anger, a place beyond fear. I am on my way to a place of healing, and I take a new step every day.'

I didn't say the Victims of Crime mantra. It was way too cuddly for me. I didn't know what Megan's story was, but if she'd made up the mantra herself it sounded to me like she was making a big deal of being bag-snatched or something. There is no place beyond anger. Everybody's angry to some degree. Nuns are angry at sinners. Kindergarten teachers are angry at the government. When you've come up against violence, real violence – you get punched by your husband for the first time, or someone pulls a knife on you in the regular, sunny traffic of a Thursday morning commute – you realise there is no place beyond anger. It's in there. In everyone. No matter what you put on top of it, no matter how long you starve it or lock it up or deny it. Anger is primal. It's in our DNA.

'We've got a couple of new members with us tonight,' Megan said as Justin, the group kiss-ass, brought her a paper cup of green tea. Justin had been gay-bashed to within an inch of his life on Mardi Gras night when he was twenty-one. Victims of Crime was his life. 'This is Aamir and Reema.'

The Muslim couple with their backs to the door nodded. Reema was looking deep into her empty paper cup like she'd found a window out of the room. I was jealous. She adjusted the shoulders of her dress nervously, and her husband sat forward in his seat, a big man, his hands clasped between his knees.

'Hi, Aamir,' everyone said. 'Hi, Reema.'

'Now you don't have to share,' Megan assured them. 'No one has to share in these groups. Sometimes it can be healing just to listen to the stories from those around us and to recognise that the trauma we have experienced in the wake of serious crime is not unique, and neither is the journey to wellness. Sometimes we like to start the meeting with some "triumphs of the week" or with some readings. But it's a pretty fluid structure here.'

'We don't mind sharing,' Aamir said. He shrugged. The anger tight in his shoulders and jaw. I could see it. Anthony, beside me, could see it. You get to know the look of a man on the edge of punching someone when you're a young cop wandering among groups of homeless in the Cross, Blacktown, Parramatta. Bopping around the clubs on George Street while groups of men hoot and holler at women from cars. It becomes like a flag.

'Well, good.' Megan smiled. 'That's great. Like I said, there's no pressure. Some of our members have never shared.' She glanced at me. I felt nauseated. 'This is a supportive environment where we have attendee-centric mechanisms –'

'I'll share.' Aamir stood up suddenly. He was even bigger standing. No one bothered telling the huge man that standing wasn't part of the group dynamic, that in fact it intimidated some of the rape survivors. He rubbed his hands up and down the front of his polo shirt, leaving light sweat stains. 'I'll start by asking if anyone here in the group knows me? If you know my wife?'

I was confused. It was great. I hadn't felt anything but nausea and boredom in all the sessions I'd attended, so this was a novel start to the night. The group members looked at each other. Looked at Aamir. Aamir shrugged again.

'No? No? You don't know me? You've never seen me before?' Aamir's stark black eyebrows were high on his sweating brow. He did a little half-turn, as though members might recognise his back, the little tendrils of black hair curling on the nape of his thick neck. His wife wiped her face with her hand. No one spoke. Anthony examined the man's face.

'I don't think they underst–' Megan chanced.

'My son Ehan was abducted one hundred and forty-one days ago,' Aamir said. He went to his chair and sat down. 'One hundred and forty-one days ago two men in a blue car took my eight-year-old son from a bus stop on Prairie Vale Road, Wetherill Park. He has not been seen since.'

He paused. We all waited.

'You don't know me, or my wife, because there has been little or no coverage of this abduction in the media. We've had one nationally televised press conference and one newspaper feature article. That's it.'

Aamir was a lion wrapped in a man. The woman across the circle from him, who'd been in a bank hold-up and now suffered panic attacks, was cowering in her seat, pulling at her ponytail. Megan opened her mouth to offer something, some condolence, some segue back into the normality of group sharing, but Aamir raged on, a spewing of well-practised words with which he had assaulted anyone who would listen since his son disappeared.

'If Ehan was a little blond-haired white boy named Ian and we lived in Potts Point, we'd still be all over the national news.'

'Oh, um.' Megan looked at me for help.

'We'd have a two hundred thousand dollar reward and Dick Smith flying a fucking banner from a fucking blimp some-where. But we've had nothing. Two days the phone rang off the hook, and then silence. I forget sometimes that he's gone. Every night at eight o'clock, no matter where I am, no matter

448

what I'm doing, I think, *It's Ehan's bedtime. I have to go say goodnight.*'

Megan widened her eyes at me.

'What are you looking at me for?' I said. The sickness swirled in me.

'Oh, I wasn't.' Megan snapped her head back to Aamir. 'I wasn't. Sorry, Frank, I was just thinking and you were in my line of sight and –'

'Are you a journalist?' Aamir turned on me. I didn't know how I'd been brought into the exchange until Megan buried her face in her notebook. The same thing she'd done when I signed on to the group.

'No,' I said. I looked at Aamir. 'No, I'm not a journalist. My girlfriend was murdered. I'm the only other person in the group who's here for murder-victim support. That's why she's staring at me. She wants me to say something hopeful to you.'

'Our son wasn't murdered,' Reema said.

'Well, Megan sure seems to think he was.'

'I never said that!' Megan gasped.

'Your girlfriend was murdered.' Aamir sunk back down to his seat. He was so far on the edge of it I didn't know how he was upright. He hovered, legs bent, inches from me. His huge black eyes were locked on mine. He knew his son was dead. And he was angry. White-hot-flame angry at everyone he laid eyes on.

'She was murdered. Yes,' I said.

'What was her name?'

'Martina.'

'And what happened after she was murdered?' Aamir asked.

'What do you mean?'

'What happened?' he insisted. 'What happened then?'

'Nothing,' I shrugged. Everyone was looking at me. I licked my lips. Shrugged again. 'Nothing. She was murdered. She's gone. There's nothing . . . afterwards, if that's what you mean.'

Aamir watched me. We could have been the only people in the room.

'Nothing happens afterwards,' I said. 'There's no . . . resolution. You go to work. You come home. You come to these groups and you –' I gestured to the coffee machine. 'You drink coffee. You say the mantra. There's no afterwards.'

Everyone looked at Megan to deny or confirm my assessment. She opened her folder, shuffled the papers, collected her thoughts. One of the urns started reboiling itself in the taut seconds of silence and I heard the spitting of its droplets on the plastic table top.

'Let's look at some handouts,' Megan said.

Anthony was waiting for me by the vending machine after the meeting. We walked up the stairs and onto the street.

'That was a bit harsh,' he said.

'What?'

'The whole "there's no afterwards" thing.'

'Reality is often harsh,' I said. We paused to watch Aamir and Reema walking to their car. The big angry man glanced back at me as he opened the passenger door for his wife. His expression was unreadable. It was the first time that his expression had been unreadable since I had laid eyes on him an hour earlier. The rage was gone, replaced by something else. His shoulders were inches lower. I didn't know what had taken over from the boiling hot fury that I saw in the meeting room, but whatever it was, it was cold.

'Do you really believe that?' Anthony asked me. 'That it means nothing?'

'Murder?'

'Yes.'

'Yes,' I said, 'I do. You don't get over it. You don't realise the mystical fucking meaning in it. You don't accept that it, like everything, happens for a reason. Come on, Tone,' I scoffed at him. He exhaled smoke from his cigarette.

'Every night at eight o'clock that guy tries to say goodnight to his dead kid.' I nodded at Aamir's car as it pulled into the street. 'And he'll be doing it until the day he dies.'

She always felt better when night was falling. The darkness folded over her like a blanket, protective. Light had never been a friend to Tara. It seemed to fall on all of her at once, seemed to wriggle into her creases and folds and dance around her curves, to expose her every surface. Tara always had plenty of surface. She'd never been able to keep track of all there was of her, and Joanie was there to point out the parts she forgot, those bulges and bubbles and handles of flesh that slipped and slid from under hems and over belts.

Pull your shirt down, Tara. Pull your pants up, Tara. Pull your sleeves down, Tara. Jesus. Everyone can see you.

Everyone can see you.

At the dinner table Joanie would grab and pinch and twist a slab of flesh Tara didn't know was exposed, a roll above her jeans or the tender white flesh on the backs of her arms. You couldn't cover Tara with a tent, Joanie said. She could feed an African village. Getting downstairs to dinner became a journey she couldn't take, so she began to take her meals up in her attic bedroom, staring at the park, the runners going round and round between the trees. Sometimes getting from the bed to the computer was too much. Tara simply lay between the sheets and dreamed about African people cutting her up and sharing her, carving down her thighs in neat slices like a Christmas ham until there was only bone – gorgeous, strong, light bone. Bone that shone, redemptive and clean. Tara lost herself dreaming.

The girls at school giggled at her bulges, the blue bruises that peppered them. Though decades had passed, their voices still bumped and butted around the attic room, red balloons of hate floating.

Why do you call your mum 'Joanie', Tara?
Doesn't she love you?

Tonight Tara stood by the windows looking over the park and watched the night falling, the bats rising, and remembered her mother. It was nine months since Tara had woken from her coma, nine months since Joanie had gone, but Tara could still hear her voice sometimes, hear her footsteps in the hall as she readied herself for some party or dinner or charity function, as she pulled on her silk-lined coat and checked herself in the hall mirror. Joanie with her elegant ash-blonde hair falling everywhere in filigree curls.

In time, all the light of the warm day dissipated, replaced by a wonderful darkness. Tara stood by the window and watched the runners on the paths in Centennial Park recede into shadows, only blinking lights indicating their jolting journeys as they continued, round and round, round and round. Then rolled away.

The Tara who watched them now was very different from the one who had watched them when her parents were still alive. Tara hugged herself in the little window, let her fingers wander over the new landscape of her body. Bumps and ridges and flaps of flesh as hard as stone, lines of scars running up her arms where the fatty flesh had been sucked dry, cut, pulled taut, stapled. Bones poked through the mess at her hips and ribs and collarbones. Her face was a mystery. She hadn't looked at herself since that first glimpse as she was waking from the coma. She spent the first month in the hospital in silence, lying, feeling herself. Neurologists came and played with her, confirmed that she could, indeed, understand them. Then a nurse had emerged from the fog and quietly told her what she'd done to herself. Tara had looked at her new self in the mirror. Touched the glass, made sounds. To her it had been laughter, but to the nurse it had sounded like snarls.

The first novel in the the Archer & Bennett series

Hades

The killer is in sight, but who is behind you?

Homicide detective Frank Bennett feels like the luckiest man on the force when he meets his new partner, the dark and beautiful Eden Archer. But there's something strange about Eden and her brother, Eric. Something he can't quite put his finger on.

At first, as they race to catch a very different kind of serial killer, his partner's sharp instincts come in handy. But soon Frank's wondering if she's as dangerous as the man they hunt.

arrow books